Zypheria's Call

ISBN-13: 978-1-940575-06-3
ISBN-10: 1940575060
BISAC: Fiction / Fantasy / Historical

For more information, or to leave a comment about this book, please visit us at:
http://www.lammaswood.com

PRINTED IN THE UNITED STATES
Second printing: January, 2015

To June Gray

who first showed me that the world of arts existed

and that even a kid from the sticks could appreciate it.

Table of Contents

Zypheria's Call

NATHAN LOWELL

Durandus

CHAPTER 1
DIRTY DEEDS

Tanyth woke with the pale morning light shining around the cracks in her door. Outside the sounds of oxen, carts, and the men who used them drowned out the sounds of morning birds. She growled in the back of her throat. They hadn't considered that building an inn for the village would mean an end to quiet mornings. She sighed and flung the covers back.

The sudden chill struck her and forced her to scurry to the hearth where the banked coals still offered a bit of warmth. The equinox might have been right around the corner but nights were still cold and she wanted her morning tea. Her footfalls on the woven mats should have warned her. The scritch-scratch of talons on the floor should have prepared her for the black wings that waved to fan the flames, wafting light gray ash from the stones and into the air, into her mouth, coating her throat until she coughed with a hoarse *caw-caw*.

Her heart pounded in her chest as she tried to force herself awake. It was just a dream. It wasn't real. She'd wake and all would be well. The horny beak that made her lips would be gone, the wings would be hands again.

She turned back to her cot. Perhaps if she got back into bed, it would end.

A man-sized shape, his gray hair sticking out of the covers, stirred in her bed. Frank mustn't see her like this. He couldn't. If he saw her, it might be real.

Frank Crane rolled over and blinked at her several times before smiling.

"G'mornin'. You're up early," he said. "Sleep well?"

Unable to catch her breath, Tanyth struggled to make sense of her surroundings. The fine ash had settled on her glossy black wings, mottling them and dulling the sheen. Behind her the warming fire felt too warm, too hot. She peered over her shoulder—her black-feathered shoulder—to see the tip of a long tail feather nearly brushing the coals.

Her scream was a raucous caw.

Frank pushed himself up, alarm on his face, "Tanyth? What is it? Tanyth? What's the matter?"

Something shoved her, shook her. A hand on her shoulder where nobody stood and suddenly she was in her bed looking up at Frank's terrified eyes.

"Tanyth? Talk to me, old woman. What is it?" he said.

Tanyth sucked in a breath, feeling the cold air burning through her raw throat.

"Were you dreaming?" he asked.

Tanyth struggled to get her arms free of the tangled covers and Frank shifted his weight to let her bring her fingers up in front of her face—tanned and wrinkled though they might be—they were her fingers.

"Yeah," she said, testing the word, afraid of the sound that might come from her throat. "Yeah, it was the dream." She looked up into his face searching for something, but she didn't know what. "You were there. You saw me."

He hugged her then, wrapping strong arms around her and holding her close and warm against him. "It was just a dream, Tanyth," he murmured.

"Why am I havin' it, Frank?"

"You're not goin' mad," he said, pressing his cheek to the top of her head. "If I'd been through what you've been through in the last half year, I'd be havin' nightmares, too."

She felt like she wanted to cry but the sobs wouldn't come.

"Besides," he said, a lilt in his voice. "Every woman I ever met that was goin' through the change thought she was goin' mad. Between the mood swings and hot flashes, every one of 'em was ready to bark at the moon at some point. I figger you're just following in the tradition."

She let him hold her, taking comfort in his strength, in his warmth. She heard the calls of the drovers with their ox carts outside in the inn's yard. She knew he had no better answers than she did and all her answers pointed north, pointed to Gertie Pinecrest.

☽〇☾

Golden morning light filtered through the treetops, slashing the yard with bands of sun and shade. Tanyth shrugged her winter coat closer to her body even as the sun's rays offered the promise of summer. The back of winter may have been broken, but its cold fingers still dug into her old bones. She leaned back against the rough planks of her cottage and lifted her mug of tea to sip, savoring its minty bite as she watched man and beast struggling to sort themselves into order in the sea of mud that used to be the inn's dooryard.

Frank came out of the inn, down the log steps, and picked his way around the soggy circus. He joined her on the higher ground. "I didn't think about that when we were plannin'," he said, nodding at the tangle of man, animal, and cart.

"The mud, you mean?"

He gave a half shrug. "Well, the mud, no. Not that either. We'll have to get some gravel to fill in there." He grimaced and rubbed a hand across his mouth. "I was thinkin' about the number of people."

"What? You didn't think people would stop?"

"Not that so much. I thought it would start out kinda slow, ya know?" He looked at her, a rueful smile curving his lips. "A few here, a couple there. It'd give us a chance to get things settled."

Tanyth chuckled at his expression but nodded her understanding. "It's been pretty steady since they opened the doors. We prob'ly shoulda figured that would happen."

"The timing is just about perfect, I guess." Frank squinted his eyes in thought. "Three days from Mossport to the north and three more down to Fernsvale to the south. I just never figured that there'd be so much traffic willin' to spend the night on the way."

"After two or three days on the road, you don't think folks would be lookin' for a night with a warm fire and somebody else's cookin'?" She shot him a pointed glance out of the corner of her eye. "I thought you were a travelin' man."

He laughed and wrapped one strong arm around her shoulders. "I never really thought of it that way. I always stop here." He kissed the top of her head.

"Yeah, but you live here."

"That's why we needed you to stop and tell us. I'd have never thought of it on my own and the rest don't travel enough to think of it."

The chaos in front of them sorted itself into a semblance of order as the lead drover stood at the front of his team and raised his staff. "Hoy!" he cried.

The other teamsters responded by raising their hands and an answering shout of, "Yah!"

The team boss used his free hand to count the raised arms. Apparently satisfied, he gave a short nod and nudged his team into motion. "Giddup, there," he said. His voice carried clearly to where Tanyth and Frank stood watching.

One by one, the teams heaved themselves out of the muck and trundled down the path to the Pike, each making the turn southward. In much less time than Tanyth thought possible, the yard was empty except for Jakey's old yellow dog snuffling the ground where the oxen had left their droppings.

"How long before you head north?" Tanyth asked.

"Well," he said, drawing the word out as he considered. "Didn't get much clay packed last fall so we gotta make up for that. Another week. Prob'ly two before Jakey and the boys get a load ready."

A raven cawed loudly. Both Tanyth and Frank looked up to the inn's roof where the raven strutted back and forth along the ridgepole.

"I can't convince you to stay." Frank's voice trailed off at the end, more statement than question.

Tanyth sighed and laid a hand on his arm. "You know I can't. It's not you."

"It's her," he said, jerking his chin in the direction of the raven.

"Yeah."

"That dream scares you that much?" he asked.

"Yeah," she said, looking down at the toes of her boots, damp from the morning dew. "After this mornin', I need to go even more. If I get stuck in a dream, I might never be human again."

He arched one shaggy eyebrow at her. "You don't believe that."

"No." Her voice caught in her throat. "But it scares me spitless to think it could happen. I'm guessin' Gertie Pinecrest can tell me one way or the other if I'm going mad."

"You're not goin' mad." His frustration sounded clearly in his growl. "Why Gertie Pinecrest? You never met the woman. How can you be so sure?"

Tanyth shrugged. "I don't know, Frank. I can't be sure. I'm not sure. But she's the only answer I got at the moment. Could be I'll get up there and I can't find her. Or she won't teach me. Or she'll tell me I'm really—" Tanyth's voice cut off. The sudden emotion of it squeezing her throat shut.

"You're not crazy," Frank said, his voice firm and his arm hugging her to his side in an oddly reassuring gesture.

Another voice spoke up, startling them both. "You're not crazy, mum. I know it." Rebecca stood at the corner of the hut, her eyes downcast and her fingers twisting together like small animals in a nest.

"Rebecca! You gave me such a start," Tanyth said, hand to her chest and willing her heartbeat to settle down.

"Oh, sorry, mum." She gave a small, contrite smile. "And good mornin', Frank."

"Morning, Becca."

"It's all right," Tanyth said. "Just took me by surprise."

Rebecca nodded. "Sorry. I just wanted to ask..." Her voice petered out.

"Ask what, my dear?" Tanyth asked, shooting a curiosity-laden glance at Frank who only shrugged in return.

"Mum? You're leavin' when the shipment goes?"

Tanyth gave a little nod. "Yes. When Frank takes the first load."

"Take me with you, mum."

Tanyth shared another glance with Frank. "Take you with me? To Kleesport?" she asked.

"No," Rebecca said, her words tumbling out in a rush. "Well, yes, but beyond. To see Mother Pinecrest."

Tanyth cocked her head to one side and regarded the younger woman. "You want ta see Gertie Pinecrest? Why?"

Rebecca shuffled her feet in the damp grass and looked at her writhing hands. "Well, mum, it's not so much to see Mother Pinecrest."

"Are ya tired of livin' in Ravenwood then?" Frank asked.

Rebecca frowned at that and shot him a look of apology. "Not exactly, but maybe a bit."

"Then what is it?" Tanyth asked.

Rebecca shrugged. "I'd like to travel with you, mum. Go where you go. See what you see."

Tanyth shuddered at the image of black wingtips where fingers should be and had to blink back the spike of fear. "What makes you say that?"

The morning sun tipped over the tree line to the east and flooded the village with golden light. Tanyth turned to bask in the warmth for a moment, letting Rebecca gather her thoughts. When the younger woman didn't respond, she said, "It's likely to be dangerous, my dear. And I don't know if Mother Pinecrest will take me on. We could get all the way up there and have to come back."

She felt Frank stiffen and looked up to see him gazing down at her, hope in his eyes.

"Would you come back?" he asked.

"Might have to." She smiled at him and reached over to pat his chest. "But don't plan on it."

She saw the light fade as he looked away and nodded.

"More dangerous than Andy Birchwood and his boys trying to burn us out, kill us in our beds?" Rebecca asked, her quiet voice almost lost in the breeze.

Tanyth shifted her weight and rubbed fingertips over her lips as if to wipe away a bad taste. "Possibly," she said at last, "but mostly long days, cold nights, and not knowing where we're going or what we're doing." She paused and considered the young woman for a moment. "Why do you want to go?"

"Well, mum, you're going off somewhere special and there's nothing here for me." The younger woman raised her head and jutted her chin out in the direction of the inn. "I can wait tables, and help out in the inn, sure, but it's not something I wanna spend my life doin'."

Tanyth looked to the hulking building just as Sadie came out with a straw broom and began sweeping down the porch and steps, clearing away the tracked in dirt from a long night and morning of traffic. The scritch-swish sound of the straw on the rough boards sounded much closer than it was.

Tanyth lowered her voice a bit. "What do you want, my dear?"

Rebecca sighed and shrugged, pulling her hands away from each other as if to force them to be still. "I don't really know, mum." A cawing from the ridgepole of the inn's roof nearly drowned her voice.

All eyes went to the heavy, black bird. She cawed once more before launching herself into the warming air and with three powerful pumps of black wings glided into the shadowed forest behind the inn.

"It's just that, well, mum, when we came out here there was a lot of people. It was an adventure, you know?" Her eyes went from Tanyth's face to Frank's and back again. "People my own age all startin' out to leave the city behind and start fresh."

Tanyth smiled and nodded. "And now?"

"Well, almost everybody left now is married or claimed—" Rebecca's glance went to Frank, before looking down once more, "—or otherwise occupied."

"Too old?" Frank asked.

She shot him a smile that held equal parts chagrin and agreement.

"Lot of the quarrymen are still single," Frank said. "Karl, Matt? Good men."

Rebecca shifted her weight from side to side, and gave a half-hearted shrug. "Yeah, but Karl and Matt think of me as their little sister. Richard is too old and David's too young."

"He's two winters older than you are," Frank said.

Rebecca shot him a venomous look from under her eyebrows. "You know that's not what I mean," she muttered.

He uttered a single laugh, and said, "Yup, I know."

"So, you think this is another adventure then?" Tanyth asked.

"Well, in a way, yes, mum, but not really." Rebecca took a deep breath and blew it out through her nose, turning her head to scan the village and surrounding forest. "When we came out here, I thought perhaps, I'd find a husband, start a family of my own. It might have happened. It could have. But it never did, you know?" She looked in Tanyth's eyes.

"Oh, yes, my dear, I know." Tanyth shot a sideways glance at Frank.

Rebecca saw the look and blushed. "Yes, well, I've been thinkin' about it for awhile. Then this fall and winter with you here, mum. And Birchwood came and I was so scared, but you were here and everything was all right."

"I was scared, too," Tanyth said, breaking in on the flow.

"Yes, mum, I s'pose we all were, but you helped us anyway." Rebecca's head came up. She gazed directly at Tanyth. "You stood up and helped us. Even after you got cut up and we all took turns tendin' you. You got better and kept going, kept pushing forward, mum. Even when you thought you were goin' mad, mum. Even after that horrible man—" Her voice broke.

"Josh, my dear. He had a name. Josh," Tanyth said. The words sounded rough to Tanyth's own ears.

"Even so, mum. He kidnapped you and dragged you out into the wood. And you got away. And you—well, you got away. You're strong. You're movin' on. I—I—" Rebecca's fingers had found each other again and took one last writhing twist before she pulled them apart, holding her hands at her sides. "I want to go with you, mum. To see what happens next." Her voice fell, almost to a whisper. "To maybe find something of my own."

Tanyth regarded the younger woman for several heartbeats, before glancing up at Frank, who merely shrugged. Tanyth turned back to meet Rebecca's eyes. "Give me a day to think about it."

"I can be helpful, mum. I've been learning stuff from Thomas about woods craft and such." Rebecca's eager voice trailed off as Tanyth held up a hand.

"I'm sure you can, my dear, but this is more about me than you. I'm used to travelin' by myself. It's sometimes

8

dangerous and frightenin'. I don't now how I feel about leadin' somebody else into that."

Frank took a breath as if to say something but when Tanyth looked up at him, he merely coughed into his hand and reached for his handkerchief.

"I understand, mum."

Tanyth smiled at her. "Thank you, my dear. Just give me 'til tomorrow. Come see me in the morning."

Rebecca's face brightened. "Thank you, mum."

"No promises!" Tanyth cut in. "I need to think about it."

Rebecca nodded several times. "O' course, mum. I understand. I do. But you didn't say no, yet. That's somethin'."

Tanyth huffed a laugh out and nodded her agreement. "True. Now, scoot."

Rebecca smiled and nodded to Frank one more time before scampering off toward the inn.

Tanyth watched the young woman go before glancing up to see Frank looking down at her. Something in his expression made her frown at him. "What is it?"

"You're gonna to let her go with ya?" he asked, looking at Rebecca's retreating back.

Tanyth gave a non-committal shrug. "I really don't know," she said. "Honestly, I've been travelin' on my own so long, I wouldn't know what to do with her."

She felt Frank stiffen slightly.

"Is that why you won't stay here?" He didn't look down at her, just continued gazing off into the village.

"Stay with you, you mean?" Tanyth said, poking him in the ribs with one sharp finger.

He looked down and gave her an abashed-looking smile. "Yeah. Well, with me and the rest of the people here." He paused, his eyes searching her face for something. "You've a home here, you know. Yours for the takin'."

She laid one hand against his weathered face and caught his wandering gaze in hers. "You know I can't do that." Her voice was barely louder than the winds whispering in the pine tops behind the cabin.

He lifted one shoulder in acknowledgment. "I know what you say, Tanyth, but I still don't believe it. You're not goin' crazy."

Her single bark of laughter echoed off the inn.

"You're not," he insisted.

"Frank, normal people do not see things through ravens' eyes. It's not natural." She withdrew her hand and scrubbed her lips again with her fingertips. "When I woke up this morning and couldn't pucker to blow on the fire because I had a beak—" She closed her eyes and shook her head as if to rid herself of the memory.

"But that was a dream, Tan. You and I both know that."

"Nightmare, more like."

"Exactly, and you woke up."

She scoffed.

"You did. You woke up and it was just a dream," he said.

"What if I hadn't? What if it wasn't?" Her eyes searched his craggy face in turn. "What if it was a warnin'?"

"Warnin'? Warnin' of what?" He sounded curious and a bit frustrated.

She sighed and folded her arms under her breasts as if hugging herself for warmth. Her eyes scanned the now familiar landscape of the village, stopping here and there with no apparent reason. Finally she turned her gaze back to his. "If I knew that, Frank Crane, I wouldn't have to go now, would I?"

Frank drew a deep breath and blew it out before screwing his mouth into a grimace. "No," he said. "I don't suppose you would."

The sound of a horse's whinny wafted on the morning breeze. "Sounds like I'm needed at the barn," Frank said, glancing down at her once more. "And prob'ly just as well."

He took three steps before she asked, "What do you mean by that?"

He gave her a devilish grin over his shoulder but didn't stop walking. "Anytime a woman uses a man's full name, it's time he finds a place to hide. The barn'll do for now."

Under other circumstances the comment might have earned him a sour look, but Tanyth saw the twinkle in his eye and a chuckle bubbled out of her.

Frank gave her a wink and a nod and his long legs soon

carried him out of sight around the inn.

She stood there for a few more moments, her fingers seeking her lips once again. Somewhere in the forest a squirrel chittered and drew her gaze in the direction of the noise.

"You're a foolish old woman," she muttered to herself, but her fingertips continued to reassure her that her lips were still lips, that her fingers were flesh and blood, not feathers. "Foolish," she repeated before rousing herself to go back into the hut.

She slipped the latch and ducked her head as she'd done a hundred times. The lintels on the doors were low and she had to step down three steps to enter the cozy hut. She'd managed to get in and out of that very door untold numbers of times all winter long. Yet she clipped her head on the top of the door and the bright pain pushed her off-balance. Her foot missed the first step, heel catching on the second as she pitched forward into the room, empty teacup flying, holding out her arms to break her fall.

The dry twig snap of her forearm seemed loud in the quiet room before the sharp pain blossomed.

She lay there on the woven grass mat of the floor, cradling her arm, and cursing herself silently until the pain made her pant the words aloud. "Foolish. Old. Woman."

CHAPTER 2
WINGED

The next couple of hours passed in a fog of pain. Broken bones were common enough in the village. The quarrymen managed to break at least one bone a year among them and rambunctious children fell out of their share of trees. When Tanyth showed up at the inn cradling her left arm, Sadie and Amber plopped her into a chair and had the bone set, splinted, and nearly wrapped almost before the three swallows of rum burned down to her belly.

"Poultice," she said, eyes still streaming from the combination of pain and rum.

Amber blinked. "Poultice?"

Sadie said, "Bone stitch, of course. You taught us, right? Comfrey. Make a poultice?"

Tanyth nodded, pleased that the younger woman had remembered.

"We got some growing just outside, mum," Sadie said, heading for the back door.

"Too young yet," Tanyth said, breathing deep and pushing the air out, willing the pain to go out with each breath. "Get dried from my hut. Grab a whole bundle and bring it back."

Sadie changed course and bolted through the connecting door to the common room. Tanyth heard her footsteps slapping on the steps as she went out the door.

Amber held the loose end of wrapping. "Should I continue, mum?"

Tanyth looked down at her arm. The flesh was already turning a nasty color and looked puffy from swelling. "It's

13

set, thank the Lady," Tanyth said. "Long's I don't move much, it should be all right like this."

"We'll have to wrap it eventually, mum."

Tanyth poked her skin with one finger above and below the obvious bruising, wincing a little at the pressure. "Yeah. But wrappin' it now, I'll just swell under the wrappin'. Best let it fill in a bit before you go squeezin' it with that."

Amber nodded and pulled a pot down from the hanger, filling it halfway with water and putting it on the stove. "Sadie will be back in a minute, mum. You just rest easy."

Tanyth tried to relax. She closed her eyes and pictured the woods behind her hut, cool and damp. She concentrated on breathing in the rich forest smell, even while her nose told her that bread baked nearby.

In moments, they heard Sadie's hurried steps. She burst through the door with a bundle of gray-green plant material in her hand. "Sorry it took so long. Had to use the broom to get it down."

Tanyth smiled. "I had to use the broom to put it up there, so seems fair."

Their winter of training showed as the two broke the stalks of comfrey into the pot, the musky smell of it not quite able to beat back the scent of fresh bread. Amber pushed the leaves into the water with a large wooden spoon and swirled them around a few times.

Sadie looked to Tanyth. "Willow bark tea?"

Tanyth sighed but nodded. The sharp pain in her arm throbbed with each beat of her heart and she tried to think of anything else. Even the bitter taste of willow bark would distract her.

"How wet do we want this, mum? Pasty?"

"Make a thick paste of it. Soak the bandages in the water before you wrap me."

Sadie and Amber nodded and set to their tasks, Amber fishing the hot, soggy herb out of the pot and placing it in the cheese cloth that Sadie held open above a bowl. The gray-green liquid dribbled into the bowl with a faint splashing sound.

The back door burst open, startling them all. The sudden

flinch made Tanyth wince. Frank strode into the kitchen, his eyes raking the room.

In three strides he knelt beside her chair, his gaze alternating between the swollen, discolored limb on the work surface and her face. "You fell down?"

She laughed in spite of herself and rubbed her head with her free hand. "Bumped my head, too."

He leaned over to look at her scalp but didn't touch it. "Got quite an egg there."

She nodded, the rum making her at once giddy and drowsy as her body's reaction to the emergency passed and the two women finished constructing the poultice.

"Stand back, Frank," Sadie said. "We need to get this on her arm."

"What is it?" he asked, even as he rocked back and stepped out of the way.

"It's called bone stitch," Tanyth said, steeling herself for the heat and pressure that would probably hurt.

"Can I help?" he asked.

Amber tutted and shooed Frank out of the way with backward flicks of her fingers. "Go clean the barn or something. She's not going anywhere for half an hour or more. Come back then and you can help her get home."

"That'd be a trick," Tanyth muttered considering that she didn't really have a home at the moment.

"You hush," Sadie said. "That rum'll turn you into a chatterbox and you don't wanna be sayin' things you're gonna regret later."

Tanyth blinked and looked at Sadie. "How much did you give me?"

Sadie poured another dollop into Tanyth's mug. "One more shot oughta do it." She thrust the mug into Tanyth's free hand and lifted it up to her mouth. "Drink up. Doctor's orders."

While Amber and Sadie positioned the soggy mass along the length of Tanyth's arm, she up-ended the mug and felt rum roll over her tongue and burn down her throat. "Much more of that and I'm going to pass out."

"We don't want that now, and not so much as to make

you sick, either, mum, but you need to go lay down in a bit. That'll help keep you in bed."

Tanyth grinned. "Oh, I think Frank can keep me in bed jes' fine on his own."

The two younger women giggled. "I'm sure he can, mum, but you'll need to be careful about that arm for a day or twelve until it's had a chance to start knitting," Sadie said.

Tanyth felt her eyes blinking slowly as she tried to think about Sadie's words, peering down at the hot poultice resting on her arm. Even the faint weight of it made the bone throb but the heat and moisture felt good on the swollen flesh.

"Be better cold, fer swellin'," Tanyth said. "Never snow around when you need it."

Amber giggled. "Not much ice this time o' year either, mum."

"You just relax, mum," Sadie said, and patted her good shoulder. "You'll be right as rain in a few weeks."

Tanyth looked down at her splinted and poulticed arm. "This isn't good."

"No, mum. Looks like you're going to be stayin' a bit longer than you planned," Amber said.

Tanyth frowned at that. "Can't. Gotta get north."

Sadie poured Tanyth's mug full of tea and placed it on the table within easy reach. "That may be, mum, but you can't go anywhere with your arm the way it is, so you may as well sit back and enjoy it."

"Hurts," Tanyth said glaring at it.

"It'll do that for a few days," Amber said. "Then it'll itch like crazy."

Tanyth nodded. "Yes. It will." She said the words carefully, aware of a growing numbness in her nose and cheeks.

"Frank should be back shortly ta take you to your hut," Sadie said.

"Not yet," Tanyth said. "Wait a bit, then wrap with them shoggy bandageses." Tanyth smacked her lips and wet her whistle with a bit of the hot tea. "No willow bark in that one."

Sadie grinned at her. "It's steeping, mum. We want it good and strong."

Tanyth nodded. The pain in her arm receded a bit. It still hurt like the blazes but the odd appendage lying on the table seemed to be part of somebody else. "Jes' as well," she mumbled.

"What's that, mum?" Sadie asked, leaning closer.

"Nuthin'. Prob'ly want that willow bark now. Maybe splash some rum in it?"

Amber frowned in concentration. "Will that make it work better?"

Tanyth shook her head slowly, gently so as not disturb her arm. "But I won't be able to taste it."

Sadie laughed. "You've had enough, I think. And if you can taste anything after that much rum, I'd be surprised."

Tanyth blinked and tried to sit very still. The room had an odd rocking feeling to it. She looked at her arm. It wasn't moving, so that was good.

Amber thrust a mug into her free hand and Tanyth sniffed before gulping down the whole mug.

"Gah, that's awful," she grumbled.

"You could taste that?" Sadie asked, eyes wide in amazement.

Tanyth rolled her tongue around in her mouth, realizing that some part of her face was feeling quite numb and that the bitter taste in her mouth was more memory than flavor. "Not really," she said after several moments consideration.

Sadie snickered. "Didn't think so."

"How long should we leave this on, mum?" Amber said waving a hand in front of Tanyth's eyes.

"What?"

"The poultice, mum. How long?"

Tanyth started to shrug but thought better of it. "Half hour or so. No more than that. Need to do it again tomorrow. Grind the roofs up."

"Roofs, mum?"

Tanyth ran her tongue around inside her mouth again and focused on her numb lips. "Roots. Mash up the roots."

"You have some roots?"

Tanyth shook her head gently. "I got no roots jes' now. But I dug comfrey root las' fall. Show you when I get back to my hut."

"Should we wrap you up, mum?" Sadie asked.

"Been half hour yet?" Tanyth blinked down at her arm. It looked terrible. "S'all swollen. Hurts."

"Yes'm. It's been a half hour. Let us wrap it up and we'll get Frank to help you back to your hut," Sadie said, lifting the bundle of cheesecloth and herb off the top of her arm.

Tanyth nodded slowly and felt her lips purse in thought. "That would be good."

Between the two of them, Amber and Sadie got a solid wrapping around the splint and Tanyth's arm. With it solidly wrapped, they were able to readjust the splint's bindings at wrist and elbow, easing the pressure on swollen flesh.

"That's not too tight, is it, mum?"

Tanyth looked at her arm and considered it for a long moment. "Should be fine," she said, sure she needed to be more concerned by the events but unable to muster the strength. "Any tea left in the pot?"

Amber dribbled a bit into the empty mug. "Anything else we can do for ya, mum?"

Tanyth lifted the mug and took a loud slurp off the top. "I'll be fine. Jes' need to lay down, I think. Roots tomorrow, then maybe we can cast it up." She peered around the inn's kitchen looking at each of the two women in turn. "Half hour yet? Where's Frank?"

Amber grinned and crossed to the back door. She had a quiet conversation at the doorway that Tanyth couldn't hear and came back with Frank in tow. "Here's Frank. You ready to go lay down?"

Tanyth considered it as the dull throbbing in her arm took on a sharper urgency. "Yes. I think I better do that." She looked at Frank and spoke very carefully. "Can you loan me one of your hands? I seem to have only one I can use right now." She tried to lift the injured arm and stopped. The movement of the muscles under the binding made her gasp, "Ow."

He helped her stand, holding her good arm firmly under his. "Let's go get you comfy, shall we?"

Tanyth nodded, vaguely aware that she was already too

drunk. "That'd be good," she managed to say and then focused all her attention on holding on to Frank's arm with her good one and steadfastly ignoring the jolts of liquid pain that splashed through her body with each step.

It felt like an awful lot of steps before Frank finally got her stretched out on her cot, damp bandages safely wrapped in a bit of canvas to keep them from leaking onto the covers. She let the darkness sweep her away.

☽○☾

She opened her eyes on the rising of the moon. Silvery talons raked the shadows. The old owl across the vale reminded her that he still lived. All was quiet below. She would hunt in the morning, but she dropped off the branch high in the spruce and glided to the ridgepole of the big building. The cold time was almost over, and the chill of night didn't dig so deeply. She wondered if the man had left a rabbit. Sometimes he did and they were tasty. She would like a rabbit.

She soared off the roof and explored the base of her tree. There was no rabbit and she crooned a call in the darkness. The bright moon showed the way back to her branch and she returned to her roost. When the bright returned, she could hunt. The food time—the warm time—she felt it coming on the night wind.

Fluffing up her feathers, she sidled up to the trunk of the tree and tucked her head under a wing.

☽○☾

She woke with a start and the sudden movement awakened the pain in her arm. No longer sharp, dulled by familiarity, it still made her sweat.

"Easy, there." Frank's quiet voice came out of the dimness.

Tanyth saw him rise from a chair beside the banked hearth and cross to her.

"You all right?" he asked.

"No, you old fool," she croaked and the sound alarmed her, reminded her of the dream. She put her free hand up to her lips to make sure the fingers were really fingers, that her mouth had lips.

Frank held a mug up to her mouth and slipped a solid arm under her shoulders to help her lift. "Here. A bit of water.

Sadie gave you a good dose of rum. Some water'll help." His voice sounded like he might be soothing a spooked horse.

She leaned up and took a few sips. Rum would explain the heaviness in her head, the queasiness in her gut and the sour taste in her mouth. She took another sip.

"Better?" Frank asked, offering the mug again.

"'Nough for now," she whispered, not trusting her voice to speak aloud.

Frank lowered her gently to the cot and knelt beside her, gazing into her face in the little light that the fire provided. A sadness spread across his face that Tanyth could read even in the near dark. "You had a dream," he said.

"Yeah," she whispered. "Not that dream. Different one."

"Bad?"

She gave her head a small shake. "She wants a rabbit."

Frank's teeth glowed in the gloom as he smiled. "She always wants a rabbit."

His amusement made Tanyth smile in return. She lifted a shoulder in a half shrug. "She likes rabbits, and they're not easy to catch."

"We're spoiling that bird," Frank grumbled, his smile still gleaming against the dark.

"She saved my life," Tanyth said.

"She's the reason you think you're goin' mad."

Tanyth sighed and settled back on her pillow. "That, too."

"You can't have it both ways, you know," Frank said, reaching out to stroke her cheekbone with one calloused fingertip.

She looked at him, brow furrowed as she tried to piece together his meaning. "Both ways?"

He nodded, the movement almost lost in the dark. "She either saved your life, or you're goin' mad. Those two things don't work at the same time."

Tanyth thought about that, but before she could come to any conclusions, sleep claimed her again and, pain and all, dragged her down into the dark.

☽○☾

The moon's pale light parted the darkness and shimmered on crystal water. Tanyth saw small pebbles rolling, rolling along the streambed, their shadows jumping and tumbling as they moved. A darker shadow that she couldn't make out lay along the flow, and at first she thought it must be a root, but as pebble after pebble rolled on the shadow, it disappeared. As she watched in the silvery moonlight, the shadows and flickers made it difficult to see but slowly, slowly, the darker shadow filled. A gouge, then, in the bed of the stream. The water pushed pebbles and some rolled past but others fell. She could almost hear the burbling of the water and the faint ticking of the pebbles as they rolled and struck each other. The moon sailed across the sky and slid down behind the trees at last leaving the stream and its curious pebbles in darkness.

CHAPTER 3
CHANGE OF PLANS

The following days bled together. Sleep came sporadically and Tanyth found herself lying in the dark, her broken arm cradled and throbbing against her chest. Frank brewed endless mugs of willow bark tea, but the constant frustration from trying to use just one hand left her nearly sobbing. When Frank needed to tend to the horses or work with the quarrymen to fill in the muck hole with rock and gravel, Rebecca took his place. Between the two of them they kept her quiet, dosed with willow bark, and as comfortable as she could be with a broken arm and a burning need to be on the road.

"How much longer before you're ready to make the first run into Kleesport?" Tanyth asked.

He didn't look at her, but offered a half shrug. "Jakey thinks they'll have a load in another week. Maybe a little more. Ten days, prob'ly."

Tanyth looked at her arm, now wrapped in a plaster cast, and flexed the fingers on the captured hand. The pain had gone down to a bearable level—enough that she was able to refuse yet another mug of willow bark tea as being worse than the pain itself.

"You could wait for the next trip," Frank said, filling in the obvious choice for her. He glanced at her over his shoulder as he stacked the clean dishes on the mantel board.

"Aye, I could, but I need to go on this first trip."

"Why are you being so stubborn about this?" Frank's question carried no heat. He stood with his back to the hearth and curiosity painted his face. "The season's still early. I doubt that the ships have had a chance to get north yet."

That caught her attention. "Not get north?"

"Ice. North coast's prob'ly still icebound. Will be until the Zypheria blows and shoves it out to sea."

Tanyth frowned at him. "You're not makin' that up to keep me here another month, are you?"

He shook his head, the truth of it plain on his face. "No. I'm not clever enough to make it up, and I doubt that it would work for long. You'd have the truth of it when you get to Kleesport."

"So, the ships are just sitting' there? Waitin'?"

"Some are. Some are workin' the southern coast until the season gets a little further along, There'll be a big rush to be the first to make it to North Haven when the Zypheria clears the way."

"When'll that be?" Tanyth asked.

Frank shrugged. "Not usually a'fore the equinox."

"That's comin' right up."

Frank raised a hand in a calming gesture. "Yup, it is, but not for another week and it'll be a few weeks after that. Shearin' Moon or later most likely. I might have time to make two trips before the way's clear."

"Or I could get there and find all the ships goin' north have gone, if I wait too long," Tanyth said, watching Frank's face closely. "Then where'd I be?"

He pursed his lips but gave a grudging nod. "'S possible. But once the season starts there'll always be ships goin' north." He sighed and looked at her for a moment before turning away to poke at the fire. "Best bet is get to Kleesport before Shearin' Moon and try to book passage on one of the ships waitin' there." His voice carried a ragged edge.

Tanyth looked at the cast on her arm and considered the problems.

"I'll take you on the first trip to town. Should be plenty of time," he said.

She looked up and saw he'd turned to face her again, his mouth turned up in an expression that approximated a smile, but the spring of his smile couldn't overcome the winter in his eyes.

"Thank you," she said, feeling the sting of tears herself. She looked away.

"How you gonna manage?" he asked.

"Manage?" she asked, surprised by the question.

He jerked his chin at her cast. "One handed?"

She twiddled the fingers that stuck out and shrugged. The simple movement gave her twinges. "Didn't really think about it."

"I could go with ya," he said.

She sighed. "Frank, we've been over this."

"That was before you got hurt."

"Things haven't changed that much. The village still needs you here. Who's gonna drive the wagon?"

Frank sighed and shook his head, swiping at the back of his neck with a hand. "What if somethin' happens to me? They'd have to find somebody."

"Frank, I don't even know if Mother Pinecrest is goin' ta be willin' ta take me on, let alone you."

He gave her a weak smile and flexed an arm. "I can chop wood, fetch water..."

She laughed. The jiggling made her arm twinge so she stopped with a wince.

"All right, well if not me, then Becca," he said.

"Rebecca?" Tanyth felt at a loss for a moment and then remembered. "Oh."

Frank leaned back against the mantel board. "She wants to go. She'd be able to help ya."

She snorted a little laugh.

"It's not gonna be easy goin' when you get to North Haven, Tanyth. A woman alone is a target."

She snorted again, but with less humor. "Nothin' new in that."

Frank gave her a little shrug.

"I could get her killed." Tanyth's words were low but sharp.

Frank's expression hardened. "You could get yourself killed, too, but I don't hear ya talkin' about that."

"I'm an old fool, Frank," she smiled to take the sting from her words. "There's little enough of my life left to take chances with. Rebecca's got a long life ahead of her. Riskin' that...?"

She shook her head and let the thought peter out.

Frank shifted his weight and thrust his hands deep into his trouser pockets, leaning his shoulders back against the mantel. "And how old were you when you started, then?"

"I was a lot older than that girl—"

"When you got married?"

"Well, no, course not. I mighta been a winter or so older."

"Well? You risked your life then, didn't ya?" Frank gave her a half shrug. "What's the diff'rence?"

Tanyth's brow furled in a frown. "Well, I was goin' off to be a grown woman. To be a wife..." Her voice trailed off.

"You went off to live with a man who beat ya, abused ya, mighta killed ya if you'd 'a stayed." Frank's murmur was barely audible over the low crackling of the fire.

She sighed, his gentle words bringing back a hard reality that she managed to ignore most of the time. "That was different," she said.

"How?"

"Well, it's what people do, isn't it? Grow up, get married, have a family?" Tanyth jerked her head toward the door. "That girl out there hasn't done any of that."

"And leavin' your husband? Takin' to the road, alone, for twenty winters or more? That's what people do?"

Tanyth looked up at his words and saw the gentle warmth in his brown eyes. He surprised a soft laugh out of her. "Not exactly, no."

"But it was your choice, right? You coulda stayed?"

"Yeah, I coulda stayed but I don't understand. What are you driving at?"

He shrugged and his mouth screwed into a brief grimace. "It was your choice. You picked your path."

"Well, course. Who else?"

"Then why're you so dead set on keeping Rebecca from pickin' hers?"

Tanyth lay very still on her cot as his quiet words took root.

Frank let her consider while he fetched the hot water from the hearth and filled the teapot to steep.

"Is that what I'm doin'?"

Frank rolled one shoulder and gave a negligent toss of his head. "Seems like. To me." He leaned back against the mantel again and peered at her through the afternoon's gathering dusk. "One woman alone's a target, right enough. Two? Two strong women on a mission from the Mother?" His weather-seamed face crinkled into a smile and mirth danced in his eyes as he shook his head from side-to-side. "Not something I'd wanna tangle with."

A soft laugh escaped her lips. "You're supposed to be tryin' to talk me into stayin'," she said after a moment. "Not pointin' out ways for me to go."

The smile remained but his expression turned to sadness. "Is that what I'm s'posed to be doin'?"

"Well, I thought that's what you were tryin' for."

He shook his head again. "Yup, well. I'd be lyin' if I said I want you to leave. That I didn't think we had somethin' here worth keepin'."

"Frank—" Tanyth didn't like the pleading tone in her voice.

Frank held up one hand, palm out. "Lemme finish."

Tanyth huffed but settled back on the cot.

"I'd also be lyin' if I said I didn't understand why you gotta do it. Some things in this world are bigger than me, bigger than you even." He shot her a mischievous look.

She snickered at his blatant attempt to tease her along.

"You got a road you got to follow," Frank said, his voice pitched low. "I know that. It's part of why I love you. I don't have to like it, but I do have to honor it. Without it, you wouldn't be the woman you are and I couldn't stand the thought that I might be the cause."

Tanyth felt the tears starting to sting her eyes and she fumbled for a handkerchief. "Now, Frank Crane," she said, pausing to wipe her eyes then swipe at her nose. "You got no call tossin' around words like 'love' and 'honor' at this late date."

He crossed to her and crouched beside the cot, gathering her fluttering hand into his calloused grip. He tilted his head to catch her eyes in his. "Seems like I gotta say 'em now or it'll be too late to say 'em at all, won' it?"

His tone wheedled its way into her heart and she leaned over to kiss his brow. "Dear man," she said, and turned her cheek to press against him. After a few moments, she said, "I'll talk to Rebecca tomorrow."

"I'd appreciate it," he murmured.

With the decision made, Tanyth's mind started rolling the idea around, probing for flaws, considering options. "We'll have to outfit her a bit."

She felt his brow move under her cheek and she pulled back to see his sad smile. "Yup. S'pose we will."

They sat like that for several moments before Tanyth wrapped her good arm around his neck and pulled him onto the cot beside her.

The tea turned bitter and cold before they remembered it.

☽○☾

The moon cast its light on the shimmering stream once more. She'd seen it many times before. Each time the moon showed her the same stream, the same clear water and rolling pebbles, always tiny pebbles along the stream bed, along the dark shadow, filling it slowly, slowly. Each dream a little more shadow filled, a little less darkness, but always pebbles in the clear, cool stream. The moon fell below the trees again and Tanyth could hear the clicking of the pebbles in the darkness—always the clicking under the gurgle of the stream.

CHAPTER 4
PREPARATIONS

Tanyth surveyed the pile of goods arrayed on her small table and shook her head.

"What's the matter, mum?" Rebecca asked, her hands twisting together in front of her body.

"Is that what you think you need to take?"

Rebecca frowned at the array of clothing and gear. "You said to bring everything I thought I'd need on the road, mum."

Tanyth smiled and nodded. "Indeed, I did, and it's prob'ly just as well." She eyed the clothing in particular. "Ya know you're gonna have ta carry all this, don't cha?"

A flash of surprise blinked across the younger woman's face. "I thought we were ridin' on the lorry."

"Only as far as Kleesport."

"Well, yes, but then we'll be on a ship for North Haven."

Tanyth nodded to grant the point. "But after that it's on our backs or left behind until we find Mother Pinecrest somewhere up in the Lammas Wood."

"Oh." Rebecca looked crestfallen. "I hadn't thought that far ahead."

"You could stay in Kleesport, ya know," Tanyth said, offering the girl a way out.

Rebecca shook her head. "No, mum. I've been in Kleesport and there's less for me there than here, I think."

Tanyth grinned. "Well, there are more men there. Single men ya might fancy once you get to know 'em."

A pink flush crept up Rebecca's neck and she shook her head. "Well, be that as it may, mum, I want to go find Mother

Pinecrest with you."

"Why?" Tanyth asked.

Rebecca shrugged in the offhand way of youth who don't want to answer difficult questions. "I've never done anything half so excitin', mum. In all my life, I've always ever done what people said I should do. Now?" she paused to shrug again. "Now, it's different. I wanna do what *I* wanna do. And besides, you need my help, mum." Rebecca nodded at the cast on Tanyth's forearm.

Tanyth grimaced inwardly at Rebecca's unconscious echo of Frank's comment. "Very well, but you'll have to cut this pile down to somethin' you can carry on your back. Where we're goin', there may not be much in the way of road and the only pack animal I count on is me."

"Why's that, mum?"

"What? The pack animal?"

Rebecca nodded, eyeing the pile of clothing dubiously.

"Have to feed 'em, care for 'em. That takes silver and time that I gen'rally don't have. If I carry what I need, I don't have to worry about takin' care of some poor beast." Tanyth paused for a moment to consider. "And it's a lot easier to pass as an old man without the added incentive of havin' a pack animal that somebody might take it into their heads to steal."

Rebecca looked up with a frown. "An old man, mum? You?"

Tanyth grinned and thrust her good hand deep in the pocket of her trousers. "You don't see me wanderin' around in a dress, do ya?"

Rebecca looked down at her homespun and then over at Tanyth, eyes squinting as if seeing her for the first time. "You don't look like a man, mum. I hate to tell ya."

The right side of Tanyth's mouth curled up in a grin. She crossed to the hook beside the door and, with her back to Rebecca, straightened out her clothes, fumbling to button the top of her shirt one-handed. She slipped into her wide-shouldered, cloth coat, settling the left shoulder gingerly over the sling that held the cast against her chest, and letting the left sleeve hang. She pulled her hat off the peg, tugging the brim down over her eyes. Last she took the staff in her right hand and turned to face the young woman again. She stood with her hips shot to the side and leaned forward on the staff.

Rebecca blinked several times, taking in the transformation. "Somebody who knows ya wouldn't be fooled, mum."

Tanyth smiled and tilted her head back to see out from under the hat brim. "I'm not worried about them. It's the stranger on the road who might think an old woman might be easy to rob or even have a bit of sport with. Those are the ones we need to worry about."

"That why you keep your hair short, mum?"

"Partly. Partly 'cause it's just easier to care for on the road." She felt the length of her hair. "Reminds me, I should clip off a bit of this before we head north."

Rebecca's hand went to her own head pulling the heavy, brown braid forward over her shoulder and running it through her hands, a far-away look in her eyes.

Tanyth saw the look on the young woman's face. "We need to figure out who you'll be on the road."

Rebecca's eyes focused on Tanyth. "Who I'll be? Can't I be me?" Her voice held a faint quaver.

Tanyth stood the staff back in its corner and slipped out of hat and coat while she thought. "Per'aps, but think of what we'd look like on the road."

"You mean after we get to North Haven?"

"Yeah. We'll be fine as far as Kleesport. We won't fool anybody aboard ship, but when we leave North Haven, we don't wanna be lookin' like an old man and his pretty granddaughter, miles from civilization."

Rebecca smiled at the compliment but stopped stroking her braid. "I've seen lots of boys with long hair," she said.

Tanyth nodded. "I was just thinkin' that, but none of the quarrymen do."

"The clay gets everywhere, mum. They shave regular, too. Same reason."

Tanyth squinted her eyes, trying to envision how her young charge might disguise herself. After a few moments, she gave up with a shake of her head.

"We can put you in boy's clothes, rightly enough. Bulky

coat and a loose sweater would cover your chest."

Rebecca looked down at herself. "Yeah. Little enough to cover there."

Tanyth gave a low laugh. "You'd be surprised how little it takes for some men, my dear. Even saggy old biddies like me can get too much attention."

Rebecca looked up, an expression of horror on her face. "You don't mean..."

Tanyth shrugged. "Why d'ya think I walk the roads looking like an old man. A poor old man, at that."

Rebecca cocked her head for a moment. "I never really thought of it."

"Well, think of it."

Rebecca cast another look down at her dress and then began bundling up the clothing on the table. "I got an idea, mum. We can take more to Kleesport, can't we? I mean on the wagon?"

"Sure. With Frank, we don't have a lot to fear. Not many would cross him without a few boyos at their back."

Rebecca nodded, her brow furrowed in thought. "Of course, mum. It's all about the look, i'n't it?"

"The look? Yeah. I s'pose it is."

"All right, then." Rebecca nodded once. "Lemme go see what I can do."

Rebecca headed for the door, the bundle of clothing wrapped in her arms. Tanyth opened the door with her good hand and held it for the young woman while she clambered up and out into the bright spring afternoon.

Tanyth watched as the young woman strode purposefully across the yard and up the stairs to the inn. She met Frank coming out and he held the door open for her as she bustled into the building.

He saw Tanyth watching from the door of her hut and gave her a big smile.

She waved and closed the door. "That fool man'll be along lookin' for his tea shortly," she muttered. She crossed to the hearth and busied herself with the familiar routine of boiling water, and setting the pot—fumbling the water into the kettle one handed and measuring tea into the pot. She did her best not to think about how much she was going to miss that fool man.

While she waited for the water to boil, she slipped her arm out of its sling, lifting it experimentally, testing the muscles, flexing her hand. The pain was still there, but not as bad as it had been. She tried to stick a finger down the top to scratch the back of her arm, but it wouldn't fit between her flesh and the cast. She cast around the hearth, looking for something—a piece of stick, anything—that she could use to scratch with.

Outside, somewhere off in the woods, the raven cawed loudly three times. Her hoarse squawks carried easily in the still afternoon air.

Tanyth looked to the direction of the squawking. "Yeah. And a good afternoon to you, too," she said.

The small kettle came to a boil, the burbling sound reminding Tanyth of something that she couldn't quite recall. She straightened and let her eyes roam around the small hut that had been her home for the past few months. The woven reed mats on the floor looked nearly new. The shelves of medicinals in the back stood ready for most common ailments. Tanyth smiled when she remembered the large pot of honey she'd hidden back there for Amber and Sadie to find after she left. The foodstuffs in the larder and on the pantry shelves would go back to common stores and the herbs drying in the rafters wouldn't go to waste now that she'd taught what she could to those she'd be leaving behind.

The sense of melancholy nearly overwhelmed her just as the kettle boiled over and started spitting on the hearth.

"Foolish old woman," she scolded with a sniff. "You know better."

Still, as she poured the boiling water over the dried leaves in the little china teapot that she'd have to leave behind, she couldn't help but feel a bit of wonder at how much a clinker-built hut in the middle of nowhere meant to her.

She heard footsteps outside and the quick two-rap knock that was Frank's nod to propriety. He slipped the latch, folded his lanky frame under the lintel, and stepped into the hut. He stood for a moment, the bright sunlight behind him, and she knew it wasn't the hut that meant so much to her after all.

He pulled the door closed, blocking the dazzling light and turned to her, a brilliant smile shining against skin so tanned it looked like leather. "Tea ready?"

She nodded, and opened her good arm to him, not trusting her voice to speak. His strong arms wrapped around her and pressed the hard cast against her breastbone. She didn't mind. At least while he held her, the blasted thing didn't itch.

CHAPTER 5
EQUINOX

Tanyth stood facing the tree line to the east. The black of star-studded night had faded to a predawn gray already. The villagers had gathered around her in the chill mist of morning A pair of travelers joined them—a tinker and a cloth merchant who'd stopped at the inn overnight.

She leaned on her staff, standing awkwardly with her left arm in the sling. The earth beneath her feet quickened with new life, awakened from a long winter sleep, ready for the flush of growth that longer days would bring. She emptied herself into the morning letting her mind relax and her body feel the faint breeze from the pine-scented forest to the east, waiting for the moment when the first rays of morning sun would creep through the trees and grace them all with its golden light.

She felt her heartbeat slow and heard her own breathing loud in her ears. The taste of new leaves, of fresh growth, washed across her tongue with each in-drawn breath. As the moment approached, stretching like a fiddle string with its own barely perceptible sound, she turned and faced the north. She waited for the flash of heat on her cheek and when it came, she spoke, her voice carrying readily on the sun-lit air. She didn't raise her arms or her voice, but simply spoke, chin upraised, eyes on the cusp of the heavens where day and night blended.

"I call upon the Guardian of the North, Bones of the World, to protect this place and all who live here, to provide the foundation for a new season, new growth, new life."

Pivoting around her staff, she faced the east and the golden light streaming between the trees to rake the yard before the inn with talons of glory.

"I call upon the Guardian of the East, Breath of the World, to protect this place and all who live here, to cool the land with your breezes and give your strength to the new growth, protecting it from harm and strengthening it by your presence."

She pivoted again to face the south and the dark line of forest on the far side of the village.

"I call upon the Guardian of the South, Soul of the World, to protect this place and all who live here, to fill their hearts with passion, to burn away that which no longer serves, and to warm that which strives to grow with the fire of life."

She pivoted again to face the west and the looming bulk of the inn. The sky behind it brightening with the rising dawn.

"I call upon the Guardian of the West, Blood of the World, to protect this place and all who live here, to wash away the hurts, to heal the ills, and to lend your strength to all that grows here."

She closed the loop by pivoting once more to the north.

"In the name of the Lady, Mother to all, I beg these boons that all who live within this place may be healthy, happy, and prosperous in the coming season. So mote it be."

With that, she raised her staff from the ground and stamped it back down. The thump of iron-shod wood against graveled soil seemed to reverberate in the still air for a moment before the sun cleared the tree line and flooded the yard with light and heat.

Tanyth's legs felt a bit weak and she found herself leaning on her staff for support. Frank was at her side in an instant.

He murmured, "You all right?"

She looked up into his concerned face. "Well, 'course. Just need to catch my breath a bit. This early mornin' stuff is tough on a body before breakfast."

He smiled, but the concern didn't leave his eyes.

The villagers around them started rustling about and Tanyth turned to find them lined up facing her and, solemnly, each stepped up and bowed before heading off to the inn for the celebration breakfast. Tanyth returned each bow with a nod of her head as a stand-in for the Lady while the ceremony played out. When the final pair, the two travelers, approached, Tanyth felt self-conscious at the looks of awe on their faces. They bowed and she cradled her staff in the crook of her arm so she could raise a hand in benediction. "Safe travels, friends," she said.

The shorter one, a tinker with a wiry frame and hair that sprouted from the sides of his bald pate, blushed and stammered, "Th-th-thank you, Lady."

His companion, slightly taller and with arms that bulged from many seasons of heaving bolts of cloth around, offered a smile that seemed almost shy and oddly out of place in such a well-dressed merchant. "My thanks, mum," he said.

Together the two strolled off toward the inn, their heads together and one or the other casting occasional glances in her direction.

Amused, Tanyth turned to look up at Frank. "What d'you s'pose got into them?"

Frank's mouth curled into a sideways smile and his eyes widened in feigned innocence. "I can't imagine."

She scowled at him. "Are you makin' fun o' me?"

He chuckled. "Not while you're carrying that staff."

She grinned and turned to cross the short distance to her hut.

Frank matched her stride for stride, arm out as if to catch her if she fell.

"You're treatin' me like an invalid, Frank." Her voice came out sharper than she intended. "I broke my arm, not my leg."

He simply grinned at her. "And if you trip and fall? How you gonna catch yourself with only one arm and your hands full?"

She snorted a laugh but had to admit he had a point. "I'm not likely to fall as long as I got my stick to lean on."

"I'm just a foolish old man," he said, eyes dancing in the morning light.

She stood her staff against her hut and smiled up at him. "True, but now that I've got no stick, maybe I can lean on

37

you?"

"As long as there's breath in me," he said and held out his arm for her to grab.

The words hammered in Tanyth's heart and she didn't trust herself to speak, simply wrapped her good arm around his and let him drag her across the yard, up the broad stairs, and into the maelstrom of breakfast in the common room.

Inside Tanyth sat at the place of honor, in front of the hearth, with the open doors of the inn allowing the golden morning to shine on her. The heat and hubbub nearly overwhelmed her, but Frank kept her mug filled with hot tea and after sampling a variety of pies, pasties, and stewed grains, she felt her strength returning.

"That prayer musta taken a lot out of me," she murmured to Frank, biting into a second helping of venison pie.

He leaned down to her. "You put a lot into it, Tanyth. Gotta expect it to take a toll."

"Just words," she muttered. "Don't see why that would be so taxin'."

He leaned back to look at her from a distance. "Is that what you think? Just words?"

She frowned. "Well, isn't it? Not like I'm doing anythin' out there but yammering."

Frank laughed gently. "You're funny."

"I don't see the humor." The feeling that he was laughing at her stung and made her feel prickly. "I'm just tryin' to help out and you got no call to laugh at me, Frank Crane."

Sadie leaned across the table. "Uh, oh, Frank. She's usin' your full name. You best apologize now and try to save yourself."

Tanyth shot Sadie a frown that set her back in her chair.

"Sorry, mum." The younger woman looked contrite and Tanyth immediately felt sorry for taking her pique out on an innocent bystander.

Tanyth reached her free hand across to pat Sadie's hand. "Nothin' to be sorry about, my dear. I'm just feeling a bit...tired. And this galoot is laughin' at me." She elbowed Frank none to gently in the ribs.

"Sorry, Tanyth. I'm not mockin' you. I mean it," he said.

She leaned over and gave him a kiss on the cheek. "See that you don't," she said. "Is there any more tea?"

She didn't really want more tea, but the conversation made her uncomfortable. She made a mental note to find out what he found so funny later, when they weren't surrounded by people.

"Excuse me, mum?"

The voice came from behind her. Tanyth turned to find the two travelers standing there.

The tinker spoke again. "Me 'n' Herm here, well, we wanted ta thank ya."

At the mention of his name the burly cloth merchant ducked his head in a quick semi-bow. His eyes looked anywhere except at her.

"That was a proper ceremony, right enough." He glanced up at his larger companion and then back at Tanyth. "Thank you for lettin' us be part of it."

"You're certainly welcome." Tanyth looked from one to the other of them, a bit confused by their obvious discomfort.

The tinker elbowed his friend who twitched like he'd been stabbed. "Yar," he said, "I hain't seen da like since I wuz a tad back ta Dermton." Each word seemed to fight its way from the larger man's chest and out his mouth.

She smiled again. "Dermton? One of my teachers lived in Dermton."

The man looked startled. "Ya know it, then? Dermton?"

"On the banks of the Ryme Flow? Just where the foothills start up to the Whitehorn Mountains?"

The man nodded, wonder in his eyes.

"Indeed I do. Spent a whole winter there with Mother Abigail Hilton. Must be..." she had to think for a moment as her memories swirled back through the miles and the winters. "Ten winters ago now. Maybe fifteen."

Herm shifted his feet and glanced at his friend before speaking. "Mother Hilton, aye, mum. You know'd her?"

She smiled and nodded. "Lovely woman. Do you know? Is she still there?"

A cloud passed across his face and the tinker answered for him.

"No, mum." He glanced up at the larger man before continuing. "She passed over some time ago. Seven, maybe eight winters since."

Tanyth sighed. "I can't say as I'm surprised. Mother Hilton was on in years when I stayed with her. A good woman, wise in the way of the woods and waters."

The tinker nodded. "Yes'm. She were."

"Mother Hilton was like a gran to us all, growin' up, mum," Herm said, the slow plod of his words rumbling through the breakfast hubbub that continued around the table. He paused and looked at his boots before casting a glance at Tanyth again. "She knew how to say a prayer, mum. You learned good."

The two stood there, shuffling their feet but making no move to leave.

"Is there somethin' else?" Tanyth asked.

Herm looked to his friend and shook his head, but the smaller man took a deep breath and looked to Tanyth. "We wuz hopin'—if it's not too much to ask, mum..."

The room quieted down and Tanyth could feel more eyes turning in their direction as the tinker seemed to stumble over his tongue.

"That is, mum. Could we beg a boon? A small blessin' for the road, mum?" He looked up at Herm who looked simultaneously abashed and hopeful.

The expression almost made her laugh but something about them made her hold her mirth in check. She glanced at Frank and was startled to see him watching her, not the travelers.

"I'm not much on blessin' and all," she said turning back to look at the two men, tugging self-consciously at the sling that held her cast. As she did, her eyes picked out a small, star-shaped spot on the hearthstone. A spot she knew was her own blood and the memory of it jolted her.

The two men bit back whatever it was they were about to say and merely nodded. "Well, thank ya, anyway, mum."

Together they started to turn away, but Tanyth stood and faced them.

"Wait," she said. "What are your names?"

They blinked in confusion for a moment but the big man

recovered first.

"I'm Herm, mum. Herm Ridgewood."

The name struck a chord in Tanyth's memory. "Your people run the Ridgewood Mill? Just down stream on the Ryme Flow?"

He smiled. "Yes, mum. Best mill on the Ryme."

Tanyth bit back a smile. If her memory was correct, it was the only mill on the Ryme.

The big man elbowed the tinker, jarring him out of his stupor.

"Oh, I'm Willum Grits, mum. You pro'ly never knew my people."

She closed her eyes to picture the tiny village. Something tugged at her memory. She imagined what the town must have looked like to a raven flying overhead. As she turned away from the river, out into the thistle and scrublands she remembered the Grits.

"You had a small place west of the town? Was it your mother who raised flowers?"

His jaw dropped. "How can you remember that far back, mum?"

She laughed and shook her head. "It's a gift, I s'pose. The All-Mother blessed me with a good memory. And while I remember the house, I can't remember your mother's name. I can see her face. I know I know it, but I just can't remember."

"Eloise, mum. Her name was Eloise."

"Was?"

He shuffled his feet. "Aye, mum. She passed over a couple winters back."

Tanyth sighed but, again, wasn't surprised. Even when Tanyth had been there, the woman had been little more than a rag and bones. She tried to support the family on what she could get from raising the flowers and the odd vegetable crop scratched from stony ground that nobody else wanted.

The two men stood side-by-side, light from the rising sun on equinox morning casting their shadows dark across the hearthstone that had been colored with Tanyth's own blood. They waited patiently while Tanyth considered.

"Farewell, then, Willum Grits and Herm Ridgewood. May

the All-Mother's blessing bring you peace on your travels and keep you safe until you find your homes once more." She reached over and pulled the small tinker toward her, her free hand on his shoulder. She was surprised to find him barely taller than she was. She kissed him once on the forehead. "Farewell, Willum," she said. She had to reach up to pull the burly cloth merchant down. She kissed his brow as well, murmuring, "Farewell, Herm."

She stepped back and time itself seemed frozen for one crystalline instant before a raven's loud caw broke the mood. The silence in the common room was so complete, they heard the heavy bird land on the ridge of the roof, heard the scratch-scratch of talons on wood shingles as she settled down.

Tanyth looked up and smiled. "Thomas? Have you put out a rabbit lately?"

He laughed. "No, mum. I'll find one today for her."

The joyful breakfast noise resumed then and Tanyth looked back to find the two travelers staring at her.

"Thank ya, mum," Herm said.

"Yeah. Thank ya, mum," Willum echoed.

"You're welcome, I'm sure. Now, daylight's burnin'. Don't you men have someplace to be before night falls?"

The two looked almost startled by the realization. "Yes'm," Willum said, pushing the larger man ahead of him toward the door. "We does, indeed, and thank ya. Most kindly."

"Blessed be," Tanyth said.

The two disappeared out the door and down the steps.

Tanyth's legs felt a bit rubbery and she sat, perhaps more heavily than she intended. She reached for her mug and found that somebody had refilled it for her. She took a grateful slurp and felt better.

The group looked to be in the final throes of breakfast, and she saw Jakey gathering the quarrymen with his eyes. They'd head out soon and the celebration would be over.

She turned to find Frank's deep, brown eyes smiling at her.

"Still think it's just words?" he asked.

Tanyth started to laugh at him, but she caught sight of the stained hearth and paused. Above them on the roof, the raven cawed again. She heard the wagons rolling out of the yard over the breakfast noises. She closed her lips over the retort she had planned and looked back at Frank.

He gave her a wan smile and an affectionate pat on the shoulder, but didn't say anything else.

"Hey, Frank," Jakey called from the other end of the table. "We'll have the load ready in three days."

Frank nodded. "I can bring the wagon up today, if ya wanna start loadin'."

Jakey flashed a grin. "'At's what I hoped. Thanks." He turned his attention to the quarrymen grouped around the table. "Now if you lovelies can tear yourselves away from your troughs long enough to earn your crust..."

His pronouncement was met with jeers and catcalls. Several crusts sailed through the air toward Jakey's head. He caught one on the fly.

"All right, you lot. Daylight's burning. Let's get some work done today." He gnawed the end of the crust he'd caught and headed for the door into the kitchen and the inn's back door beyond.

Around the table, the quarrymen snatched final swigs of tea and took what food they could carry to eat on the way. As a group, they followed Jakey through the door to the kitchen and on out of the inn, the hubbub of young men in good health fading into the distance.

Frank looked to Tanyth. "Three days, mum. Probably leave on the fourth. You gonna be ready?"

Tanyth lifted her cast in its sling and considered it. The low ache in her arm had subsided to a maddening itch. She wriggled the fingers and thumb experimentally. "It's gettin' there," she said, then nodded. "Yeah. I'll be ready."

He turned his gaze toward Rebecca who was helping Amber and Sadie to clear the table of the wreckage of breakfast. "What about her?"

"Dunno. She said she had some ideas, but I haven't found out what they are yet."

"Ideas?" Frank asked, eyebrows arched in surprise. "About what?"

"Well, she thought we should have a pack beast, but I

turned that down."

"What's wrong with that?"

"Care and feedin' on a long road. Hard enough to care for myself let alone an animal."

Frank sucked air through his teeth and squinted. "Could be. Lemme think on it. What else?"

"We don't wanna look too enticin' to anybody we meet on the road. We talked about why I wear trousers instead of a dress. I think she didn't quite consider how dangerous it might be to look like an old man and his daughter out travelin' on their own once we get to North Haven."

Light seemed to come on behind Frank's eyes. "That's why she wanted the sword, I bet."

"Sword?"

"One of the weapons we took off Birchwood's men. She asked William if she could have one."

Tanyth frowned and watched Rebecca back through the door to the kitchen with a pile of dirty crockery in her hands. "Carryin' a sword and not knowing how to use it is just askin' for trouble."

Frank's head bobbed slowly. "Yup. I think so, too. And I think I see what you mean about the pack animal. If you got so much to carry that you need it, it might be worth stealin'."

"Yeah. That's why I never travel with more than I can put on my back. The animal itself is worth stealin' for some. A poor, old man travelin' alone? What's he gonna have?"

"Well, you'll be a poor, old man travelin' with his beautiful granddaughter if you're not careful," Frank said.

Sadie leaned down, clearing away the dishes. "I don't think you'll need ta worry about that," she said.

The two looked up at her. "Why's 'at?" Frank asked.

Sadie just smiled. "Talking about Rebecca?"

They nodded almost in unison.

"She's got some surprises."

"I hope she's not plannin' on carryin' that sword," Frank said.

Sadie shook her head. "William convinced her t'would be more dangerous to carry than to go without."

"Then what...?" Frank asked.

Sadie shook her head again. "That's her surprise. I s'pect you'll be satisfied with the result."

Sadie finished clearing the dishes and disappeared into the kitchen, passing Amber at the doorway.

"You two still here?" Amber asked. "Go pack, shoo. Whatever you need to do. Scoot." She made shooing motions with her hands.

"You sure I can't help with the clean up, Amber?" Tanyth asked.

Amber cast a pointed look at the sling and shook her head. She gathered the last dirty bowls and mugs in her capable hands. "You've done enough for one day, mum, and I've got all the help I can handle in the kitchen right now."

A shriek of laughter punctuated her words and she rolled her eyes in mock annoyance.

"See what I mean?"

Tanyth stood and tottered on legs that lacked strength. Frank caught her arm and steadied her.

"You all right, mum?" Amber asked, eyes narrowing in concern.

"Oh, yes, my dear. Just sat too long and my legs need some stretching."

Amber shot a knowing look at Frank. "I'm sure he'll be happy to help you, mum."

The comment shocked a laugh out of Tanyth even as Frank groaned.

"Off with ya, then," Amber said. "We all got work to do."

Tanyth turned toward the door leaning more heavily on Frank's arm than she really thought necessary.

"You gonna be all right walkin' the roads?" Frank asked as they stepped out of the inn and into the brilliant morning sunlight.

Tanyth drew a deep breath filled with the scent of moist earth and blew it out slowly. "I don't know why I'm feelin' so weak. Not like I've done much."

Frank snorted. "Yup. Nothin' at all."

"Well, nothin' to speak of."

"Well, do me a favor?" he said, patting her hand where it wrapped around his arm.

"If I can."

"Don't go sayin' any more prayers until you get your strength back."

She looked up at him, eyebrows beetled in confusion. "Prayers? What's a few words got to do with anything?"

He snorted and shook his head before looking into her eyes. "Just promise me? Please?"

She read the concern there. "I don't get what you're so worried about. It's just words."

"Promise me."

She gave a little nod. "All right. I promise."

"Thank you."

"You're welcome. I guess."

"Now about that leg stretchin'..." he said with a grin.

She blushed, but grinned and tugged at his arm. "Now, you behave yourself. It's not my legs you're thinkin' of stretchin', and you got horses to harness and a wagon to drag up to the quarry."

He threw back his head and laughed. "Aye, that I do," he said as they reached the door to her hut.

She unwrapped her arm from his and gave him a little push. "Git. You got work to do and I need to do some organizin' myself."

He stood there for a moment looking down at her. "All right." He reached in to peck her on the cheek. "You be careful this morning. You're a lot tireder than you think."

She shook her head in mock exasperation. "Just a few words, Frank. Stop being an old woman. That's my job. Go play with your horses."

She lifted the latch and slipped into the cool dimness of her hut. At the foot of the short stair she turned to watch him walk away toward the barn.

"Frank?" she called.

He stopped, turning to look back at her.

"When you get done with the wagon? You could stop back here. I think I could use a little help stretchin' after all."

His brilliant grin all but sparkled in the morning light. He gave her a jaunty salute with two fingers and turned back toward the barn. He seemed to be walking a bit faster than before.

Tanyth smiled to herself and eased the door closed. She started to stoke up the banked fire in her hearth and found a long, splinter of kindling in her hand. Before tossing it on the blaze, she pulled the cast out of its sling and struggled to get the rough bit of wood under the top edge. The almost-there feeling of not quite scratching the itch had her pushing harder and harder until something gave and she was able to stick the whole length of the splinter down her arm. With a whimper of relief she worked the rough wood up and down, scoring her arm with scratches where the cast stopped, but getting to the itch at long last.

CHAPTER 6
SURPRISE

Frank brought the laden lorry wagon down from the quarry late in the afternoon. William and Thomas helped him unhitch the horses. Tanyth watched from the back stoop of the inn as the two men led the team to the barn, then she slipped inside to join the dinner preparations.

"You sure I can't help?" she asked, inhaling the homely smell of sourdough and spices that permeated the new building, already beginning to overwhelm the new wood scent of fresh construction.

Sadie had been baking all day and a wisp of sandy hair fell down across her face and stuck in the sweat honestly earned in front of a hot oven. "Yes, mum, we're sure."

Amber straightened from the kettle of stew that bubbled over the fire and gave Tanyth a warm smile. "You're the guest of honor, mum. Wouldn't be proper for you to do the work."

"Don't be silly. It's your last chance for cheap help," Tanyth said, waving her free hand as if to bat away the objections.

"Well, if you must do something," Amber said, "check that teapot. It should be about steeped. You'll prob'ly have to try a cup to make sure it's all right."

Tanyth chuckled at the blatant ruse, but did as the younger woman bid, settling on a stool in the corner out of the way.

"So, you both know what's in the hut? How to use it?" Tanyth asked.

Sadie pulled the last loaf out of the oven and slid it onto the worktable. "Yes, mum. We been over it a few times

49

already."

"Few dozen, more like," Amber added. She smiled at Tanyth. "We'll be fine, mum. Don't you fret."

Tanyth blew across the mug before taking a sip of the hearty tea. "Well, just so long's you're not sendin' after me because somebody got the flux again." She grinned at them and they laughed in return.

"No worries on that score, mum," Sadie said. "We're in good shape to weather the summer and who knows? By fall, maybe we'll find another healer to move out here with us."

"Frank's goin' ta put the word out in Kleesport, mum," Amber added. "We'll miss ya, right enough. You're part of the family, but we'll get by until you come back."

Tanyth sipped again and felt her heart beat heavily in her chest. "You know I'll prob'ly not be comin' back, don't ya?"

The two younger women shared a glance before Sadie answered. "Yes, mum. We know, but..." she shrugged. "Ya never really know what's gonna happen 'til it does, now do ya?"

Amber said, "And there's always Frank. You'd be hard pressed to find a better man to fill your wood box." Her eyes twinkled over a sly smile.

Sadie giggled and scrubbed a bit of butter across the tops of her fresh loaves.

"Oh, you two and your wood box fillin'," Tanyth said, her own laugh escaping in spite of herself. "I'm more interested in what Rebecca's up to and I'd feel a lot better knowing what she's planning before we have to get on the road."

Amber glanced at Sadie who gave a small shrug in return.

"You two know what she's plannin'?"

"She asked us not to tell, mum," Sadie said.

Amber added, "You'll see soon enough, and you'll have plenty of time on the way to Kleesport to fix anything that's wrong."

Tanyth looked back and forth between the two for several long moments. "Long's she's not planning on haulin' any more than she can carry."

"Well, I don't know about that, mum," Amber said. "She's packed up her goods and will be droppin' off a couple of trunks full when she gets to Kleesport."

"Frank already left room for 'em on the lorry wagon," Sadie said.

"Does she have a bedroll and a backpack?" Tanyth asked.

"Yes'm. William and Thomas gave her one out of stores, along with travelin' gear. She and Thomas been practicin' for the last week and if Thomas says so, she's set," Sadie said and Amber winced.

"Practicin'?" Tanyth asked, eyeing Amber with a raised eyebrow.

"Oh, you know, mum. Lightin' fires, layin' out a bedroll, cookin' without a hearth. Like that," Amber said.

"Uh, huh." Tanyth wasn't convinced but judging from the narrow-eyed glances the women shot back and forth, she wasn't about to find out from them. The uncertainly made her uneasy.

"What about you, mum? Are you ready?" Sadie asked. "You figured out how to put on a pack around that sling?"

Tanyth grunted. "Won't be pretty, but we can do it. Just have to put the sling over my head, put on the pack and then put the arm in the sling after that."

"And your coat?" Sadie asked with a wry grin.

"That's a bit more trouble, but it has to go on over all of it." Tanyth sighed. "I'm just hopin' I'll have this cast off by the time I need to wear the coat and carry the pack."

"Got supplies and all?" Amber asked, following Sadie's lead in trying to change the subject.

"Oatmeal, tea, a bit of cheese. I'll stock up in North Haven before we leave there. Not much sense in carryin' food all that way." She nodded at a crate tucked in the corner of the kitchen. "Frank's got enough food in there to feed half the village, I think. More'n enough for the three of us to get to Kleesport."

Amber snorted. "And back most likely."

They heard the sound of boot heels in the common room and Amber frowned. "I didn't hear anybody come in."

Just as she turned to investigate, the connecting door swung open. A youth slipped through and froze, mouth poised to speak. Tanyth had just time enough to register the homespun trousers and deer hide vest before she recognized the face staring out at her.

"Rebecca?" Tanyth said.

"Well, that kinda spoils the surprise," Sadie said.

"Oh, mum. I figured you'd be in your hut packin'." Rebecca sighed and let the door close behind her. "You'd have seen at dinner anyway, but we were gonna surprise ya."

"Well, I'm surprised right enough," Tanyth said with a short laugh. "What've you done?"

Rebecca stood with her arms out from her sides and gave a shuffling turn. "Got the clothes from the quarrymen. Mostly they're Kurt's stuff that the others couldn't use. Got a spare pair of pants and a couple of shirts."

"You cut your hair?" Tanyth felt a pang of guilt for the woman's sacrifice. "You had such a lovely braid."

"Thanks, mum, but it's just hair. It'll grow back. Charlotte cuts the quarrymen's hair. She did a good job with it?"

A leather thong held a small, ruddy-brown ponytail back off Rebecca's face. Charlotte had chopped her bangs off square in the front and it emphasized Rebecca's chin by taking some of the roundness out of her face. She'd never pass close inspection, but at a distance, she should fool most.

"You got a hat?" Tanyth asked.

"Yes'm, a wide brimmed one and a kerchief to hide my neck."

Tanyth made a little twirling motion with her fingers and Rebecca twirled slowly around again.

"That vest does a good job hiding your chest," Tanyth said.

"Well, I learned that from you, mum."

Tanyth's eyes widened in surprise. "From me?"

"Yes'm. You wrap your chest when you're travelin', don't ya?" Rebecca cast her eyes down and gave a little shrug. "I noticed when you were cut up."

Tanyth nodded her head slowly in approval. It was a habit she'd fallen out of since the run in with Birchwood, but it was one she'd need to start again.

"The vest hides her hips," Amber said with a smile.

Tanyth blinked and looked again.

"Slip your vest off, Becca," Sarah said.

With a grin, Rebecca slid the deer hide off her shoulders and did another little twirl. Even the bulky shirt and home-spun trousers couldn't disguise the very feminine roundness of the young woman's hips and backside. Rebecca put the vest back on and Tanyth noticed that it fell just far enough to mask the top edge of the curve and making her seem much more masculine.

"My face is still too clean, but a little soot and dirt on the sides..." Rebecca scrubbed at the edges of her cheeks, "and it'll look more realistic."

Tanyth squinted her eyes a bit and nodded again. "Yeah. A few days on the road and you'll look grubby enough. You're still lookin' too young to be my son, but you could be my grandson." She smiled. "You still lookin' forward to the trip?"

"More'n ever, mum." Rebecca's face brightened. "I've packed up what I've got that nobody else wants and I'll leave a trunk with my auntie in Kleesport. I've got a rucksack and bedroll and all my gear fits in it."

Tanyth grinned. "Yeah, I heard you were practicin' with Thomas."

Rebecca shot an angry look at Amber.

"Yep," Amber put in quickly. "We happened to mention you were practicing your fire makin' and such so you'd be ready for the road."

Rebecca nodded. "Oh, yeah. Right. He's real helpful on packin' and unpackin'. What to put on the bottom of the pack and all."

Tanyth hid the grin behind her mug and sipped the cooling tea. "Per'aps you'd like to come help me pack, then," she said. "Might be you learned a trick or two I haven't stumbled on."

Rebecca blinked a couple of times but surprised Tanyth by nodding agreement. "I'd be happy to, mum, if you think I can help."

"Dinner's still a couple hours away, mum," Amber said. "There's time if you wanna. Save some time in the morning."

Sadie gave her a knowing smirk. "And you'll prob'ly be too busy after dinner to do much. Now'd be a good time."

Her curiosity piqued, Tanyth finished off the last of her

tea and stood. "All right. Let's do that."

Rebecca led the way out of the kitchen, back through the common room, and out of the inn.

"You'll be fine as long as you're standin' still, I think," Tanyth said following the younger woman down the steps.

Rebecca glanced over her shoulder. "Standin' still?"

Tanyth smiled. "You'll need to practice walkin' without the wiggle."

Rebecca colored. "Oh, mum,..."

Tanyth laughed. "It's all right, my dear. We'll have plenty of time to practice and after the first twenty miles, you'll have it under control, I'm sure."

"True enough," Rebecca said.

Tanyth nodded to herself. The threat of miles hadn't bothered the woman. Perhaps it would work out after all. A lot would get settled by the time they got to Kleesport.

"What'll I call you on the road, mum?" Rebecca asked as they crunched their way across the newly laid gravel.

"Call me?" Tanyth's mind went blank.

"Yes'm. I can't call you 'mum' or people will know."

Tanyth snorted. "You don't think people will know as soon as you speak?"

Rebecca grinned and shook her head. "No, mum. I'm pretty sure they won't." The husky tenor voice that came so naturally from Rebecca's mouth could have come from any young man. "I've been practicin'."

Tanyth laughed then from the sheer surprise of it. "You'll have to do the talkin' for us both then," she said. "I've never been able to do much with my voice."

Rebecca grinned. "The boys from the quarry think it's pretty funny. I just mimic Jakey. It comes out like this."

Tanyth caught a hint of the gruff supervisor's tone in her voice. "But you don't sound that much like him. You sound like one of the quarrymen trying to imitate him, and badly."

"Yes, mum. I sound like one of the quarry*men*."

Tanyth lifted her face to the sky and her laughter echoed around the huts. "Indeed you do, my dear. Indeed, you do."

Tanyth slipped the latch and led the way out of the fading afternoon sun and into the cool dimness of the hut. She had arrayed her traveling gear on the table and around the hearth. Clothing lay folded on the bed. She turned to Rebecca. "Well? What did you learn about packin'?"

"Heavy on the bottom," she said. "Light on the top. Stuff you need fast on the outside." Rebecca cast her eyes over the array of goods scattered about the hut. "You're going to carry all that, mum?"

Tanyth shook her head. "Not all of it. Some is staying here in the storage room for others to use." She waved a hand at the table. "All that, and everything that's set along the edge of the hearth. That pile of small clothes, and this pile of outer wear," she said, pointing out the goods. "The rest I'll leave."

Rebecca's eyes narrowed as she looked around the hut. "You're leavin' the teapot?"

"Yeah. China is heavy and it can break. On the road we'll just brew tea in the kettle." Tanyth pulled her battered rucksack off its peg and held it up for Rebecca to see. "What do I put in first?"

"What's heaviest, mum?"

Tanyth gave a little nod of approval and crossed to the table. "This." She hefted a canvas wrapped bundle about a foot long, half a foot wide, and nearly four inches tall.

"What's that, mum?"

"Notes. Pressed leaves. All the things I've collected over the last twenty odd winters on the road."

Rebecca frowned. "Twenty winters, mum? In that?"

Tanyth held it out in one hand and Rebecca took it, her two hands drooping from the weight. "Lord and Lady, mum, you're gonna lug that around with you?"

Tanyth grinned. "Been carryin' it all this way. Can't see any good reason to stop now."

"Can I look?" Rebecca asked.

Tanyth held out her hand. "Not much to see, but sure. A quick peek before it goes into the bag won't hurt."

Rebecca handed the bundle back and, with the younger woman's help, Tanyth gently unfolded the canvas wrapping. As the stained covering opened, it revealed bundles of papers bound in leather thongs. Each individual bundle looked much like the next. Small, neat lettering covered each page. As she flipped through the bundles, Tanyth displayed small sketches, the occasional pressed sample, and even pages written in an obviously different hand.

"I suppose I should sort through this and see what's there," Tanyth said, "but there'll be plenty of time for that when I get where I'm goin'."

Rebecca shook her head. "That's a lot of stuff, mum."

Tanyth nodded. "When I get done travelin', I'm gonna write a book. Fill in all the stuff I learned about herbs and medicinals. Make it so other people can learn without havin' to spend twenty-odd winters to find out."

"When'll that be, mum?"

"Gertie Pinecrest is the last. I've visited all the others."

Outside the raven called raucously.

"If I don't go mad first," Tanyth added.

Rebecca gave her a quick hug. "You're not goin' mad, mum. You've gotta be one of the sanest people I know."

Tanyth pressed her cheek against the younger woman's hair. "I hope so," she said. "I surely do."

Rebecca pulled back. "All right, then. Let's see. Pack that bundle on the bottom?"

Tanyth nodded, immersing herself in the mundane tasks of getting ready for the road after months of habitation. The activity didn't completely distract her from the raven's intermittent calling, but it helped.

CHAPTER 7
DEPARTURE

Tanyth stood at the foot of the short stair and opened the door to let in the morning light. The cot stood naked along the back wall, the bedroll lashed to the bottom of her pack once more. The hearth wasn't cold yet, but the ashes had been brushed back against the stonework. Only a few glowing coals continued to smolder. The china rested on the mantel board along with the single oil lamp, its glass chimney finding the gray dawn and reflecting it. Beside it, a small white china teapot glowed against the dark stone of the fireplace. The table stood cleared. All her worldly possessions had gone into the pack or been scattered around the many pockets of her trousers.

In spite of herself, she sighed. She pulled her coat on, draping it over her left shoulder and slipping her free arm down the right sleeve before shrugging it into place. "You're lucky your shirts are cut so full in the sleeve, old woman," she muttered. A couple of tugs settled the coat around her. With a single smooth movement and a small grunt, she heaved the pack up onto the door-sill one-handed. Her hat came off its peg for the last time and onto her head. Grabbing the staff in her free hand, she levered herself up and out of the hut.

As she was trying to work out the mechanics of carrying pack and staff at once with only one hand, a man's voice said, "I'll get that, mum." Thomas leaned down to grab her pack and hooked it over one shoulder. "You'll have plenty of time to carry it when you get on the road."

"Thank you, Thomas, but you didn't need to worry about

that."

He started walking toward the inn and simply shook his head. "No, mum, but I want to." He cast a glance at her and stopped. "You comin'? Sadie and Amber got breakfast ready. You got time to eat before Frank finishes with the team."

She latched the door and nodded. "I hope they made enough. I'm hungry as a bear in springtime this morning."

Thomas' peal of laughter echoed off the front of the inn. "I think you'll be able to find a stray crust or two if you ask nicely," he said. "Per'aps a half a mug 'o tea as well."

Tanyth huffed a quiet laugh of her own. "Well, we'll just have to make do."

When they stepped into the common room, Tanyth wasn't at all surprised to find the whole village, except Frank and William, gathered around the long table. Tanyth found a place near the hearth and was soon elbow deep in hot tea, honeyed bread, and a bowl of oatmeal flavored with apples, currants and raisins.

The village had started eating a communal breakfast as soon as the inn's dining room had been completed. Amber and Sadie found themselves surrounded by plenty of help in the kitchen and seemed to enjoy the hubbub that nearly twenty adults and children could make while still waking up in the morning.

Tanyth found herself sitting a bit back from the festivities, watching the homey meal unfold. Rough quarrymen helping young children with over-sized utensils. Some of the older children with their heads together at one corner of the wide table, furtive glances toward adults hinting at mischief in the making. Amber and William's boy, Riley, appeared to be the ringleader, as always. Jakey's dog snaked through under the table, looking for scraps, drops, and hand-outs—all readily available.

Amber took a break from hostess duty to pull up a stool. She did a quick survey of her own before turning a sad smile toward Tanyth. "Not gonna be the same without you, mum."

Tanyth sniffed and leaned over to the younger woman. "Don't you start on me. You know I can't stay, much as I'd like to." She tried to sound gruff.

Amber tapped a fingernail against Tanyth's cast. "You can bluster all you want, mum. And I know you can't stay." She slipped an arm around Tanyth's shoulders and pressed their cheeks together. "There'll always be a place for you here, mum," she whispered.

Tanyth returned the hug as best she could with only one arm and while seated. "Thank you, my dear," she murmured. "Thank you." Her throat closed up then and she couldn't say anything more.

Amber released her grip and sat back, her smile no happier, but a look of understanding on her face. Without another word she stood and headed for the kitchen again.

Before she could reach the door, Frank opened it from the other side and stepped into the common room. His eyes found hers almost immediately and he gave a quick nod.

"You still here, Frank?" Jakey shouted. "I thought you'd be halfway to Foxrun by now."

"Daylight's burnin' right enough, but I'm not leavin' without a full load."

With much good natured jeering and cat-calling, Tanyth soon found herself clambering up on the wagon seat, her pack and staff stowed close at hand in the bed of the lorry. She turned to look at the sea of faces smiling up at her, some with tears coursing down suntanned cheeks. She scanned the crowd and smiled back, feeling self-conscious with all the attention. Her free hand tugged at the sling as if to assure her that it was still there.

She twisted around in the seat looking for Frank and found him working his way through the small gathering with William, Amber, Sadie, and Thomas in tow.

Jakey grabbed Frank's arm and they put their heads together. William stepped up beside the big wheel and leaned over toward her, Amber and Sadie right behind.

"So, you're ready to go?" he asked. "We haven't convinced you to stay?"

She shook her head, not trusting herself to speak.

He gave her a wistful looking smile. "I understand, mum. You're on a strange road, to be sure, but it's your road to walk, right enough."

Tanyth felt touched by the understanding look in his eyes. She knew he'd had to make some of those decisions himself when they started the village that would become Ravenwood. It couldn't have been easy to leave friends and family behind and strike off to carve a life out of wilderness.

He shared a look with his wife before reaching into his pocket and pulling out an envelope. "Here, mum. This is for you." He held the envelope out to her. A bit of red wax and an ornate seal featuring a sailing ship and a tree sealed the flap.

She took it and saw it was addressed to a "George Pendelton, Esq." She looked down at him with a question on her lips.

"George is our factor. He's at the Royal Bank in Kleesport. Frank knows him and can show you the way," William offered by way of explanation.

"But what is it?" Tanyth asked.

"It's a draft on the village account, mum. Should be enough to get you a ticket to North Haven with a bit left over for some supplies and such," he said.

She started to give it back, but Amber reached up and blocked her hand. "No, mum. This is something from the whole village. We all want you to have it."

"But you can't—" she started to say.

"Mother Fairport?" William interrupted. "You gave us this." He spread his arms out to encompass the inn. "You and your visions saved us from Dandy Andy and his gang."

She started to protest but he cut her off again.

"You did, mum, much as you try to deny it." His eyes dropped to her chest for a moment before looking back at her face. "You bled for us, mum, and you nearly died protectin' us. That's just a bit of something to help you along the road. It's not a lot and we have it to spare. Please, mum. Take it along with our thanks and the promise that you always got a home here."

Tanyth looked from face to face, each earnest smile telling her volumes. She looked at the envelope once more and pulled her hand back. "Thank you, all," she said before her throat closed up again.

William gave a small cough and nodded. "I'll just go give Frank a hand with the team." He gave Amber another peck on the cheek before joining Frank and Jakey.

Tanyth looked at the envelope and at the earnest faces peering up at her.

"Please, mum," Amber said. "Take it. The village can certainly afford it and you've given us so much."

Tanyth tucked the envelope into her tunic. "Thank you," she said. She swallowed and looked around at all the faces smiling up at her. "All of you."

Leaving Jakey, Frank walked around the team—up one side and down the other, speaking softly to each animal in turn, giving each a pat on the neck or a smoothing stroke down the croup, checking each buckle and shackle of the harness as he passed.

When he made it all the way around he turned to William. "Looks like we're ready, bossman." He stuck out his hand.

William shook it. "Take it easy, ole timer. We need them horses back safe and sound."

Amber handed Frank a folded pack of paper. "Shoppin' list. No gingerbread this time," she said and leaned in to give Frank a peck on the cheek. "Come back safe."

He smiled and nodded. "I'll do my best," he said. He nodded at Tanyth, "She'll protect me at least on the ride into town."

Tanyth couldn't think of anybody who needed less protecting than Frank Crane, but she laughed along with the villagers.

With a heave and grunt, Frank climbed up beside her and took his seat, a foot on the brake lever and gathering the broad leather ribbons that guided the team. He looked to her with a boyish grin. "You finally ready?"

She laughed in spite of the weight in her heart and looked around. "Where's Rebecca?"

"You mean Robert?" Frank asked, a quizzical expression on his face.

"Robert? No, Re—"

Her words cut off as a figure carved through the small group gathered around the wagon. Rebecca in her full kit strode around the side of the wagon and slung her pack over the low sideboards before vaulting aboard. She stood there, leaning against one of the clay barrels, hip-shot and grinning. Tanyth saw the pommel of a dagger gleaming under the edge of the woman's vest. A quiver full of arrows hung on her back and she carried a bow slung over her shoulder.

"Robert," Frank said.

"Robert," Tanyth repeated.

"'At's me," the young woman said, her voice the practiced tenor that shouldn't have sounded so fitting coming from her mouth.

Frank looked over his shoulder at Rebecca. "Well, boyo, you're gonna wanna find a seat. We got a few rough patches to get through before we get out on the Pike."

"Can you use that thing?" Tanyth asked, jerking her chin at the bow peaking over Rebecca's shoulder.

"Ask him," Rebecca said, pointing at Thomas.

Tanyth looked to Thomas who nodded. "She'll do. Make her practice on the way to Kleesport. If she don't get enough game to feed ya, make her go hungry." He winked at Rebecca. "Keep your gut dry, and your eye on the target."

"Anything else?" Frank asked, a smile that carried equal parts understanding, sympathy, and urgency pasted on his face.

"You always this excited to get on the road?" she asked him.

"Only when I'm with you, mum."

"That eager to be shut of me then?" she asked.

He shook his head. "Get you away from this rabble so's I can have you to myself," he said loudly enough that the people in the back of the crowd could hear.

"Hey, I'm still here!" Rebecca said.

"You'll be huntin'," Frank said over his shoulder and waggled his eyebrows in Tanyth's direction. "Now, siddown a'fore ya fall down. We're rollin'."

With that, Frank lifted his foot off the brake lever and gave the reins a gentle snap. It was enough to get the lead horse moving and the rest ambled along behind. The team with its heavy wagon eased around the bulk of the inn, crunched across the newly graveled yard and rolled out onto the Pike. A flock of children ran along beside, Riley in the lead waving and shouting, "Goodbye. See ya in a moon. Goodbye."

Tanyth turned in her seat to watch the village disappear, a small group of adults—William and Amber, Thomas and Sadie among them—waving as the screen of trees blocked her line of sight and they disappeared from view.

She straightened around and looked up at Frank, settling her hat firmly on her head. "Well," she said.

He glanced down at her with a half smile before turning his attention once more to the backsides of the horses ahead of them. "Yeah," he said.

"Oh, I can see you two are going to be loads of fun on this trip," Rebecca said, clambering over the back of the seat to plop down beside Tanyth. She leaned forward and grinned at them both. "How long before we get to Kleesport?"

Frank laughed. "We ain't there yet. Be a while."

"How much of a while? Ten days?"

Frank shook his head. "Two weeks, more like."

Rebecca nodded. "Good." She sat quietly while the horses clopped along, their heavy hooves sounding hollow in the still morning air.

After a few moments the wagon rolled by a distinctive looking tree beside the road. Tanyth tried to remember why it looked so familiar, until a dark shadow soared silently through the woods and landed on an outstretched branch with a flare of black wings.

"Think she knows?" Rebecca asked, nodding at the bird.

Tanyth stared for a long moment, trying to remember what it was like to see through her own eyes and the bird's eyes at the same time.

"She knows," Frank said.

Curious, Tanyth turned to him. "How can you be so sure?"

He smiled down at her. "She's here."

The rumbling crunch of wagon wheels filled the gaps between hoof beats as they watched the raven watching them. Long after they'd left the bird behind, Tanyth thought she heard the hoarse *caw-caw-caw* that reminded anything within earshot that she owned those woods.

"Hope Thomas remembers to give her a rabbit now and again," Tanyth said.

"He will, mum. He will," Rebecca said, patting Tanyth's forearm. "He likes her almost as much as you."

Frank snorted a short laugh but offered no other comment.

☽○☾

As the afternoon sun began sliding down behind the trees, Rebecca sat up in her seat, startling Tanyth out of a sleepy revery. "I don't know how you two can sit on this hard bench," she said, shifting back and forth.

"You can always get down and walk," Frank said. "I do sometimes."

"Can I?"

"Sure, you can probably walk faster than the horses anyway. Grab your bow and get in a little practice, if you want."

The surface of the Pike was level enough that she didn't have any problem clambering into the bed of the wagon. Taking up bow and quiver, she lowered herself from the tailgate, letting the wagon roll away from her while she strung the bow.

"Be careful, Robert," Frank called.

Rebecca raised a hand and stepped off to the side of the road, vanishing into the undergrowth.

"Will she be all right?" Tanyth asked.

Frank shrugged. "Thomas thinks so and she's been hunting with him all spring."

"How do you know he thinks so? He tell ya?"

"Where ya think she got the bow?"

Tanyth looked over her shoulder to the place where "Robert" had disappeared into the woods. "Oh."

He grinned and sidled closer to her. "Now that I've got you alone, old woman..."

She grinned and wrapped her good arm around him, leaning against his comforting warmth.

"Can't leave you two alone for a minute, can I?" Rebecca said, stepping out of the bushes just ahead of them. As the wagon rolled by, she tossed a spring-mottled hare over the side of the wagon. "How hungry are you?"

Frank eyed the hare. "That's enough for me. What'll you eat?"

Rebecca grinned and disappeared back into the woods.

"This was a good idea," Tanyth said.

Frank cuddled a bit closer. "Yes, I think so, too."

She blew a small laugh through her nose and hugged him back. "Yeah, but I was talkin' about her." She jerked her chin at the woods. "She's been huntin' with Thomas?"

Frank's eyes followed her gaze and he nodded. "After Birchwood, Willam and Thomas thought it be a good idea to have another archer or two trained. Thomas asked a couple of the boys in Jakey's crew but they couldn't spend the time. She heard about it and talked Thomas into teachin' her. Took to it right sharply. Even made Thomas give her some exercises to build up her arms so she can hold the draw."

Tanyth sighed, "And now she's leavin' the village to go with me?"

"She's never really been at home in the village, I think."

"She seemed to fit in well enough."

Frank shrugged. "Mebbe. I'm just an old fool myself, so what do I know."

She hugged him again. "You're the smartest old fool, I know."

He looked down at her, pulling away slightly to get a good look. "How many old fools do you know?" The mock serious-ness on his face made her giggle.

"Well, not that many. Mostly just me—besides you, that is."

He resettled beside her. "Beside me is just where you belong, I think."

The noises of horses hooves and iron-shod wheels on gravel hid the sound of his sigh, but Tanyth felt his frame expand and collapse. She closed her eyes and nuzzled his shoulder, drinking in the musky scent of him, the texture of his sleeve against her cheek. She wanted to remember him on the cold, lonely nights that lay ahead.

They rode in silence. The sun slipped lower in the sky, sending streaks of brilliant gold into the puffy white clouds drifting over head.

"You gonna drive all night?" she asked, shifting her backside against the hard plank seat.

He shook his head. "Horses need to rest and eat. Campsite's just 'round the bend. We'll stop there."

As they rounded the bend, Tanyth made out the flicker of a fire through the trees. "Looks like we'll have company," she said.

Frank grunted. "Mebbe."

She felt him tense. "Trouble?"

He sucked air through his teeth for a moment before answering. "Have ta see who's there first. Not likely, but ya never know."

The gathering dusk masked the campsite but as they approached, Tanyth slid away from Frank, giving him room to maneuver, and pushed her hat firmly onto her head. She glanced over her shoulder to see where her staff lay behind the bench seat. When she turned back to face the road, only a small stand of trees blocked her view. She didn't see any sign of animals or wagons.

As they cleared the trees, a lone figure stood from the far side of the fire. "'Bout time you two made it. What'd ya do? Stop and neck?" Rebecca yelled.

Frank laughed. "No, we don't have ta stop ta do that," he shouted back.

By the time Frank got the wagon situated, and the horses relieved of their tack, Tanyth and Rebecca had a respectable meal of fresh rabbit, hot tea, and pan bread ready.

☽○☾

"You keep huntin' like this, and we won't use half the supplies I got on the wagon," Frank said, leaning back on his elbows and patting his belly in appreciation.

Rebecca beamed, her smile nearly as bright as the fading fire.

"Will we have to keep a watch?" Tanyth asked.

Frank leaned his head back and gazed up at the starry sky. "Normally, I'm here by myself, so I can't," he said. "Don't see any reason to start now. I 'spect we're all light enough sleepers that nobody'll be sneakin' up on us in the night." He nodded at the wagon. "Sling the bedrolls under the wagon. It's shelter if it rains."

"Bet it leaks," Rebecca said, eyeing it with a dubious expression on her face.

"Yep, but a leak here and there is better than a soakin'," Frank said with a grin.

"Bitter voice of experience?" Tanyth asked.

He chuckled and gave her a nod. "Too many nights on wet ground."

"Why don't you sleep in the wagon?" Rebecca asked.

"You remember how hard that seat was?"

"Yeah."

"You only sat on it part of the day. My bony backside has put up with it since early mornin'. I got a chance to get off the wagon? I'm takin' it."

Rebecca laughed and stood to fetch her pack and bedroll out of the bed of the wagon.

"She's gonna be a big help to you." Frank's voice was barely loud enough to be heard over the breezes sighing through the spruces all around.

She looked over at him and saw his mouth twisted in a half grin. "I hope so," she said. "I still feel bad about puttin' her at risk. My arm's almost healed. Might be good enough by the time I get to North Haven."

He snorted. "I doubt that. But what if it is? You'll send her home? Alone?"

Tanyth sighed. "That's not likely, is it?"

He shook his head slowly. "No more likely than you stayin' to begin with."

The hollow clunk of head against wood, followed by a low voiced mutter, reached them from the wagon. They laughed softly and Frank clambered to his feet, brushing the back of his trousers off, and mounding dry soil around their fire pit with the side of his boot. "You all right, over there, Robert?"

"Fine. Just fine."

Frank laughed again and held out is hand. "Come on, old woman. Best get some sleep. Mornin' comes a'fore breakfast."

☽ ⭘ ☾

The moon showed her the shallow creek again. The dark

shadow along the stream bed was barely visible. Shadows of new pebbles marked where it lay buried. Only a small dark seam remained. The pebbles kept clicking together and the burbling of the water seemed to laugh in the darkness as the moon's light faded again.

☽○☾

Tanyth woke with a start and a pressure in her bladder. "Damn runnin' water," she grumbled.

"Hmm?" Frank asked, not really awake.

"Nothin'," she whispered. "I'll be right back. Save my place."

"Mmm," he said.

She snickered and slipped out of the bedroll to go crouch behind a bush. The moon smiled down at her between the treetops to the west. It would set soon. Business complete, she crawled back into her bedroll and snuggled into Frank's warm embrace, letting the cold and the moon and the silly little stream all fade away.

CHAPTER 8
HORSES' BEHINDS

Life on the road soon fell into an easy rhythm of rising with the dawn, caring for the animals and themselves, then wheeling the heavy wagon out onto the packed gravel surface of the Kleesport Pike. They rolled along through the day, occasionally stopping at streams and waypoints to water the horses. Every so often they'd pass a hamlet or village. When the sun set, Frank guided them to the next in a string of campsites and lay-over points where they'd make camp, fix dinner, and stretch weary bones out under the scant cover of the wagon.

Occasionally they'd meet a wagon coming the other way. Twice they were passed by the jingling mount of a King's Own messenger bound north for Kleesport. When he heard the bells on the harnesses, Frank guided the team to the side of the road until the rider had passed.

"I don't know how they do it," Rebecca said after the second one rode by in less than three days.

"What's that?" Tanyth asked.

"Ride day after day with them bells goin' jingle-jingle-jingle all the time. It would make me crazy after the second day," she said.

Tanyth snorted. "You hear the tack jangle on these horses?"

Rebecca looked at her with furrowed brow. "Well, of course."

"Do ya? Really? Clop, clop, jingle, jangle, jingle, jangle, clop, clop? All day? Every day?"

She rolled her eyes. "No, that's just the sound of the team."

Tanyth jerked her chin in the direction taken by the messenger. "And that's just the sound of his horse. Prob'ly pays no more mind to it than you do. Only time he notices is when it stops."

Rebecca frowned but gave a slow nod. "Prob'ly so." After a moment she said, "It'd still prob'ly drive me crazy."

Frank added, "Me, too."

They laughed and Rebecca vaulted the back of the seat to get her bow. "Well, I'm gonna try for some grouse today. Rabbit's are getting a bit old."

"Be careful. We're comin' up on Foxrun," Frank said. "You're apt to find another hunter or two out to fill his own pot."

She nodded once. "Thanks for the warnin'. Will we be stayin' there over night?"

Frank eyed the sun's position in the morning sky and shook his head. "Might stop for water, catch up on the news, but too soon to stop for the night."

Rebecca gave another short nod and dropped from the tail board onto the road, disappearing into the undergrowth in moments.

The drumming of heavy hooves coming fast from behind alerted them and Frank guided the wagon to a wider spot on the Pike and reined up. In a few moments, a passenger coach hauled by a four-in-hand rattled by. The driver waved from his high seat and pale faces peered out of the dimness as the coach rumbled past. They were gone in an instant, disappearing around the bend ahead.

"May as well water the team now we're stopped," Frank said, and set about suiting action to word by dipping from the barrel of fresh water and giving each horse a brief slurp.

Tanyth kept her seat and twisted around to watch the road behind.

"What're you lookin' for, old woman?" Frank asked, clambering back aboard and taking up the reins once more.

"King's Own."

Frank frowned and cast a glance over his shoulder. "That's odd, all right. I didn't notice. Usually there's a pair not too far behind the coach." He shrugged and snapped the reins.

"Gi'up, there."

The horses took up the slack on the harnesses and soon had the lorry rumbling along again.

"How long we been on the road, Frank?" Tanyth asked once the team had settled into their plodding rhythm again.

Frank squinted at the sky. "Lessee. Four nights? Five?" He shook his head, "We're coming up on Foxrun so must be five nights. Why?"

Tanyth nodded. "Not even half way, then."

He gave her a sad smile. "So eager to be shut of me, are you?"

His comment found a home in her heart and she leaned over to hug his arm with a sigh. "No, dear ole fool. Just wonderin' how much longer I can enjoy your company."

He nodded and leaned into her. "Yeah. Another week and a few days, we'll be in Kleesport. Road's in good shape for spring so we're makin' good time. We'll have a few days there before I head back."

She sighed again. "In that case, I better start movin'."

"How's that?"

Tanyth stood and followed Rebecca's path over the seat into the bed of the wagon. "Time to get the walkin' muscle in shape. Been a long winter without exercisin' it."

"You want me to stop?" Frank asked.

Tanyth shook her head. "I can manage."

She made her way to the back of the wagon and laid her staff down in the corner before stepping over the back, letting herself down, one hand on the tailgate and stepping onto the roadway, letting the wagon pull her forward for a step or two before letting go and snatching her staff.

Frank grinned at her as she strode up and along side him. "For a poor old lady, you seem pretty spry."

She grinned. "My walkin' muscle needs a work out but some foolish ole man been keepin' my hips limber all winter," she said with a wink.

Frank's face clouded for a moment and Tanyth wished she hadn't mentioned it.

"That foolish old man's gonna miss you," he said.

She pulled her arm out of its sling and reached up to

rap the side of the seat with it, her fingers idly tracing the numbers carved into the wood. "That foolish ole man's gonna be missed," she said, turning her eyes forward and letting the brim of her hat block his sad, sharp eyes from seeing her tear up.

They went on like that for a mile or two. Tanyth easily kept pace with the plodding draft horses, her staff striking the earth on every other step, striking sparks now and again on bits of rock. She found herself lulled into the rhythm of it, her body moving her as it had for season after season. The weight of the cast swinging on her arm felt good after being caught in the sling for so long, a counter weight to the heft of the staff in her right hand. The steady movements set her mind free to wander in ways that it hadn't while riding on the hard, wooden seat.

Dark green spruces began to hug the road's shoulders and occasionally a grouse flushed from the verge, wings whirring loudly as it disappeared between the trunks of the trees. Once a deer stood just inside the forest, stalk still and watching as they paraded by.

"Did you see that?" Frank asked after they'd passed, his voice low against the cloppity-clop of the horses' shoes.

"Is that unusual?"

"Not normal for them to stand still like that, but it happens once in a while. Usually I see 'em bouncing across the Pike when I come around a bend in the morning or late in the afternoon."

Tanyth looked up at him, his sun-seamed face alight with the excitement of seeing the buck watching them. "You love this, don't you?"

He glanced down and Tanyth saw the truth in his eyes. "Sometimes I think I was born on a wagon's seat." He paused to scan the road ahead and cast a quick glance over his shoulder to the path behind. "At least I get to sit up a bit and look out over everythin'," he said.

Tanyth cocked an eyebrow at him. "Sit up a bit?"

Frank nodded. "Yeah. Take the team, fer instance."

Tanyth glanced at the six heavy horses but then back at Frank. "What about 'em?"

"Well, the two in front have it pretty good."

"You mean the dust and all?"

Frank rolled a shoulder in a shrug, and Tanyth saw the twinkle in his eye.

"Well, that, too, but I was thinkin' about the scenery. Up here I get to see all around. Lead horses get to take in the view."

She chuckled a little then. "View must get kinda boring for the rest of the team," she said.

Frank nodded. "Yep. Every day, all day, starin' at the same horse's behind."

Tanyth, from her vantage at ground level had to admit the wisdom of his observation. "But you stare at all six."

He nodded and screwed his mouth into a wry smile. "Why do ya think I don't travel with a mirror for shavin'?"

She glanced up at him. "Why?"

"So I don't make it seven," he said, his eyes fixed straight ahead.

Tanyth laughed and the sound of it fell like bells on the still morning air.

Just ahead, where the dark spruces spread branches nearly into the road, a man stepped into view from around the bole of a tree. "Well, ain't that sweet," he said. He slouched and stuffed his hands in his pockets. The pommel of a sword gleamed in the shadow.

The team flinched away from the sudden movement. "Easy there," Frank said and pulled the team back in line.

Ahead, three more men stepped out of the woods and formed a rough line across the Pike. Their rough leather vests, homespun shirts and trousers looked stained and dirty even from where Tanyth stood.

"You'll wanna stop that team a'fore you get to the boys," the man said.

"Or?" Frank asked.

"Or they'll stop 'em for ya." The man gave a nod in the direction of the men and a fourth stepped out of the woods and drew a bow. "Be a shame to waste fine animals like that 'cause you were stupid, now wouldn' it?"

Frank pulled in on the reins and put a foot on the brake

to stop the wagon. He turned to the bandit. "What is it you want, exactly? I'm not carryin' any money."

"Well, for a start, you got a nice team. We'll take them. Then there's the wagon." He stretched his neck up as if to survey the contents. "And you got somethin' in them barrels? Could be somethin' we can use? Or sell. Don't matter."

Frank and Tanyth shared a glance. Tanyth saw something like an apology in his face that she didn't understand.

"All right," he said. "Just let us get our gear."

The man guffawed. "Well, that was a lot easier than I expected." He turned to the brigands standing in the path who joined him in rough laughter. The bowman lowered his bow, but kept the arrow knocked. "Don't ya wanna fight a lil about it? You just gonna hand over them horses and cargo and all?"

Frank shrugged. "Not my team. I'm just the driver. Wagons can be replaced. So can horses."

"Well, if ya gonna be all reasonable, what'll we do for sport?" the man asked. "How d'ya feel about your woman, here? Can you replace her?"

Something clicked over in Frank's expression and Tanyth saw his hands tense on the traces. "You got no cause to worry an ole lady like that," Frank said, his voice under as tight a rein as the team in front of him. "Let's just keep this civil and there's no need for anybody to get hurt."

The men laughed again.

"Who's gonna drive this, then?" Frank asked, looking at the ruffian. "You? You ever drive a six-horse team?"

The man shook his head, still grinning. "You just tie them reins off and jump down like a good fella, huh? We'll talk about who's gonna drive afterward."

Tanyth leaned on her staff, feeling the connection of the wood to the iron at its foot and the ground beneath. She felt the earth under her, felt the trees like a dark cloud gathering before a storm. "I don't think that's a good idea, Frank," she said.

The man turned his attention to her. "You don't think it's a good idea? Frank? She doesn't think that's a good idea." His mirth spilled over to his men who nudged each other and grinned in response. "And what are you gonna do about it then?" he asked taking a step toward Tanyth.

Tanyth held her ground, twisting her staff and hearing the iron grind against the gravel under her feet. The sun beat down on her back where the roadway's broad slash through the forest let the midday heat in. She shook her head but didn't speak, wasn't sure she could speak.

"Tanyth?" Frank said, his voice low. "We can replace the horses."

She shook her head again without looking up.

"No? She says 'no,' Frank," the bandit leader said. "You can't replace the horses?"

She bared her teeth in an expression that might have been mistaken for a smile. "We might," she said. "But you're not gonna let us live."

The man's expression of jolly-good-cheer melted off his face to be replaced with something sly, more vicious. "Now, why would we want to harm the likes of you two old people? We respects our elders, don't we boys?" The man spoke half over his shoulder to his men and took another step toward Tanyth.

"Tanyth." Frank's voice held a warning.

Tanyth shook her head. "No, you don't. Maybe you should."

Humor broke across his face again and he smiled broadly. "Well, the old bat's got some spine," he said and looked up to Frank. "That where you keep your backbone, old timer? She keep it for ya?"

The horses pranced in the traces, unused to being held to rein and uneasy about the strange men around them. Even they felt the menace that Tanyth saw sliding off their oily faces and pooling around them on the ground like some greasy fog.

"Tanyth," Frank said, "we don't need to fight them."

Tanyth heard the unease in his voice. "They're not going to let us walk away, Frank. Look at 'em."

The bowman stood with an arrow nocked and the bandits in the road loosened their swords. The leader's face broke into a snarl. "Aw, and we was just gettin' to know each other. We coulda had a lil fun. Now you gotta go and spoil it all." He took another step toward Tanyth and glanced over his shoulder. "Ethan?"

The bowman lifted his weapon and drew a long shaft back to his ear.

Tanyth saw the point rise and knew that the target was no longer the lead horse.

"Frank," she said.

"I see it," he muttered.

"Now, why don't you two old farts be reasonable about this?" the leader said, a storm cloud on his face. "We can make it easy on you. No need to suffer. We'll even give you a nice burial in the woods after. Won't we, boys?" His voice took on a steel edge and he took another step toward Tanyth. "Now, do you wanna be reasonable? Or do you wanna watch Ethan here put a shaft through your man's shoulder so he can bleed to death watchin' us have our sport with you, huh? What ya say?"

Tanyth glanced at the bowman, measuring the distance and angles with her eyes. She pulled in a breath—redolent with spruce, warmed by the sun, dry as the dust on the road—and turned her gaze back to the leader. It was not a look of surrender she gave him.

"He's not that good," she said, her voice a low growl.

A look of surprise flashed across the man's grimy face. "You're a bettin' woman, I see," he said, amusement and something like scorn in his tone. "You bettin' your life he can't hit from there?"

Tanyth shook her head. "No, I'm bettin' Frank's."

The man scoffed. "And what makes you so sure?"

Tanyth ground her staff down into the soil, feeling the power swelling under her feet. "It's a long shot and he's not accounted for the wind."

The bandit looked confused for a moment, his eyes casting up to the tree tops. "What wind?"

A soft fluttering sound ended with a meaty thunk and a cry. The man looked to see his bowman down in the dirt of the road, bow beside him and an arrow sticking out of his thigh.

"The wind an arrow makes in flight," Tanyth said.

When the bandit turned to look at her, he met the iron end of her staff as she swung from the ground, staff pivoting in her good hand and propelled by the power behind the cast on her left. The strength of her swing took him over and laid him out in the weeds with barely a grunt before the surprised look faded from his face and the light went out in his eyes.

Rebecca stepped out of the woods, arrow nocked and ready. With her tenor voice she said, "Anybody else want a shaft?"

The bandits all held hands well clear of their sword hilts and backed away.

Frank held down a hand for Tanyth. She tossed her staff into the wagon's bed and scrambled up to the seat beside him. Her legs turned to rubber and darkness clouded her vision, reducing her view to a tunnel.

"Gi'up, there," Frank said and flicked the reins.

The restive horses stepped out with a will and the sound of horses' hooves and iron wheels was the only noise besides the wounded man's whimpers. Even the birds had stopped chirping.

Rebecca released the tension on her bow and vaulted into the bed of the wagon as it came up to her, standing tall, leaning her hips on the barrels for balance against the unevenness of the road to watch the cowed men.

"What about him?" one asked pointing to the wounded man.

"What about him?" Tanyth called back.

"You'll live to regret this!" another man shouted.

"I already regret it," Tanyth said. "I hate havin' to kill a man before lunch. It puts me off my feed."

The men looked startled and after a few furtive glances for the departing wagon, scuttled across the road. Tanyth watched them examine the body, and then one man stood and stared after them, a look that might have been disbelief on his face. The wagon eased around the next bend and the heavy, green trees blocked the view.

Rebecca blew out a breath and clambered over the seat to settle beside Tanyth. She looked back and forth between Tanyth and Frank. "You both all right?"

Frank shook his head. "She's not."

"Tanyth?" Rebecca took Tanyth's slack hand in hers and stared into her face. "What's the matter?"

Tanyth took a breath, savoring the flavor of the warm, dusty air and the warm scent of horse. The darkness stopped creeping across her vision. "I'm all right," she said. "Just a lil weak right now."

Frank snorted. "A lil weak, she says."

"What is it?" Rebecca asked.

Frank glanced down at the two women and cast a glance over his shoulder behind them before answering. "Fool woman been sayin' prayers again."

"I never said a word," Tanyth said. "Not a word."

Frank snorted and shook his head. "Well, I was prayin' as hard as I could. I figured you'd be prayin', too."

Tanyth smiled up at his worried face. "I didn't have time for prayers. I was just hopin' that Rebecca wouldn't get caught."

Frank nodded and smiled at the young woman. "Good shootin', by the way."

She scoffed. "I hit his leg."

"From what? A hundred yards?"

She shook her head. "Maybe fifty. And I was aimin' for his eye." She grinned. "Thomas always says I shoot low." She spared a glance for the road behind. "Think they'll come after us?"

Frank twisted his head to look himself. "Naw. They lost the brains of the outfit, such as he was. And they'll have to deal with the wounded guy. That'll slow 'em down."

Tanyth's breath started to come a little easier as they rolled along.

"Think they'll report us for attackin' 'em?" Rebecca asked after a few moments.

Frank shot her a look. "They attacked us."

She shrugged in return. "Our word against theirs."

Tanyth chuckled.

"What's so funny, old woman? You scared me nearly to death back there."

Tanyth reached up to stroke his leathery cheek. It felt

almost hot to her touch. "I was so afraid they'd kill you," she said, her voice barely audible over the clop and crunch of travel.

He nuzzled her hand. "And I was sure he was gonna grab you and put a knife in you while I was tangled up in reins, but what's so funny?"

"Well, what are they gonna say?"

Rebecca and Frank shared a look of puzzlement.

Rebecca shrugged. "I still don't get it."

"Can you see them walking into town and saying 'we got attacked by two old fogies in a lorry wagon. The old woman bashed Joe's head in with a walking stick and some kid with a bow wounded...' what was his name? Ethan?"

Frank nodded. "Yeah, I think so."

"Some bandits if two old farts and a kid can best five of 'em," Tanyth said. "You think they're gonna admit that?"

Rebecca laughed at that, but Frank didn't look that convinced.

"You think they're gonna cause you trouble on the return trip?" Tanyth asked.

He freed a hand to scratch his chin. "Prob'ly not. By the time I get back here, they'll mos' likely be long gone." He glanced behind them again. "Still, when we get to Foxrun, we should probably let 'em know at the way station there."

"What if they're from Foxrun?" Tanyth asked.

Frank took a deep breath and then blew it out through his nose. "Yeah. That's what I'm worried about."

CHAPTER 9
FOXRUN

Long before she saw the village, Tanyth smelled the smoke and the sour aroma of people. She wrinkled her nose at the scent.

"Should be Foxrun," Frank said. "Musta had a rough winter."

Tanyth looked up to see him looking down at her, concern in his eyes. "I'm all right." She stirred herself on the seat and rubbed some of the dust out of her eyes. "Just needed to rest a bit. Guess I'm not used to walkin'."

She saw Frank and Rebecca share a glance over her head, but before she could ask about it, the wagon rounded a shallow bend and she saw the source of the smell. A collection of buildings huddled around a crossroad. What should have been the town square was an unremarkable intersection of roads on either side of the hard packed Pike. On the far side of the crossroad, a coach pulled out of the waystation's yard and thundered northward, disappearing in a cloud of dust that slowly settled in its wake. The driver looked like the same one that had passed them earlier on the road.

"Foxrun," Frank announced. "Mind your purse and keep your valuables hidden."

Rebecca laughed at his off-hand tone. "Is it really that bad?"

He cast her a sidelong glance but rolled one shoulder in a shrug. "There's worse, but it's always a good idea to keep your eyes open when travelin'."

"I was expectin' somethin' more...prosperous," Tanyth said,

eyeing the ramshackle collection of hovels.

Frank's eyes narrowed as he surveyed the village. "Somethin' ain't exactly right."

"What's wrong, Frank?" Rebecca asked.

"Not sure. Inn here brings in money. They gen'rally do a good custom. Tap room serves a fair pint."

"This don't look like a prosperous town," Tanyth said. "Not the best of times?"

Frank shook his head slowly from side to side. "I been drivin' this road for five summers now. That was the first time I ever been threatened." He paused to glance over his shoulder at the road behind. "That wasn't somethin' I expected, so no, not the best of times."

Rebecca said, "First Birchwood. Now them? What's next?"

Frank shrugged again. "Dunno, but maybe Rupert's got some ideas."

"Rupert?" Tanyth asked.

Frank nodded, jerking his chin at a squat, solid-looking building beside the Pike on the other side of the crossroad. "Rupert Peabury. He runs the way station here. Good man with the animals. Keeps his eyes open, his mouth closed, and his ear to the ground."

"Sounds uncomfortable," Tanyth muttered.

Frank huffed a short laugh and Rebecca smiled.

As the wagon rolled by the village, Tanyth saw big-eyed children peaking out of darkened doors. In one hut, a woman pulled the child out of the open door and back out of sight before closing the door. Here and there a chicken scratched and pecked in the dirt. Early summer weeds had taken hold and grew wherever careless feet hadn't trampled them. The place was quiet enough that Tanyth heard the occasional grunt of a pig somewhere on the backside of the village even over the sounds of the wagon.

"Not real friendly," Rebecca said.

Frank nodded but said nothing.

On the other side of the crossroad, a wide barn with watering trough at the front and a paddock behind squatted beside the Pike. As the wagon approached, a solitary figure walked out of the way station and leaned against the open barn doors. The man kept to the shade so Tanyth couldn't see much of him in the afternoon's glare.

"Rupert?" she asked.

"Prob'ly," Frank said.

Frank steered the team into the yard and pulled up just in front of the building.

"Well, well, well," the man said, a crooked smile twisting his mouth to the side of his face. "Must be springtime afta all."

"Hey, Rupert. How was the winter?"

Rupert sighed and shook his head. "Been betta," he said and spit into the dust beside the barn's footing.

Frank turned his head to look the village over. "Seems kinda quiet."

"Yep. We had a spot o' trouble. Kinda quieted things down a bit." Rupert scratched his jaw where a patchy beard tried to grow. "Can't be sure it's ova, if you get my drift." Rupert looked at his boots, lifting one to check the heel.

Frank nodded. "I do."

Rupert squinted up and nodded slowly. "You stopppin'?"

Frank shrugged. "Daylight's burnin', but the horses could use some water and the barrel could use some freshenin' if you got it to spare."

Rupert grinned. "Water—we got plenty o' that." He turned his head and shouted back over his shoulder. "Daniel? Bran? You boys grab a couple buckets and get your lazy behinds out here."

Tanyth heard a grumbled response from the depths of the barn and two rangy boys in their middle teens shambled out, each with a bucket in his hand and a surly expression on his face. They wore tired denim overalls that lacked the stains and dirt that Tanyth expected to see. Rupert wore the same.

"Mr. Crane's team needs waterin'," Rupert said. "And when you're done, toss a couple of buckets in his water butt."

The two nodded and shuffled off to the watering trough.

"Manners, boys," Rubert said, crossing his arms over his chest and leaning a shoulder against the barn.

The two turned faces toward Frank, and nodded. "Howdy,

Mr. Crane. Mum..." They didn't know how to greet Rebecca, so just nodded once in her direction and kept walking.

Rupert ran a weathered hand over his mouth as he watched the pair of them drag themselves to the watering trough. Tanyth thought he hid a grin behind the hand and became sure of it when he glanced up at Frank, shaking his head.

"I see they're growin' up," Frank said, a grin on his face.

Rubert nodded and tsked. "Slowly. They keep growin', sure enough. I think it's all the manure in their boots, but their maw says it's 'cause we keep feedin' 'em reg'lar."

As the two worked either side of the team, offering their buckets to the huge draft horses a pair at a time, Tanyth saw them forget to be sullen. They knew their business and took pains to keep the horses from drinking too much, giving each a scratch on the ear and a pat on the flank as they moved along. By the time they finished and drew fresh water for the wagon, they had recovered from the sulk enough to be casting shy glances at Rebecca.

Frank reached into a pocket and flipped a pair of silver coins through the air. Each boy caught one even as Rupert stirred himself.

"Here, now! No need for that," he said.

Frank scoffed. "Boys earned it, Rupert. Simple business."

"We don't charge for water here, Frank Crane. You know that."

Something in the man's face, some hint of distress made Frank's mouth close against whatever he was about to say. After a moment, he said, "Nope. Ya don't and I'm grateful for the water." He jerked his chin at the boys. "I paid for service and them two did a fine job of it. They do ya proud, Rupert."

The wind went out of Rupert's sails and he raked a hand through thinning brown hair. He blew a breath out and nodded. "Sorry," he muttered and turned to the waiting boys. "Say thank you."

"Thanks, Mr. Crane," the taller of the two said, nodding his head.

"Yeah. Thank ya," his brother chimed in.

"Now you two go take those silvers and stash 'em in the

house. See if your mother has any chores for ya."

"Aw, pa," the taller one said but turned to do as he was told.

The two boys scuffed their way through the large barn and out the back door, disappearing in the direction of the village.

Rupert snorted in what might have been a laugh and might have been exasperation before turning back to Frank. "You don't have any of your own, do ya, Frank?"

Frank grinned and shook his head.

"Y'ever think you wanna start? Get a hound instead," Rupert said with a shake of his head. "He'll crap on the rug, piss on the floor, and gen'rally behave like a kid, but he don't eat as much and after ten winters or so he'll die and leave ya in peace with fond mem'ries."

Frank laughed and even Tanyth chuckled at the woebegone tone.

"You love them boys more'n you love horses, you old coot," Frank said, shaking his head. "And you'd die yourself if'n you couldn't tend horses."

Rupert grinned and gave a shrug, wiping his mouth with the back of his hand. Tanyth saw the truth of Frank's words reflected in the man's eyes.

"Now that the boys're gone, you wanna tell me about it?" Frank said.

Rupert's expression turned sour. He spat on the ground again. "Last summer things went all to hell. We had trouble with some yahoos. They came to town, rode right up to Zack and Eloise's demandin' protection money."

Frank stiffened.

"What? You, too?" Rupert said.

"Birchwood and his boys?" Frank growled.

Rupert shrugged. "Never heard the names. Zack knew but he didn't spread it around."

"Four riders. Leader wore a fancy coat with a red silk lining in it? Pranced about like the crown prince himself?" Frank said.

Rupert nodded. "That's them. They disappeared just afore you came through that last time in the fall."

Frank shook his head. "They just moved on to greener pastures."

"Your place?" Rupert's eyes narrowed.

Frank nodded. "You see all the help I had that last trip?"

"Oh, I saw you go rollin' by here right enough. Half a dozen guys with ya?"

"Yep. Didn't stop. We were in a hurry."

"I wondered." Rupert nodded, chewing the inside of this mouth. "Makes sense now."

"What'd they do here?" Tanyth asked.

Rupert scrubbed his mouth with his hand again, as if trying to clean up what he might say. "Zack paid 'em off. They rode away."

Frank shook his head and leaned down, resting his forearms on his thighs. "Then what?" The sadness in his tone said he already knew.

Rupert shuffled his feet a little and gave a shrug. "A week later they came back. Rode right up to Zack's and there was some kinda row. We had a carriage in at the time, and things got busy. Passengers. Horses. Ever'body wantin' somethin' right now, you know how it is," Rupert shrugged.

"Aye," Frank said with a nod.

"By the time we got the carriage out of here, they was gone. I see them hightailin' down the Pike, but didn't think anythin' of it until I heard Eloise scream."

Frank nodded. "Sounds about right."

Rupert shrugged and looked south down the Pike. "They haven't been back since. Don't know whether to be glad or mad."

"They won't be back," Frank said.

Rupert turned a surprised look up at the older man. "You sound pretty sure."

Frank shrugged. "I know where his body's buried."

Rupert's face went slack for a moment and then recovered as he saw the look on Frank's face. "That would make a man pretty certain, I guess."

"So what happened after Zack?" Frank asked. "That ain't the end of it, is it?"

"Couple of the boys got ta talkin'. Decided that stealin'

must pay pretty good." He looked up at Frank, an uneasy expression on his face. "Why'd ya ask?"

Frank shrugged. "Well, in all the years I been driving this stretch of road, I never been held up before."

"Before?" Rupert shook his head and raked a hand through his hair again. "How many?"

"Five. Leader, stocky guy with a smart mouth. Three swords and a bow."

"Ethan," Tanyth said. "They called him Ethan."

Rupert closed his eyes and slumped back against the barn, his eyes on the ground and his head shaking side-to-side. He took in a deep breath and blew it out. "What'd they get?" he asked, his voice hollow and tired sounding.

"Ethan got about a yard of cedar," Frank said.

Rupert looked up, puzzlement on his face. "A yard of cedar?"

Rebecca held up her quiver in response.

"He's dead?" Rupert asked, eyes wide.

Frank shook his head. "Thigh. He'll limp for a while, but if they get the shaft out and get him back here, he'll be fine."

"Aw, Frank, I'm sorry about this. We shoulda told the King's Own what was goin' on but they never...that is, I didn't know they was doin' more than talkin' about it."

Tanyth saw a shadow in the man's eyes.

"Well, they won't be doin' any more," Frank said.

Rupert nodded. "When the next messenger comes through, I'll tell 'em myself." He took a deep breath and blew it out. "I shoulda turned that bastard in last fall when he started spoutin' off."

"Which bastard is that?" Frank asked.

"Everett Hampton," Rupert said. "He took it pretty hard when them buggers killed Zack. He's been lordin' it over the town ever since. Thinks he's some kinda grand high protector. Spoutin' off about how he'll see to it nothin' like that happens again, he knows how to take care of a village, and the like. Mostly it's just the ale talkin' but..." Rupert sighed and shook his head. "'Nough's enough."

"He won't be botherin' ya anymore, either," Frank said.

Rupert's agitation stilled and he stared up at Frank. He

had to clear his throat before he could speak, and even then his words came soft on the breeze. "You sound pretty certain."

Frank nodded.

Rupert squinted his eyes closed and opened them wide again as if trying to wake up from a bad dream.

Frank said, "T'were me, I'd get the village together and see if a few wiser heads might not be able to find a new leader afore Ethan and his friends get here." Frank looked over his shoulder, back down the Pike. "Carriage just been through. I figure you got a couple hours. Might be you should use that time ta figure out what to do next without their help."

Rupert's brows knitted together. He crossed the narrow gap between barn and wagon and held up a hand. "Good advice. Thanks."

Frank shook the hand and nodded. "Good luck," he said, then clucked his tongue and snapped the reins. The horses pulled against the harness and the wagon began to roll once more.

As they pulled out onto the Pike, Tanyth looked over her shoulder. Rupert stood there, staring at the ground. He raked a hand through his hair and turned, quick strides carrying him into the barn and out of view.

She settled back into her seat and faced forward again.

"Think there'll be trouble, Frank?" Rebecca asked.

Frank shrugged. "Been trouble. Maybe now it'll get fixed."

CHAPTER 10
THE WINDING ROAD

After Foxrun, Tanyth started each day on foot. She abandoned the sling, preferring the freedom of movement that the unfettered arm gave her. She kept the splinter she'd picked up in Ravenwood tucked inside the cast and used it regularly.

"You could ride, you know?" Frank said on the third day after the attack.

"I need to get my walkin' muscles back in shape," she said, smiling up at him. "You could get down and walk with me. Do ya good."

Occasionally Frank did just that but as they got closer to Kleesport, traffic on the Pike became too heavy for Frank to spend much time at the head of the team walking with Tanyth.

Tanyth felt herself losing her connection with him as every day passed, with each mile closer to the city and the port. Part of her wanted to drag her feet, to savor what she'd found even as she looked forward to the new adventure.

After a week on the road, the thought of a solid bed, a meal that didn't include game, and a roof that didn't leak as much as the bed of the wagon did had her grumbling as she walked. "Gettin' soft, ole woman."

Her broken arm had not yet healed. Every so often, she'd forget the cast and clunk her hipbone with it, or pull too hard with the freed fingers. The resulting pain told her that it wasn't quite time to take off the cast.

As they made camp one night, Frank said, "Two more days. We'll be in Kleesport day after tomorrow. Probably be at the gates by mid day."

Rebecca grinned, her face alight from excitement and the glow of the fire. "It'll be good to see the old place again," she said. "My auntie will be surprised to see me."

Frank grinned. "I thought you didn't get along with your auntie."

She shook her head. "I don't get along with my mother. She thought I was throwin' my life away goin' along with William and Amber. Wouldn't s'prise me if she'd had a funeral already."

Tanyth cocked her head. "Funeral?"

"Yes, mum. 'Cause she thought I'd go out there and die at the hands of some bandit or in the slatherin' jaws of some fearsome beast."

Tanyth laughed at the younger woman's characterization. "She didn't talk like that did she?"

"Yes'm, she surely did." Rebecca shook her head. She held up a bit of rabbit meat and tore the flesh away from the spit with her teeth. She had to pant air through her open mouth because it was so hot. "She'd pitch a fit if she saw me like this," she said when she could chew and swallow again.

"You mean eatin' rabbits you killed yourself?" Frank asked, his eyes bright with mischief.

Rebecca shook her head. "Wearin' pants and shootin' a bow. Hunkered down around a fire and eatin' with my fingers."

"Well, it's not very ladylike," Frank said.

Rebecca made a rude noise and they all laughed.

After the meal, while they sipped their tea and the ruddy glow of sunset faded to black, Rebecca asked, "So, what're ya goin' ta do in Kleesport?" She looked back and forth between Frank and Tanyth.

Frank took a deep breath and blew it out. "I'll take the lorry wagon around to the yards and leave it to be unloaded. They'll take care of the horses and such for me on the first night. While that's goin' on, I'll have to do a bit of shoppin' for William. He's given me a list of stuff we need. I usually stay in town for three or four days takin' care of village business." He shrugged. "Then I'll harness up and head back down the Pike."

"And you, mum?" Rebecca asked. "Given it any thought?"

"Well, we've got to find passage to North Haven. Prob'ly restock travelin' supplies in the city. Don't know how long it'll take."

Frank grunted. "Hard to say how long. If the Zypheria hasn't blown the ice out yet, could be a while."

Tanyth started to say something but Frank held up a hand and gave her a gentle smile. "I don't think it's happened yet," he said.

"Why d'ya say that?" Rebecca asked.

Frank jerked his chin at the empty road. "Not enough traffic. When the ice opens up the passage north, there'll be a lot more people wantin' to take custom. That's a good market up there. Lotta folks be anxious to make money off it." He sipped his tea before continuing. "Once the ice is out and the ships are sailing again? There'll be a lot more wagons, some goin' north with trade goods and more goin' south."

"Wouldn't it be easier to just sail south?" Rebecca asked.

Frank nodded. "Some will. Bulk goods like lumber, ore. Some'll go south around the cape to the factors down in Port Darby. Some will load up wagons and head down the pike for the inland markets south of Ravenwood."

Rebecca grinned. "And a lot of 'em will stop at the new inn."

"Yep." Frank's grin shone white in the glow of the fire. "The town's gonna grow so fast you won't recognize it by this time next year. You sure you don't wanna ride back with me?" Frank directed his question to Rebecca, but Tanyth felt the tug of it in her chest.

"Gotta go where Mother Fairport goes now, Frank," Rebecca said with a cheerful grin, either unaware or unmindful of the real intent of the question.

Frank's grin faded and he buried his muzzle in his mug, draining it out before upending it on a flat rock beside the fire. "Yep. S'pose ya do," he said. "I better go check the team."

Rebecca watched him go before turning to Tanyth. "He wasn't askin' me, was he, mum?"

Tanyth sighed. "Yeah, he was, but he was also askin' me, indirectly."

Rebecca fiddled with a bit of stick, flecking the dried bark from it before tossing the naked wood onto the coals. "You're not goin' mad, mum."

Tanyth watched the stick smolder and then catch fire, the small flare throwing the younger woman's face into contrast against the darkness of the trees behind her. "Somethin's happenin'. I need to find out what I can."

"And you think Mother Pinecrest can tell you?"

"She's the only chance I got right now."

Rebecca glanced in the direction of the horses. "He loves you."

Tanyth nodded.

"You're gonna walk away from that? From him?"

"Some things can't be helped. Things...happen. You get old, you get sick. Sometimes you get sick and die. Sometimes it's worse when you don't."

"Don't what, mum? Don't get sick?" Rebecca cocked her head.

"Don't die." Tanyth tried to smile, but couldn't bring it up as far as her eyes. It felt hollow and wrong pasted on her mouth so she let it go and gazed into the fire instead.

After a few moments, Rebecca asked, "Is that what you're afraid of, mum? Getting...sick?"

Tanyth felt her eyebrows flex in time with her lifting shoulders. "Somethin' like that." She drew in a deep, slow breath and let it out gently through her nose. "Some of my teachers, they just kinda drifted off. They weren't quite all there all the time." Tanyth glanced at the young woman, saw her eyes gleaming in the firelight. "Happens to old people sometimes. They get so they don't know who they are. Where they are."

Rebecca nodded. "My great grandpa. I've seen it."

They sat without speaking for a time. Rebecca found bits of leaf and twig to toss on the coals. The smoke from them curled around the campsite on the fading evening breeze. It tickled Tanyth's nose, mingling with the scent of horse and human, adding to the moist smell of springtime.

"If that's what you think's happenin', mum, why don't

you stay with...?" Rebecca nodded her head toward Frank.

Tanyth bit down on a flash of anger. It wasn't the girl's fault so she took a couple of breaths before speaking. "I started somethin' and I aim to finish. Gertie Pinecrest is the last link in a long, long chain, my dear." She glanced over to see if Rebecca was listening. "I mean to finish that chain before..." She paused, trying to think. "Before I can't any more."

Rebecca nodded. "I see that, mum." She sighed and glanced over to see Frank dusting off his hands and heading back to the campfire. "I can't say I understand, but I'll take your word for it."

Tanyth smiled, feeling the sadness in it but unable to stop. "You could go back with Frank," she said. "Back to your place in Ravenwood."

Rebecca seemed to consider it and then gave her head a little shake. A half smile crept around the corner of her mouth. "Guess we both got things ta do."

"What things?" Frank asked stepping up to the fire and hunkerin' down.

Rebecca grinned at him. "I got a bed roll to spread out. You two, well, you'll find something, I'm sure." She gave Tanyth a cheeky wink before pulling her bedroll out of the wagon and ostentatiously spreading it out on the ground well away from them.

Frank snickered a little, puffs of laughter hissing out of his nose. He settled down beside Tanyth. Close enough to touch, but not touching. "She seemed to think we've got things ta do."

Tanyth leaned into him, letting her head rest against his shoulder, using his solid strength. "She's a good woman."

She saw Frank's head nod and felt the muscles in his shoulder flex with the movement. "I didn't know better, I'd say she looks up to a certain old fool," he said.

"Who you callin' an old fool, old fool?" Tanyth said, giving him a playful slap.

He pulled back and looked down at her. "Me, o'course. Who you think?"

Tanyth smiled and hugged his arm. "That's all right then."

"You thought I meant you, didn't ya."

She nodded. "Well, yeah." She thought about it for a time, just savoring the moment, smelling the horse scent on him, feeling the strength of his arm in the homespun shirt under her fingers. "She prob'ly does."

"She prob'ly does what?" Frank asked.

"She prob'ly looks up to ya."

He gave a little chuckle in his chest that Tanyth could feel as well as hear. "Everybody's favorite uncle, I am." His voice carried a note that seemed out of character.

Tanyth hugged his arm tighter, nuzzling against his shoulder. "Not mine."

He reached over and laid one calloused paw over hers where it gripped his bicep. "No. Not yours."

Tanyth thought he might say something else but he didn't, simply sat staring into the fire, holding her hand, and thinking his own thoughts without sharing them. After a time, he patted her hand and shifted his weight.

Tanyth released her grip and caught herself in a yawn.

"Must be time to call it a night," Frank said with a grin. "I'm borin' ya to sleep."

She shook her head. "Been a long trip and I'd be lying if I said I wasn't lookin' forward to a proper bed at the end of it."

A sly grin spread across Frank's face and his eyebrows waggled suggestively. "Now that you mention it," he said and let the statement go unfinished.

Tanyth laughed as she clambered up from the ground. She gave his butt a fond pat before heading for the wagon and her own bedroll. His quiet promise made her wish the trip were a little closer to done.

Or that Rebecca slept more soundly.

That thought made her giggle and she spread her bedroll out so that it touched Frank's. Spring or not, night got cold and the man generated enough heat to warm two sets of old bones.

☽O☾

The moon showed her the shallow creek once more. The dark shadow along the streambed had disappeared. A ridge of pebbles lay in its place, a gently curving line of tiny stones, each resting firmly on the next, each settled in the stream's sandy bottom. This time there were no pebbles clicking together to disturb her slumbers, only the gentle laughing of the water as it bubbled over the pile of stones, a new ripple in the surface to catch the glimmers of fading moonlight.

Chapter 11
Kleesport

The heavy wagon rumbled to a halt beside the road, Frank's foot on the brake and his tanned hands holding firm on the reins. A farmer with a cart full of caged chickens steered around the large lorry wagon with a curious glance at the trio on the seat.

"Trouble?" he called.

"Nope. Just settin' a bit," Frank answered with a nod. "Thanks, though."

The farmer waved a hand in salute and headed down the shallow slope toward the city.

Tanyth stood and stretched, hands at the small of her back as she bowed backwards and tried not to stare at the sprawl that waited ahead.

"Somethin', ain't it?" Frank asked after a few moments.

"That it is, but what exactly?" Tanyth gave him a grin.

Frank's quiet laugh drew her eyes to him. "That's a good question," he said. "Lotta people. Lotta business happenin' there."

Tanyth turned to eye the chimneys, most spewing some kind of smoke—from black to pale gray—into the blue spring air. Beyond the haze on the other side of the city, the blue-green of ocean stretched to the horizon. The tall, bare trees of ships' masts were just visible through the haze. Near the horizon a spot of white marked a ship underway, only her sails visible at such a distance. Above it all arched a crystalline sky with a hint of white clouds far to the eastern horizon.

As if reading her mind, Rebecca leaned over and said, "It's

not so bad, mum. I grew up there. It'll be fine, you'll see."

Tanyth smiled at the earnestness in the young woman's face.

"Tanyth?" Frank's voice drew her gaze. "Are you gonna be all right down there?"

She sat back down on the seat beside him and patted his arm. "It's where I need to go," she said, eyes turned once more to the distance. "And across that water to boot."

"It's not exactly a safe place," Frank said, his gaze following hers. He didn't mean Kleesport.

She snorted. "Name somewhere that is."

He barked a short laugh.

"I'll be all right, Frank, but thank you for askin'." She looked over at him. "How long before we get into town?"

Frank eyed the carts and wagons on the road ahead and craned his neck around to see who and what was coming behind. "Prob'ly be there just before dark. Don't wanna be dragging this load too fast in that crowd."

She eyed the heavy barrels of clay in the bed of the lorry wagon and turned to look at the city. "Where's a good place to stay?"

Frank frowned. "Well, I usually stay at the Broken Gate. It's handy to the unloadin' and they keep things clean and orderly. Matt Esterhouse keeps a fine stable."

"Good beer?" she asked, a knowing twinkle in her eye.

"Well, that, too, and Mabel Esterhouse makes a darn fine kidney pie." He gave her one of the grins that made her eyes laugh with him.

"They know ya there, do they?"

Frank cocked his head to the side and shrugged. "Yeah. I'm a reg'lar. Spend a few days there every few weeks during the season. Why?" His eyes narrowed as he looked at her.

Tanyth leaned over and pecked him on the cheek. "See you there, then."

"What d'you mean?"

Tanyth hopped down from the wagon and pulled her pack out of the bed with her good hand, easing it up over her cast and onto her shoulders.

"Tan? What do you think you're doin'?"

She took up her staff in her good hand and pressed her wide hat firmly down on her head with cast on her forearm. "I'm walkin'. What's it look like? You comin' Reb—ah, Robert?" Tanyth eyed the travelers around her but no one seemed to be paying her any mind.

"But you can't walk all that way by yourself," Frank said.

She laughed at the expression of horror on his face. "Why not? I've spent twenty-one winters wanderin' all over Korlay by myself."

"And she won't be by herself," Rebecca said, climbing into the bed of the wagon and gathering her gear. She buckled on her pack and slipped her bow through the straps before lowering herself over the side to join Tanyth beside the road.

Frank sighed. "Well, yeah, but you could ride..."

Tanyth laughed again and shook her head. "You'll be all day getting' this rig into town. I can walk it in half the time. And besides, that seat is getting awful tired of my bony old backside sittin' on it." She reached back and rubbed the backside in question.

Frank laughed and shook his head. "Bony is not how I'd describe it, but I know what you mean." He shifted his weight back and forth on the seat. His foot on the brake and his hands tangled in the reins hampered his freedom of movement.

She smiled at him and gave him a nod. "All right then. We'll see you 'round dinner time. The Broken Gate, you said?"

"Yup, head straight in on the Pike, Potters Road crosses it just the other side of the coach station. Head west and you'll see the broken gate hanging in front. Big yard out back for the horses."

She nodded and repeated, "West on Potters Road, broken gate in front. Got it." She gave him a smile and saluted with her staff before turning toward the city. She heard him sigh and chuckle before getting the heavy wagon rolling once more. Her long strides soon left the slower wagon behind as she and Rebecca swung along the hard packed surface toward the largest city she'd ever seen in her life.

"I hope you know what you're doin', old woman," she

99

grumbled.

"What's that, mu—ah, mister?" Rebecca said, with a quick glance around.

Tanyth just shook her head and kept walking. "Just grumblin'," she said. "Nothin' serious."

"If you're gonna talk to yourself, least you could do is speak louder so I know," Rebecca said, her grumbly tone belied by the twinkle in her eye and the smile on her lip.

"If I spoke up, then it wouldn't be to me, now would it?" Tanyth asked.

Rebecca laughed softly and strode along with her.

☽○☾

The city looked closer than it really was. Tanyth and Rebecca picked their way along the verge of the road, often walking past slow moving carts and wagons laden with produce. Most people smiled and nodded as they went by—some offering a greeting as well. Their ground-eating strides soon left Frank and the lorry wagon behind in the throng. As they got closer to the city, the traffic grew thicker. In addition to cargo laden wagons and the occasional rider, they found themselves in the company of laden bearers, plodding along with huge bundles of sticks on their backs or yokes across their shoulders with heavy loads on either end. They had to slow their pace to match the tide of people flowing into the city.

Before they were halfway to the broad plaza that seemed to make a kind of entryway to the city, Tanyth found her pack straps had started to bite into her shoulders. She shifted the weight as best she could but began to regret not staying with the lorry wagon and Frank.

"Yer just out of shape from all that soft livin' over the winter is all," she muttered.

Apparently she wasn't as quiet as she thought because a porter with a pair of cheeses on a yoke over his shoulders shot a dark look in her direction.

"Whazzat?" he asked.

She glanced over at him, momentarily at a loss, before realizing what she'd said. "I'm sorry," she said with a small shake of her head. "I was just muttering to myself. I got soft over the winter." She indicated her pack straps. "Just a lil walk and already my pack is chafin' my back."

The porter rolled his eyes and shook his head.

"You might wanna not talk to yourself so loud right here, mum," Rebecca said, leaning close to speak almost in Tanyth's ear. "The locals can be a bit testy."

Tanyth snorted a short laugh and stepped off the Pike to walk around a cart filled with baskets of apples that rested on the shoulder.

"Apples! Who wants a nice juicy apple?" a woman standing in the bed called to the passing throng. "Apples. A penny a piece. Three for two pence. Apples!"

The porter carrying the cheeses moved around the obstruction on the other side and shot the woman in the cart a look darker than the one he'd given Tanyth.

The thought of fresh apples made Tanyth's mouth water and she stepped up to the cart to look in the baskets. Springtime and apples didn't really go together. She expected to see wizened knots of fruit in the baskets. Instead she saw gleaming red-gold skins on taut, full fruit.

She looked up at the young woman. "How is it you have fresh apples in spring time, miss?"

The woman smiled. "We keeps 'em chilled, mum, all winter long they's restin' like in our cold rooms." She slipped her belt knife from its sheath and carved a slice off the fruit she had in her hand. "Try a bite, mum?"

Tanyth took the piece of apple and bit into it. Not as firm as a fall apple, but solid enough to chew on and filled with sweet juice. Tanyth popped the rest into her mouth and fumbled for coppers in her pocket. "You want one, Robert?"

Rebecca had her hat brim pulled low on her forehead and nodded without speaking.

"I'll take two, please." She held out two coppers.

"You sure, mum? Two pennies buys you three apples. Good deal on a great fruit." The young woman held out three apples in offering. "Tuck one in yer pocket?"

Tanyth turned and looked back up the road. She couldn't see Frank or the horses in the crowd. With a nod to Rebecca she said, "We'll take two to eat along the road, thanks, but my friend's coming along in a lorry wagon with six-in-hand. Big grays and the man at the reins wears a leather vest and green pullover. Can you see him from up there?"

The woman straightened her back and shaded her eyes with a raised hand, squinting into the distance. "Only see one big wagon comin' up the Pike, mum. Looks like an old geezer in the seat." She looked down at Tanyth who'd taken off her hat to mop her brow. Getting a good look at Tanyth's face and graying hair for the first time, the woman's eyes widened in alarm. "That is...I mean, mum..."

Tanyth laughed. "No, you've the right of it. He's an old geezer." Her voice softened. "But he's a good old geezer. When he gets here, toss him the other apple. His whistle probably needs wettin' by now."

The woman looked up at the line of people on the Pike and then back at Tanyth. "Done, mum," she said and scooped up the coppers, placing a large apple in Tanyth's palm and tossing another to Rebecca, who caught it neatly on the fly.

Tanyth took a big bite and felt the juice escape down the side of her chin. She grinned up at the woman and saluted with the apple.

As she started around the cart, the woman called, "Ain't you afraid I'll cheat ya and not give yer man his apple, mum?"

Tanyth chewed and swallowed before answering. "Nope."

"Yer awful trustin', mum."

Tanyth laughed. "I've been called worse, my dear. Much worse." She nodded again and took another bite of the apple, sucking on the fruit to capture as much of the sweet nectar as possible, before turning and resuming her walk toward the city.

The woman in the cart shook her head and resumed her calling. "Apples? Who wants a nice juicy apple? A penny a piece or three for two pence. Apples?"

)O(

As they approached the plaza, Tanyth noted that several of the King's Own stood watching the flow of travelers in and out of the city. One of them stepped up to them and nodded a greeting.

Tanyth nodded back and noticed the downy fuzz on the soldier's cheek. She smiled and took off her hat. "Good day," she said and waited for him to speak.

"Good day, mum. Can I ask your names and what your business is in the city?"

Tanyth blinked. "Of course, you can ask. My name is Tanyth Fairport and we're headin' to the port to take passage to North Haven."

The trooper turned to Rebecca. "Your name, son?"

Rebecca pulled off her hat, breaking the disguise and leaving the soldier blinking.

"Rebecca Marong. I used to live here."

"Marong? Any relation to Richard Marong?" the guard asked.

"My...uncle."

The guard nodded and turned back to Tanyth.

She watched his eyes work from her gray hair down to her boots. "And how long are you planning to stay in the city, mum?"

"Only as long as it takes to get passage." She cocked her head and leaned on her staff.

He nodded at the cast. "What'd ya do to your arm?"

Tanyth controlled a rising temper with a deep breath before replying. "Broke it."

With an uneasy glance at Rebecca, he took a breath as if he didn't want to say whatever he was about to utter. "There are vagrancy laws in Kleesport, mum. Do you have sufficient coin for lodging and food while in the city?"

"I believe so, young man, but until I get into the city and see how much things cost, I won't really know, now will I?" She tried to keep her voice level but the young man's questions began to annoy her.

"Do you have five silvers on your person, mum?" the guard asked.

"Yes." Tanyth bit the word off and let it lay there for a moment before asking, "Do you need me to show them to you or will you take my word for it?"

He smiled and held his hands out to his sides. "No offense, mum. I'm just doing my duty."

She watched the wagons and bearers entering the city un-hindered, pointedly watching them walk by and even around them where they stood on the side of the plaza. "And them?" she asked.

"Tradesmen and vendors, mum. Not travelers." He pointed to a drover with an oxcart laden with baskets of vegetables. "He wears a vendor tag. He's heading for the market."

Tanyth noted that the man did, in fact, wear a wooden tag on a thong around his neck. As she looked about, she saw that all the tradesmen and carters wore them.

"Everyone doing business in the city has a tag, mum. For taxes." The youth looked a bit apologetic. "I meant no disre-spect, mum. Just doing my duty."

Tanyth glanced over at Rebecca who merely shrugged an apology. "It's been a while since I've been home."

Tanyth frowned and wondered if Frank had a tag and she'd just never noticed.

"If you intend to do business in the city, mum, you need to register with the city clerk and get a tag like those."

Tanyth shook her head. "I'm just passin' through." She bit her tongue on any sharper comments.

"Do you have a place to stay, mum?"

"I'm planning on staying at a place called the Broken Gate."

"Yes, mum, I know it." He eyed her once more and point-edly did not look at Rebecca. "That's a place that caters to drivers and carters, mum. Are you sure?"

"Well, we're meeting a driver there, and he's been there many times. I'm sure he'd not steer us to a place that's too rough for a little old lady like me." Her eyes dared him to make another comment.

He bit back the follow up question and nodded once, giving her a polite salute. "Thank you, mum, and I'm sorry to have bothered you. Enjoy your stay in Kleesport."

"You have a name, soldier?" she asked.

"Yes, mum. Footman Milo Carver, mum."

"Thank you for your courtesy, Footman Carver," she said. "May we go now?"

He stepped back with a flourish of his arm. "Of course,

mum."

She eyed him but he appeared to be sincere and she strode off without another glance, Rebecca tugged her hat brim as she paced along beside. Behind her she heard the lounging guardsmen laughing and calling out to the young man. She heard their voices but couldn't make out their words in the hubbub going on around her. Whatever they were saying, she was sure it wasn't pretty.

"Well, that was close," Rebecca muttered as they crossed under the tall gate.

Tanyth cast her a sidelong look. "Close?"

"Yeah. He didn't make us prove we had five silvers."

Tanyth shook her head. "I have five silvers, my dear. What...?"

Rebecca grinned. "You may, mum, but I don't."

Tanyth laughed, her cackle making heads near-by turn in amusement. "We'll see you have a few to put in your pocket as soon as we get settled, my dear. I have a few set aside."

Rebecca shook her head. "My auntie will take care of that, mum. Don't you fret."

Tanyth shrugged and they continued on into the city.

They hadn't gone twenty paces before shouts started behind them, "Make way! Make way!" Tanyth felt, rather than heard the heavy hoof beats, and stepped to the side of the plaza, moving with the flow of the crowd. Traffic stopped and a messenger of the King's Own cantered past, his harness bells jingling a warning, and his orange sash marking him as a courier. When he'd passed, the crowd surged forward filling in his wake. Tanyth stood in her spot for a few moments watching the carters and drovers jockeying for position on their way to market. A pair of men, better dressed than the rest and carrying walking sticks, strode along with heads together. The nearer one banged Tanyth's cast and shot her a venomous look.

"Watch where you're walking!" he snapped before turning back to his companion.

Tanyth heard him say, "Bad business. Avram should have listened and now the whole cargo's lost."

The other tsked and shook his head before the crowd swallowed them up.

"Busy place," she muttered.

"Yes'm," Rebecca said glancing around. "Always was."

"This tag business?"

Rebecca shrugged. "I never noticed, but then I wouldn't'a, would I?"

"Your uncle, he's important?"

Rebecca shrugged again. "Father, really. And, I just didn't want them carrying the word to him. My uncle's not so important."

"Why's 'at?"

"He doesn't run a big company."

"No, why don't ya want your father to know?"

"He wasn't happy I left the first time. I don't s'pect he'd be happy to learn I'd left again and goin' in the opposite direction this time." She gave a little grimace and glanced around at the people flowing by them.

Tanyth nodded once before joining the northbound flow, looking for the carriage station and the intersection of Potters Road.

CHAPTER 12
THE BROKEN GATE

The woman behind the bar eyed Tanyth and Rebecca up and down before speaking. "Beggin' yer pardon, mum, are you sure you wanna stay here?"

Tanyth looked around the nearly empty taproom. Groups of men sat at tables scattered around the room. Every so often one or more would cast eyes in her direction, more curious than threatening. "It seems well-tended, my dear. Why wouldn't we?"

"Well, mum, mostly we get drovers and carters in town on business. They can get rowdy sometimes, mum." The woman paused. "And it's hardly seemly for a woman travelin' alone, if you get my drift, mum."

Tanyth turned a pointed look to Rebecca before looking back at the barkeep. "I'm hardly alone."

"Well, no, mum, but this...your son?"

Rebecca took off the hat and shook out the leather thong that held her cropped hair back. "I'm just the lady's maid," she said, a challenging look in her eye.

The woman blinked several times, and Tanyth saw her eyes flicker to the pommel of Rebecca's dirk then up to the fletched arrows over her shoulder. "I...ah...well, that is, I'm not sure we have room just now. Busy season. Everybody waitin' for the Call, you see."

"The Call?" Tanyth asked, reclaiming the woman's attention.

"Zypheria's Call, mum. The wind? Blows the ice off the north shore."

Tanyth nodded. "Heard of it. We're waitin' for it, too."

The woman nodded, her hands twisting a damp rag on the bar while she looked back and forth between the two of them. "Can I ask how ya found us?"

"You're not exactly hidden, are ya?" Rebecca asked. "First left on Potters Road, just inside the main gates."

Tanyth held up a hand and quelled Rebecca's outburst. "We got your name from Frank Crane. Drives a lorry wagon with a six-horse team. You know him?"

"Frank? Comes to town every few weeks drivin' a clay wagon? Old guy? Gray...um." The woman frowned and looked at Tanyth's gray hair. "You're with Frank?"

"Yeah. He's bringin' in a load of clay now. Should be here later tonight."

The woman's eyebrows shot up at that news. "Are you his wife, mum?"

"D'you ask all your guests these kinds of questions?" Tanyth asked, a bit of pepper in her tone.

The younger woman blinked and leaned back, surprise showing on her face. "No, mum, but we don't get that many travelers ta begin with. Mostly regular custom."

Tanyth took a deep breath and let it out before stepping closer and leaning an elbow on the bar. "All right, then. No, I'm not his wife. I'm just passin' through. My friend here is goin' with me to keep me company and help out while my arm heals." Tanyth held up her forearm to display the now ragged-looking cast. "I wintered in the village and Frank offered us a ride to town. I got tired of sittin' on that hard seat and walked on ahead while he dealt with the clay. He recommended this place. Said I should get a room, maybe a bath. And he'd be along soon's he's done with the load. Now? Do you have any other questions?" She tried to keep her voice calm and her temper in check but the young woman's frown deepened as Tanyth spoke. She sighed and ran a hand through her hair. "I'm sorry, my dear. I'm tired and dirty, and not on my best behavior. I've traveled back and forth across Korlay for more'n twenty winters and I've never been questioned so much in my life as I have been in the last hour." She smiled in apology. "It's made me into a cranky old woman."

The woman's frown cleared a bit, but she still looked uncertain. "Well, mum, rooms are a silver a night and comes with breakfast...nothin' fancy, mind. Tea and oatmeal, pancakes, toast." She paused and added, "Baths are an extra silver. Paid in advance."

"Sounds fine." Tanyth pulled out her purse and counted three silvers out onto the bar. "There's enough for two nights and a bath. I need to visit the banker tomorrow and then see about getting' passage to North Haven. I'll know more about how long I'll be stayin' then. That all right by you?"

"Yes, mum." The woman scooped the coins off the bar and into a ceramic jar where they rattled as they fell. "If you'd just sign the book, mum, I'll have Elly start drawin' your bath." She pulled a leather-bound book from behind the bar and handed Tanyth a pen, placing a small jar of ink close at hand.

Tanyth eyed the pen and ledger.

"Can you write, mum? I can sign for you if you can't."

Tanyth shook her head. "No, I can write. I just..." Her voice trailed off as she examined the pen and the quality of the paper in the bound ledger. "I just never had to sign into an inn before. Usually just paid the bill."

"Taxes, mum," the woman shrugged as if that explained it all. "City takes its tithe and this is how they know how much it should be."

"You have to buy your own pens and ledgers?" Tanyth asked as she penned her name on the next open line.

"Yes'm."

"Sounds expensive," Tanyth said, holding the pen up to get a look at the craftsmanship.

"Not as expensive as not payin', mum," the woman said, a bitter shadow behind her words.

Tanyth looked up at that and saw a barely concealed anger in the younger woman's face. "I dare say," she said and handed the pen back. "Will that do?"

The woman turned the ledger around and looked. "Yes'm. Thank you." She took the pen and added notations for two nights, and a bath, then inscribed a three in the last column. "There," she said, and pulled a key attached to a block of wood from under the counter. "Room four, mum. Up the stairs, turn right, end of the hall." She leaned in and lowered her voice. "Easier to sleep away from the stairs."

Tanyth took the key and nodded her thanks. "Thank you. Are you...Mazie?"

"Mabel, mum. Mabel Esterhouse."

"Ah, yes, then you and your husband own this place."

"Yes, mum." The woman seemed confused by the change in their conversation.

"Frank said you keep a good stable and run a clean house."

Mabel smiled at the compliment. "Thank you, mum. We try."

"He also said you brew a nice ale."

She practically beamed. "Well, mum, not to brag, but folks do say it's the best ale west of the boulevard."

"Do you suppose we might have bit while we're waiting for the bath?"

"Of course, mum. Two coppers a pint or five for a pitcher..."

Tanyth dropped four coppers on the counter and watched as Mabel scooped them up and dropped them into a metal box. They rattled as they fell.

Mabel saw her watching and gave a small shrug.

"Taxes?" Tanyth asked.

"Yes'm. Don't have to make marks in a ledger but the coins gotta make a noise when they fall."

Tanyth frowned at that. "Make a noise?"

Mabel's mouth screwed into a grimace. "Yes'm. Sometimes the taxmen come and sit and listen and keep tally by the sound the coins make. They check."

Tanyth's face must have shown her incredulity.

Mabel shrugged. "It's how it works here, mum. Part of doin' business in Kleesport."

Before Tanyth could answer, one of the men spoke from across the taproom. "Oye! Mabel, me love! Another pitcher here, eh?"

"Keep your braces up, there, Bernard! I'll be right with ya." Mabel gave Tanyth a small shrug and went to the taps.

The man called Bernard nodded and turned back to the table. The three men with him all had frowns on their faces and leaned on their elbows, heads together.

"Cheerful bunch," Rebecca muttered.

Tanyth shrugged and nodded.

Mabel came back with a pair of pints and gave a little nod at the men. "They've lost a friend today. They're entitled to a little grievin'." She slid the pints across the bar. "You can take them up with you, mum. Elly will be right along with the bath water."

"What happened?" Rebecca asked, picking up her glass.

"Longshoreman. Reggie Winters. Lovely young man. Wavy black hair. Gorgeous eyes. Had shoulders...well, never mind that." Mabel shook herself and focused. "He sometimes drove lorry for one or t'other of the carters around. Got tired of liftin' and tuggin' so he signed on as a deck hand and shipped out."

Tanyth sipped her ale. "He not comin' back?" she asked, idle curiousity driving her tongue.

"No, mum. Not like that. The ship went down."

Rebecca gave a little, "Oh, no," sound.

"That common?" Tanyth asked. "Losin' ships like that?"

Mabel glanced around the room and used her rag to wipe down the bar. "Too common, some say."

Rebecca and Tanyth shared a look. "Why's 'at, mum?" Rebecca asked.

"All I'm sayin' is, when you book passage to North Haven?" She looked back and forth between them, staring first at Rebecca and then at Tanyth. "Make sure the ship's insured."

Rebecca sucked in a quick breath.

"That helps them that are left behind a bit," Tanyth said, taking another sip of the nutty ale.

A sour expression crossed Mabel's face. "Helps with the odds of survival, too, mum. Helps a lot more'n it prob'ly should if you catch my meaning."

"Oye! Mabel? You run out of ale or somethin'?" Bernard and his companions were all looking in their direction.

Mabel waved her rag at the man in a dismissive gesture. "'S'cuse me, mum. Some around here's got too little patience and too few manners."

Tanyth nodded her thanks, but Mabel was already drawing off a fresh pitcher and didn't see.

☽○☾

Tanyth felt much better for having bathed and Frank was right about the ale. Rebecca helped get her clean and kept the water off her cast. "Just like ole times, eh, mum?" she said, helping Tanyth out of the bath and into some cleaner clothes.

Tanyth smiled remembering the days that one or more of the young women in the village had helped her after Birchwood's knife had carved a long scar up her center. "Well, not exactly," she said but smiled. "I appreciate the help."

Rebecca grinned and skinned out of her own clothing to take advantage of the warm water. "You just relax, mum," Rebecca said. "I'll just scrub up a bit and do a little laundry. We'll be fresh as daisies when Frank gets here."

Tanyth smiled at the young woman's cheerfulness.

"An' thanks for payin' for the room, mum," Rebecca said. "I can pay ya back."

The comment caught Tanyth unaware. "No, no. You're helpin' me. Least I can do is pay for the room."

Rebecca shot her a knowing grin and rolled her shoulders in a shrug. "Well, you prob'ly won't get much use of it until Frank heads back down the Pike."

"Not get much use of it?"

Rebecca's giggle filled the small room before Tanyth realized what the girl was getting at.

"Well, if you're trying to make an old woman blush, you're gonna have ta do better'n that," Tanyth said with a snort and a laugh. "Sadie and Amber cured me o' that with all the talk of woodboxes."

Rebecca just giggled some more and ducked her head to rinse off the soap. "Still, mum," she said. "I don't think you'll be spendin' much time here once Frank arrives." She made little shooing motions with her fingers. "You scoot. Go rest your bones downstairs and keep an eye out. I'll finish up here and be down in a bit."

Tanyth shook her head at the smiling girl and headed back down the stairs. Her legs complained at the unfamiliar movement of walking up and down the narrow stairs. "Funny how riding is so much harder on a body," she muttered.

In the taproom, she found the crowd had grown a bit and a couple of serving girls had joined Mabel. The light outside had faded to late afternoon and sturdy lanterns mounted on the posts and walls gave the room a warm, cheerful glow. A heavy stone hearth to one side had a small fire kindled for warmth, but few sat by the blaze. She took a seat at a small table just back from the hearth to rest her bones a bit.

One of the serving girls came over immediately. "What can I bring ya, mum? Nice bit of tea?"

Tanyth's stomach grumbled but over the hubbub, she didn't think the girl had heard it. "What's on for dinner then?"

The girl shook her head. "Stew for now, mum, but there's a joint of lamb roastin' for later. There's bread and cheese, o' course."

"Bread and cheese then, and another pint of your ale, please."

The girl looked at her in surprise. "Ale, mum?"

Tanyth laughed. "Ale, please."

The girl shrugged. "Ale it is, mum."

In moments the girl returned with a rough loaf of dark bread and a slab of hard cheese on a board. She slid the board onto the table, and slapped a tankard of ale down beside it. "Four coppers, please, mum."

Tanyth counted out five and the girl smiled. "Enjoy your meal, mum."

Tanyth took a sip of the ale and used her belt knife to hack an end off the loaf. She was startled by a rattling of metal on metal. She looked over to see the serving girl throw another handful of coppers into the metal can. She huffed a laugh and muttered, "Wonder how they count that?"

A man at the next table leaned over and spoke to her. "As a successful afternoon, how would you count it?"

Tanyth looked over at the man. He seemed innocuous enough, but something in his air set her teeth on edge. His clothes were a bit too new, a bit too clean to belong to a carter or driver. His hands seemed too white. "Aye, that would be, I suppose," she said and turned back to her bread and cheese.

The man didn't appear to take the point. "New in town?" he asked.

Tanyth looked at him and nodded. "Yeah. Just got in this afternoon. First time here. On my way to North Haven."

The man nodded and sipped his own ale. "Long way for a woman on her own."

Tanyth took a bite of cheese and washed it down with ale. "Not as far as all that."

"Ships don't come cheap." He took a swig of ale without looking in her direction.

She chuckled. "Lucky I only want a ticket. Not in the market for a whole ship this season."

"Tickets aren't cheap either."

Tanyth turned to the man and gave him a look up and down. "So I've heard," she said.

The man returned her look and took another sip of his ale.

"And the city clerk takes a dim view of people doing work for wages that don't get taxed?" Tanyth asked.

The man shrugged. "Well, that's true everywhere."

Tanyth nodded. "At least true here."

"Yes, definitely true here."

"Well, if you see the city clerk and he asks about me, please give him my regards and tell him I'll be gone soon's I can get a ticket out." Tanyth turned back to her bread and cheese.

The man didn't answer for a long while. Tanyth heard his cup snap down on the table and he stood. As he walked by, he looked down at her. "You'll be awhile yet, mum. North Haven is still ice bound and probably won't be taking traffic for at least a couple more weeks."

Tanyth frowned up at the man. "So I've heard."

He gave an oily smile that didn't reach his eyes. "Enjoy your stay in Kleesport, mum." He left with a mocking salute with his index finger before heading for the door.

The barmaid came over with a fresh mug of ale. "You all right, mum?" she asked, her eyes darting to the door and back again.

"Yes, my dear, fine. Is everybody in Kleesport so interested in how much money you're worth?"

The girl shook her head. "Only the tax collectors and the

King's Own," she said. "Might as well be one and the same, if ya ask me." She sniffed toward the door as if smelling a foul odor. "Ale's on the house, mum. Sorry he bothered ya."

"He was no more bother than the average flea on a dog," she said, "but I don't want you to get in trouble." Tanyth slipped a couple of coppers onto the table.

"We only get in trouble when we charge for it, mum. So far they ain't figured out a way to tax what we give away for free." The girl gave Tanyth a saucy grin and a quick wink.

Tanyth laughed at the girl's cheek and toasted her with the fresh mug of ale. "In that case, to your health, my dear."

"Thank ya, mum. You just holler for Betsy if you need something. I'll take good care of ya."

Tanyth inclined her head in thanks, noticing that Betsy palmed the coppers before she left the table.

Tanyth bent to carve another chunk of the heavy, dark bread when another person walked up to her table. "You stayin' out of trouble, old woman?"

She looked up to find Frank looking down at her, a crooked grin on his face and a half eaten apple in his hand. "Who you callin' old?" She stood and gave him a hug. "Seems like a long time since I left ya this morning. Pull up a chair. I'll buy you an ale," she said.

"Was this your doin'?" he asked holding up the apple.

"Yeah. I see you got it all right."

"Lady nearly beaned me with it. Good toss but I had my hands full of reins."

"How'd you catch it?"

"She hit me in the chest and it fell into my lap. I caught it with my legs." His bemused expression made her giggle. "You get us a room?"

"Well, I got me and Rebecca a room," she said. "Mostly people been pretty concerned about how much money I got and why I'm not shackled to some likely male."

Frank arched an eyebrow. "Bad as that?"

Tanyth gave a shrug. "Go see what your friend Mabel has to say, get settled. I'll hold down the table and tell ya about it when you get back."

Frank's mouth screwed into a grimace. "Deal," he said.

"Be right back."

Tanyth watched him amble over to the bar and get a warm greeting from Mabel. They glanced in her direction and she raised her mug in greeting. She couldn't hear the conversation over the growing babble in the taproom, but Mabel looked serious and Frank nodded a lot. Eventually, they came to some kind of agreement and Frank sauntered back to her table with an amused expression.

"Apparently, they aren't much on unmarried women sharin' rooms with men," he said, hooking a chair with his foot and pulling it out to sit on.

Tanyth snickered. "Probably wonderin' how they tax that."

Frank barked a short laugh.

"She happy now?" Tanyth asked, glancing at Mabel who watched them from her vantage at the bar.

Frank nodded. "Yeah. But I'm on the other end of the hall from you."

"Just as well," Tanyth said. "Rebecca's got enough to giggle about without noises through the walls."

Frank laughed. "Well there's that." He looked her up and down. "You been here long enough to get a bath?"

She smirked. "Rebecca, too. She's doing a bit of laundry now. You probably wanna look into one yourself."

He looked down at himself and nodded. "Two weeks on the Pike'll do that to ya."

She laughed. "Speaking of two weeks on the Pike, how'd you get the lorry wagon into town?" she asked.

He cocked his head. "Drove it. Why?"

"I got stopped at the plaza by the King's Own and asked my business. Everybody goin' in with goods had a tag on. I never saw you with any tag."

Frank scowled. "They stopped you? What for?"

"Warnin' about vagrancy laws and to tell me about the taxes."

Frank sighed and shook his head. "I swear it gets worse every year."

"So? Where's your tag?" Tanyth asked.

"I don't need one. William registered the wagon and the tax number's carved into the wood beside the driver's seat."

He shrugged. "I also drove around the plaza and went in the brickyard gate. Less traffic and they all know me over there."

Tanyth offered the board with bread and cheese. "Snack?"

He shook his head. "I'll go get cleaned up a bit before eatin'. Mabel says they're roasting lamb tonight. It's a house specialty." He stood and, with a nod, went off in search of his bath.

CHAPTER 13
GETTING DOWN TO BUSINESS

Tanyth woke with the dawn and rolled over to find Frank still asleep and snoring softly. She grinned and slipped from beneath the covers. After sleeping on the ground, the beds at the Broken Gate were a welcome change. The tick smelled relatively fresh and if not filled with the same sweet grass she'd been used to in Ravenwood, it appeared to be free of vermin and broad enough to accommodate them both without undue crowding.

"Not that you mind a little crowdin'," she murmured. She glanced at Frank again but he'd barely stirred.

She slipped into some fresh clothes and stepped into the hall, closing and locking the door behind her. She pocketed the key and followed the smell of baking bread down to the taproom to see what kind of breakfast came with the room. She found Mabel bustling about with a pair of the girls sweeping the floors and cleaning off the tables.

"Good morning, mum!" Mabel called as she saw Tanyth coming down the stairs. "You're an early bird, aren't you?"

Tanyth smiled. "Comes from too many winters on the road. Travelin' don't get done while you're curled up in bed."

"Guess that's true, mum, but I do enjoy the occasional lie about with the mister. Kinda decadent like." She looked around at the taproom. "Course, that don't happen much with all this."

Tanyth nodded in sympathy. "I can see why."

Mabel finished wiping down the table and tossed her rag into a bucket on the floor. "Well, can I get you some tea, mum? A roll and cheese?"

"Thank you, Mabel, a bit of tea would be most appreciated. Get my brain in gear this morning."

Mabel nodded, took her bucket and elbowed through to the kitchen. "I'll be right back, mum. Won't take but a moment."

Tanyth watched the two girls—Elly and another that she didn't recognize—working on the last of the tables. They smiled at her as they took up brooms and set about sweeping down the large room, shepherding the dirt toward the hearth, their straw brooms making little scritch-scritching sounds on the worn floorboards. Tanyth stepped aside and took a seat out of harm's way just in time for Mabel to come back from the kitchen with a sturdy china pot and two mugs.

"Here we go, mum." She set the pot on the table and took a seat with her. "I'm ready for my tea as well. Do you mind if I join you?"

Tanyth smiled. "It's your place. Help yourself."

Mabel grinned back. "Well, I don't wanna impose, but I do so miss conversation..." She stopped, coloring a bit about the ears as she covered her confusion by pouring tea into the mugs.

The two girls finished sweeping and put their brooms away. Mabel saw and called to them. "Thank you, girls. Your tea's on the work table in the kitchen."

They each gave a short curtsey then scurried off to their breakfasts.

Mabel looked across at Tanyth. "They're good girls, really. Just need a bit of direction now and again." She blew across the mouth of her mug before taking a sip. "And somebody to keep 'em on the straight and narrow, if you know what I mean, mum."

Tanyth took a sip of her own tea, nearly scalding her tongue on the hot brew, and nodded. "I suspect it's hard with so many men here all the time."

Mabel gave her head a little sideways shake. "Odd but the carters and drivers that we get behave pretty good. Most are too fat or too old..." Mabel fetched up on that with a glance across at Tanyth. "No offense, mum."

"None taken."

"Your Frank's a fine gentleman, he is. Been comin' here for three or four years, I think."

"Well, he's not *my* Frank." Tanyth said over the top of her mug. "I'm just kinda borrowin' him for a time. I need to give him back when I'm done."

Mabel blinked at her as if not quite sure what to make of the statement.

"I'll be taking passage to North Haven as soon as I can. He'll be heading back to Ravenwood when he finishes his business."

"Ravenwood, is it? That what they decided on for a name?"

"Yeah. Seems to suit. They built an inn out there last winter. Should make things a little easier for 'em."

"Do tell! Sounds like it's turning into quite the little township." Mabel sipped her tea. "Frank don't talk about it much, but once in a while we get him chattin' in an evenin'."

They sipped tea quietly for a few moments before Mabel asked, "What's in North Haven?"

"Just passin' through on the way north. I need to visit somebody up there."

"My goodness! Nothin' north of North Haven that I ever hear tell of," she said. "Nothin' but woods and mountains and more woods and mountains."

Tanyth grinned. "Well, I'm heading up to Lammas Wood, so I guess that's part of the woods."

"Just you and the girl out into the wilderness like that, mum?" Mabel seemed shocked.

"You know Lammas Wood?"

Mabel shook her head. "Not me, mum. Only what I hear. Stories and whatnot around the fire."

"What kinda stories?" Tanyth asked, making conversation and not really expecting any answers.

Mabel leaned in and lowered her voice. "Well, mum, I hear there's bears there. And wolves."

Tanyth smiled at the seriousness of the woman's tone. "Can't say as I'm surprised. That's where the bearskins and wolf pelts come from. Figger they must grow up there."

Mabel nodded and sipped her tea. "Still, mum, some of the stories the men tell 'bout what happens up there..."

"Well, men. You know how they can be. Strong enough in groups, but scared of the dark by themselves, some of them."

Mabel rocked back in her chair with a hearty laugh and took a deep pull from her tea. "Well, that's true enough, mum. And they do come up with some outlandish stories at times, I swear." She gave a half smile and arched an eyebrow in Tanyth's direction. "Still, good to snuggle up to on a cold winter night, eh, mum?"

Tanyth toasted the younger woman with her mug. "I'll drink to that," she said with a smile.

A man wearing a dark green shirt rolled up to his elbows and a pair of work pants held up with suspenders walked into the taproom from the kitchen. He nodded a greeting to Tanyth and Mabel reached out to take his hand. "Mother Fairport, this here's my husband, Matt. Matt, this is Mother Fairport. She's stayin' with us for a few days."

Matt knuckled his forehead, the scent of horse wafting from him. "Good mornin', Mother Fairport. Pleased to meet ya."

"Matt," she nodded. "Nice to meet you, too. Frank tells me you run a fine stable."

"Frank Crane?" he asked. "Nice of 'im. Got a crack team, he does. And 'e knows how to treat 'em. Better'n some treat their wives."

Mabel coughed and looked up to her husband. "Something you needed, my dear?"

"Oh, yeah," he said, reminded of his errand. "When Toby comes down, tell him his mare's set. Your brother finished shoeing last night and she's ready to get back on the road."

Mabel nodded. "Sure will. He'll be glad to be movin' again."

"Thanks," he said and leaned down to kiss her on the cheek. "Pleasure to meet you, mum," he said to Tanyth. As he turned to walk back through the kitchen, Mabel gave him a pat on the backside. He smiled back at her from the door.

Mabel saw Tanyth looking and gave her a shy smile. "Fifteen winters we been together. He still warms me just by lookin'."

Tanyth smiled and thought of the old man asleep in her bed. She took a pull from her mug and remembered that she'd locked him in. "Speakin' of men. I better go let Frank out. He'll want to be getting' on with his day, I wager."

Mabel snickered. "You locked him in?"

Tanyth stood and smiled down at her. "Well, good man like that, you don't want him wanderin' around loose on his own now, do ya?"

Mabel laughed and waved her off. "We'll have a full breakfast here in another hour or so. Bring him down and we'll feed him up for ya. He'll need his strength."

Tanyth laughed at that and headed back up the stairs to see if the man in question was awake. As she climbed, she pondered how she might wake him if he weren't.

☽◯☾

Tanyth's staff echoed a bit in the cavernous office belonging to George Pendleton, Esq. She felt a bit unsure of herself among the fine furnishings and walls with paintings on them. A large, glazed window gave George Pendleton, Esq. a fine view of the docks over the roofs of a few low buildings. Tanyth turned to face the florid-faced man standing behind the ornate carved-wood desk.

"Mr. Crane, always a pleasure. How can I help you today?"

Frank shook Pendleton's offered hand. "Nothing for me, Mr. Pendleton. This is Tanyth Fairport. She's the one you need to help today."

Mr. Pendleton looked from Frank to Tanyth and back again. "Certainly, and what might I do for Mother Fairport today, Mr. Crane?"

Tanyth stepped in front of Frank and said, "You can start by talking to me directly, young man."

Mr. Pendleton looked Tanyth up and down once very slowly. The touches of gray at his temples told Tanyth he probably wasn't used to being called young man. His sour expression told her he didn't much like it.

"Madame, it is simply not appropriate for you to take that tone with me."

Tanyth smiled. "Good. At least we agree that tone is important. I have business with you, Mr. Pendleton. I've brought Frank along to vouch for me. You know he's an agent of William Mapleton's company?"

Mr. Pendleton blinked rapidly several times, glancing up at Frank and then back at Tanyth. "Yes, madame. He is."

"Excellent," she said and pulled the sealed envelope from her coat pocket. "I was instructed by Mr. Mapleton to present this to you so I can arrange passage to North Haven."

Mr. Pendleton looked at the envelope as if it might be a snake, or perhaps a mud pie. "Madame, this is the Royal Bank, not a booking office." He scowled at Tanyth as if mortally insulted.

"Mr. Pendleton, perhaps you might read the letter from William?" Frank suggested. "I believe it will clear up any misunderstandin's you might have about Mother Fairport here."

Tanyth was mildly put out with Frank for interfering, but Mr. Pendleton looked at Frank and then back at the envelope before taking it gingerly between thumb and forefinger. "Very well," he said in much the same tone that Tanyth had heard children agree to eat vegetables.

He tilted the envelope up to the light, pushing his spectacles up to peer closely at the seal.

"It's valid, Mr. Pendleton," Frank murmured.

Mr. Pendleton shot a look at Frank. "Do you know what's in this?"

Tanyth heard Frank shuffle his feet but fought the urge to look back at him.

"More or less."

"So you'll know if it's been tampered with?" Mr. Pendleton looked at Tanyth with a barely concealed accusation in his eyes.

"Oh, yes, sir. Without a doubt," Frank said.

Pendleton sighed, took a seat behind the desk, and broke the wax seal. He removed a single sheet of paper. As he read it, the color on his face drained away and then refilled again in a rich scarlet. "This is preposterous," he said. He looked over Tanyth's head at Frank once more. "Mr. Crane, you cannot believe that the Royal Bank will honor this request.

It's simply not done."

"Are you certain, Mr. Pendleton?" Frank asked. Tanyth recognized a quiet, dangerous tone in Frank's voice and turned to look at him. He smiled down at her.

"Quite positive, Mr. Crane." Mr. Pendleton jumped to his feet and shook the letter in the air. "To give this much to a woman? It simply is not done, sir."

Tanyth felt caught between a whirlwind and the deep blue sea. She thumped the iron heel of her staff once on the wooden floor. "You might try talking to me, Mr. Pendleton, and explain what the issue is."

Mr. Pendleton looked up to Frank and back at Tanyth. "Madame, Mr. Mapleton has asked me to withdraw from his accounts a sum which is completely inappropriate for a woman to have in her control."

"How much, Mr. Pendleton?" she asked, more curious than furious, although she suspected her fury would come along soon enough. The closeness of the office after over a week on the road, the cloying scent of furniture wax, and the ludicrousness of the situation added fuel to a temper that was already dangerously close to breaking lose.

"Twenty gold crowns, madame."

"And does his account not hold twenty gold crowns, Mr. Pendleton?" Tanyth asked.

"Of course, of course, madame, but that's not the point."

"What *is* the point, Mr. Pendleton?" Frank's voice, calm and deceptively quiet cut through the office.

"Mr. Crane, you know as well as I that handing that much money over to a woman is completely inappropriate."

Frank laid a hand on Tanyth's shoulder. She felt him vibrating through it. "So if, for example, I was to request that amount, there would be no problem?"

Relief washed over Mr. Pendleton's face. "Exactly so, Mr. Crane. I'm so glad you—"

Frank held out a second envelope. "Then perhaps you might read *this* letter, Mr. Pendleton."

Mr. Pendleton smiled and took the letter. "Of course, Mr. Crane." He broke the seal and began reading even as he talked. "Royal Bank stands ready to..." His voice trailed off and he sat back down, gingerly balancing on the edge of his chair. Tanyth could see his eyes trace and retrace the words on the page.

"Is there a problem, Mr. Pendleton?" Frank's voice chilled even Tanyth.

Mr. Pendleton took off his spectacles to stare at Frank over Tanyth's head. He opened and closed his mouth several times as if looking for and failing to find the words.

"Is there?" Frank repeated.

Tanyth watched Mr. Pendleton fumble his glasses back onto his face and take a moment to smooth his shirtwaist. His hands shook visibly. "No, Mr. Crane, no problem. Just one moment, please."

Mr. Pendleton rang a small silver bell on his desk and a youth entered the room almost immediately. "Bolton, please fetch twenty gold crowns for me."

"Twenty gold crowns, Mr. Pendleton. Yes, sir."

"A moment, if you please?" Tanyth said.

Mr. Pendleton's color lost some of its pastiness and he was able to almost look at her. "Yes, Madame Fairport?"

"Correct me if I'm mistaken but a gold crown is rather a heavy and unwieldy item?"

Frank snorted behind her in something that she suspected was a laugh.

Mr. Pendleton looked at her with an expression of disbelief. "Well, madame, perhaps so. Why do you ask?"

She sighed and turned to Frank. "Mr. Crane, should a frail old woman like myself be wanderin' the streets of this fair city with that much gold on my person?"

Frank's eyes danced and his lips twitched in what threatened to be a grin. "No, mum. That might be a bit unwise."

"I thought so myself." Tanyth nodded as if making up her mind about something before turning to Mr. Pendleton. "Sir?"

"Yes, madame."

"Do you think that the Royal Bank might be willing to accept a deposit from a woman like myself?"

Mr. Pendleton blinked several more times. "Well, madame, it would be somewhat irregular. You'd need to have your husband countersign and you would need to find a factor to manage your account and to make certain that only..." He saw the look on her face then and his voice petered out.

"But not as impossible as, say, giving me twenty gold crowns and letting me walk out the door with them?" she asked.

Mr. Pendleton looked up at Frank and then back at Tanyth. "Well, no, madame."

Tanyth looked to Frank who shrugged in a "why not?" gesture and nodded.

"Then perhaps I might draw out, say, fifty silvers and leave the rest on account until I need it to book passage to North Haven? Would that be less irregular still?"

"Yes, madame, but you would still need to secure a factor to manage your account," Mr. Pendleton said. "Under the circumstances, I can recommend any number of our people—"

"How about you, Mr. Pendleton?" Tanyth asked, breaking into his ramble.

"Me?" his voice almost squeaked. "Madame, I feel that you might find some of our other factors more to your liking."

Tanyth looked at him. "Why?"

"Well, madame." He sighed and saw that his secretary still stood in the doorway, ears flapping. "That will be all for now, Bolton."

"Yes, sir." Young Bolton removed himself but Tanyth felt certain he would be listening at the keyhole.

"My apologies, madame. We have a reputation at the Royal Bank and perhaps I took that too far." He looked like he might strangle on his tongue. "Under the circumstances, I felt that you might find one of my colleagues less..." He groped for a word.

"Argumen'ative?" Tanyth supplied.

"Uh..."

"Hide bound, per'aps?"

"Well, um. Yes, madame." Mr. Pendleton finally had the grace to look her in the eye and look as sheepish as a Royal Bank factor might when seated in his own office staring down his nose—at least figuratively—at a poorly dressed little old lady.

"All right then, Mr. Pendleton," she said. "Now that we have an understandin', I think you'd make a splendid factor, assuming you'll have me?"

Mr. Pendleton sat back in his chair and cocked his head. "Madame?"

Tanyth leaned forward and tapped the front of his desk with her fingertips. "Please, call me Tanyth? And we got off on the wrong foot. I think we understand each other now, don't you?"

Mr. Pendleton seemed taken aback. "Madame...er...Tanyth, I've never had a woman with her own account before." He looked almost embarrassed.

"And how many of your colleagues have?"

He examined his hands. "None that I know of...Tanyth." He looked at her apologetically. "I could make some discreet inquiries..."

"No, I don't think that will be necessary." She looked to Frank who merely pretended not to notice, staring straight ahead as if nothing in the room involved him. "How do we proceed then, Mr. Pendleton?" she asked.

☽○☾

Half an hour later, Frank and Tanyth left the imposing stone edifice that was the Royal Bank and began working their way toward the docks. A skirling wind whipped down the alley between two buildings and carried the tang of dead fish and cold salt water. Tanyth shouldered her coat closer around her body.

"That went well," Frank said.

"Yes," Tanyth agreed. She looked up at him. "I do have one question, though."

He grinned. "I expect you do."

"What was in the letter?"

"Which letter?" He wore his innocence like a cloak.

"I will hit you with this stick, sir." Her words delivered calmly, but Frank had no doubt that she might do just that.

"We had a little talk back in Ravenwood," Frank said. "William is rather naïve."

"William?" Tanyth nodded. "He thought that the bank might not deal with a woman?"

"No. He thought they would."

"But you thought different?"

Frank nodded with a rueful grimace. "You met Mabel." It wasn't a question.

"Yeah. Of course."

"Have you met her Matthew yet?"

"This morning. Just for a minute, why?"

"Mabel's got the brains in that marriage. Matt's a good man, keeps a good stable, but..." Frank shrugged.

"So?"

"So they needed to open an account for the inn. They wouldn't take Mabel's signature even though she brought in the money."

"They made her fetch Matt?"

Frank nodded. "It was easy enough for him, but..." he shrugged again.

"So you figured they'd give me trouble if I tried to cash that note from William?"

"I was pretty sure of it."

"Why didn't William have you withdraw the money then?"

He grinned down at her. "Would you have taken it from me?"

Tanyth grinned back. "Prob'ly not."

He shrugged as if that were all the answer he needed.

"What was in the letter, then?" she asked.

"Instructions to withdraw all our money and close the account."

Tanyth stopped in the middle of the street and looked up at Frank. "You'd have done that?"

Frank stopped and looked back at her. "Naw, I knew he'd give in."

Tanyth shook her head. "Why in the name of all that's holy...?"

"What? Why would he give in? Greed. He makes a nice cut from the money we spend through the Royal Bank."

Tanyth frowned. "Can I ask?"

"How much money?"

She nodded.

"The village has something over forty in the account. It

grows a little bit each year as we make more than we spend. We have some investments that pay well."

Tanyth gasped. "Forty gold crowns? You gave me half of Ravenwood's money?"

Frank laughed and Tanyth nearly beaned him with her staff after all.

"What's so funny? We have to go back there right now. This is impossible."

Frank held his hands up, palms out in a placating gesture. "No, no, Tanyth. Not forty crowns."

"What?"

"The balance isn't forty crowns. It's forty thousand."

Tanyth felt like she'd been punched in the chest.

"The twenty crowns is about what we get for two barrels of clay." Frank held out his hands to the sides. "It's not a problem, Tanyth. Really."

She stared at him.

"What is it?" He stepped closer to her and took her hand. "Are you all right?"

"You fought Andy Birchwood? Risked it all when you could have paid him off?"

Frank folded her in his arms, holding her close to his chest.

She tried to push him away. "You risked all those lives? Kurt got killed!" Her anger threatened to boil over but he held her tight.

"Tanyth, we would have paid him if it would have helped. You saw what he did at Foxrun," Frank's voice sounded muffled, vibrating through his chest. He held her against her struggles until she stopped pushing, then he stood back and looked down at her.

Tanyth saw what looked like tears in his eyes when she looked up and her protests died unspoken. "What? What aren't you tellin' me, Frank Crane?" She wanted to be angry but the look on his face made her voice come out soft.

"Andy Birchwood killed my sister."

"All-Mother, help us."

"After he collected all he could, he killed her and her husband. There was no proof, but we all knew the kind of man he was. We thought we were shut of him."

Tanyth let him hold her then, and she wrapped her own strong arms around his chest, hugging back but being careful not to clunk him in the back of the head with her cast. "You never said..."

"No," he said. "We knew what he'd do. We knew he was a murderer."

"Did William know?" she asked, pushing back to look up into his face.

Frank nodded his head. "He knew Andy was a killer, but not who he killed. Not until..."

"Until?"

"Until after."

"After I killed him, you mean?" Tanyth asked.

"After he almost killed you." Frank held her close once more. "I thought he'd come after the wagon. It made more sense. I thought I was going to get a chance at him myself. When he didn't—" His voice caught in his throat.

After a few moments, he regained his composure and took a large red handkerchief out of his pocket and blew his nose loudly, not looking at Tanyth.

He cleared his throat a couple of times and turned toward the docks, carefully linking her casted arm in his, before resuming the story. "So, we could have paid, but we knew—I knew—that as soon as we stopped, he'd kill us." He looked at her, walking alongside him. "All-Father forgive me, mum, but that's the truth of it. I'd have brought the gold back in my teeth if I'd thought it would have saved anybody."

Tanyth felt shaken and confused. All she could do was walk alongside and shake her head. Finally she said, "But you live in huts."

Frank's laughter echoed off the fine, stone buildings and his laughter infected her. "Yes," he said at last, "but they're excellent huts."

That set them off in more peals of laughter and they chuckled all the way to the docks, ignoring the curious looks their laughter earned them.

Chapter 14
Delayed Freight

Frank held the door for her and she sailed into the harbor master's office, a cluttered little lobby with chalkboards around the walls and a wet wool smell that clung to her nose. A cheery bell tinkled as the door opened and closed. The clerk behind the counter looked up and glanced back and forth between the two of them. He seemed a bit confused when Frank lounged beside the door and Tanyth approached, her staff making hollow clunks as she walked.

"You're not going to give me any trouble about buying passage, are you, young man?"

Her fierce expression must have made an impression on him. He goggled a bit but stammered, "N-no, mum. Where would you like to go?"

"North Haven."

He nodded. "All right, mum. When would you like to go?"

"How soon can I leave?"

The clerk looked up in surprise and scanned the chalkboards. "Mum? You know North Haven is still not open, yeah?"

She looked at him with a frown. "I heard there's a windy something we're all waitin' on?"

The clerk laughed politely before apparently realizing she hadn't made a joke. "Yes, mum. The Zypheria."

"How much longer?" she asked.

The clerk shrugged and shook his head. "We don't know, mum. Everybody's waiting for the Zypheria's Call. Could be any day. Might not be for a month."

"I've been hearin' about this zypher thing for a couple weeks now," she said.

"Zypheria, mum. Warm wind that comes down of the mountains out on the western end of the bight, mum. It blows the ice out along the north shore. Can't get a ship in there until then."

"And when it does?"

"There's four ships in port ready to sail with supplies." He pointed to the boards displayed around the office. "Them boards there, mum? That's all the ships comin' in, getting' ready to leave, or just fillin' in time. That board on the end? That's ships bound for North Haven."

She saw that the departure dates were blank and somebody had scrawled "Iced In" across the top in red chalk. She turned back to the clerk. "I see. And do any of those ships carry passengers?"

He nodded. "Oh, yes, mum. Most of 'em, but they won't accept passage until they know when they're leavin'."

"Which they won't know until...?"

"Until the Zypheria starts blowin'," the clerk finished. "Could be any day but nobody knows for sure."

"Seems kinda haphazard to me," she said.

The clerk simply shrugged.

"So, if I come back in a week?"

"You prob'ly should check every day now, mum." The clerk gave her an apologetic smile. "We just don't know and I'd hate for you to miss it."

"Can you send me a message?" She looked at the boy. "You do have messengers in this city, don't you?"

"Well, yes, mum, but it'll cost a silver—"

She slapped two silvers onto the counter. "Tanyth Fairport. I'm staying at the Broken Gate. Think you can get me a message?"

He gulped and pulled a blank envelope from under the counter. In a labored scrawl he wrote "Tanith Fairport, Broken Gate, North Haven bound" on the front and tucked the silvers into it. He then folded the envelope closed and tucked it into the side of his window. "Yes, mum."

She smiled. "Blessed be, lad. Thank you kindly."

"Yes'm. I'll be sure to send it."

Frank held the door for her and she sailed out of the office into a brilliant afternoon.

Tanyth stopped on the walk outside and surveyed the wharfs, wondering which of the many ships tied up at the various piers were waiting to go to North Haven.

"How does a body know about this wind shift?" she asked, looking up at Frank.

"You mean, how can you tell if he's not sent the message?"

Tanyth grinned.

He pointed to the flags and pennants flying from the various masts around the harbor. "See how all the flags are pointin' south?"

She nodded. "That means somethin'?"

"It means the wind's comin' from the north. The westerlies come in the spring, blow all summer long. The flags'll all be pointin' east most o' the time. In the fall it'll shift north'ard again and the wind's mostly out of the north or nor'east until the followin' spring."

"So we're waitin' for them flags to swing around when the wind changes?"

"Well, mostly we're waitin' for it to change on the north side of the Bight. The shift in wind along the north shore blows warmer air up into the bays up there. Changes the direction of the waves. Between the waves and the wind, the big ice sheets break up and get blown off shore." He shrugged. "It'll shift up there first but it'll get down here sooner or later. When it does, the ships'll start goin' north again."

"What's the Bight?"

Frank jerked a chin at the open water beyond the piers. "That's what they call that stretch of ocean—the Bight of Korlay. Big round bay. Takes days to sail across. Flows into the open sea to the east. Got mountains runnin' right down to the water on the west. North Haven's on the other side."

"I see," she said, and gingerly wrapped her cast around Frank's offered arm for the stroll back across town.

As they walked away Tanyth noticed that he was trying to hide a smile. "What's tickled your funny bone this time,

Frank Crane?"

He looked down at her and shook his head. "You're a wonder, you know that?"

She frowned at him. "Hardly a wonder, Frank. I'm just a poor little old lady who's strayed too far from home."

Frank snorted. "Well, then come on, old lady. I think we need to get back to the Gate for tea."

"Tea?" she asked, looking up with concern on her face. "Why? Do you think they've run out of ale?"

"No, mum. I just figured a poor old lady like you might not be up to ale at lunch."

She looked up at his poorly hidden smirk. "I *will* hit you with this stick," she said, but hugged his arm to her side.

"Don't hurt me too badly. I promised Rebecca we'd deliver her trunks to her auntie this afternoon."

Tanyth leaned her head on his shoulder for a step before looking up at him. "She's an odd girl. Not at all what I expected."

Frank glanced down and nodded. "She walks her own road, no question there. Kinda reminds me of somebody else. Can't think of who off hand."

Tanyth's laugh barked and echoed off the buildings. She pulled on his arm. "You know her family?" she asked after a few steps.

"Her family's had a hand in runnin' the city about as long as it's been here. Ole man Marong didn't take kindly to Becca joinin' up with the band of gypsies that left here to start over in the woods." Frank sucked air in through his teeth. "Her aunt's the kind that wants everybody to get along. Nice enough lady."

"She'll keep Rebecca's secret?"

Frank shrugged. "I s'pect that by the time it leaks out that she's in town, she'll be gone again." He grinned down at her upturned face. "The Broken Gate ain't exactly included in the social circle that the Marongs would run in."

"Not top drawer, is it?" she asked.

"Not even in the same dresser."

She laughed again. "When we get back I need to talk to this Matt fellow."

"Really? Change your mind about a pack animal?"

She shook her head and lifted the cast. "I need to get this off. I'm tired of dealin' with it and it's time."

Frank looked down at her. "It's only been, what? Three weeks since you broke it? That's not nearly enough time to heal."

She shook her head. "More like four and a half and it's comin' off."

"Now, Tanyth..."

"Don't you 'now Tanyth' me, Frank. This bone is healed and I need to get the arm workin' again a'fore I need it up north."

He scowled. "That's not a good idea. Takin' it off too soon..."

She shook her head. "It's healed, Frank."

"Hasn't been enough time."

"It's healed, I tell you."

He started to object but stopped, his mouth open as if to speak.

"Flies. You'll wanna close that," Tanyth said.

"You been sayin' prayers again?" he asked.

She gave a small shrug. "Somethin' like that."

"How can you know—?" His question cut off. "Dreams. You been dreamin'?"

"Yeah. Ever since the first night."

"You think they're real?"

She shrugged. "Arm hasn't hurt for a few days. Itches a bit but not under the skin like it did while it was healin'."

"It's still too soon for it to have healed up...unless you did it."

"I'm no healer."

Frank snorted.

"I'm not. I know a little bit about herbs and what they can do. That's all," she said.

"But you know a broken arm takes longer than a couple weeks to heal. Even for a youngster."

She shot him a look. "Careful with the 'youngster' comments, old man."

He grinned at her. "Sorry."

She grinned back.

"Still, you know it takes awhile."

She nodded without answering.

"And you want to take the cast off anyway?"

"Yeah," she said. "It's time."

"'Cause you dreamed it was healed."

"Yeah."

"Or you healed it in your dream," he said after they'd taken a few more steps.

Tanyth scowled up at him. "You keep makin' these silly claims about me, Frank. I never claimed I healed anybody. Least of all me."

He hugged her arm to his side and offered a smile of apology. "Never said you did, but ya have to admit..." He paused to look into her eyes. "You have to admit, you don't know for sure."

It wasn't what she expected him to say and the surprise escaped in a laugh. "No," she said. "I guess I don't know."

"Well, there you have it. We'll just go see Matt when we get back and have him snip that thing off and then we'll see, huh?" He grinned down at her.

She grinned back at him and hugged his arm once more as they fell into an easy walking rhythm back across the city.

CHAPTER 15
SEPARATE ROADS

For the next three days Tanyth fell into a lazy pattern of eating and sleeping, lounging around the taproom with Rebecca while Frank tended to the village's business. Each day saw strength and flexibility returning to her injured arm. One day she accompanied Frank out to make some of the village purchases and delighted in adding several small tokens to the crates of supplies.

On the morning of the fourth day, Frank rose early and put on his traveling clothes. Tanyth watched him pull on his heavy cord trousers, warm tunic, and over it all, a leather vest. He stuffed the rest of his gear into a canvas bag with a clever strap and toggle arrangement that fit neatly under the seat in the wagon.

When he was done, he came to sit on the side of the bed. She reached for his face with her free hand and ran the ball of her thumb across the crows-feet beside his eye, cupping his face in her palm. "Time to go, old man?"

He nodded and started to say something, but stopped.

"Give them all a hug for me when you get back," she said.

"I will." He gazed at her for a long moment. She couldn't read the expression on his face.

She sighed and closed her eyes, seeing the raven's visions in her memory, remembering the drop of blood and the ship from her dreams. She opened her eyes to look up at him.

He smiled then. Tanyth thought it a sad smile, but it warmed her for all of that. "You're always welcome in Ravenwood," he said. "If you ever decide to settle down, I'll..." He stopped and cleared his throat.

"I'll remember," she said and pulled him down for a kiss.

He stood then and gathered his bag, stopping at the door for a look back. "Be careful, old woman."

"Watch yourself, old man. Blessed be."

He left the room and she heard the door latch behind him. In the quiet of the morning, she heard his footsteps fade down the hall.

She lay there for a time, staring at the rough boards of the ceiling, watching the growing light of day creep across the splinters and knots, seeing the way the light played over the saw cuts in the wood. When she thought it safe, she rose and dressed. The room echoed with his absence.

"Don't go getting' all goopy, old woman," she muttered to herself, but part of her just laughed at that and got goopy anyway.

She finished dressing and straightening out the covers on the bed. She looked around for something else to do before realizing that she was just wasting time, delaying the moment when she'd leave the room on her own.

She crossed to the small window and peered out at the morning. She looked down into the yard behind the inn and out across the city to the north. The rising sun gilded the edges of rooftops and chimney pots. Smoke from countless fires drifted across the sky but couldn't obscure the silver edge of the sea beyond. Bubbles and ripples in the windowpane made the view waver and dance but she saw the white seabirds soaring over the rooftops. Occasionally fat pigeons flapped by in pairs or small flocks.

"You could go back with him," she murmured and rested her forehead on the cool glass, breath from her nose fogging the view. She closed her eyes and felt very tired. The raven nightmare still haunted her and the only clues she had pointed to the north. She opened her eyes again and leaned back from the window to gaze across the roof tops to where the land was so cold, it was still locked in ice. She drew in a breath and blew it out through her nose.

"Moon calf," she grumbled. The grumbling felt familiar.

Her stomach grumbled back and it made her smile in spite

of herself. With a final look to the north, she left the room and headed for breakfast.

In the taproom, she found Rebecca halfway through a bowl of oatmeal at a small table by the hearth. The morning activity was already winding down. The carters and drivers with road ahead had already gone. Those with nothing much to do until their loads were ready hadn't bothered to rise. Tanyth had seen the pattern often enough to recognize it. She took her customary chair across from Rebecca, who offered a small smile.

"Saw Frank goin'," she said.

Tanyth nodded, not ready to speak about it.

Rebecca wolfed down the last of her oatmeal and sat back in her chair. "You sure about this, mum?"

Tanyth drew in a breath and blew it out in a sigh.

"All right," Rebecca said with a small, tight smile. She leaned across and patted Tanyth's arm. "Just askin'. I go where you go."

"You wanna go back?" Tanyth asked.

Rebecca's smile grew. "No, mum. Never been on a ship before. I'm kinda lookin' forward to it."

Elly brought them a small pot of tea without having to ask and smiled at her brightly. "Mornin', mum."

"Good morning, Elly. Busy morning?"

The young woman gave a careless shrug. "Not so's you'd notice, mum." She paused and asked, "You want breakfast this mornin', mum?"

"Just my oatmeal would be good, my dear."

"Of course, mum. I'll be right back." She left with a bright smile and a flurry of skirts.

Tanyth smiled inwardly and felt tired. "All that cheerfulness so early in the day," she muttered.

Rebecca laughed quietly. "She likes her job," she said and leaned in with a conspiratorial whisper. "And she's sweet on the butcher's boy."

Tanyth smiled.

Elly returned with a heavy bowl filled with steaming oatmeal. "Here you go, mum. There's some dried fruit in it this mornin'. Hope you like it."

Tanyth's mouth started to water at the rich, warm smell. "Thank you, Elly. I'm sure I will."

"You just holler if you need anything, mum." Elly gave a small curtsy and hurried back to the kitchen, only to return almost immediately with a large teapot. She went from table to table, refilling mugs as she went, smiling and joking with the few customers scattered about.

Tanyth smiled at the young woman's energy and dug into the oatmeal, almost burning the roof of her mouth on the hot grain.

It didn't take long for her to work through the bowl and just as she spooned the last bit of cream from the dish, Mabel came out of the kitchen and surveyed the room. She made a slow circuit, speaking with the new faces and greeting the regulars. She ended at Rebecca and Tanyth's table and helped herself to an empty chair.

"Good morning, mum," she said with a smile. "Are you well?"

A shadow in the woman's face made Tanyth pause. "Good mornin', Mabel. I'm feelin' quite fit today. Why d'ya ask?"

"Oh, just...you look a bit peaked this morning."

Tanyth shrugged. "Per'aps a little tired," she admitted. "At loose ends today, what with Frank gone and the ships not ready."

Mabel gave a sideways glance at Rebecca then looked at her hands. "Frank's a good man, ain't he, mum?"

"Oh, yes. He's that."

Rebecca cleared her throat and drained her tea with a sudden toss of the mug. "If you two would 'scuse me?" She rose from the table and grinned at Tanyth. "Need to pick up the room a bit now that you're movin' back in."

Mabel snickered and Tanyth felt her color rise.

Rebecca chuckled as she climbed the stairs and disappeared.

Mabel glanced after her. "She's somethin' else, ain't she?"

"Rebecca? Yeah. Thinks we're on a grand adventure."

Mabel shrugged. "Well, you are, aren't ya?"

Tanyth laughed. "I s'pose so."

"She been with ya long?"

Tanyth shook her head. "Just a few weeks. She was tired of livin' at Ravenwood. Wanted to see some other sights."

"Well, she's seen Kleesport now."

Tanyth grinned. "She grew up here. She's lookin' forward to North Haven."

Mabel cocked her head. "She's from Kleesport? You know who her people are?"

Tanyth nodded. "I do, but it's not my story to tell."

Mabel arched an eyebrow at that but nodded and lowered her gaze to where her fingers twisted together on the table. After a few moments she looked up from under lowered lashes. "Can I ask, mum...?"

"Ask what, my dear?"

"Why you didn't leave with him? With Frank, I mean." Mabel seemed almost embarrassed to ask, but Tanyth saw the curiosity in the younger woman's eyes.

"We got different roads to travel. The village needs Frank more'n I do right now." She offered a helpless shrug.

Mabel seemed scandalized by the revelation. "Really, mum? You two seemed like quite the item. You sure you don't need 'im?" The last question had a bit of sly grin behind it.

Tanyth smiled back. "Oh, he's a good 'un to have about, no question." She paused and sipped her tea, not sure what she should be admitting to the younger woman.

"So? What's more important than havin' a good man about, mum?" Mabel seemed perplexed. "I don't know what I'd do without my Matt." She paused and looked at Tanyth with narrowed eyes. "You don't strike me as the spinster type, mum."

Tanyth sighed and sipped her tea. "I've got a son out there somewhere." She waved her mug in the general direction of the door. "He left home when he was only about fourteen winters. Joined up and got away."

"Where is he now, mum?"

She shrugged. "Dunno. Never heard from him after that."

Mabel's eyes grew large. "Not once? He never wrote home to his mother?"

"Not that I know of." Tanyth paused for a moment. "I left soon after. Been on the road ever since."

"Left, mum? Left what?"

"House, home..." Her voice trailed off.

"Husband?" Mabel's voice almost squeaked.

Tanyth gave a small shrug and took another sip of cooling tea.

Mabel's look of astonishment cleared in an instant. "Got away, you said."

Tanyth nodded.

Mabel sat back in her chair, arms hanging limp at her sides. "Whoosh, mum. That's a story."

Her exclamation drew a low chuckle out of Tanyth. "You have no idea, my dear. No idea at all."

Mabel leaned in. "Was he a drunk?"

Tanyth gave another shrug. "No more'n a lot of men. He liked his ale in the evenin'. Sometimes too much. He had a temper, though. Quick to heat and slow to cool. Ale didn't help that, but it was the temper that drove me away."

Mabel looked into Tanyth's eyes and, for once, she didn't look away. Tanyth didn't like the look of pity that came into the younger woman's face, but she accepted it.

"How long ago was this?" Mabel asked.

"Over twenty winters gone."

Mabel's eyes got wide again. "And you never went back?"

Tanyth shook her head. "Nothin' to go back to."

"What'd you do, mum?"

"I spent that first winter with a woman lived nearby. Holed up in her spare room, doin' chores and the heavy liftin' she couldn't. She started teachin' me about the herbs and plants. It was interestin' and she said I had a gift for it. When winter broke, I moved on to another old woman who taught me more. Been going from hearth to hearth ever since. Every new hearth I learned more. They showed me how to use the plants and which plants did what."

"So now you're going north," Mabel said. "What's up there?"

"Another hearth, I hope. Last of the old healers lives up that way."

Mabel frowned. "I know a few healers here in town. Men-folk mostly but I s'pect there's midwives and some wise-women, too."

Tanyth nodded. "Most cities attract healers. Not a pretty callin' but one that's needed. I may take it up myself when I'm done travelin'."

Mabel's face took on that sly, teasing look again. "Maybe go settle down with Frank?"

Tanyth smiled. "Maybe. Old woman could do a lot worse than settlin' in with a comfortable old man."

"So what's stoppin' ya, mum?"

Tanyth shook her head. "Not time, yet."

Mabel cocked her head and Tanyth could see her thinking. "Nothin' up north but hunters and trappers and lumberjacks, mum."

Tanyth smiled. "Well, must be somethin' there or they'd not be huntin' and trappin' and such."

Mabel laughed. "Well, there's the hermit, but——" Mabel's voice cut off as she realized what she'd said. "All-Mother, you're not going to hunt down the hermit, mum."

Tanyth smiled but didn't say anything.

"Mum, she's not real friendly. Drivers come back tellin' stories about this crazy old woman who lives in the wood up there. All alone. Been there for a hunnert winters."

"Her name is Gertie Pinecrest, and I'm pretty sure she hasn't been there that long," Tanyth said, twisting her tea mug in her fingers. "I don't think she's dangerous."

Mabel's mouth worked for a few heartbeats before she was able to get words in order. "But, mum, she's crazy."

"Crazy how?" Tanyth asked. "I really don't know much about her. Just the stories I've picked up on the road."

Mabel grimaced. "Well, I don't know first hand, mind. I only know what the drivers say..."

Tanyth nodded.

"She runs through the forest screaming at the lumberjacks makin' 'em stop cuttin' down trees."

Tanyth arched an eyebrow. "She got a reason?"

Mabel shrugged. "Dunno. Nobody's ever said. But she lets animals out of traps. Even busts up the traps sometimes." Mabel stared into Tanyth's eyes. "How strong do you have to be to break a steel trap, I ask ya? This just ain't right, mum."

Tanyth considered the woman's words for a few moments. "Is that all?" she asked.

Mabel sat bolt upright in her chair as if stung. "Is that all? Isn't that enough? Mum, the woman is dangerous."

Tanyth smiled. "I don't think she's as bad as all that."

"How can you say that, mum?" Mabel appeared aghast.

"Tales grow with the tellin'. You know that."

Mabel paused and sat back in her chair. "Aye, they do. You think that's what's happened with the hermit, mum?"

Tanyth shrugged again. "I been on the road for over twenty winters. Holed up in cabins with old women every year, sometimes a couple different ones in the space of a few months. I been from Easton to the Western Marches. Went as far south as Ortala once. All on my own. Heard tales all along the road."

"Weren't you scared, mum?" Mabel asked after she'd had a moment to digest.

"Sure," Tanyth said with a shrug. "Lots of times, but you musta been scared right here once in a while."

Mabel looked around the taproom. "Well, sure, mum. I s'pose everybody gets scared sometimes."

"There ya go," Tanyth said. "You get scared and you just keep goin'. Nothin' too excitin' about it."

Mabel kept shaking her head. "So, you need to go track down the hermit? And you're not scared?"

Tanyth snorted. "Of course, I'm scared, but I gotta go track down the hermit."

"Why, mum? Ain't you afraid she'll hurt you?"

"That's the least o' my worries. Why would she hurt me?"

Mabel blinked. "Really? What are you scared of then, mum?"

"Well, that she won't take me in and teach me what she knows." Tanyth sighed and leaned closer. "That old woman is the last of the keepers of the old knowledge. She may be crazy, or she may just be onto somethin' the rest of us only got hints about. There's powers in the world. Things I can hardly believe myself. Things that scare me a lot more than some jackass with his pants down and his brains in his hand. I think Mother Pinecrest knows what they are and how to use 'em. At least she might know what's happenin'—" Tanyth bit her words off, unwilling to finish the sentence, unwilling to admit what was happening, even to the well-meaning younger woman.

Mabel seemed to sense there was more behind the words. Tanyth kicked herself mentally for opening that door. Mabel didn't ask the question that Tanyth expected. "Why are you tellin' me this, mum?"

Tanyth shrugged and gave her a sheepish grin. "Don't really know. I'm a little bit at odds and ends today. I miss Frank already, I won't lie about that, and I'm nervous about getting' on a ship and hoping to get north as soon as I can."

Mabel nodded. "I can't even imagine what you're goin' through, mum."

Tanyth patted the woman's hand where it rested on the table between them. "You caught an old woman on a foolish day. I'll be fine."

Mabel seemed to remember where she was and looked around the taproom as if not aware of how she got there or what she should be doing. "Well, you tell a good story, mum. No question about—"

A clatter and short shriek from the kitchen had Mabel up and moving before the sound stopped echoing in the near empty taproom. Tanyth followed Mabel into the tidy kitchen and found one of the serving girls leaning against a work counter, a metal tray of biscuits up-ended and scattered across the floor. The oven door stood open, the heat wafting into the room.

"Wendy? What is it, girl?"

Tears coursed down the girl's face and she nodded at the mess on the floor. "I dropped the biscuits, mum. I'm so sorry."

"There, there, dearie. It's just biscuits. We can make more."

The girl's tears continued and Tanyth realized that she cradled one hand to her chest.

Mabel seemed to realize it at the same time. "Is there something wrong with your hand? Let me see." She crossed to the girl and made to reach for the injured hand but the young woman held her arm out of reach.

"I burned it, mum. Don't touch it. It hurts so." The girl's crying tapered off and she opened the offending hand to inspection.

A straight, red welt ran across the girl's palm.

Mabel gasped and looked up at the girl. "You're supposed to use a pot holder, my girl. Those pans get hot."

She nodded. "I know, mum, but when I slid the tray out of the oven it started to slip and I grabbed the side to steady it. I wasn't thinkin', mum." She sobbed again. "And now I've ruined everything."

Mabel shushed the girl and wrapped a motherly arm about her shoulders. "Now stop bein' a goose and let's get you taken care of, then we can worry about the biscuits."

The girl looked from Mabel to Tanyth, who still stood by the door. Mabel seemed to notice her for the first time. "Sorry about the excitement, mum," she said.

Tanyth smiled and shrugged it off. "Anything I can do to help?"

"Know anything about burns?" Mabel asked. "I'd just slather on a little butter and wrap it in gauze, but you're the expert here."

Tanyth snorted. "I'm no healer. Just an old lady who knows a bit about herbs and such." She crossed to the girl who offered the hand for inspection. The skin had already begun to blister. "Got a bucket of water? Colder the better."

The girl looked to the sink and clean up area. "Just pumped this morning, mum."

Tanyth led the girl to it and, taking her arm, thrust the hand into the bucket. "Leave it there. I've got some salve that should help in my pack." She nodded to Mabel and ran up to her room.

Rebecca looked up as she burst through the door. "What is it, mum?"

Tanyth shook her head and dove for her pack. "Nothin' serious. One of the kitchen girls got a burn. I got something in here that might help."

On the top of her belongings she found a new, leather-bound book. She lifted it out and rubbed a hand over the tooled leather binding. It had no title and no markings on either spine or cover. She opened and found a note inside the cover.

"When you get to where you're going, you'll need a book or two to write it all down in. This one will get you started. —F.C."

She also found one of the pens like Mabel used to sign in the guests and a new bottle of ink. She blinked away sudden tears and put the book on the bed to look at later. It took only a few moments for her to rummage about in the bottom of the pack and pull out one of the tins she kept there. The smell of it told her she had the right one. She rushed back to the kitchen to help Mabel tend to the injured girl.

CHAPTER 16
FAIR WARNING

By mid-morning Tanyth had enough of waiting around the inn. The conversation with Mabel and the injured girl bumped her out of her funk. "Enough of this sittin' around," she muttered and grabbed her hat, staff, and a jacket against the chilly spring breezes that found their way off the water and between the buildings.

"'Bout time," Rebecca said. She snatched up her own jacket and hat, following Tanyth down the stairs and out the door. "You're not goin' wanderin' alone, mum. Not while I'm here."

They set off for the market district, but soon found their path leading to the docks. Residents gave the strange old lady in trousers and a big hat a wide berth. The odd young man at her side glowered at everybody they passed. Tanyth snickered inwardly at some of the looks they got. A couple even made a warding sign against evil when they thought she wasn't looking. She ignored them and kept walking.

They were only halfway to the docks before her left knee started complaining. "Gettin' soft, old woman," she grumbled.

"What's that, mum?" Rebecca asked leaning over and casting a look of concern at Tanyth's face.

Tanyth shook her head. "Knee doesn't like the moisture. Keep goin'. It'll be fine after a bit."

A final turn brought her onto Front Street—the main road that bordered the harbor. A row of warehouses and chandleries lined the shoreward side while long, stone piers stretched

151

their narrow fingers out into the harbor on the other.

She stopped then and took in the view, drawing deep breaths of the cold, wet air into her lungs and blowing it out. The tang of salt and fish invigorated her and she wondered why Mabel served so little fish. Surely there were fisherman who could supply some decent catches.

After resting for a few moments, both hands on the head of her staff, they set off again, heading for the Harbor Master's office. As they strode along, the iron heel of her staff made rhythmic thumps on the wooden boardwalk, and she found herself admiring the view of crisp blue water, white gulls, and long piers. She probably should have been paying closer attention to her path and less to the sailing ships and seabirds.

As it was, she ran headlong into a portly man with broad shoulders and a hint of gray at the temples. The impact set him back, and would have knocked her off her feet, if it hadn't bumped her against the weathered boards of a warehouse.

"You should watch where you're going," the man snapped.

Tanyth recovered and both apology and jibe died on her lips as she saw the man's face. Even curled in a snarl, she recognized something about him. "Mapleton..." she murmured.

The man stopped dusting off his coat and pants, glanced at Rebecca, and peered at Tanyth, his eyes taking in the face under the wide hat and then her general shape fully registered. "What did you say?"

"Sorry. I shoulda been more careful to not be where you were walkin'."

"No," he shook off her apology. "You called me Mapleton." He scowled at her, taking in the lines on her face and the gray in her hair. "Do I know you?"

Tanyth shook her head. "No, sir, but I believe I know a relative of yours—William?"

The man stiffened. "You know William Mapleton?"

She nodded once. "Well, enough that I saw him in you just now."

"He's my younger brother." He squinted at her in the glare of the late morning sun. "And you are?"

"Tanyth Fairport. I spent the winter at your brother's village."

He seemed surprised. "Did you? And is he calling his little encampment a village now?"

She smiled. "No. He calls it Ravenwood now. So do the rest of the villagers."

"How's he doing, my little brother?"

She shrugged. "Amber keeps him in line. He's holding up under the strain."

"His kids? James and Matilda? They're well?"

"You mean Riley? He's goin' to be a handful when he gets older. He's already got all the kids in the village in line."

He tilted his head to one side, almost birdlike, to look at her. "You really do know William."

She laughed and nodded. "Indeed I do."

A thought seemed to slap into the man's head and he looked about, staring first at Rebecca and then around the quayside. "Is he here? Did he come to town with you?"

Tanyth shook her head. "No, sir. He's needed in Raven-wood. I rode in with the first load of clay for the season."

"Ah, Frank is here then? Frank Crane? You know him?"

She smiled. "Oh, yes, I'm quite familiar with Frank Crane. He left this morning to take the lorry wagon and supplies back."

"And left you behind?" The man seemed astonished.

"I'm heading north, Mr. Mapleton. Going back to Raven-wood wouldn't do me much good."

"North?" He turned and looked at the ships as if seeing them for the first time. "What? Sailing to North Haven?"

"Well, it'd be rather a dampish walk from here, now wouldn't it?"

He looked at her and, for the first time, smiled. "Yes, mum, I supposed it would." He held out a hand. "Stephen Mapleton, at your service, mum."

She shook the offered hand and noted that for all his foppish dress, his hand was strong and callused from labor. He was not the office-bound dandy she'd first taken him for. "Pleased to meet you, Mr. Mapleton. This is Rebecca. She's—"

"Mr. Mapleton," Rebecca broke in and shook the man's hand. "Nice to meet you."

"And you," he said eyeing the young woman's apparel with

curiosity. "And you, too, Mother Fairport. Please be more careful on the docks. It's a dangerous place here. You could fall off the pier and drown." His concern seemed genuine to Tanyth, if a bit condescending.

"Thank you, Mr. Mapleton. I'll watch my step."

He tipped his hat to her and started to walk on when he stopped and looked at her, then at the ships lined up at dock. "You're booking the first ship north, I take it, mum?"

"That's my plan."

He nodded, as much to himself as to her, before speaking. "A word of advice, mum?"

"Yes?"

"Pick a ship that's insured."

She frowned at the unexpected answer. "Insured?"

He nodded once, very sharply. "Insured." He looked around as if to see who might be watching or perhaps near enough to hear. "Just be sure." With that, he hurried off, leaving Tanyth and Rebecca standing on the boardwalk staring after him.

"How odd," Tanyth said.

Rebecca pursed her lips but kept her own counsel.

With a small shrug, Tanyth straightened her hat and set out again along the boardwalk, Rebecca keeping pace alongside. The harbormaster's office lay just ahead and she had a mind to stop in.

When they got there, a barrel-chested man with a heavy beard stood behind the counter. His eyebrows shot up when he saw her enter. Tanyth saw him settle a welcoming smile on his face like a mask and fold his hands on the counter, as if he'd been up to something that he wanted to pretend he wasn't doing.

"Good day, sir. How may I help you today?" he said while Rebecca was still closing the door.

Tanyth smirked and took off her hat, letting her hair fall free and stepped up to the counter. "You could call me Tanyth as a start, young man. We can see what happens after that."

She saw his face sag in surprise, saw him glance at Rebecca who also removed her hat, and then watched him puff himself up again. She sighed.

"I'm sorry, mum. Tanyth. Of course, mum. How can I help you today...Tanyth?"

"Is North Haven open yet?"

He blinked, clearly not expecting a direct question. "North Haven, mum?"

"Yes, the port that's to the north? Last I heard it was still closed because of ice, but should be clearing any day. Have you any news?"

He grumped about for a moment, stroking his beard and stretching his braces. "Well, certainly, mum. That is to say, no, mum. There's been no recent news. North Haven is still iced in. Prob'ly. When the Zypheria blows, we know when to send the ships north again, but no, mum. It hasn't started yet."

"Thank you." She started to put her hat back on but paused to ask, "Where is the other young man? Bright lad, tow-head, about eighteen or nineteen winters?"

"Parkins, mum? Why he's havin' a bit of lunch. He'll be back shortly."

"I see," she said. "Can you tell me which of the ships will be heading north when the time comes?"

"Oh, I couldn't do that, mum. That there's what we call confidential information." He puffed up his chest and smiled in a way that made Tanyth want to poke him with the iron end of her staff and let some of the air out.

"Indeed," she said and settled her hat on her head. She turned and scanned the chalkboards mounted on the wall. "Then all these markings here? They have nothing to do with the ships or their ports?"

"Um, well, mum. Those are just notes we use to try to keep track. 'Tis a busy port, you know. A lot of trade from here goes out to the eastern kingdoms and the island nations to the east. Lots of cargo in and out."

"I imagine that's true," Tanyth commented and noted the vessels on the board marked North Haven. Just as before four names were scrawled in chalk, three on pier two and one on pier three. "Tell me, young man, have you heard of a vessel named the *Zypheria's Call*?" She turned to the man and saw his eyes flicker toward the board and then back at her.

"*Zypheria's Call. Zypheria's Call.*" He fingered his beard and made a big show of trying to recall. "I believe that's a coastal packet, mum."

"So, she's not in port now then?"

"Oh, no, mum. Certainly not."

"Do you expect her soon?"

"Well, mum, she's a coastal packet and keeps her own schedule. Rather independent these ship captains. One never knows." He cleared his throat and glanced at the board again before looking back at Tanyth. "One never knows for sure, mum. Never for sure."

"I see," she said. "Tell me, young man, can you read? Write?"

He pulled his head back on his neck and peered down his nose at her. "Well, of course, mum. You can't hold this job without knowin' your letters and your numbers." He said it with a degree of pride.

"Well, it might interest you to know that I can both read and write as well."

His face took on a pasty look where it showed around the face moss. "Zat so, mum?"

"Quite well, in fact." She gave him a hard look for a few heartbeats. "You might want to keep that in mind the next time you have confidential information that you don't want just anybody to read off these large boards around the entry."

"Err. That is, mum. You have a good point."

"Are you the actual harbor master?" she asked.

He shook his head. "No, mum. He's my uncle." His voice lost some of its timbre and a great deal of its volume.

"And your name?"

"Wesley, mum. John Wesley." He lowered his head.

"Well, John Wesley, when Parkins gets back from lunch, you might be nice to the lad and ask him about the ships. He seems quite knowledgeable."

Wesley looked up at her. "Yes, mum. Excellent suggestion."

She smiled and, with a nod, followed Rebecca out of the office.

Outside she shook her head and sighed. "Why is it they

have to be such idiots?"

Rebecca giggled. "You handled him quite well, mum."

Tanyth just sighed and shrugged a shoulder. "Be better if they didn't need quite so much handlin'."

A seabird soared overhead and uttered a call like a rusty hinge shuttering open. It dropped a large white deposit on the boardwalk in front of her.

She snickered. "Exactly my point," she called to the bird then set off down Front Street in search of Pier Three, Berth J.

CHAPTER 17
A TALL SHIP

They walked along Front Street and noticed a large sign with a number at the foot of each pier. She lead Rebecca down pier three, walking by large letters painted on the bollards in a regular off-set pattern with A on one side and B across from it. Berth J was near the end closest to the harbor's mouth. A cold wind blew steadily along the length of the broad stonework and they soon walked with hats clutched in hands rather than risk losing them to wind and sea.

Tanyth spotted the ship by its position and the nameplate across the stern. She was able to read it from some distance because two berths behind it were empty. The *Zypheria's Call* looked poised to sail, her bow aimed almost due north by Tanyth's reckoning.

The ship appeared well maintained, her metal parts gleaming in the sun and the painted bits looking bright and solid. Tanyth didn't know much about ships, having sailed only twice before in her long trek, and never across open ocean. As she drew alongside, the ship itself seemed to have an odor—clean and pungent smelling, at once familiar and foreign. It took her several minutes of taking deep breaths to place it as tar and rope.

A reinforced plank stretched from the deck of the ship onto the pier itself. It seemed to Tanyth to be a rather steep climb up to the deck. A rope ran along either side like a kind of handrail and she eyed it dubiously as more problematic than proper. Perplexed as to what to do next, she stopped at the end of the plank and looked up toward the ship and then higher still to where the empty masts and rigging stretched into the cloudless blue sky. The sight thrilled her and she really couldn't explain why.

Footsteps coming along the pier behind them made her turn and look to see who approached. A man of medium years and darkly tanned skin nodded politely and smiled. He carried a leather-bound book under his arm and wore a tasteful wool suit against the chilly breeze. "Good morrow, mum. Miss."

"Good day, sir. Blessed be."

"And to you, mum." He stopped beside them and looked up, much as she had, admiring the lines and the rigging. "She's a beauty, isn't she?"

Tanyth nodded and allowed her gaze to follow his up and into the tall, gently swaying rigging once more. "She seems quite lovely, but I don't know much about 'em."

He glanced at her out of the side of his eyes for a moment. "I know a bit. Have you any questions?"

"Do you know this vessel? *Zypheria's Call*, I believe."

"I do, mum. She's a gaff-rigged schooner, a hundred and twenty feet from bow to stern and twenty-five feet at the beam. She ships fifty tonnes of cargo in her holds, draws only nine feet of water, and carries a crew of twelve." He rattled the information off without taking his eyes off the masts.

She turned to face him, lifting her hat to shade the bright sun from her eyes. "Seems rather more than a bit, sir."

He looked at her, glanced at Rebecca, and grinned a most charming grin. "Yes, mum. While I know a bit about sailing and ships, cargo and the like, I confess to know a bit more than average about this particular ship."

"Are you a member of her crew, then?"

"Yes, mum. First mate."

"What does the first mate do on such a ship, if you don't mind an old woman askin'?"

His grin never faded. "Whatever the captain says, mum, of course."

She barked a laugh at that and he winked at her like she might be thirty winters younger.

He let his jocularity fade but not his pleasant demeanor.

"I'm second in command, mum. Captain is first, of course, then me, then the second mate."

"Then who?"

"Then the crew, mum. Bosun heads them up and the seamen do the heavy lifting while we officers enjoy the fruits of exalted rank and station."

She caught the twinkle in his eye, in spite of the bright sun. "That duty includes teasing old women and pullin' their legs, too, does it?" she asked.

"Yes, mum. Yes, it does." He turned to her and gave a half bow. "Forgive me, mum, for enjoying myself so much with you. I'm Benjamin Groves, First Mate. May I know your name?" He offered a handshake.

"Tanyth Fairport, potential passenger," she said, accepting the hand and noting calluses that belied his claim of exalted rank. "This is my travelin' companion, Rebecca. You take passengers aboard *Zypheria's Call*, I trust?"

Her statement wiped the jest from his face and he frowned at her. "Well, yes, we do, mum. But we're bound for North Haven."

"Yeah, I know. I just came from the harbormaster's office."

Groves's eyebrows shot up. "And he sent you down here?"

She smiled a smile of her own and shook her head. "Not exactly, no. I'm rather a stubborn old boot, though, and quite capable of readin' a chalkboard."

"So you and your party need passage to North Haven..." Groves let his statement trail out rather than turning it into a question.

"Yeah. Somethin' like that."

"North Haven is still iced in, mum."

"Yeah, I've heard all about it. Everybody's just waitin' for the wind to shift?"

"The Zypheria, mum, yes."

"Yeah, Zypheria. When it does, then I'm assuming you and those other three boats—"

"Ships, mum. They're ships."

"Ships, then," she said with grin. "You'll have to pardon an old lady for not knowing the right lingo."

"Not at all, mum. Everybody has to learn sometime."

"So the way I figure it, you'll all be rearin' to take off out of here as soon as this Zypheria blows. You all want to be the first one there and get the best prices for whatever it is you're takin'." She eyed the man to see his reaction.

"More or less correct, mum."

She nodded. "And then you'll be able to get the best prices on a winter's worth of furs, wood and whatnot to bring back?"

His mouth twisted into a grudging smile. "For an old lady who doesn't know the lingo, you've got a pretty fair idea of what's going on, pardon my saying so, mum."

He cast a glance at Rebecca who merely grinned back at him.

"I'm old, Mr. Groves. Not stupid." Tanyth looked up into the rigging again. "Don't need to be a sailor to know which way the wind blows, eh?"

"Quite true, mum."

She turned back to him. "So the sooner you get out of here, the sooner you'll get back. The less waitin' around you have to do for passengers and such, the quicker you'll be gone?"

"Well, we don't carry many passengers, mum. We've none scheduled for this trip because we don't know when we'd need to leave." He stopped then and looked at her. "But I take it you'd like to be on this trip?"

"You know anything about the other three ships waitin'?"

He looked over to the next pier. "Those three in a row, right there, mum."

To Tanyth's eye they looked like they were all cut from the same mold, right down to the weathered paint on the masts.

"Would you let your mother sail on them?" she asked.

He coughed and Tanyth suspected it was to cover a laugh. "My mother, mum?"

"Yeah, Mr. Groves. You do have a mother? Most men do."

He started to chuckle. "Yes, mum, I surely do. She lives here in Kleesport."

"Well, would ya?"

He stopped laughing and looked at the ships across the narrow passage for a long moment before turning back to Tanyth. "No, mum. I wouldn't."

"Then, yes, Mr. Groves, we'd like to sail with you when you go north. How much will it cost and what do we need to do?"

He looked at her hard, looking for something in her face that she didn't understand. "Well, mum," he said at last. "I think you need to talk to the captain and work out those arrangements with him."

"And where might I find your captain, Mr. Groves?"

He turned and looked back down the pier to where a bow-legged man in a deep blue frock-coat ambled along in their direction. "Here he comes now."

The captain was perhaps twenty winters older than Groves with the same deep tan and laughing eyes. A neatly trimmed white beard graced his jawline. As he got closer, Tanyth noted other similarities and Groves caught her looking back and forth between them.

"Aye," the younger man nodded. "The captain sleeps with my mother whenever he's in port."

Rebecca seemed scandalized by the remark, but Tanyth grinned. "And why shouldn't he sleep with his own wife?"

Benjamin shook his head. "No good reason I can think of, mum."

They were still chuckling when the captain got to them.

"What have you been doing to my first mate to tickle his fancy so, mum? If I might be so bold as to ask?" His dancing eyes belied his gruff words.

"We were just comparin' ships, Captain. He seems to know quite a lot about them."

"And you found that humorous, the two of you?"

"Oh, indeed, Captain. I know so little he's able to amuse and inform me quite handily."

The captain turned to his son. "And you? Have you no comment on this matter, my fine first mate?"

"Mother Fairport is a woman of infinite kindness and possessed of rather a dry wit, Captain."

"Is she now?" He regarded her anew. "Dry anything is

good at sea and wit one of the rarest commodities. I salute you, madam."

"She'd also like to book passage to North Haven for her and her companion, Captain."

The quiet statement caught the captain's attention and he looked back and forth between the two of them, a speculative look in his eye. "Does she now?"

"Yes, Captain," Tanyth said. "She does."

A faint smile tickled the edges of his mouth and he eyed her up and down. "Sensible trousers. Sturdy staff." He peered into her face for a moment. "Strength." He nodded. "Very well, mum, I assume you don't mean to work passage?" He left the question hang in the air for a moment.

Young Mr. Groves leaned in. "He's just said he thinks you probably don't want to be a deck hand for the voyage."

She leaned toward him and answered with a question of her own. "Is that possible?"

The young man shrugged. "Yes, mum, but I wouldn't recommend it. It's usually reserved for those who have less wit and experience than you do, mum."

"Younger, you mean?"

"Yes, mum." He shrugged apologetically. "Unless you're used to the hard labor, it's rather a strain."

"I see. Thank you, sir."

"My pleasure, mum."

"Yes, Captain, you assume correctly," Tanyth said loudly as if the captain hadn't been observing their conversation the entire time.

"Capital," he exclaimed. "It's time we had a passenger or two to liven up this voyage."

"Wait," Rebecca said. All eyes turned to her. "Can anybody work passage?"

The captain looked from Tanyth to Rebecca and back for a moment before looking to his son who simply shrugged.

"You, miss?" Captain Groves asked, not unkindly.

"Yes, sir. I'm strong and I don't much like relyin' on Mother Fairport for everything."

"My dear, you know that's not a problem for me," Tanyth said, laying a hand on Rebecca's forearm.

Rebecca smiled but there was a firmness in her jaw. "Yes'm, but it's a problem for me. I didn't ask you to bring me along so's I could be a hanger-on or a lady's maid."

"Well, no, but..." Tanyth saw the look in Rebecca's eye and let her voice trail off.

"Thank you, mum," Rebecca whispered before turning to the captain once more. "Yes, Captain, I'd very much like to work passage."

The Captain frowned and eyed her up and down. "You strong?" he asked.

"I can draw a bow," she said.

That sparked the captain's interest and he smiled. "You any good?"

"I gen'rally hit what I aim at."

He peered at her. "Can you run?"

"If I need to, Captain."

The Captain tilted his head back and looked up at the rigging. "See that set of ratlines?" Pointing at the ship's mainmast.

"That net thing?"

"Aye, that 'net thing' is called the ratlines. It's how the crew gets up to the tops. Think you can climb that?"

Rebecca tilted her head back and looked up. Tanyth saw her swallow once. "Yes, sir."

The captain pulled a heavy, gold pocketwatch out of his vest and flipped the cover open with a flick of his thumb. "All right, missy. Prove it. Up to the top and back again. Fast as you can."

Rebecca looked at him, her eyes wide. "Now?"

"Now, girl! Tide's running and you should be, too. Go!"

Rebecca went. She bounced across the plank and up onto the ship startling a sailor who lounged out of sight beside the rail. She threw herself up and grabbed the net, pulling herself to the outside of the lattice with only one look down. She started climbing the ratlines like a ladder.

The startled sailor spoke to her and made a grasping motion with his hands. "Like that!" he called.

She looked at her hand placement on the horizontal bars and realized that the sailor wanted her to grasp the verticals.

She shifted her hands and looked down.

The sailor grinned and waved his arms. "Now, go! Go!"

She lost her footing a couple of times and Tanyth felt her heart skip a beat each time, but she got to the top and looked down at the captain who gave a broad nod and waved her to come back. She paused then, looking down at the deck and stood there for a long moment.

Then she lifted her head and looked around the harbor. Tanyth saw the smile break across the young woman's face and she clambered down the ratlines even faster than she'd gone up. At the bottom she swung off, stepped down from the rail to the sailor's cheerful laughter and raced back over the plank to skid to a stop where she had started. Her lungs pumped and she leaned over to rest her hands on her knees but the grin pasted on her face tickled Tanyth down to her toes.

"Well, Captain?" Rebecca panted. "Fast enough?"

The captain examined his watch, latched the cover down, and put it away before speaking. "To be honest, my girl, I just wanted to see what you're made of."

"You make all your passengers do that?" Tanyth asked.

The captain nodded. "Aye. If they wanna work passage and we don't know 'em from bein' around the docks or the like, we send 'em up the ratlines. If they go, we'll book them."

"If they go?" Tanyth asked.

Young Mr. Groves grinned. "Yes, mum. Some won't go. Or they'll get up on the rail and freeze."

"Then what?" she asked.

"Then we charge 'em a reduced fare and let 'em help on deck once in a while."

"What about me then, sir?" Rebecca asked, straightening up and flexing her hands. Tanyth could see they were chafed and red from the lines.

The captain exchanged looks with his first mate before turning to Rebecca. "Tell me, missy. How was the view up there?" He jerked his chin up at the masthead.

Rebecca turned her head to consider the top and her smile grew. "Glorious, sir."

"You weren't scared?" he asked.

She looked at him and shrugged but the smile didn't dim. "When I got up there and looked down at the deck? Yeah. That looked a lot further down than it felt like lookin' up. That was a bit scary, Captain."

"But...?" he said.

"But when I looked around—across the harbor? Out into the bay? Up at the sky? With the wind blowin' and everythin'?" She took a deep breath and blew it out before giving a small shrug. "I wasn't sure I wanted to come down, sir."

The captain's eyes crinkled up as he smiled. "Well, Mr. Groves? Will you accept this one for working passage?"

The younger Groves nodded. "Yes, Captain. She'll do."

"Very well, missy. You're a working member of the crew." He eyed Tanyth and the ship and then looked back at Rebecca. "You'll share a compartment, I s'pect?"

Tanyth and Rebecca nodded.

"And the fare, Captain?" Tanyth asked.

"Five crowns plus an extra crown for food. And you must be ready to board on an hour's notice, day or night."

Young Groves coughed into his fist.

His father shot him a sour look.

Tanyth bit back her laugh and countered, "Two crowns and we move aboard this afternoon."

The Captain blinked. "You'd move aboard now, mum?"

She shrugged. "As I understand it the Zypheria...?" She looked to Mr. Groves.

"Yes, mum, the Zypheria."

"This Zypheria could start blowin' at any moment. Correct?"

The captain nodded. "Yes, mum, that's true enough, but it might not happen for several days."

"If we're already aboard, then you'll have no need to fetch us and wait for me to drag my poor, tired carcass all the way across the city, correct?"

The captain's eyes danced again. "Your poor, tired carcass, mum?"

She gave a small shrug.

"Does that work on anybody older than twelve winters?"

"Hasn't yet, Captain, but I keep tryin'."

He looked down at his boots and then up the rigging. "It could be a long wait, mum, and the quarters are not exactly luxurious," he said. "Are you sure that's what you want?"

Tanyth looked at the ship and then turned to look out to the clean blue line between sky and sea. When she turned back, she could feel her smile all the way to her toes. "Yes, Captain. I believe it is. And it'll give Rebecca here a chance to learn her new duties."

"Three crowns," the captain said.

Tanyth started to speak and young Mr. Groves cleared his throat loudly.

"Who's side are you on, boy?" the captain muttered.

"Me, sir? I'm just the first mate, Captain."

"Uh huh," he said. "Save it for your mother."

"You think she'll start believing me, sir?"

"I doubt it, lad, but sometimes fish have wings." He cast an arched eye toward Tanyth.

"Meals, Captain?"

The captain looked to the first mate who made a big show of looking out to sea. "Included," he muttered.

"In that case, I accept," she said. "Four crowns and not a copper more."

Both men looked at her with identical expressions of consternation.

Young Mr. Groves recovered first and leaned in again. "Mum, the last offer was three crowns, not four."

"Yes, I know, dear boy. I'm old, not deaf. At least not yet." She paused long enough for him to look a bit chagrined. "I also am smart enough to know that you'd really rather not have to cart us all the way out to North Haven, and that havin' to feed a pair of extra mouths may not exactly be easy if you can't send to the butcher's for an extra chicken. Am I right?"

The young man nodded and the captain looked at her with an oddly calculating look.

"It's worth a crown to have you take very good care of us until we get ashore."

"Oh, we'd do that anyway, mum, even at our normal—"

His father coughed loudly.

When they looked in his direction, he put on an innocent face. "What? It worked for him. Please, don't let me interrupt. Four gold crowns, you say?"

Tanyth smiled and discovered that she was already quite fond of the old man and his son. "I realize it's unusual and I appreciate any extra effort ya might undertake on our behalf since I really don't know what we're getting into."

That seemed to strike a chord in the younger Mr. Groves but before he could ask, the Captain spoke. "Most generous, mum, and thank you. We will take excellent care of you both."

"Do you have a preferred method of payment?" she asked.

"The usual payment is half on boarding and half on arrival," the Captain said.

"Would a Royal Bank draft on boarding suffice?"

"You want to pay it all, mum?" the younger Mr. Groves asked.

"Yes. It's more convenient and I don't have to carry around those heavy coins."

"Heavy coins, mum?" the elder Mr. Groves asked.

"Yes, the gold crowns. They're rather a burden."

The two men shared a quick glance before the captain thought to ask, "Mum? Have you ever seen a gold crown?"

She shook her head. "No. I can't say that have. Why?"

The Captain fished around his trouser pocket and pulled out his hand. He held it palm up. In it were three coppers, four silvers, and two gold coins only half again bigger than the silvers.

She looked at the coins and then into the faces of the two men. "Crowns?"

They both nodded.

Tanyth started to laugh. "Yes, I can see I need to have a talk with my banker."

"You do have the fare, mum, don't you?" Mr. Groves asked.

Tanyth nodded. "Yes, Mr. Groves. Assuming Mr. Pendleton at the bank will let a poor frail woman like me walk out with it."

The captain cocked his head. "George Pendleton? The Royal Bank?"

"The same, Captain."

"If he gives you any trouble, just tell him to talk to Captain Saul Groves." He paused and looked at her afresh. "How did you get crowns in the Royal Bank without ever seeing one before?"

She smiled and shook her head. "They were a gift. When I retained Mr. Pendleton, I was told that twenty gold crowns was too much of a burden for an unattended woman to be carrying around."

"Yes," the captain said. "Yes, I can see where that might be the case." He shot a look at her. "It was a wise choice, mum."

"I can see that, Captain, just not in the way that I expected."

The captain clapped his son on the shoulder with one weather-roughened hand. "See that, lad? There's always something new to learn."

"Yes, Captain."

The captain turned back to Tanyth. "Do you need any help fetching your luggage, mum? I can send a couple of the crew with you."

She shook her head. "It's a lovely day and I can use the exercise. I'll stop in for a visit with Mr. Pendleton and we'll be back in a couple of hours."

The younger Mr. Groves smiled and nodded. "We'll be ready for you, mum."

"Thank you, both." She gave them a nod and started back down the pier, Rebecca strolling along beside. She had a very good feeling about the next stage of her journey. The good feeling reminded her of something. She turned back to the two men. "Oh, one more question, Captain?"

"Yes, mum?"

"Is this voyage insured?"

Captain Groves glowered at the question and Tanyth almost took a step back in surprise.

Young Mr. Groves laid a hand on his father's arm and answered for him. "No, mum," he said. "Is that a problem?"

She considered the matter for a moment, then nodded her head at the three ships lined up on the next pier. "Are they?"

The two men looked and Tanyth thought the captain might spit on the dock but the younger Groves said, "Probably, mum."

Tanyth shook her head. "No, Mr. Groves, I don't believe it is."

"Thank you, mum," he said. "May I ask...?"

"What? Why I wanted to know?"

Mr. Groves nodded once.

"I hear odd things, Mr. Groves. Two brothers and an inn keeper all had words about ships and insurance. I thought perhaps a direct question would tell me somethin' new."

Captain Groves' face lost most of the angry redness and he cocked his head to the side. "And did it, mum?"

Tanyth smiled at him. "Yes, Captain Groves. I think it did. Thank you." With a wave she turned, and they headed off to tie up loose ends.

CHAPTER 18
TAKING STOCK

The sun passed mid-afternoon by the time Tanyth and Rebecca returned to the *Zypheria's Call*. The walk back to the ship with her pack on her back warmed Tanyth and left her a bit breathless. As she approached the ship, she noted that the vessel rode considerably lower. The long plank from dock to deck had a very slight downward angle and she eyed it with interest.

"There you are, mum," a cheery voice called from the ship.

She held up a hand against the sun's glare and saw the younger Mr. Groves walking along the deck toward the plank. "Took a bit longer than I expected, but I trust we're still in time, Mr. Groves?"

"We're all ready for you, mum. Come aboard."

She eyed the plank once more and realized that the roped railing was too low for her to hold onto and still stand upright. Tanyth stepped back and let Rebecca march across, alighting on the far side with the help of Mr. Groves' offered hand on the last step.

Tanyth watched the two young people share a smile, Rebecca suddenly shy and Groves smiling at the toes of his boots while holding the hand a heartbeat longer than Tanyth thought quite necessary.

Rebecca turned and smiled too brightly. "It's easy, mum. It's got a bit of bounce in the middle, but just keep goin' and you'll be fine."

She scowled at the board and shifted the grip on her staff, trying to picture the plank as just another narrow piece of

173

trail.

"You'll be fine, mum," Mr. Groves called by way of encouragement. "It has a bit of spring in it, but nobody's fallen off it yet."

"How encouragin'," she muttered.

"What's that, mum?" he asked.

"Thank you, Mr. Groves," she called.

Rebecca gave a small laugh.

Tanyth fixed her eyes on the far end and began a careful walk across the plank. After a couple of steps she got the feel of it and was able to finish the passage without further difficulty. She got to the other end and took Mr. Groves' hand for the last step onto the smooth planks of the deck. The scent of tar and rope was more pronounced there under the rigging, the waves lapping against the hull sounding louder.

"And here we are, mum. Safe and sound." His bright smile seemed to gleam against the dark-tanned cheeks. He cast his eyes back along the pier. "But where is your luggage, mum?"

She turned slightly and nodded over her shoulder. "This is all I got."

He turned to look at Rebecca who pivoted to show the rucksack on her own back.

His brow furrowed in a frown as he eyed the packs and then looked at her again. "That's it, mum?"

"It's all I need."

"Pardon my askin', mum, but what all do you have in there?"

"Clothes, a bit of tea, some oatmeal, cooking pots. Bedroll."

He bit his lower lip as if uncertain about his next course of action.

"Spit it out, Mr. Groves. I'm relyin' on you to keep us out of trouble."

He rubbed a hand over his mouth and shot her a sideways look before asking, "Do you have any warmer clothing in there, mum?"

"Warmer clothing?" She considered the question for what he hadn't asked. "How warm?"

"Mum, at sea? The wind cuts."

"I thought this Zypheria that everybody's waitin' on was

a warm wind."

He grinned. "It is, mum, but only by comparison. It's wet and miserable on a good day in high summer. We're heading north. We'll be sailing around chunks of ice floating in the water. There'll be days when it'll feel colder than mid-winter here."

"What do I need?" she asked.

He looked them both up and down. "Heavy wool coat, some heavier trousers. Do you have any sweaters or knit pullovers in there? Either of you?"

"Got some of my winter things still. Haven't switched to summer weight yet." She considered his words. "I've a heavier canvas coat, but I'm suspectin' that's not what you're talkin' about."

Rebecca shook her head. "I'm wearin' the warmest I got."

"Come this way, ladies. Let me show you to your quarters and perhaps you can show me what you have for warm clothes?"

He led them toward the back of the ship and through a narrow door. "Mind your step and your head here, mum. Three steps down and you're clear."

She ducked her head and used her staff to feel her way down the steps in the dimness after being in the open deck.

At the foot of the steps, Rebecca paused and looked back. "It's just like one of William's huts, mum."

Tanyth nodded. "Watch your head and step down. It's a bit easier here. S'pose he modeled 'em after this?"

Rebecca turned, scrubbing her pack against the wall of the narrow passage. "Hard tellin', mum."

Mr. Groves waited for them a few steps down the passage. He held open a door and Tanyth entered the small room, Rebecca on her heels. A pair of built-in bunks stood level with her waist and she saw some cupboard doors with smooth handles under each. Several pegs decorated a very short wall and a small circular window, no bigger across that the splayed fingers of one hand, brought in light from the outside.

She stood her staff in a corner, hung her hat on a peg and unslung her pack, bumping it on the bed and then on the wall as she struggled to get the straps off her shoulders. Rebecca followed suit and for a moment they struggled to stay clear of each other until Rebecca managed to heave her pack up onto a bunk.

"Sorry about that, mum." Groves leaned in the doorway, standing well back to give them as much room as possible. "Quarters aboard are a bit tight," he said, apology written on his face.

"I'll step out on deck if I need room to change my mind." She grinned at him. "I'm just glad we don't have more baggage than this." She dropped her own pack on the empty bunk and realized that there was a lip along the edge. What had looked like a very flat ticking was actually well-padded. She pulled the top of the pack open and pulled out her heaviest coat. Holding it up for his inspection, she realized that her warmest cover wasn't as substantial as his woolen frock-coat.

He worried his lower lip between his front teeth as he considered the garment.

"This won't do, will it, Mr. Groves?"

He swallowed once before looking at her with a small shake of his head. "You're probably going to want a lot more than that, mum. Even just wanderin' around North Haven will be a bit nippy in that. At sea?" He shook his head.

"Can I buy one?" she asked. "And how much would something like that cost?"

"Oh, certainly, mum. There's a chandler just off the head of the pier. He'd sell you a nice solid watch coat. You could even get some wool lined canvas trousers for no more than a dozen silvers."

"And you'd recommend I get some of these trousers and pants?"

"'Fraid so, mum. Otherwise you're going to be a tad chilly before we get there and I don't know that we'd be able to thaw you out on arrival."

She chuckled and rummaged deeper in her pack, pulling out her pullovers and knits. "What d'ya think of these, then, Mr. Groves? I don't much like bein' cold. The All-Mother knows I've spent enough of my life chilled to the bone without addin' any more days to the tally."

He considered each garment, sometimes weighing the fabric in his hand. After a few minutes they'd sorted her clothing into "probably warm enough" and "you'll want warmer" piles.

"Those lighter ones will be good for wearing under stuff, mum," Groves suggested, "but you'll want some good dense wool for bulk." He took a moment to look at Rebecca's much smaller pile of clothing and shook his head. "You'll need to find something warmer, miss. You'll need to be on deck and working. Sometimes you'll be active enough to keep warm, but you'll want some jerseys. Perhaps some rain gear."

"Anything else you'd recommend, Mr. Groves," Tanyth asked, reclaiming Groves' attention from his consideration of Rebecca's assets.

He rubbed his fingers across his mouth, frowning at the piles as he thought. "Only other thing for you, mum, might be some oil-cloth for heavy weather, but when we run into squalls, you're not going to want to be out on deck at all." He glanced at her. "In fact, we'd ask you both to stay in here if the weather gets bad. It's just a lot safer."

"Even as crew?" Rebecca asked.

Groves nodded. "There'll be plenty enough to do before it gets ugly, but we don't want anybody on deck that doesn't need to be there when it gets bad."

"And is there anything else we should get while we're ashore that would make this passage more enjoyable?"

He rolled a shoulder in a shrug. "Any special treats you might want on the voyage, mum. Some like to travel with their own ale, a bit of something stronger maybe. Food aboard is good, but it's plain and simple fare. Lots of stews, breads..."

"Oatmeal?"

"Yes, mum. Oatmeal with apples and dried fruits most days. Salted fish and pork. Lots of beans."

"Beans, you say? Baked beans?"

"Yes, mum. At least few times a week. Cook makes a mean pot of beans and the biscuits to go with 'em."

She beamed. "I'm likin' the sound of this voyage already, Mr. Groves. Now, where did you say this clothing merchant—"

"Chandlery, mum."

"Yes, this chandlery? Is it near?"

He jerked his head toward the deck. "I can point it out from the deck, mum. Easy to find. You walked by it twice already."

She left her hat on its peg but took staff in hand and let Rebecca lead the way out of the stateroom, following the lithe young woman back up onto the deck. She paused at the opening, her hand resting lightly on the coaming to steady herself, looking out at the wood and rope. Odd doors and strange metal fittings made her smile at the novelty. She looked up at the tall masts with their heavy booms and the deep blue sky beyond. She nodded to herself before following Rebecca and Groves across the gangway and back onto the dock. She didn't even think about the narrow plank until she'd already crossed it in his wake.

He grinned at her. "We'll make a sailor of you yet, mum."

She snickered and looked down the pier. "Where's this place?"

He pointed to the harbormaster's office and then counted three buildings to the left. "That's it, mum. Harris will fit you up right. Just tell him you're going to North Haven and Ben Groves says you need some warmer clothes."

"Seems simple enough."

"It's nothing complicated, mum. Warm is warm and dry is dry. There's precious little that's warm or dry about sailing these waters. Harris knows."

"For me?" Rebecca asked.

"Same. Some jerseys and maybe a slicker."

"I thought you said she wouldn't be out in rough weather," Tanyth said.

Groves grinned. "Well, there's rough weather and then there's rain, mum. They don't always go together."

Rebecca grinned and Tanyth had the uneasy feeling that the younger woman was actually looking forward to rough weather at sea. With a quiet chuckle to herself, she set off down the pier, Rebecca trailing along in her wake.

Chapter 19
At The Chandlery

Tanyth didn't know quite what to expect from a chandlery. The door opened with the requisite jangly bell on a spring, but after that her shopping experience took a left turn. Inside the door she found, not a shop, but a warehouse. The ceiling disappeared into the shadows above, with only the occasional beam and cross-brace visible in the gloom. Huge spools of rope stood around like spindles in some giant's sewing box. Folded bolts of canvas, piles of chain, and barrels of all shapes and sizes formed a higglety-pigglety maze that she hesitated to enter. The place smelled of tar and rope, of wood and lamp oil.

A man's voice boomed from deep in the maze somewhere. "Just a minute!"

She heard footsteps echoing in the rafters and a barrel of a man with shoulders like hams and hands like a fistful of sausages loomed out of the dark. "What'cha need?" He squinted against the light coming in from clouded windows at their backs.

"Are ya Harris?" Tanyth asked and watched his face crinkle in consternation.

"And who else might I be in Harris's Chandlery?" He turned his head and squinted against the light. He took a few more steps forward until he was close enough to get a good look at her. "Mum? Miss?"

"Excellent. Pleased to meet you, Mr. Harris." Tanyth held out her hand.

His huge paw engulfed hers and he gave it a firm shake

179

but didn't pull her arm from the socket as she first feared. "You be in the right place, mum?"

"I believe so, Mr. Harris. Mr. Benjamin Groves recommended you."

He face lit up at the name. "Ah, lil Benny, sure. I know the lad. He's first mate now on his da's vessel." The way he said it, Tanyth thought he couldn't have been prouder if the young man in question were his own son.

"Indeed he is, and the *Zypheria's Call* is heading to North Haven soon."

"Oh, aye. She and every other dog's body with two feet of mast and a good bilge pump. It'll be a race for certain."

"We've taken passage, and Mr. Groves suggested we need some warmer clothes and sent us here to be outfitted."

Harris blinked several times and worked his mouth open and shut once before actually speaking. "Well, mum, this here's a ship chandlery. We don't stock much in the line of ladies' fittin's if you know what I mean." He frowned at each of them in turn and shook his head. "No, mum. Nothin' fine enough for you ladies here."

"I'm not lookin' for frills, Mr. Harris. Benjamin seemed to think I needed a watch coat and some wool lined canvas trousers."

Harris stood straight, pulling his head back, and eyeing her up and down. "He did, did he?" He scratched his chin in thought and squinted his eyes at them again, stepping a half step away to get their measure. "Well, you seem to be comfortable enough in trousers, mum."

"I am that, Mr. Harris. I do a lot of walking. Trousers work better for me."

"Not real lady-like, mum." He seemed to realize that he'd spoken without thinking and hurried on to say, "No offense, mum." The look of horror on his face might have been comical in another circumstance.

"None taken, Mr. Harris, and you're right. Isn't lady-like, but it's practical." She smiled. "I'm kinda known for bein' a practical old boot."

Half his mouth curled up in a grin. "I see, mum. I do see, indeed."

"So can you help us? I hate bein' cold, and Mr. Groves assures me that the voyage north will be nothin' if not cold."

"Oh, aye." Mr. Harris nodded several times. "Yeah, it'll be cold and windy and wet, like as not."

"So I'm led to believe, Mr. Harris." She let him stew in his own cogitation for a time.

He looked them up and down again, rubbing his chin in what looked like a well-practiced gesture. Finally, he pressed his lips together in a line and scowled fiercely. "Yeah. You really ain't much smaller than average. I should have a watch coat that'll fit ya." He headed into the dimness and raised a hand in summons. "Come on back. Let's see what I got here to keep a body warm."

He led her through the maze of crates and barrels. She saw that skylights high in the roof of the building let in a substantial amount of light. Even from the floor she saw the seagull streaks and grime on the outside that blocked a good portion of the sunlight. The place only looked dim because she'd come in from the full light of day. Her eyes adapted rather quickly to the lowered lighting.

"Here we go, mum. Miss." Harris held a door open and she found herself in a dim side room filled with piles of large boxes. Harris fumbled with a match and got a lantern going, which he hung on a bracket on the wall. "Slip off your coat, mum, and let's see if I got sommat that'll suit ya."

She did as he asked. He took it from her, hanging it carefully on a peg in the wall as if it were some fine cloak rather than a somewhat ratty wind breaker.

He measured her with his eyes again, then pursed his lips and began rummaging in an open crate. He emerged holding a coat so deep blue, it appeared almost black in the lantern light. He held it aloft in one meaty paw, turning it so the light caught black wooden toggles down the front. "Hmm, yeah. Maybe," he said. He turned to Tanyth, handing her the coat. "Here, mum, try this 'un on."

Tanyth was surprised by the weight and nearly dropped it before she got a good grip.

Harris barked a short laugh. "Quite a lot heavier than that wind breaker you're wearing, eh, mum?"

"Indeed it is." She swung the coat around her body and thrust her arms into the sleeves. The heavy coat wrapped itself around her like a warm hug. Her fingertips just showed at the ends of the sleeves, and when she held the front closed, there seemed to be too much fabric.

"Just a second, mum," Harris said and showed her the trick to crossing the fabric over itself. "See? It wraps around here in the front a bit," he said. "Keeps the wind from blowing in between the buttons."

She pushed the sleeves up to free her hands and soon found the knack of using the wooden toggles as buttons.

Harris stepped back and looked at her. "That's a tad largish on ya, mum." He shook his head and scowled. "Might fit your...um...helper." He looked at Rebecca who merely shrugged and helped Tanyth slip out of the heavy coat, wrapping it around her own shoulders and sinking into its folds.

Harris eyed the toggles critically and nodded once. "Yup. Fits there. I think there's a size smaller here somewhere." He all but disappeared head first back into the crate of coats, one foot off the floor and waving around in the air.

"Ah, hah!" The woolens muffled his cry but he struggled up out of the box, his prize clutched in his hand. He held it out to her. "Here, mum. Try that one!" His face, reddened from the exertion, beamed in jubilation. "I knew there was an extra small in there somewhere."

She took the second. It felt almost as heavy as the first, but she was prepared for the heft and slipped it on without difficulty. The sleeves fell below her wrists but above the base of her thumbs. She had no trouble finding the buttons or getting the front of the coat closed. She felt as if she cuddled in a big, blue blanket.

Harris smiled and nodded, tugging the sleeve and straightening the collar. "That looks right smart, mum. Right smart." He stopped fussing at the coat and looked at her askance. "How's it feel, mum?"

"Delightful," she said with feeling. "This will do nicely."

Harris turned to Rebecca. "And you, Miss? 'At suit ya?" He gave her coat the same tug and critical inspection he'd given Tanyth.

She held her arms out from her sides a bit and looked down at the coat. "It's quite warm and seems to fit fine."

Harris looked closely at her face. "You look familiar. What'd you say your name were?"

"Rebecca," she said, offering a hand.

Harris took the hand and shook it, not looking away from her. "You remind me of somebody. You got a family name?"

"Marong," Rebecca said, her voice low.

Astonishment swept across Harris' face and he tugged on the young woman's hand, using it as a lever to turn her left and right. "I'll be..." he said. "You're Richard's daughter? His youngest?"

She pulled her hand away and brushed it down the front of her coat with a small shrug. "Please don't say anything to him," she said.

Harris beamed and nodded. "'Course not," he said. "Course not." He cocked his head this way and that. "I'll be hung for a horse thief," he said, "but you're the spittin' image of your mother. You know that, don't cha?"

Rebecca blinked, her eyes wide. "You knew my mother?"

Harris grinned and nodded several times, still peering at Rebecca's face as if it were some precious painting he wanted to memorize. "Oh, aye. Victoria. A wonderful woman. Too good for your father, I always said." He seemed to come to himself with that comment and gave himself a shake. "Ah, that is..." He looked down and pulled a large blue bandana out of his pocket, wiping his face with it and blowing his nose before continuing. "Yup. Spittin' image."

He glanced at Tanyth with something like longing in his eyes. "You ever meet her mother?"

Tanyth shook her head.

"Pity. Lovely woman." He glanced down again and blew out a sigh. "Too many tides come and gone now," he muttered. "Too many tides."

He stood like that for a moment, but before Tanyth could speak, he started rummaging in a crate across the room, mutterin', "Trousers, trousers." He soon came up with two pairs of dark blue pants that matched the coat. "Here we go, mum. I'll just step outside and give you ladies a bit of private. You try them on and lemme know when it's safe ta come back, yeah?"

She slipped the jacket off and laid it on top of an unopened box. "That sounds quite proper, Mr. Harris," she said.

He slipped out, closing the door behind him with a bang.

It took on a couple of minutes for them to discover which pair of pants fit whom. The smaller pair was too small for Tanyth but the larger pair slipped over her hips with a bit of room to spare. The smaller pair fit the slim-hipped Rebecca without a problem.

"We'll need belts to hold them up," she muttered, "but they'll do." She pulled the trousers off and laid them on top of the coat, before slipping her own tinker's pants back on. "All clear, Mr. Harris," when they'd made themselves presentable once more.

He bustled in and looked back and forth between them. "Fit, did they?"

"Yes, Mr. Harris. Quite well. What's next?"

He pursed his lips and looked her up and down a couple of times, his eyebrows raising and lowering a couple of times. "You're not fishin' so you don't need boots..." He eyed her short, gray hair. "You got a hat?"

"Nothin' suitable for a windy day, I'm afraid."

"Ah, ha!" He dug into a box and pulled out what looked like a pair of knit sacks. He gave one to each woman. "Try 'em on."

The bag turned out to be a hat that pulled down over her forehead and around her ears with a lot of material left to spare.

"Fold up the edge, mum. Make a bit of a roll of it." He pulled out another hat and showed her, pulling the hat on his own head.

She did and found that the hat fit snug around her ears, gripping her head without binding. Rebecca looked snug in hers. Tanyth looked at Harris and he beamed in response.

"Just so, mum. Just so." He looked back and forth between them. "Anything else you ladies need?"

Rebecca said, "I need some warm sweaters. Perhaps a sailor's jersey? And a slicker."

Harris' mouth twisted in a grin on the side of his face. "Got just the thing, just the thing. He crossed to the back corner of the room and lifted the lid on a smallish crate. He pulled out a fistful of jerseys, and fumbled through the pile until he found the one he wanted. He glanced at Tanyth. "How 'bout you, mum? Finest wool. Softer than silk." He held the fabric out for her to feel.

She brushed a hand across it and was surprised by the smooth texture of it. "What kind of sheep gives that kind of wool, Mr. Harris?" she asked, almost unable to pull her hand back from the soft warmth of it.

He grinned, showing a gap in his teeth that made him look more rakish than he had before. "Not sheep, mum. Goats. Special kinda goat gives this really fine wool."

"I'll take two," Tanyth said. "And two for her."

He nodded and started shuffling through the pile, holding up the turtle-necked jerseys against each of them until he was satisfied with the sizes, muttering to himself the whole time. He soon had four picked out and stacked up with the rest of the clothing.

"And a slicker, ye say?" His head tilted back and forth. "You plannin' on bein' on deck in the rain?"

Rebecca grinned. "I'm workin' passage, Mr. Harris. Mr. Groves said it might get wet."

His eyebrows shot up in surprise. "You are? Working the deck on the *Call*, ya say?" He looked back and forth between Tanyth and Rebecca.

"Yes, sir. I am." Rebecca's voice carried a ring of steel in it.

Harris's smile, when it came, lit up the small room. "An' jes' like your mother, too, so why should I be surprised..." He slapped a thigh for punctuation and started pushing crates around. "I got a shipment of ponchos in the other day. Be just the thing, I'm thinkin'. Now if I can just remember where they are."

He struggled and fussed and furrowed his brow, examining the floor as if the answer might be in the grit between the boards.

"Ah! Of course." He banged out through the door and returned almost immediately, pushing a crate across the scarred floorboards with a dreadful grinding. "Forgot to bring it in," he muttered, a little breathless from his exertion.

He grabbed a pry-bar from a nail in the wall and soon had the cover off and pulled out a drab green bundle of fabric that smelled of linseed oil and sheep's wool. He grabbed one corner and shook it out revealing a kind of tent. He held it out to Rebecca. "Put that on."

She took it and held it up, turning it this way and that. "I'd be happy to, Mr. Harris, but how?"

He guffawed. "Pull over. Stick yer head through the hole."

With that bit of instruction the purpose of the rectangular garment became clear. Rebecca opened the wide bottom and pulled it over her head, sliding her arms into roomy sleeves. A hood of the same fabric covered her head and neck, leaving only her face exposed in the front.

"This will keep me dry?" she asked holding her arms away from her body and looking down at herself. She wrinkled her nose.

"Well, dry is a relative term at sea, miss," Harris said with an apologetic shrug. "Drier than without but if it rains enough, it'll soak through. The linseed oil in the outer cover will shed water a bit and the lanolin on the wool inside will help more."

"So sailors wear these?" Rebecca asked.

Harris rubbed the palm of his hand across his lips. "Well, mostly no, Miss. Truth told, they can't be bothered with 'em. They're good in a little rain, but they get heavy fast and then when you're wet through...well, you're wet."

Tanyth frowned a bit at the logic. "So, what do they do?"

Harris grinned. "Well, mum, they get wet. Out there, wet's pretty common. The trick is to stay warm."

"What would you give to a new deckhand, Mr. Harris?" she asked.

"A pile of cotton undershirts and a tin of liniment," he said without a beat.

The two women shared a glance and a frown.

"Can you explain that, Mr. Harris?" Rebecca said.

"Wear a couple of the cotton undershirts. Toss on one of

them goat wool jerseys over it all and add a windbreaker like your watchcoat. They're actually good at holding water off you for a while. Light rain, you pro'ly won' notice. When it gets really damp, you'll get wet through but the cotton will hold the water close to your skin."

"How's that help?" Tanyth asked.

"Your body heat will warm it up. You'll be wet, but as long as it stays next to your body, it'll be warm enough. Just keep workin' and get out of the wet clothes as soon as ya can."

"And the liniment?"

"Rope and salt water will dry your hands out somethin' dreadful. Liniment will help keep them from crackin' and bleedin'."

"Bleedin'?" Rebecca said, her voice rising to almost a squeek.

"Oh, aye. Liniment will help keep your skin from dryin' out. That'll keep it from getting' chapped and cracked. Salt water in the cracks hurts like blazes. Liniment. Yes'm. Benjamin didn't mention it?"

They shook their heads.

Harris scoffed. "Pro'ly don't use it himself so didn't think. Once your hands get used to the ropes and canvas and such, it's nothin' to be concerned about, but a new deck ape? Yeah. That's what I'd give 'em. Pile o' cotton undershirts and a tin o' liniment."

Rebecca nodded her head. "If you'd find some that I could wear, Mr. Harris? And you stock this liniment?"

He grinned. "O'course, miss. Be just a minute."

He rummaged and fumbled about, pulling out shirts from one crate and pulling a squat, square can of liniment out of a cubby. He stacked the lot on top of Rebecca's pile then turned to Tanyth. "And for you, mum?"

She shook her head. "I'll go with what I got. She's workin' passage. I'm just along for the ride."

He chuckled and nodded. "Aw-right, then. Is there anythin' else?"

"Thank you, Mr. Harris," Tanyth said. "And how much for all this?"

He nodded and held up one fat digit. "A moment, mum.

Lemme just look." He fished in his pocket and pulled out a bit of chalk. He puttered about with the crates, smudging out numbers and making new marks, squinting at notations on the sides of the boxes. He did a fair amount of muttering and nodding to himself. "All right, mum. The coat's s'posed to be six silver, but I'll never sell that size out so, I'll give ya both coats for ten. Pant's are five each." He shrugged in apology. "Less wool, but more work. The jerseys are four silvers, but I'll throw in the last one for free so twelve there."

"Very fair price, Mr. Harris." Tanyth winced to herself. She hadn't owned clothes that cost more than a silver in her life. She had to admit to herself that she also made most of her clothes and she lacked the skill and knowledge to work that kind of heavy wool. "And the hats?"

He made a dismissive gesture. "I'll throw that in to sweeten the deal, mum. I'd hate to think of ya out there freezin' yer ears off."

"And my shirts and the liniment?" Rebecca said.

"Add a silver for the shirts and another for the liniment."

"Done, Mr. Harris, and thank you kindly."

They shook hands and Tanyth counted out the silvers from her dwindling supply, glad that she'd had the presence of mind to fill her pocketbook when she'd gotten the golds for passage.

Tanyth and Rebecca bundled the heavy clothing up as best they could and followed Harris back through the maze to the front of the chandlery.

"You've rather a lot of goods here, Mr. Harris."

"Oh, aye, mum. Pretty much anythin' a ship might need to get out and back again safe." He looked around proudly. "Canvas to paint, lines to linens. Just about anything."

She paused at the door. "Food? Tea?"

"O'course, mum. Can't sail without tea. And barrels of flour, hard tack, salt fish." He waved a hand in the air to help him think. "Beans, oatmeal, cornmeal. Beans. I already said beans."

"I could use some tea. Mr. Groves said I should stock up on anything special I might like..."

Mr. Harris grinned. "Oh, aye, but you don't need to worry about tea. Ole Saul Groves, he likes his tea too much to risk runnin' out." Harris nodded. "He's got at least a hun'erd weight of tea aboard already, mum."

The number took her by surprise. "A hundred pounds of tea?"

"Aye, mum. Sailors drink a lot of tea."

"How long is this voyage?"

He blinked at her. "You don't know, mum?"

She shrugged. "The subject's never come up."

"Usually takes a week and a half to two weeks to make the passage. This time of year, watching for ice and all, probably two, two and a half."

"Thank you, Mr. Harris. You've been very helpful."

He knuckled his brow. "Thank you for your custom, mum." He shook his head. "Don't get many womenfolk in here."

She stopped with her hand on the latch. "You get some then?"

He'd already started back into the depths of the warehouse but stopped with a shrug. "Well, no, mum. You're the first." He glanced at Rebecca. "First since her ma used to sneak in to buy fishin' gear from my da." He rolled his mouth up as if to prevent himself from saying more.

Tanyth felt Rebecca stiffen and looked to her, but she just shook her head. Even in the dimness of the chandlery, Tanyth saw her eyes gleam wetly.

With a nod to Harris, Tanyth said, "Well, thank you for your assistance, Mr. Harris."

"My pleasure, mum. My pleasure. Safe voyage." He raised a hand in salute and disappeared around a pile of barrels.

Tanyth followed Rebecca out of the shop, hearing the bell jingle again. She still wore the knit cap and reached up to tug one side down over her ear. The afternoon breeze had an edge to it and she was glad to have the protection. "Shoulda got one of these ages ago," she muttered.

Rebecca smiled at her, and tugged her own hat down a little. "They are practical, aren't they, mum?"

Tanyth nodded and cast Rebecca a sideways look. "You wanna talk about it?"

"My mother?"

Tanyth nodded. "Yeah."

Rebecca shook her head. "No, mum. I'd rather not. Can I help you lug some of that?" She nodded at the bundle of woolens that Tanyth had wrapped in her arms.

Tanyth snickered. "Well, you got more to carry than I do, my dear. If I can keep from droppin' my stick, we should be all right to get back to the ship." They started walking back down the pier. "But I don't know where we're gonna stow all this stuff."

"Under the bunks, prob'ly, mum."

Tanyth shot her a look. "You been on a ship before?"

Rebecca shook her head. "Father wouldn't allow it." She grinned at Tanyth, "But I peeked in the cupboards while you were busy with Benjamin. They're empty."

Tanyth's eyebrows shot up. "Benjamin, is it?"

"Mr. Groves," Rebecca said. "I meant Mr. Groves."

Tanyth laughed. "I know what you meant, girl. I know what you meant."

The setting sun cast their shadows across the pier as they trudged back to the ship.

CHAPTER 20
SETTLING IN

When they got there, Tanyth managed to get across the plank without falling in, even with the heavy bundle of woolens and her staff. She hung the coat on one of the pegs and looped the belt loop of the trousers on another. She looked at the mass of the two items of clothing and shook her head. "You'll never get them in your pack, old woman."

Rebecca snickered. "You're not plannin' on takin' them with you off the ship?"

Tanyth shrugged the problem aside for later and turned to laying out her bedroll on the bunk. It was a snug fit and she crawled up onto it, stretching out on top to try it out. She rolled her old heavy coat into a pillow and discovered that the narrow bunk suited her back quite well. The low overhead and solid head and foot made her feel very secure.

"Just like your own little cave, isn't it, mum?" Rebecca said from across the way.

For a moment Tanyth remembered another cave under a fallen tree but banished that thought with a grunt.

"This is much better," she muttered and closed her eyes, just for a moment, relaxing in the gentle sway of the ship and the quiet creaks of flexing wood and rope.

☽○☾

The nest had been damaged a bit but nothing a little repair couldn't fix. The dimness protected them and the warmth of their bodies kept them comfortable. They'd run out when things got quiet and find food. Food would be good. Water would be good.

First, find something soft, something to unravel to fix the nest.

☽○☾

Tanyth's eyes fluttered open. She glanced over and saw Rebecca still stretched out, her hands folded across her stomach. She heard steps on the deck outside followed by a light tread in the passage outside her door.

A double tap followed by "Mother Fairport?"

"Yes?"

"It's Benjamin, mum. The Captain requests the pleasure of your company in dining ashore with us this evening."

"Just a moment, Benjamin."

She clambered out of the bunk, and scrubbed her face with her palms, still off balance from the brief dream. With a twist on the handle she opened the door and faced the first mate. "We're not exactly supplied with fancy clothes, Mr. Groves."

The young man nodded a greeting and flashed a smile at Rebecca who leaned out of her bunk. "What you're wearing is fine, mum. There's a tavern just off the pier. Mother's coming to sup with us. It's mostly a sailor's dive but the stew is good and it's handy to the ship. Not exactly a fancy eatery, but we like it."

She considered her options, glanced at Rebecca who gave a small but eager nod, and realized that she didn't want to spend the rest of the evening in the tiny cabin herself. "All right," she said. "When?"

"Four bells, mum."

Tanyth cocked her head. "And when would that be?"

"Oh, sorry, mum." He nodded at the tiny window. "Should be just about dark but you'll hear the ship's bell ring four times. It'll sound like ding-ding, ding-ding."

"You do a lot of this ding-dinging?"

"Every half hour, mum. It's coming up on two bells. You'll hear it, then three bells, and at four bells, I'll come and collect you."

"All right, then."

He caught sight of the blue coat on the peg. "I see you found Mr. Harris."

192

"Oh, yes. Very nice man. I should be warm enough now, I think."

"You'll be warm as the rest of us, I expect, but you'll be glad for the extra clothing."

"You're not makin' an old woman feel very comfortable about this trip, Mr. Groves."

He gave her a short laugh but his face took a serious cast. "It's the first trip of the season, mum. The next one will be warmer and easier, but this first one?" He shook his head. "Normally, we don't take passengers on this trip at all."

"Too dangerous?" she asked.

"Not that so much. Every trip is dangerous to a degree." He shrugged. "The sea's a powerful thing and man's but a poor, fragile shell, as you probably know better'n me, mum."

"Then why?"

He laughed again. "Because it's just so miserable that if it weren't for the profit we stand to earn, none of us would go either."

She found his laughter hard to resist and soon laughed with him. "Well, we'll all ride it out together then, I guess," she said.

In the distance she heard, "ding-ding."

"There! That's two bells," Groves said. "I'll be back in an hour."

She nodded. "I'll look forward to it."

She started to close the door but stopped. "Oh, one more thing, Mr. Groves?"

"Yes, mum?"

"Is there a place aboard where I can wash up a bit?"

"Oh, of course. Let me give you the tour, mum."

The tour, such as it was, took only a few minutes. The narrow space under the deck held the captain's cabin across the width of the stern and a small cabin that the first and second mates shared.

Rebecca blinked at that arrangement. "There's only one bunk?"

"We never sleep at the same time. When we're underway, one of us is always up."

"Sounds tirin'."

Groves laughed. "It can be, but that's life at sea. Between tiring and terrifying, most of us pick tiring."

"I can understand that, Mr. Groves," Tanyth said. Having been through her own share of terrifying, her agreement carried plenty of freight.

He showed her the "water closet" as well. He shrugged, clearly embarassed. "We don't get many women passengers, mum. Facilities are a bit rough."

She grinned at him. "Try sharin' a privy with twenty other people."

He barked a laugh. "It'll get a bit ripe, but the bucket gets changed out regularly underway. And it's always colder in here because of the vents."

She nodded. "The alternative would be much more unpleasant, I think."

He laughed again. "I believe you're right, mum."

They returned to the stateroom and he showed her where to find a small tin basin and a pitcher. "If you take this to the cookhouse on deck, mum. You can draw hot water from the tank on the stove."

"That's pretty handy."

He shrugged. "Dirt and disease kill more sailors than salt water, mum. We try to avoid it where possible. Bring your pitcher and I'll introduce you to Cook. You two should get on famously."

She took up the metal handle and followed him out onto the deck. A small deckhouse between the two masts held a tidy kitchen. A rotund, clean-shaven man looked up from a pot of something when the door opened. "Mr. Groves," he said, nodding to each of them in turn.

"Cook? This is Mother Fairport. She and her companion have taken passage to North Haven and will be staying aboard until we leave. I've come to show her where to get hot water."

"Welcome aboard, mum."

"Thank you, Cook?" She looked back and forth between the two men. "Is that the correct form of address?"

"Aye, mum. Most just calls me Cook. It's been so long now I almost forgot my other name."

"Almost?"

"Aye, mum. James, mum."

"No one calls you James, then?"

"Only my mother, mum." The man laughed. "O'course, she's also Cook, and I learned from her before I joined up and went to sea." The man laughed again. "We blame my father, mum."

"Your father?" Tanyth looked to Mr. Groves who hid a smile behind a hand and tried to look innocent.

"Aye, mum. He's the reason they call me Cook."

"Why's that, then?"

"Well, because he married my mother, mum. She was a Wilson before she was a Cook, and if he'd not married her they'd call me a—"

"Yes, Cook," Mr. Groves interrupted. "We've a lady aboard."

"Oh, sorry, mum," Cook looked abashed. "I forget my manners sometimes."

"It's quite all right. I've heard much worse."

In the distance they heard the ship's bell ring twice and then once. "Three bells?" Tanyth asked.

"Just so, mum," Mr. Groves agreed. "I'll leave you to the tender mercies of the ship's comedian and see to my own duties now, if that's satisfactory?"

"Thank you, Mr. Groves. I think you were right. Cook and I will get on famously."

He smiled and left the deckhouse, latching the door behind him.

"Well, Cook, if you'd show me where to get the water, I'll get out of your way."

"Oh, right here, mum. This spigot?" He handed her a towel. "Use this, mum. That gets a tad warm when the stove's on."

She filled the pitcher about half full with water so hot it steamed even near the heat of the stove. She was careful to hold the pitcher's handle after nearly burning her hand on the metal base.

"There's sweet water in that cask there, mum." The cook pointed to a tapped barrel near the door. "You can use that for drinkin' and washin' up and such."

"Sweet water?" she asked.

"Yes, mum. Not to be confused with salt. Don't drink the salt water, mum."

She looked about the cookhouse but saw only the one barrel. "And where would I find salt water, Cook?"

"Why, all around the outside of the ship, mum. Just drop a bucket anywhere. You'll find all you need."

She turned to look at him and saw his eyes twinkling. She laughed aloud and was still chuckling when she got back to Rebecca.

"What's tickled ya this time, mum?" Rebecca asked.

"You'll want to watch out for the cook, my dear. He's a certain way with words that'll tickle ya when you're not expectin' it."

Rebecca frowned at the cryptic remark but took her turn at the warm water without asking for an explanation.

CHAPTER 21
A SHIFT IN THE WIND

Mr. Groves rapped on their door at the fourth stroke of the bell and offered her his arm as they walked the pier toward the city. Rebecca walked beside Tanyth and occasionally leaned in to look at Groves.

"It's easy to forget the city's here sometimes, mum," he said.

Tanyth looked at the hulking mass of warehouses along the quay and the buildings climbing the low hill beyond. Around them, a forest of masts and spars stood out in sharp relief against the darkening sky. "I can see why. It's quite peaceful out here at the end of the pier. None of the hurly-burly of the city and such."

"The ship itself is a spot of comfort on its own," Mr. Groves said. "This pier seems almost too weak to bind her."

Tanyth smiled up at her young escort. "Mr. Groves, I believe you're a romantic."

He smiled back. "All sailors are romantics at heart, mum. Else we'd stay at home and tend farms."

In no time they found a well-lighted tavern named The Sailor's Cradle that sported as its sign a full hammock strung on a standard and swinging in the breeze. Tanyth looked up at it as they approached. "A hammock?"

"Indeed, mum. The crew in the fo'c'sle—that's up in the bow beyond the cookhouse—they sleep in hammocks, not bunks."

"Why is that, Mr. Groves."

He shrugged. "Part custom, part convenience. Part com-

197

fort, truth be told."

She eyed the open weave net that formed the body of the hammock on display as they walked under it and into the tavern proper. "Comfort, Mr. Groves?"

"Aye, mum. Hung on both ends like that, when the ship rocks, the cradle doesn't. You're less likely to be tossed out of a hammock in heavy seas than you are a bunk."

"Not to be an alarmed old lady, Mr. Groves, but is that likely?"

He grinned. "No, mum. Bunks on the *Call* run cross-wise in the ship. If we rock side to side, you'll barely feel it and if we start climbing seas big enough to rock us that much bow and stern, we'll have bigger problems than falling out of our bunks."

Her mouth twisted into a grimace. "You're not makin' me feel all that comfortable in this voyage, Mr. Groves."

"Well, that's part of my plan, mum."

"You tryin' to scare me into stayin' here?"

He shook his head. "No, mum, but I want you expecting conditions so dire that when they're merely miserable, you'll count it a blessing. Is it working?"

She couldn't help but laugh. "I'll tell you when we get to North Haven, Mr. Groves."

"That'll work out fine then, mum." Benjamin gave Rebecca a wink that made her blush as he held the door.

They found Captain and Mrs. Groves in a quiet side room set with a large table and several people already in attendance. The space itself was more alcove than room and offered a commanding view of the bar through a wide arch with curtains bunched to either side.

When they stepped into the alcove, Captain Groves raised his glass in welcome. "Benjamin! Excellent, you've arrived." He addressed the table at large. "Gentleman and lady," he said, the last directed to a white-haired lady on his left, "most of you know my son, Benjamin, first mate on the *Zypheria's Call*."

Most of the men raised a glass or nodded to Mr. Groves who gave a small bow in return.

"And the lovely woman on his arm is the most adventurous Mother Tanyth Fairport who has taken passage with us to North Haven along with her traveling companion—" The captain stopped in mid sentence. "I'm sorry, my dear, but I've forgotten your name."

"It's Rebecca, Father," Benjamin said.

"Of course, of course," the captain said. "My apologies, Rebecca."

Rebecca smiled and murmured, "Not at all."

The men rose and gave small bows before resuming their seats. The Captain's lady patted the empty chair beside her in invitation, and Mr. Groves seated Tanyth in it before helping Rebecca into an empty seat beside her. He then took his own place on the Captain's right.

Seating established, the captain continued. "Mother Fairport, this collection of rogues and scalawags are my partners, bankers, and with the exception of my lady wife, not to be trusted while I'm out of the sight of land, which is why she stays ashore to keep track of them all."

There was a general laugh and considerable good-natured jeering at this pronouncement but the company soon quieted and servers appeared with large bowls containing a stew of fish, potatoes, and milk.

"So pleased to make your acquaintance, Mother Fairport." The captain's wife greeted her with a broad smile. "Since Saul's manners don't include introducing me by name..." She directed that jibe directly at her husband, who toasted her with his mug and an apologetic look on his face. "Call me Murial, if you like."

Tanyth offered a handshake and said, "Please, Tanyth. All this Mother Fairport business just makes me feel older than I am."

Murial chuckled and patted Tanyth's forearm. "I can imagine only too well."

Servers placed bowls in front of each person and withdrew to stand ready in the background.

Tanyth nodded her thanks and noted that everyone looked to the Captain.

"Thank you all for coming," he said as the table quieted. "Some of you know this is a tradition with us, to break bread together before we sail. The wind might shift any day now and we'll be getting underway as soon as practicable after that. Thank you, gentlemen, for your continued support and belief in the vessel and her crew." He held up his glass and was joined by all the men at the table. "Fair wind and following seas!"

They all repeated the phrase and each took a deep swallow of whatever was in their mugs and glasses.

The captain lifted his spoon and took a sip of the stew whereupon the company passed the baskets of bread and dug into their own meals.

While the men discussed ships and cargoes, riggings and hulls, Murial turned to Tanyth. "You're going north then?"

"Yeah. The last leg on a long journey, I hope," Tanyth said between spoons full of rich stew.

"Oh? You've traveled far?"

Tanyth nodded. "All over Korlay. This will be the farthest north but I've been the length and breadth, I think." She nodded to the Captain. "The mainland anyway."

"My goodness, how long has that taken?"

"This marks my twenty-first winter," Tanyth kept her voice low to slide in under the table discussion of the relative merits of dried fish over salted pork which seemed to be occupying at least half the men in a lively debate. "And how do you fare? Wife of a sea captain?"

Murial turned a fond eye toward her husband before replying. She leaned in to put her head near to Tanyth. "Frankly, if he didn't go to sea, I'd probably brain him within a season." Her eyes twinkled as if in jest, and Tanyth chuckled. "He can be such a fusspot, but he's a good man." She reached over and patted him affectionately on the arm and he returned the favor by catching her hand and kissing her fingers with barely a break in the discussion.

"And this wind they're all wound up about?" she asked.

"Yes. There's something about that westerly wind that brings an unfortunate change to otherwise sensible menfolk." Murial glanced over at her husband with a smile. "He worked for years to earn enough to get a ship of his own. Bless him, he wanted to christen her *Murial*."

"After you?" Tanyth asked. "Why's that?"

Murial snorted a soft laugh. "A lot of captains name the ship for their wives. I think it makes 'em feel less guilty. Mother knows they spend all their time with one or t'other. Per'aps it cuts down on the confusion over names when they only have to remember the one."

Tanth laughed.

"But Saul? He's always answered Zypheria's call so when it came time to name the ship, I made him name her that." She took a bite of her chowder and offered a small shrug. "It's the lot of a sailor's wife and one I knew full well when I married him."

"How's that?"

"My father was a captain. I saw it in my mother."

They ate in silence for a time, letting the men's conversation wash around them.

"Your son seems a good man," Tanyth observed.

"Thank you, he wasn't always such a good boy." She tsked and took a spoon full of soup. "When he was a lad, he vexed me something terrible. Playing pirate in my vegetable patch. Chasing the girls in the school yard." She leaned over to speak to Rebecca. "Some of them let him catch them, too, and if you don't think there wasn't hand-wringing and lamentation aplenty over that!"

Tanyth couldn't help but like the blustery woman.

"Still, he turned out quite fine. Now, if he'd just find a nice woman of his own and settle down. I'm getting old and want to see my grandbabies before I cross over."

Tanyth looked to the young man in question and shook her head. "Some woman will set her cap for him, you wait and see. He'll be a catch but it'll take a strong woman to land him, I wager."

Rebecca coughed, but waved off Tanyth's concerned look, holding a napkin to her lips as she recovered. "Swallowed wrong," she said. "Sorry. I'm fine."

"No doubt, my dear. No doubt," Murial said, a shrewd look in her eye as she measured the distance between Rebecca and her son across the table.

Benjamin seemed to realize they were talking about him

and smiled, shaking his head as if chiding them. "Not fair, you three with your heads together," he said.

"Oh, hush, boy. We're just planning your future between us," Murial said, much to the delight of the table at large.

"Father, I knew it was a mistake to get Mother Fairport and that woman in the same room. We're doomed, sir."

Captain Groves laughed and patted his wife's hand. "That woman is your mother, boy, and I've been doomed for more winters than you've been alive." He turned to his wife. "And glad to be, my dear." He reached in to kiss her on the cheek amid table thumping and catcalls.

"How charming!" A new voice cut through the babble and all eyes turned to see a tall man standing in the arch.

The mood turned cold. Captain Groves said, "This is a private party, Malloy. I don't recall you were invited."

"Ah, I beg pardon, Captain. The view of such matrimonial harmony fills my romantic soul and I couldn't help but comment."

"Spare us your bilgewater. You've business here? Spit it out. If not, shove off."

The man just held up his hand in a placating gesture. "No need to be gruff, Saul. I'm just here to let you know, I'll be happy to accept your congratulations when you get back from North Haven."

"My congratulations? For what?"

"Why for being the first one up and the first one back, of course."

"Good luck with that, Malloy. And unlike some, I will congratulate you in the unlikely event you manage to beat me north and south again." Groves stood and shook a fist at the man. "But so help me, by the beard of the All-Father, if you ever lay a hand on another of my crew, I'll personally—"

"Saul." Murial's voice cut into the growing tirade. "He's not worth this."

Captain Groves looked down at his wife. He took a deep breath and let it out. "You're right, my dear." He turned to address the table. "My apologies to everyone." He looked up at the man still standing in the arch. "And good night to you, Captain Malloy. Fair winds and following seas."

"Ah, the brave captain. Hiding behind his lady wife's skirts as always."

"Good *night*, Captain Malloy." Saul Grove's face held an impassive stare that Tanyth was happy not to be receiving.

A burly man wearing an apron stepped up beside Malloy. "Is there a problem, Captain Groves?"

"Captain Malloy, here was just leaving. Buy him a drink for me before he goes, would you, Carson?"

"Be my pleasure, Captain." The burly man turned to Malloy. "Shall we, Captain?"

The two men moved off and Captain Groves resumed his seat. "My apologies, again," he said, scanning the assembled party with his eyes.

The servers cleared off the stew and brought a joint of roast mutton. By the time plates were doled out and glasses refilled the jocularity of the party returned, if not quite to the same level.

Tanyth looked to Murial who sighed and shook her head. "Two years ago, Saul and Malloy reached North Haven almost at the same time. They were loaded and ready to go, but three of the *Call*'s crew turned up missing and Saul was delayed." She shrugged. "Everybody blames Malloy for being the cause, but there's no proof."

A discussion regarding the benefit of sloop-rigged over square-rigged schooners erupted around the table with much noise and laughter.

"And did the missin' crew show up?" Tanyth asked.

Murial nodded. "Very hungover and locked in a root cellar."

"Seems kinda clumsy to get locked in a root cellar."

"Yes, which is why Saul, among others, thinks Malloy is behind it."

Tanyth sipped her tea and picked at the mutton while the discussion of sail rigs wound down around the table. During the lull that followed, a gentleman on the other side of Rebecca leaned forward and spoke around the women. "Saul, did you register with the syndicate?"

Captain Groves turned and Tanyth sat back a bit in her seat. "Now, Peter, we've been over this before. You know my feelings."

Tanyth looked to Peter, a youngish man of perhaps thirty-five winters. He seemed well dressed, as far as Tanyth could tell. "I know you have, Saul, but you really should reconsider. What if something happened to *Zypheria's Call?*"

"Well, then we'd just have to deal with it." The conversation around the table cut off as the two men talked. "I went and talked to them just last week. What they're charging for premiums makes doing business with them unprofitable. I'd be better off selling the ship and taking up farming."

"It's just business, Saul. You know that. They calculate the risks and underwrite the voyages based on past performance and the law of averages."

"So they say, Peter, but I'm not so sure anymore."

"I wish you'd reconsider. Particularly after that unfortunate incident with Avram's *Elizabeth*, I'd think you'd be more concerned."

Captain Groves shrugged his shoulders and dug into his trencher of mutton. "My mind's made up, Peter. We're sailing as we are. That's all there is to it."

Mr. Groves turned to his dinner companion, an older gentleman with white muttonchop whiskers. "When do you think the Zypheria will call, Mr. Chelton?"

Chelton looked up from his meal and shrugged. "I'd bet on tomorrow."

"Do you have some ideas, insider knowledge, sir?"

The elderly Chelton grinned at the younger Groves. "Well, lad, it hasn't arrived yet and each day is a little warmer. Eventually, if I keep sayin' it, one day I'll be correct and everybody will forget I was wrong twenty days in a row, they'll be so anxious to get underway."

The party all laughed at the logic and yet Tanyth saw a glimmer of slyness in the old man's eye. She toasted him with her teacup and he gave her a small wink and a nod across the table.

The conversation turned to more general topics then and consumed the men in a discussion of taxes and the crown. Tanyth took the opportunity to ask Murial, "What's this syndicate that's causin' such a stir?"

Murial tsked and leaned close. "A group of money people insure voyages against loss. In return for a share of every cargo that goes out, they agree to pay off the business for the loss of a ship in the event it never arrives."

"Is this the insurance I've heard tell about?"

Murial nodded. "It is, indeed."

"How does that help?"

"All these men have a stake in the voyage. They put up money that helps pay the costs and they stand to make a lot of money in return when Saul gets back. If the ship is lost, they lose all they've invested. The syndicate will guarantee some minimum payout if the voyage is a failure."

Tanyth looked around the table and noticed that the man called Peter was just picking at his food and shooting dark looks at Captain Groves.

"Who pays you if you lose your husband and son?"

Tanyth saw the pain in the other woman's face and reached out to pat her forearm.

"That's what I thought," she said.

Some change in atmosphere washed through the tavern. It started in the other room but even Tanyth could tell something had happened. Everyone at the table went silent, looking out through the arch to try to see what was going on.

The burly man who had shown Malloy away appeared as if by magic in the arch. "The wind," he said. "It's shifted."

The change was startling. Captain Groves pulled his pocket watch from his vest, flipping the case open with his thumb. "Ben, we've two hours until the tide turns. We need to be outside the breakwater by then. We're casting off at eight bells. Pass the word. Anybody not on board by then gets left."

"Aye, aye, Captain." Mr. Groves stood and with a muttered apology headed out of the tavern.

Saul turned to the headwaiter. "Peters, give these ne'er-do-wells a bit of dessert, a tot of rum, and then kick them out. Put it on my bill."

"Of course, Captain."

He leaned over and kissed his wife, and Tanyth sat close enough to see her kiss him back.

"All-Mother watch over you, husband."

"I'll see you in six weeks."

The captain seemed to notice Tanyth still sitting at the table. "I'm needed at the ship, Mother Fairport. You and Rebecca have time to finish your meal and take dessert, if you've a mind."

She stood and picked up her coat. "I'm ready now, Captain. If you've got time to walk me to the ship."

Rebecca followed suit.

"We're off then."

With a flurry of good-byes, Tanyth found herself striding down the pier between Rebecca and the captain as men ran along Front Street and funneled into the piers, racing around them in some cases to beat the captain to the vessel. Shouts echoed around the harbor and up into the streets above.

His eyes gleamed in the light of the moon and Tanyth thought he looked exuberant. "Good thing you moved aboard this afternoon, mum."

"I see that, Captain."

A few high clouds raced across the sky, hiding and then exposing the first quarter moon where it rode in the south-western sky. The wind that had driven straight in from the end of the pier before now roiled sideways across the dock. Tanyth felt the warmth against her face and a bit of damp-ness in it as well. She had little time to consider the changes. In moments they boarded the ship and the captain started barking orders.

"Bosun!"

"Aye, Captain."

"Single up all lines. Clear away the running gear. Get the running lights lit and tell Cook to put on the tea."

"Tea's already on, Captain!" Tanyth recognized Cook's voice coming from the deckhouse.

"Good lad!"

"Jameson!"

The bosun answered, "He's not aboard yet, Capt'n. Said he'd be back by seven bells."

"How many others are missing?"

"Scooter, Rand, Nichols, and Franklin, sir."

"Franklin's here!" came a voice from the gangway as a gangly youth in a striped jersey pelted aboard. "Scooter's right behind me and Nichols's with Jameson. They'll be along sharply."

Benjamin appeared out of the night. "That's the lot, Captain. Everybody's either here or on the way."

"Bosun! Get those lines singled up. We'll need a spring line to push the bow out against the tide. Send three aloft to the tops and get those gaskets off the main and for'ard."

"Aye, aye, Captain." The man started bawling orders and cuffing heads.

The captain saw Rebecca standing beside Tanyth. "Scooter!" he yelled.

"Aye, Captain?" The lanky crewman appeared as if by magic from the gloom.

The Captain waved a hand at Rebecca. "She's workin' passage. Show her what do to."

"Aye, aye, Captain," Scooter said and beckoned with a sweep of his hand and a grin. "Come on, then," he said and looked up at the rigging. "You know what a gasket is?"

Rebecca followed the youth across the deck and was halfway up the ratlines before Tanyth could blink. In a few heartbeats she was lost to view in the darkness above.

Tanyth crossed the deck and stood with her back against the deckhouse. She felt as if her head were on a swivel as she tried to watch everything and stay out of the way.

"Ahoy, *Zypheria's Call!*" The shout came from the pier.

The captain ran to the rail to squint out into the dark. "Who goes and what'd ya want?" he called.

"It's Peter. Peter Robertson! I've a package, Captain!"

"Peter?" The captain stretched his neck forward trying to see. "This isn't some more insurance foolishness, is it?"

"No, Captain. I've a shipment for my man, Wiley, in North Haven. I told him you'd bring it when the port opened."

"Why the devil did you wait until now to do this? I've neither the time nor the inclination to break out the cargo boom for one crate!"

"It's not that big, Captain. We can horse it aboard. Please, Saul. It needs to go with you this trip."

The captain spit into the sea beside the dock. "All right! Get it aboard, man!" He turned to the sailors on the deck. "Franklin, Cleeves. Give 'im a hand."

Two sailors scampered up the slanted gangway and returned in a few moments with an oblong crate between them, stepping carefully on the way back down.

"Thanks, Saul."

The captain spat again. "If you make me miss the tide, Robertson, you'll be owing me more than thanks!" He turned to the bosun. "Get the stern line in and secure that gangway."

"Cuppa tea, mum?" She turned to find Cook standing beside her in the semi-dark. He held out a heavy mug with a dark liquid in it.

She accepted it and nodded her thanks. She took a sip and nearly choked. "What's in this tea?"

Cook's smile glowed in the dimness. "Jot of rum, mum. It'll help you sleep."

Tanyth barked a laugh. "You think I'm goin' to need it?"

"You ever been out to sea before, mum?"

"Not in the open sea, no."

"Yeah. You'll thank me in about two bells, mum."

Considering the level of noise on deck and the hour, she thought perhaps he might have a point. "Thank you, Cook."

"You're most welcome, mum. And welcome aboard."

CHAPTER 22
THE ROLLING SEA

Whether it was the excitement of getting underway, the heavy meal, or the rum, Tanyth couldn't be sure, but she slept soundly. She awoke to a distant bell ringing and sun shining in the tiny window. She lay there in her nest of covers and felt the ship's slow roll up and down. As she lay there she became aware of a low rushing sound, a kind of vibration that had no tone but should have.

"Good morning, mum," Rebecca said, her voice low and sleep filled.

"G'mornin', my dear." She rubbed her eyes and peered across to where Rebecca sat cross-legged on her bunk, fully dressed and sipping a mug of tea. "You been out on deck already?"

Rebecca held up the mug. "Been workin' and just got off duty about three bells ago. Been trying to sleep but every time I nod off, they ring again." She grimaced.

"How're your hands?" Tanyth asked.

"Mr. Harris was right," the young woman said holding up her empty hand to peer at the palm. She turned it and Tanyth saw the redness of abrasion.

Tanyth winced in sympathy.

Rebecca shrugged. "Looks worse than it feels but I put on some of Harris's liniment and it feels a lot better."

Tanyth made a mental note to see what was in the liniment.

"When d'ya have to go back to work?"

"'S afternoon they said. Somebody'll come get me."

Tanyth tried to sit up and discovered that the movement of the ship made simple things like sitting up or getting down off the high bunk a bit treacherous. She focused on the slow lift and fall of the ship and, after a few moments, was able to stand without falling over. She held onto the bunk's rail until she was sure of her balance.

"It's a bit tricky at first, mum, but it gets better if you don't think about it too much." Rebecca rested her head against the wall behind her, closing her eyes and a small smile drifted onto her lips. "Kinda comfy in an odd way."

Tanyth grinned and did her best to struggle into a pair of trousers and one of her heavier pullovers. The view out the small window showed a sunny day with a few high clouds, but her breath soon fogged the glass. It took her a couple of tries to pull on her boots, leaning back against the bunk and pulling on one boot at a time between the swells.

She congratulated herself for not falling over and noticed that her staff kept rocking back and forth, back and forth where it stood in the corner. "That'll fall if you leave it there, old fool," she muttered.

"Wazzat, mum?" Rebecca asked, opening her eyes and looking toward Tanyth.

Tanyth shook her head. "Nothin', my dear. Just my staff. Wonder it hasn't fallen down and hurt somebody already."

Frowning she looked around the tiny cabin, trying to figure out where to put it where it wouldn't be in the way and wouldn't roll around. Eventually she realized that it fit nicely beside her mattress along the inner rim of her bunk and felt better for having stowed it. She looked around at the other objects and set about making sure things were either in the cupboards, hanging on pegs, or were secured somehow so they wouldn't rattle around. By the time she'd finished, Rebecca snored softly where she sat, her head lolling to one side and shifting gently in the rolls.

The ship's bell rang three times and Rebecca jerked awake, the empty mug gripped in her hand as if she thought she might spill it. She sighed in exasperation and looked at Tanyth with a small shrug.

Tanyth heard a soft footfall outside the door and a gentle

tap.

She reached over and released the latch, letting the door swing open.

Benjamin Groves stood there with a big grin on his face and a haggard look around his eyes. "Good morning, mum. Miss. Cook's compliments and he's got your breakfasts when you want 'em."

"Thank you, Mr. Groves. That's kind of him."

"Cook likes having passengers, mum. Don't spoil him too much."

"Spoil him?"

"Yes, mum, by telling him how good his food is. We like to tease him a bit. Passengers tend to be nice to him."

She laughed. "I can't promise anythin', Mr. Groves, but I'll do my best." She peered at him again. "Have you slept?"

"A bit. Getting underway like that means a lot has to happen in a hurry. I got a couple of naps in, but I need to go grab some sleep now and relieve Jameson at eight bells." He gave her a smile and a shrug. "It'll even out as we get the rhythm down, mum. If you need anything, you can ask Cook."

"Thank you, Mr. Groves. Don't worry about us."

"Good day, mum. Miss." Even in his apparent exhaustion he managed a warm smile in Rebecca's direction. "For a green hand, you did yourself proud out there."

Rebecca smiled and colored, looking into her empty cup as if there might be something more in it. "Thank you, sir."

Mr. Groves winked at Tanyth. "She did better than most of the ordinary seamen we get. 'Specially for her first time up the mast underway."

Rebecca grinned. "Oh, mum, you can't imagine what it's like up there..." her exuberance met Groves' flashing smile and she shrugged. "It was fun, sir. Thanks for lettin' me work passage."

"You're quite welcome, miss." He nodded once to Tanyth and headed down the narrow passage toward his bunk.

"Breakfast, my dear?" Tanyth asked.

Rebecca looked into her empty mug and placed a hand on her stomach. "Not just now, mum. I'm really sleepy and if it's all the same, I think I'll just try to lie down here and see if I can sleep between the dings."

Tanyth nodded and relieved the younger woman of the empty cup. "You sleep. I'll see about food."

Rebecca slumped over, dragged a blanket half over her shoulder and was asleep before Tanyth could move.

With a grin, Tanyth stepped out into the passage and quietly pulled the door closed behind her. Getting used to walking on a moving floor took a bit of concentration, but she managed to get to the stairs leading up to the deck without falling. Having walls to lean on helped. When she got up to the deck, she stopped on the top step of the ladder and took it all in.

A clear yellow sun had barely cleared the eastern horizon, gleaming brilliantly across low rolling waves. Here and there it struck sparks that glimmered and glinted against the dark water. She looked up at the curved expanse of brilliant white canvas above her head gleaming in the dawn's light and the heavy wooden boom along the bottom edge of it. With the horizon all around she realized that the deck was not just rising and falling but that it was tilted over to the side.

"That explains why I've been off kilter," she muttered.

She took the last step up onto the deck and stood there with one hand gripping the hatch coaming to steady herself against the movement of the ship.

A sailor wearing a striped shirt and blue pants walked by. "You all right, mum?"

"I'm fine, but this ship seems to be movin' about."

He grinned. "Yes, mum. She'll do that for the next couple weeks or so I 'spect."

Tanyth grinned back. "So I been led to believe." She looked at him standing there swaying in time with the deck and looking perfectly comfortable without holding on to anything. "Is there a trick to it?"

"To walkin' on deck, mum?" He shook his head. "Just something you get used to. Easier if you just stand up and let go of the bulkhead, mum. Don't think about it and you'll be fine."

"Really?"

"It's how we do it, mum." He held out his hand. "I'll catch ya if you head for the rail, mum, if'n ya wanna try."

Tanyth gathered her courage and straightened up, holding her arms out for balance but letting go of the wall behind her.

"Bend your knees a little, mum. Let the ship just kind move under ya."

Tanyth followed his advice and found that she had no problem standing still. The gentle swells were easy to compensate for and the more she relaxed the easier it became.

"There you have it, mum. Easy as pie."

"How do you walk?"

"One foot after the other, mum. Same as always. Just plow right along like you're goin' somewhere and next thing ya know? You're there."

"What's your name, young man?"

"They call me Scooter, mum."

"Would you mind walkin' with me to the deckhouse, Scooter? Just in case?"

"O' course, mum, but you won't have any problem. Just keep your head up, mum, and don't think much about walkin'."

She gave him a long stare, but he just shrugged his shoulders. She lifted her head and didn't look at her feet, but the first couple of steps were a bit shakey.

"What cha gonna do when you get to North Haven, mum?"

Tanyth looked over to where the young sailor strolled along beside her. "I need to find a woman there. I hope she'll be my teacher." She wasn't sure how much she should share about Mother Pinecrest given what she'd heard from Mabel Esterhouse.

"And here you are, mum."

Tanyth looked up in surprise to discover she'd crossed the deck while she wasn't watching.

The sailor opened the deckhouse door and held it for her. "Told ya not to think about it, mum." He gave her a cheeky grin and she looked back across the deck again.

"Thank you, Scooter. That was quite a lesson."

"'T weren't nuthin', mum. A couple bells of practice and you'll be climbin' the riggin' with the rest of the deck monkeys."

She glanced up to see a sailor hanging from the rigging high above her and the image of her being that far up was so ridiculous that she laughed aloud.

"When you're done with that jackanapes, mum, you might come in and close the door," Cook called. "You're lettin' the heat out."

Scooter knuckled his forehead and she stepped into the deckhouse, only bumping her shoulder once on the doorframe as she walked through. He closed the door behind her.

"Good mornin', Cook."

"Good mornin', mum." Cook handed her a mug of tea. "This'll help, mum. The less you think about it, the easier it gets."

She took the mug and fought the urge to reach for something to steady herself.

"Just sway with the roll, mum. You'll get it."

Tanyth wasn't so sure. She looked into the mug, sniffing the contents. "There's no rum in this?"

Cook laughed. "No, mum. You slept well, though, din't ya?"

"Yes, I did. Thank you." She blew across the top of the mug and tried a tentative sip. The hot tea felt good going down.

"Would you care for some breakfast, mum? I've oatmeal or some eggs, if you'd prefer. No beans this morning, I'm afraid."

"Oatmeal would be most welcome."

He crossed to the stove and spooned a healthy portion into a heavy crockery bowl and drizzled a bit of honey across the top. Tanyth was so busy admiring the clever arrangement of rails around the edge of the stove that she gave no thought to what she was going to do with tea in one hand a bowl of hot oatmeal in the other.

"You can take that back to your room, if you like, mum."

"What do the sailors do?"

Cook grinned. "Most of them just sit on the deck." He pointed to a corner of the deckhouse opposite the water butt. "If you prop yourself in the corner there, mum, there's a shelf you can put your tea on. It might be a bit easier than getting' down and then back up again, if you're not used to it and ya don't mind eatin' standin' up."

Tanyth eased herself into the corner and found a narrow ledge at waist height. It was just wide enough for a mug of tea and a small lip kept the cup from sliding off.

"Just like 'at, mum." Cook nodded his approval. "Get that inside ya, and if ya like, there's plenty more where it came from." He turned to his stove again, pulling open a fire door to chuck in a couple sticks of split wood before taking his long spoon to several pots.

Tanyth spooned up the rich oatmeal. The dusky sweetness of the honey brought out a nut-like flavor in the oats. Before she knew it, she was down to the bottom of the bowl and considering whether or not to take Cook up on his offer of a second bowl.

"Where do I put this, Cook?"

He turned from his ministrations and pointed his spoon at a wide tray just inside the door. "Dirties go there. I'll get some help here in a bit and we'll get them cleaned up."

Tanyth leaned over, careful not to let the rocking of the ship throw her around. The bowl wasn't the first dish in the tray but there was plenty of room for more. "The crew hasn't eaten yet?"

"Most of 'em are sleepin' yet, mum. Those that ain't on duty. Along about seven bells there'll be a reg'lar stampede through here, though, mark my words."

She leaned back into her corner, feeling quite comfortable with the sturdy walls to hold her up and the heavy mug cradled in her hands.

Cook shot her a glance over his shoulder. "You're a bit different from the other ladies we've taken aboard, mum."

Tanyth laughed. "Ya get many ladies aboard, do you?"

Cook finished whatever he was doing on the stove and turned to her, leaning easily on a bit of the bulkhead nearest his hip. "Well, not that many, no, mum. We're a freighter. Not like some of them fancy boats what takes mostly passage." He paused, glancing at the ceiling and obviously considering. "Maybe five or six a season. They don't come out much."

"How do they manage meals?"

"I have to take it to 'em. I'd be happy to, mum, but Mr. Groves said you'd probably be just as happy to come get breakfast."

"Does everybody eat on deck?"

Cook shook his head. "You're standin' in the mate's corner. When they're on duty, they just stand there and eat whatever's handy. Crew sits where they like. Cap'n Groves, now, you'll see with dinner, I wager. He likes his sit-down dinner in the cabin, such as it is."

"Sit down dinner?"

"Oh, aye, mum. He's got a regular table and chairs and all in the cabin. I usually do up a couple or three plates and low man on the ladder does the servin'. Just like a big ship." Cook smiled. "He always invites the passengers to sup with him. You'll see, mum."

"And the other meals?"

"We're not a big ship, mum. We grab what we can, when we can. Nice weather like this? It's easy pickin's. If it gets narsty? Hardtack and hot tea, if you're lucky. Hardtack and cold water, if you're not."

She finished her tea and placed the mug in the tray beside the bowl.

"Thank you, Cook. That's much better."

"Quite welcome, mum. Anytime you wanna cup of tea, you just come get it. I've always got a pot ready."

"Good ta know, Cook. Thanks."

"My pleasure, mum. Truly is."

She edged out onto the deck again, already feeling a bit steadier and braved a walk all the way around the deckhouse before the biting wind cut deep enough that she turned her steps back toward her cozy room to escape it.

"Shoulda worn the heavy coat," she muttered, glad that Mr. Groves had pointed out the shortcomings in her wardrobe. Under the circumstances, she thought she knew why lady passengers didn't spend much time on deck. "Prob'ly don't bring enough clothes."

Safely back in the compartment, she smiled at Rebecca, still curled into her bunk and took a moment to straighten the young woman's covers, drawing them up and tucking her in.

Rebecca didn't stir even as the bell dinged a few times somewhere above them.

Tanyth climbed back into her bunk as the only practical place to be and wondered if she would have to spend the entire trip sleeping. The brisk wind, warm food, and gentle rolling of the ship conspired to push her over the edge and back into slumber once more.

$$)O($$

The nest moved again. She groomed herself and then the babies. They fed now and would be quiet later. She'd be able to hunt. Bread would be good and a walk to the water. There was a smell of something new in the Big Place. Sometimes there was new nest material, things she could shred with tooth and claw. For now, there was the humming that meant she couldn't go outside. She didn't mind. It was cozy in the den with her sisters near and the male guarding them all. Later she could explore, but now the babies needed to suckle. She shifted her weight and they pressed against her.

$$)O($$

Tanyth awoke at the sound of feet running on deck and the memory of a bell dinging. She felt warm and comfortable in her nest. The thought set her heart racing and she all but threw herself out of the bunk, looking at her hands and feet in alarm until she counted the familiar numbers of fingers and saw her stocking-clad feet on the rough, wooden decking. She scrubbed her eyes with the heels of her hands and raked her hair back, feeling the coarse texture of gray, long familiar to the skin of her fingers. She took a deep breath and blew it out.

"What is it, mum?" Rebecca sat halfway up, here eyes wide in alarm. "Are you all right?"

"Not mad," Tanyth muttered. "I'm not goin' mad."

"'Course not, mum," Rebecca said. "Did you have a dream?"

Tanyth took a deep breath and blew it out. "Yeah. Dream. Scared me. That's all." She looked across at Rebecca. "Sorry to wake you, my dear. I don't know what came over me."

Rebecca shook her head. "You didn't, mum. The bell and the stompin' around on deck did that."

Tanyth crossed to the small window and looked out at the sea rushing by. Long, smooth rollers stretched to the horizon even as the water's surface dappled at the touch of the breezes flowing by. She took deep breaths and rested her forehead against the cold glass, savoring the smoothness, savoring the cool on her fevered brow.

She cast her eye around the tiny cabin. "I may not be mad now, but I might if I spend a week in here," she murmured. Her eye caught on the deep blue of her new coat.

Rebecca put her head down on her pillow again, eyes already drooping. "What'll you do, mum?"

Tanyth pushed the hair away from the younger woman's brow. "I have a mind to make myself useful. You sleep. I'll get out of here and leave you to it."

Rebecca gave a small, contented sounding sigh and her eyelids fluttered closed again.

Tanyth pulled the coat from its peg, shrugged it on and headed for the deck.

The rolling of the ship didn't bother her any more. Some part of her brain managed her feet without her knowledge. She strolled up and down the ship looking at everything. She climbed up to the raised portion of the bow and walked all the way to the front of the ship. For one fleeting moment, a dream she once had of a clear morning and a cold wind layered over her sight and gave her an odd feeling, but the low smudge of land that should be *there*—she turned her head to make sure—was missing. The ship's rise and fall was more pronounced at the bow, the distance traveled greater than in the middle of the ship where the seesaw motion found its axis. The rising bow almost flung her into the air on the upward swing and the deck all but fell out from under her boots on the downward. The feeling in her belly made her giddy. She smiled into the teeth of the wind even as a frisson of fear tickled the backs of her knees.

She turned and made her way aft, passing a few sailors sitting cross-legged against the inner rail in the sun. They looked up from their work and nodded to her, each giving a friendly smile and a nod. She was surprised to see some of them knitting while others worked bits of rope or carved small pieces of wood. She felt over dressed in her heavy, new woolens while many of the sailors seemed to be comfortable sitting in short pants and shirtsleeves.

At the stern, a pair of stairways led up to a raised deck that formed the roof of her cabin. Higher than the main deck, a large, spoked wheel held pride of place behind a fat pillar. She found Mr. Groves and the bosun standing there along with another sailor who held the great wheel by its spokes, his eyes on the bow and his legs flexing to keep the wheel steady.

Mr. Groves crossed to her even before she'd gotten all the way up the ladder. "Good day, mum," he said, offering his arm and leading her to the upper side of the slanted deck. "I see you've gotten your sea legs under you."

She smiled and nodded. "A young man named Scooter helped me this mornin' and I seem to have found the way of it."

He turned and leaned his elbow against the railing. "This is the bridge, mum. It's where we steer the ship and pass the orders to the crew."

"You spend your time up here, then, do you?"

"Yes, mum. Most of it. When I'm not needed elsewhere or sleeping."

She turned and scanned the horizon and looked forward along the length of the vessel. "It's a good view from here." She squinted up into the bright sun and then looked at the wide, foaming vee of the ship's passage. She scanned the horizon in that direction and saw nothing. "No land?"

Mr. Groves smiled. "No, mum, we left land behind sometime in the night. We should see the northern shores in a week, perhaps. In the meantime, we sail merrily along and hope for good weather."

"How far are you ahead of the others?"

"The others, mum?"

"Yes, the other ships bound for North Haven. Like that fella last night...It was just last night, wasn't it?"

He laughed. "Yes, mum. It was just last night, although

being out here has a way of making you forget the time."

A loud clang-clang startled Tanyth. She hadn't been looking in that direction but the bosun had crossed to the ship's bell and given its lanyard a pair of good tugs.

"Well, except for that," Groves said with a small smile. "The days do tend to blend together, though."

Tanyth cast her eyes forward across the sailors at the railing again and nodded. "I can see where it would. What do passengers do on this voyage?" She squinted up to see his face.

"Bored already, mum?" he asked.

"Let's just say, I'm not used ta just sittin' 'round and breathin'."

"Well," he said, "most of them stay pretty close to their compartments. Reading or writing, I imagine. Most of them are businessmen who seldom venture out much. Almost all of them take a couple turns of the deck every day. Some of them work passage, too. That keeps them busy and, if they're up to the task, works out well for everybody concerned."

"I see," she said. "I'll have to try to find something to fill the time then, won't I?"

Mr. Groves nodded with a sympathetic shrug. "Father has a small library in his cabin. You might ask for a book to read if you like. You're invited to dinner tonight as well. The evenings are a bit more relaxed."

"Mr. Groves? We're comin' up on the waypoint." The bosun's voice carved through the wind.

"Thank you, bosun. Pass the word," Groves called back.

Tanyth saw men moving even before the bosun started shouting orders and crewmen came, seemingly out of the deck planks themselves and took up stations around the deck. Scooter disappeared down the companionway and emerged a few moments later with a blinking Rebecca. They took up station holding a rope and looked to the bosun.

"Mum? We're going to come about," Mr. Groves said. "That means change direction on the ship. You need to be down below. If you stand by the companionway below, you'll be able to see everything and not be in any danger."

"You mean I'll be out of the way there?" she said, her mouth turning up on one side.

"Yes, mum, that, too." He offered his arm and took her back to the stairway that led back to the deck. "And, mum? This is the bridge. Please don't come up here again unless invited. It's dangerous for you and a distraction to the crew." He smiled. "It's nothing personal, mum."

She looked around at all the eyes on her and realized the truth of the matter. "Oh, I'm so sorry, Mr. Groves. It won't happen again."

"Thanks for your understanding, mum."

She made her way down the few steps and then stood leaning against the bulkhead near the head of the stairs into the ship. She looked up to see Mr. Groves watching her. He gave her a nod and a smile before disappearing back onto the bridge.

Several men shouted and there was a moment where nothing seemed to happen.

She heard the bosun bellow, "Ready about!"

Everybody in her sight seemed to flex and then freeze in place, some holding ropes, some apparently just holding on.

"Hard a-lee!"

Then everybody on deck seemed to explode into action. The men holding ropes all pulled furiously. She realized that some of the men who appeared to be just holding on, held the handles to winches that they strained against to turn. Tanyth became aware of the great bow of the ship shifting direction and the angle of the shadows on the deck spun as the vessel came around, leveled off, and then started heeling over on the other side.

"Belay and secure sheets and running gear!"

The ship settled on its new course and the wind that had been coming across the deck from one angle, now came across the opposite side as the ship began its stately rise and fall, but with the deck pitched to the right rather than the left.

All together it lasted only a few minutes, but the exercise left Tanyth breathless just watching it.

The sailors went back to whatever they were doing before the bosun started hollering and Tanyth took her new knowledge of the way ships worked to the deckhouse to have a chat with Cook. Rebecca passed her going the other way. She gave

Tanyth a nod and a tired smile before disappearing down the companionway.

$$\mathrm{D O C}$$

That evening, as promised, the captain invited Tanyth to dine in the cabin with him. Mr. Jameson, the second mate, joined them. He turned out to be a pinch-faced man, perhaps a year or two older than the younger Mr. Groves. With the help of a couple of sailors, Cook delivered some china chafing dishes, a platter of carved meats, and a large pot of tea before slipping out of the cabin with a wink and a nod.

"Well, mum? How was your first day aboard?" the captain asked by way of opening the evening's discussion.

Tanyth smiled and accepted a mug of tea. "It's gone quickly, I must say. I take it all the ship's departures aren't so..." she searched for a word that didn't imply criticism.

"Precipitous?" the captain suggested.

"Yes, precipitous."

The captain beamed. "No, mum, but that one's the special one. First out is generally first back."

"And are we?" she asked. "First out?"

The captain nodded and turned to Jameson. "How much of a lead do you reckon, Mr. Jameson?"

Jameson frowned in consideration and shook his head. "As much as half a day, sir. I don't think the *Red Cloud* could get her crew back before the tide changed, and she draws half again more than we do. *Sea Rover* and *Fair Wind* hadn't even recalled crews by the time I got the word. We were well past the breakwater before the tide changed."

The captain nodded. "Aye, and with that harbor and that tide? They'd have been better served to wait until full tide and sail out on the change."

They enjoyed the meal for a moment before the captain shook his head. "And what possessed Robertson to bring us that last crate? Just when we're getting underway." He tsked and sopped up his soup with a bit of bread. "You did get it secured below, didn't you?"

"Of course, Captain. It's lashed down in the main hold. Not hefty enough to matter if it shifts, but Holt and Murray lashed it good and I checked."

"Excellent." The captain turned to Tanyth. "Sorry, mum. Business is like that. No matter how much a man tries, when you work for yourself, you've either got a slave driver for a master or a fool. Either way is a problem. Murial gives me a chewing every time I talk shop at the table."

"I understand, Captain. Since our safe arrival sorta needs your attention, I'm happy to share with Mr. Jameson here."

Tanyth saw a smile flicker across Jameson's face before he tamped it down.

"So, do you think we've enough of a lead?" Tanyth asked.

The captain grimaced and gave his head a shake. "Can't rightly say. It's a big ocean and they could be just over the horizon and go by us."

Mr. Jameson said, "A lot depends on the weather—and the ice, mum. If we get a good blow, we might get pushed well off course, or maybe pushed way ahead."

Captain Groves nodded. "Too right, Jameson. Too right." He glanced up at Tanyth. "We're only on the first day, mum, and there's lots of days and nights left to go before we get there. We made it out first, and we've a good course plotted. Staying on it will be the key."

"Won't they have the same course?" Tanyth asked.

"Maybe," the captain agreed, "if the best course were a straight one. There's currents out here, mum, vast rivers in the ocean that can drag you in directions you can't always see."

"Sorta like tryin' to swim straight across a stream?" Tanyth asked

"Exactly so, mum. Exactly. If you don't know they're there, you can wind up somewhere you don't want to be."

Tanyth wondered if anybody who got to be a captain on a ship that plied these waters would likely be caught in such an error of ignorance, but she kept the notion to herself.

"And the ice?" she asked, as much to be polite as wanting an answer.

Jameson said, "When the ice breaks up, it doesn't just melt, mum. Wind and wave break it loose from the shore. Tides carry it out to sea. Sometimes it forms rafts, piled up and staying together for days, weeks even."

"So not something we'd want ta go sailin' into, I take it?" she asked.

Jameson's narrow face cracking into a grin. "That's right, mum. A bad strike could stave a hole in the side right at the waterline. Even break the stem. That's as dangerous as a fire, mum. Maybe more."

"There's nothing to worry about, mum," the captain said. "It'll be days before we're far enough north and we can usually spot big ice pretty handily." He shot Jameson a quelling look that Tanyth didn't think she was supposed to see.

"Well, it certainly sounds like an adventure," she said.

"And how about you, mum?" Jameson asked. "What takes you to North Haven so early in the season?"

"I'm goin' up to study the plants and such," Tanyth said. "I've spent over twenty winters travelin' and collectin' plant lore and the like."

"Your husband must be a very understanding man, mum," Jameson said.

"Not really," Tanyth answered before considering where that line of conversation might go. She forestalled the inevitable by turning to the captain. "You must have a lot of stories about the north lands. Do you know much about North Haven?"

He pushed his empty plate away and sat back in his chair. "Well, mum. I've not spent a great deal of time there, you understand. Just long enough to get in, unload, load up, and get out again." He smiled indulgently. "Murial gets worried if I'm gone too long."

"How about you, Mr. Jameson? Any interestin' stories?"

Jameson shook his head with a glance at the captain. "Nothing worth sharing, mum. Nothing decent."

That piqued Tanyth's interest but she tamped down the spark. Her eyes came to rest on a bookshelf built into bulkhead beside the door. "Are you a big reader, Captain?"

He glanced at the books. "I turn a page now and again on a slow voyage, aye, mum. I think I've read most of them at least once. Murial keeps finding new ones while I'm at sea and then I have to bring them out here. They help pass the time." He waved a hand. "Please, feel free to borrow anything you might fancy there. If you really like it, I might be persuaded to let you keep it. Just to make room for new books, you understand."

Tanyth spotted a twinkle in the captain's eye and even Jameson hid a grin behind his napkin. "Thank you, Captain. I travel light, but I might borrow one or two, just to pass the time, as you say."

From above they heard six bells. "Well," the captain said, "thank you for sharing my table, mum. I'll look forward to tomorrow night and you can regale me with tales of the excitement you'll undoubtedly find aboard." His sardonic smile held more self-deprecation than actual bite, as if he knew that being passenger was only slightly less boring that watching grass grow.

She chuckled. "You never know, Captain. I might find something that's worthy of a dinnertime tale or two."

He stood and bowed over her hand. "If anyone can, mum, I do believe you're the one." He waved at the bookshelf again. "Help yourself to anything you find there. I need to make my rounds, check in with Benjamin. Mr. Jameson will see you to your cabin, mum."

"Thank you, Captain."

He bustled out and Tanyth looked to Jameson who just shrugged. "Does he think I'm gonna get rolled on the way down the hall, Mr. Jameson?"

He threw back his head and laughed. It was the most animation Tanyth had seen from the man all during dinner. "No, mum," he said. "He's just a bit—pardon the expresssion, mum—old fashioned."

She grinned. "I've heard the term a time or two, Mr. Jameson." She jerked her chin at the captain's bookshelf. "Anything worth readin' in that pile?"

Jameson scrunched up his face in thought, his eyes traversing the shelves. "Murial Groves has a good eye, mum. Almost everything in there is worth the read, I think. There's a good mix of adventure stories, romantic stories, even some collections of shorter ones for those who lack the patience to wade through deeper water, as it were, mum."

"You ever read them?"

He smiled at her. "All of them, mum. It's a long, lonely season at sea. Being second mate keeps me busy, but there's still time when I need to stay out of the way. That's a good way to do it."

"What's the second mate's job, then?" Tanyth asked, settling back in her chair and helping herself to the lees in the teapot.

"Watch standing and cargo handler, miss. I have to make sure the boxes and barrels in the hold get balanced properly and tied down so they don't go bouncing around down there while we're trying to sail about."

Tanyth thought for a moment about her odd dreams. "You know a lot about below decks then?"

"Oh, yes, mum. All of us do, really, but Ben takes care of the stuff above the deck and anything below is my duty, more or less."

"Are there any small critters aboard?"

"Critters, mum?" He looked confused by the change of direction. "You mean rats, mum?"

He didn't seem as upset as she thought he might be. "Dunno. Are there?"

He drew a deep breath and blew it out his nose, before leaning forward across the table. "I never said this, mum." He looked at her with an arched eyebrow.

"Said what, Mr. Jameson?"

"Captain Groves keeps a clean ship. Clean as they come and sometimes cleaner than is right, but he's a good skipper and knows his vessel, the waters he sails in, and the realities of our chosen profession as well as any man afloat."

"But?" she prompted.

"But he has a deathly aversion to vermin of the four-footed kind. Under no circumstances are there ever any rats on the *Zypheria's Call*, mum." He paused and laid one long finger along side his patrician nose and winked at her.

"Thank you, Mr. Jameson. I'm greatly relieved."

"Why d'you ask, mum?"

"I don't know, Mr. Jameson. Just thought I might have seen one and I'm greatly relieved that I was mistaken."

"The shadows on the decks, mum. They can be deceiving."

"That must have been it then, Mr. Jameson."

"I'm certain it was, mum." He paused for a moment and then looked at her a bit sideways. "Uh, mum?"

"Yes, Mr. Jameson?"

"If you ever think you don't see one in the future, would you let me know?"

"Of course, Mr. Jameson. It would be my pleasure."

He smiled. "Thank you, mum, and please, call me Scott."

She held her hand across the table. "Tanyth when we're ta home, Scott. Nice to make your acquaintance."

Introductions complete, Tanyth nodded at the bookshelf. "Now help me pick out somethin' to read. If I have to sit around all day tomorrow, I'll go mad."

Chapter 23
Sunrise, Sunset

Tanyth woke with the sun and found herself blinking at the wooden overhead while listening to the bell ring four times. She levered herself out of the enclosed bunk and managed to get her pants on without falling over. After a quick trip to the water closet, she returned to her cabin for her heavy, blue coat.

Rebecca, apparently accustomed to the bells, snored delicately in her bunk and Tanyth left her sleeping there while she went to find something to do.

The path to the cookhouse wasn't any where as difficult as she remembered. As promised, her feet found the deck easiest when she didn't think about it. The dense wool kept the wind off her torso so she didn't feel quite so exposed. Cook looked up in surprise when she opened the door and slipped into the warmest place on the ship.

"Mum! You're up early. You looking for a cuppa?"

"I am, Cook, but I'm lookin' for somethin' to do as well."

"Something to do, mum?"

"Yeah. You need a helper?"

"Well, I have help, mum. Usually there's a sailor crossed the bosun the wrong way or just somebody drew short straw."

"You got anybody who knows how to cook?"

He blinked. "Well, no, mum, but mostly it's just scullery work. Peeling vegetables and chopping onions."

She slipped her coat off and hung it on a peg by the door. "Put me to work then, Cook. I can't stand ta sit in that cabin another day."

"Mum? It's only the second day out."

Her fierce grin set him back a half step. "Now you know how desperate I am, Cook. Whatever you need doing, long's I can do it right here and help out. That's what I need."

He shrugged and said, "All right, mum, but if you get tired of it, you just lemme know. There's not so much to do, really, but I'm grateful for the company, even at that."

She clapped her hands together. "Right. Where do I start?"

He nodded to the hot water tank. "Wash your hands and grab a knife out of the block there. There's about half a hundred weight of potatoes need peeling."

It took her only a few minutes and a bit of instruction to figure out the process. A bucket of cold water on the deck, and a clever fold-out work surface defined her space. A burlap sack of potatoes provided what promised to be endless amusement. She propped herself against the bulkhead and let her hands and blade find the peel. Each fresh white tuber plopped into the bucket of water on the deck. Eventually she had so many peeled potatoes, water slopped out of the bucket and onto the decking.

"Here, here," Cook said. "Lemme fix that! No need to be making a shambles of my galley."

His idea of fixing it was to pour some of the water off into a fresh bucket, place the fresh bucket in place of the old, and scrape the small mountain of parings off her board and into a metal pail.

"There you go, mum. Fill that and we'll find ya something else to do."

The morning unwound with the regular dinging of the ship's bell and a parade of sailors through the small cookhouse. Breakfast turned out to be a queued up affair at seven bells. The sailors lined up outside and Cook ladled beans into a heavy crockery bowl for each hand. A basket of biscuits hung from a peg in the bulkhead and spoons stood in a mug. One at a time, the sailors entered the cookhouse, took the offered bowl, stuck a spoon in the bowl, grabbed a biscuit out of the basket, and picked up a full mug of tea off the sideboard. As each sailor left, the next took his place. Cook assigned Tanyth to line up a dozen mugs and fill them up from the big teapot he kept warm on the side of the stove. In less than five minutes, all dozen sailors had food and drink. They lined up on the deck outside, backs to the railing or the deckhouse. They spoke very little but ate with gusto and apparent good humor. When all the sailors had been through the line once, a couple had already lined up for a second helping. Cook ladled until the last person in line stepped up and Tanyth saw Rebecca holding out her hand for a bowl.

"G'mornin', miss," Cook said. "You feelin' a little more lively today, then?"

She smiled. "Yeah, thank you, Cook." She looked to Tanyth. "You seem to have found a good place to hide, mum."

"Not exactly hiding, but I found something I could help with. Keep my hands busy."

Rebecca nodded, helped herself to a biscuit and stepped outside to sit on the deck. At a quick glance, she blended right in with the crew. None of them seemed too concerned about sharing the deck with a woman, so Tanyth focused on what she was doing.

"How many beans do you make, Cook?" Tanyth asked once the door closed again.

"I use ten pounds of dried beans at a time, a pound of molasses and half a pound of hard sugar. Salt pork, dry mustard, and a couple onions." He grinned. "It lasts a couple days and I swear the second day's better'n the first."

"You bake beans every other day?"

"Aye, mum. And bread in between. Biscuits whenever I have a moment. They keep pretty well in the sea air and if we run into bad weather, dry biscuits smeared with cold beans is better'n an empty belly."

"Cold beans?"

"Aye, mum. If the seas get too big, we have to shut down cooking in here. Wouldn't do to get a fire loose in heavy weather. We take it real easy."

"Does that happen much?"

He sighed and ran a hand over the back of his neck. "Not so much, but almost a day or two every trip north. Coastal routes ain't so bad, mum. We can duck into a harbor most places. Out here there's nowhere to hide."

She cast her eyes around the windows, blue-green water on every side. "I see what you mean."

"Thought you might, mum."

Tanyth looked about and asked, "So, now what d'we do?"

Cook's twinkling grin never faded. "Now we clean up."

The sailors queued up with their dirty dishes, reaching into the cook shack to place them in the tray just inside the door.

Tanyth looked at the tray and then looked at the grinning Cook. She grinned back and started pushing up the sleeves of her pullover. "I know what has to happen with dirty dishes, Cook. Show me how we do it here."

He laughed a high-pitched laugh and hefted the full tray off the deck, placing it on the fold-out table that she'd spent so much time peeling potatoes on. A splash of hot water from the tank and a bit of cold from the butt went in on top of the dirty dishes and almost filled the tray.

"Wash fast, mum, and you'll be done before the rinse water cools."

Tanyth laughed and dug in with a will. She soon had clean crockery coming out of soapy water and into the bucket of hot rinse water at her feet.

Cook entertained her by singing bawdy songs while making a rich, meat and potato stew for lunch.

The cleanup took very little time. Not having to move about and having everything immediately at hand made Tanyth's job easy and she lost herself in the homely chore.

"Mum? You're makin' these brawny sailor lads look like pikers with this," Cook said as she dropped the last of the clean dishes into the still steaming bucket.

"What do I do with this, then?" she asked, pointing to the tray full of dirty water.

Cook shook his head. "Nothing, mum. Just a moment." He pulled out another bucket and neatly upended the tray into it, pouring out all the slop water and even taking a moment to rinse the tray with fresh, clean water from the tank behind the stove. With a nod and a wink, he put the tray back beside the door and stuck his head out. "Hoy, Scooter!"

The young sailor popped into the cookhouse. "Aye, Cook?"

"Slop water." Cook pointed to the bucket.

Scooter grinned and hooked the bail with one skinny hand and disappeared out the door. He was back almost before Tanyth could blink and dropped the empty bucket at Cook's feet. Cook flipped a small, paper wrapped object through the air. Scooter caught it on the fly. "Thanks, Cook."

"Thank you, Scooter."

The young man nodded once to Tanyth and disappeared from the cookhouse almost as fast as he'd appeared.

"Hard candies," Cook said. "Any time I need something lugged to the rail, I poke the nearest sailor. He does it for me and gets a candy in return."

Tanyth laughed. "Good system."

"You want one, mum?" Cook produced another candy from his apron pocket and held it up. "You more'n earned it."

She shook her head. "Thanks, no. I'm not much for candies. Never got the habit."

"Anytime, mum." He put it back in his apron. "They're peppermints. Good for settlin' the stomach when things gets a bit bouncy."

"I'll remember." She looked around the cookhouse. "What's next?"

Cook shook his head. "Now I just stir the pot and wait for lunch, mum. You've worked me out of chores for now."

The bell rang twice.

"That's mid-morning, mum. Couple hours left until lunch. You'll have to entertain yourself until then."

"Thank you, Cook. I don't remember the last time I enjoyed chores more."

"Any time, mum." He reached for the teapot. "You want to take a cup back to your compartment?"

She shook her head. "I think I'll go lay in my bunk and read. I borrowed a book from the captain's library."

"Come back about seven bells, if you've a mind to, mum, but I'll be just lounging about the cookhouse until then."

Tanyth lifted the heavy coat off the peg and wrapped it

around her for the short walk to her cubby. She felt proud of herself for not stumbling or hesitating on her march across the deck. The smoke from the cookhouse chimney mingled with the clean air and tar to fill her head.

When she stepped into the cramped room, she found Rebecca sitting on the deck with the contents of her pack spread about. The young woman looked up with a smile.

"There you are, my dear. I'm surprised you're not hanging off the rigging somewhere," Tanyth said with a grin.

Rebecca grinned. "Prob'ly will be soon enough. Scooter'll fetch me for the next chore. We'll be swabbing the decks this afternoon."

"Sounds like fun," Tanyth said with a trace of sarcasm.

Rebecca giggled. "It is in a way, mum. I'm low man—well, I suppose low woman—on the chain o' command so I get to do the stuff that I don't need to know much about. Mostly it's do what I'm told and hold on."

"Hold on?"

"Aye, mum. One hand for the ship, one hand for me. I'm supposed ta always have the one for me wrapped around somethin' solid when I'm up there." She cast her eyes upwards.

"Sounds like good advice. I s'pect I'd have trouble lettin' go with one if 't were me."

Rebecca shrugged and rolled up a lightweight shirt, stowing it in the growing pile in her pack. "There's so much happenin', mum. It's hard to find time to be scared." She glanced up from under lowered brows. "And it's beautiful up there. Even in the dark, mum."

"You're climbin' the riggin' in the dark?"

"Well, somebody has to take in the sails or let 'em out. Don't happen by magic."

Tanyth nodded and smiled. "I s'pose not." She surveyed the deck. "What's all this then?"

"Stayin' busy, mum."

"Repackin' looks like."

Rebecca nodded. "Makin' sure I know what's here and where it's stowed. Some of them mornin's on the road we didn't pack that good."

Tanyth nodded. "I should go through mine." In a moment

she'd pulled her own pack from the cupboard and squatted on the deck beside Rebecca.

"You're carryin' a lot more'n me, mum." Rebecca cast an eye at the piles of goods in addition to the clothing that came out of Tanyth's pack. "You want me to share some of that?"

Tanyth shook her head. "I'm used to it." The thought of the heavy pack made her flex her shoulders. "Or I was. I will be again."

She pulled out the heavy, canvas-wrapped bundle of papers on the bottom and weighed it in her hand.

Rebecca caught the movement. "I still say that's a heavy brick to lug around, mum."

Tanyth nodded. "It's the most important thing in my pack."

"What'll you do with it, mum?"

Tanyth shook her head. "I'll have to sort it all out one of these days. I keep sayin' I'll do that, but I keep puttin' it off. P'rhaps after I visit Mother Pinecrest I'll finally be able to settle down and start organizin'."

"Why not now, mum?" Rebecca asked.

"What? Here?"

Rebecca gave a small shrug. "What else you gonna do?"

Tanyth considered the bundle in her hand and looked back at the eager young face. "We've got a few days, don't we?"

Rebecca nodded. "How long you think it'll take?"

"There's a lot there. Could take a while."

"Well, sooner started, sooner done." Rebecca said.

Tanyth dropped the bundle into Rebecca's waiting hand. "Be gentle with the dried leaves. They're probably a mite brittle."

"What? You want me to sort it?"

Tanyth rolled one shoulder in a half shrug and almost took the package back. "Have a look. See if you see anything interestin' in it. Lemme know what you find."

"What'll you do, mum?"

Tanyth grinned and pulled herself up from the deck with a hand wrapped around the lip of her bunk. "I'm gonna take a nap."

Rebecca giggled and Tanyth clambered onto the mattress.

She lay back and let the gentle movement of the ship rock her. She felt her eyes closing. With nothing more pressing to take up her time, she surrendered and let the darkness fill her.

$$\mathrm{D}\mathrm{O}\mathrm{C}$$

The babies slept in a pile and she needed to get out to find some food. She pattered through the narrow confines, avoiding the smelly water down below and used her clever sharp claws to pull her body out into the Big Place. She stopped and looked, testing the air with her nose. Listening for the voices of the others. There were many others. Some big, some small. Most dangerous to her, and she had babies to tend.

The male was there, sniffing at her, but there was nothing for him yet. Her time would come again before long but now she needed to find food, or something else to pad her nest, to make it warm for her and the babies. She scampered down between the big things and rooted along the edges of the Big Place. The sharp edges sometimes broke open and left cracks that she could smell and sometimes crawl in. Often she found nest things or food. She found a bit of apple behind one of the sharp edges, brown and delicious. She ate it there and kept moving.

A sharp edge clicked and she froze. She stilled even her whiskers and waited to see. There were sometimes things hiding here. Things that smelled sharp. Something hard and not food. She didn't know what the click was and that was dangerous.

The sharp edge clicked again.

Nothing happened for a long time but she stayed still. Waiting. Watching without moving her eyes. Testing the air with her nose.

There was a smell there, just on the edge of her nose. A sharp smell.

The sharp edge clicked again and still nothing happened.

She cast about looking for others, but there were no others. Nothing moved in the Big Place. The sharp edge with the click sound drew her and it clicked again. She stayed still, eyes bright in the dark and sniff, sniff, sniffing. There was something there in the sharp edge. Something with the click.

It had a sharp smell, but also the smell of fuzzy things that she could shred for her nest.

Maybe there was a way in, she sniffed around the bottom of the sharp edge and found a hole. Then another hole. And another. Too small to enter, but the smell came from the holes. Perhaps she could make the holes bigger. Big enough to enter.

The sharp edge clicked again, but she barely stopped to notice. Whatever it was, it clicked. It didn't move. Just clicked. There were no others, although the smell was there. The hard smell. The sharp smell.

She used her teeth on the edge of the hole and the wood gave a bit. She bit some more and chewed the splintery edge. Yes, she could make the hole bigger. Maybe big enough to get in. Her nose fit in the hole and part of her head, but not enough to see. She smelled and heard it click again. With her nose in the hole she felt warm, even warmer than her nest. Maybe she could make a new nest where it was warmer. She pulled her nose out of the hole and peered in to see if perhaps others hid inside, waiting for her to make the hole bigger. All she saw was a soft light, barely enough to see in the dimness of the Big Place.

She chewed and worried a bit but would have to come back. The babies would waken soon and she'd need to feed them. They would tickle her and she would groom them. She scampered back into the narrow place and pattered into the nest. Only the tip of her tail touched the smelly water and she groomed it clean before curling up with her babies.

☽○☾

The dinging of the ship's bell lifted Tanyth out of sleep and she lay there on the bedroll thinking about the life of a rat living in the bilges. She sighed. The unhurried life of a rat with her naked babies between the ribs of the ship left her feeling sleepy again. She rolled over, pulling the top of her bed roll onto her so she could be warm and cozy in her own nest.

"Rats," she muttered. "Rats and ravens. What's next? Fish in the sea?"

CHAPTER 24
A BIT OF A BLOW

On the fourth night out of Kleesport, Tanyth awoke to find herself tumbled in a corner of her bunk in the dark. The ship's even, rocking-horse movement had turned into a thrashing corkscrew that found her holding on to the edge of her bunk, legs splayed to keep from rolling while the strength of her arm was all that kept her from sliding out to land in a heap on the deck. The ship continued to rock up and down, but the up seemed to go on almost forever. When it came down, it came down hard and shuddered. She heard shouts and the shuffling of booted feet above her head, but she didn't dare move.

"You all right, mum?" Rebecca's voice sounded small and scared in the darkness and the noise.

"Just hangin' on, my dear. I'm glad you're not out in it."

"I was, mum, then when it started to get too rough on deck, Mr. Groves sent most of the crew below. There's just a small scrap of sail up there now so we'll get called back when it's time to raise more sails."

"And in the meantime?" Tanyth asked.

"Hang on, I guess, mum."

Tanyth laughed and they settled down to ride out the storm.

Through it all, every so often she'd hear the ding-ding of the bell. She heard two bells but in the darkness had no idea what time it might really be. Her chest pounded and she closed her eyes to the possibility that the ship might sink, taking them all down. When she did, the memory of a dream

239

long past surfaced behind her eyes. She saw a vision where she stood in the bow of a northbound vessel, the sun shining in a gorgeous morning and the smudge of land in the distance.

"Mother, what are you doin'?" she muttered.

"What's that, mum?" Rebecca asked in the darkness.

"Just mutterin', my dear. Nothin' important."

After an impossibly long time she heard four bells but didn't remember hearing three. Either the sound of the storm drowned it out, or the pounding of fear in her ears blocked the sound.

Her arm grew tired of holding and she used the corkscrew motion of the ship to twist around and brace her legs against the lip, pressing her back against the solid wall of her bunk. She no sooner congratulated herself on the achievement than the ship crashed down hard again and she felt the it shudder through the very bones of her spine.

"This is much better, I'n't it, you old fool," she muttered.

"I wish you'd speak up, mum."

"Nothin' of any account to say, my dear. Just an old woman mutterin'."

"Mutter louder, please?"

She listened and decided that the storm was not nearly as loud or raucous as she thought.

The corkscrew seemed to abate some and the long rides up didn't end in such a jarring crash on the way down. She dared not hope that the end of the storm might be getting closer, but then, why wouldn't it. Storms on land seldom blew with violence for very long. Certainly slow rains and long drizzles occasionally plagued a spot, but heavy winds and strong rains tended to blow themselves out fairly quickly ashore.

She heard the ship's bell ring five times and by the time it rang six, she was certain the worst was over. The hammering of her heart had likewise subsided. She was surprised to find herself quite calm, even resigned. It was as if her terror burned through her and left her weak and shaken, but otherwise, simply waiting for whatever might come.

After a time, the worst of the movement calmed. The ship still climbed too high and smashed down too far, but the terrible shuddering only happened once in a while and the corkscrew motion faded to a shadow of its original force. She found she could stretch out on her bunk and hardly slide around at all on her bed roll.

By the time she heard seven bells, she was nearly calm enough to fall asleep again. The occasional shudders and crashes jarred her, but only as a loud conversation might, and not with the soul shearing terror of the full storm. At length she heard the companionway door slam with a bang and then boots in the passage outside her door.

"Mum?" Mr. Groves' voice came to her through the panel. "Mum? Are you all right?"

She wrapped herself in her bedroll and called, "Come in, Mr. Groves."

The door opened and Mr. Groves stuck his head in. He wore no hat and his dark hair lay plastered to his skull. His torso seemed wrapped in some bright, glossy poncho and his face split in a jubilant smile, bright teeth flashing in the dimness.

"We had a bit of fun, mum, but we're fine."

Tanyth barked a laugh. "You call that a bit of fun?"

Groves shrugged a shoulder. "It blew up suddenly, but it was only a small squall. Nothing to be concerned about. Call's a sound ship and we've sailed through many much worse. Sorry, we didn't get to warn you, mum. Are you quite all right?"

"Scared the stuffing out of us, but other than that, we're fine, Mr. Groves."

"Did you get tossed out of your bunk?"

"No, Mr. Groves. I got a good hold and wouldn't let go."

"Good for you, mum. We'll have heavy seas for a bit yet, but it should calm down in a few bells. The glass is already rising and we're out of the worst of it."

"I'll take your word for it, Mr. Groves."

He laughed. "Sorry, mum. Just hold on a bit longer. You can probably go back to sleep if you like."

"What time is it, Mr. Groves? Does Cook need a hand in the deckhouse?"

"Nearly noon, mum, but the galley's secured for now. It's too wet and wooly out there to do more than curl up and stay warm and dry. Cook is in his hammock, I wager. We'll have a hot meal for dinner, but we can get you some cold beans and biscuits if you're hungry, mum. Can we bring you something?"

At the thought, her stomach threatened to do a somersault without her. She found herself suddenly awash in sweat. "I think I'll just lie here and try to sleep, Mr. Groves. Thank you."

"Rebecca? You're wanted on deck," Groves said.

Rebecca held up a hand, pale in the dim light. "I'll be right there."

"Report to the bosun when you get up there."

"Aye, aye, sir."

He gave Tanyth another broad smile. "Hold on for a little while longer. This one's almost over. You can see it's already getting lighter. The sun will be out in another bell."

As soon as he mentioned it, the light from the small port brightened almost perceptibly and Tanyth found she could see him quite a bit more clearly than when he'd first opened her door.

"Thank you, again, Mr. Groves."

He waved and closed the door with a careful slam to set the latch.

Rebecca levered herself out of her bunk and into her trousers, putting on a couple of cotton shirts and her jersey over it all. She took a moment to take a dab of liniment and rub it around on her hands before heading for the deck. "See you in a bit, mum," she called and closed the door behind her.

Tanyth stretched her neck out to get a glimpse out the port and immediately wished she hadn't. Ugly black clouds stretched to the horizon and every so often the view out the window itself was obscured by foaming, rushing, gray water.

"All-Mother, preserve us," she grumbled. "A bit of fun, he calls it. A bit of fun." She sighed and shook her head, but her eyes closed. She found that, yes, she could go back to sleep.

$$\text{)O(}$$

Tanyth's stomach woke her, insisting that it was time for a little something to go in it. She felt muzzy and a bit sore.

Wrestling with the ship for a few hours had left her muscles feeling hard used. "You're gettin' soft," she muttered and crawled out of the cozy bunk.

Rebecca's bunk was empty, but her coat and boots were missing. Tanyth figured to find her on deck.

She pulled on a pair of trousers and added an extra pullover before shrugging into her blue coat and making her way into the open air. The ship bobbed a bit more forcefully than she was used to, but a bit of extra care with flexed knees seemed to work just fine and she pushed into the cookhouse without incident.

Cook looked up with a nod. "You weathered the blow all right, mum?"

"Not somethin' I wanna wake up to every day, Cook, but I seem to be alive."

Cook's eyes twinkled and he nodded. "Wait'll we get a big blow, mum."

She shook her head and propped herself in the corner. "Anythin' I can do to help?"

He shrugged. "At the moment, I'm just trying to get the stove hot enough to cook with. Everybody's cold, tired, and hungry. They'll be looking for something filling and hot for their dinners. Stove'll be hot enough in another bell. I'm thinkin' a nice stew with a spicy broth. Should be just enough time to cook if you care to peel me some roots."

She slipped out of the coat and hung it on her customary peg. "Sounds fine, Cook, and I'd take a mug of tea if you had it."

He placed his hand on the side of the teakettle. "Next one still warmin' up, mum, but shouldn't be too long now." He leaned down and opened the fire door to peer in. He grunted and closed the door again. "It'll be hot enough when it gets there, but it takes a while to get a good bed of coals laid down."

"All right then," Tanyth said and rolled up her sleeves, pulling open the folding worktable as she did so. She fetched a bucket and put a couple of inches of water in the bottom. "Bring on the vegetables, Cook," she said, pulling a paring knife from the block. "I'm ready for 'em."

He grinned and wrestled half a bag of potatoes from the ready pantry. "A couple dozen of these, if you please, mum. I'll find you some carrots to do after that."

Tanyth dug into the potatoes and lost herself in the mundane exercise. Cook poured her tea when it was ready and a steady parade of sailors came to the door to take a cup of tea, or a biscuit, or both. When she shifted over to carrots, Cook took a pot of fresh tea and grabbed a fistful of mugs through their sturdy handles.

"I'll be right back, mum. I need to go visit the bridge and see if the captain needs some tea."

She saluted with the paring knife and kept on peeling. Three sailors came to the door while Cook was gone and accepted mugs from her with grateful smiles. All of them looked wet, cold, and tired, but every one smiled and offered a word of thanks.

Cook returned with the pot and no mugs after a bit. "All quiet, mum?"

"I handed out some tea and I've got these carrots almost done." She paused to survey the pile of unpeeled carrots. "Another few minutes. You got anything else after that?"

Cook's head swiveled in a methodical survey of the galley. Tanyth could practically see him checking off things in his mind. "I need to get the stew on and then make some biscuits, mum. A hot broth and a bit of bread will get this lot through the night. Tomorrow I can give 'em some sweetened oatmeal for breakfast and baked beans for dinner."

"I can make biscuits. If that'll help you any."

"Well, mum, that's probably—" Two bells rang and Cooks eyebrows shot up. "Thank you, mum. If you don't mind? I can get this stew simmerin' if you can make me a sheet of biscuits to go into the oven. It's probably hot enough by now." He leaned down and checked the firebox, throwing in another stick for good measure. He stood, dusting his hands together. "Aye, mum, that'd be right helpful."

He set her up on his sideboard with a huge bowl, a half barrel of flour and the rest of the fixings for biscuits. While she mixed and measured, he started browning some meat in the bottom of a caldron-sized soup kettle. They worked together, sometimes bumping hips in the confined galley, both so engrossed in their individual tasks they barely noticed.

"Tight space," Cook muttered once. "Sorry, mum."

She bumped his hip on purpose. "I've worked in tighter spaces, Cook. We got sailors to feed." She offered him a friendly grin and he laughed and set about throwing spices and redolent herbs into the stew pot.

By the time she had the large sheet pan filled with biscuit rounds, he had a pot of stew bubbling on the back of the stove. Just the aroma coming off the meat-and-vegetable rich broth warmed Tanyth as she stood there. Cook grabbed a towel and pulled open the oven door so Tanyth could slide the large tray in. He slammed it shut and checked the firebox one more time.

Three bells rang out across the ship.

Cook grinned. "Perfect timing, mum. The stew should be ready and the biscuits fresh from the oven at the next bell." He cocked his head and asked, "You'll be dining with the skipper again, mum?"

"Plenty of time to put on a ball gown and get there, Cook." Her mouth twisted into a wry grin.

He barked a couple of sharp laughs. "True. Not like you've a long way to go."

"And I've got a limited number of frills in my closet just now," she added.

"Well, thank you for the help, mum. That woulda been tight to do on my own."

"Thank you for keepin' me entertained for an hour or two, Cook." She pulled her coat down off the peg and slipped it on. "I best get back and get ready for dinner." She took another deep breath of the wholesome aromas filling the cookhouse. "Hope I can wait that long. My stomach feels like it hasn't been fed this week."

"Take a cuppa tea with you, mum. It'll keep your belly busy 'til reinforcements arrive."

She took one of the crockery mugs and he poured her a careful measure from the big pot at the back of the stove. The hot tea warmed the china and she held it up to her chin, letting the warm, moist air drift across her nose and face. A small sip felt good going down and she took another before offering Cook a small toast. She made her way back to her cabin without spilling the tea and found a place to rest the cup while she stripped off the heavy coat and hung it on its peg.

She found Rebecca carefully paging through the bundle of papers. The young woman smiled up as Tanyth turned to her.

"What ya findin'?" Tanyth asked.

"Lots of notes about herbs and such. A few leaves so far."

"Borin'?"

Rebecca considered the pile and took so long to answer that Tanyth laughed.

Rebecca colored. "Not borin', mum. Just—I never read anything like this. Notes about this or that. Some of these herbs I never heard of."

Tanyth shrugged. "That's why I been collectin' 'em."

The cabin felt cool to her, after the overheated cookhouse, so Tanyth dug into her pack and pulled out a heavy sweater. She tugged it down to her hips and felt the extra warmth almost immediately.

"Well, you're no basket of fruit, old heart, but at least you're warm," she muttered.

"Beg pardon, mum?" Rebecca asked.

Tanyth shook her head. "I'm just mumblin' to myself again, my dear. Pay me no mind. If I'm talkin' to ya, you'll know."

Rebecca grinned and held up a page. "Who's Mabel Elderberry?"

Tanyth tilted her head to look at the page. "That's the last woman I stayed with before I came to Ravenwood. Spent all that winter workin' with her on ointments and salves. You can prob'ly still smell the beeswax." Tanyth held the paper up to her nose, catching just the faintest whiff of sweetness from the page. She held it out for Rebecca to sniff.

Grinning Rebecca closed her eyes and took a long breath through her nose. "Just barely," she said.

Tanyth read the page, recognizing a recipe for the wintergreen salve that Mother Elderberry sold at market.

"What's that for, then?" Rebecca asked, nodding at the page.

Tanyth smiled. "Mostly whatever ails ya. Mother Elderberry sold a lot of it and some of the elders said it helped .their arthritis a bit, others claimed it healed blisters."

"And did it, mum?"

Tanyth gazed at the page and pictured the round, smiling face of Mabel Elderberry, skin flushed from stirring a boiling pot and her gold-green eyes dancing in the morning light of her tiny cottage. Tanyth gave a shrug. "Prob'ly didn't hurt, but mostly, it smelled good."

Rebecca laughed just as somebody rapped on their door. "Miss? Bosun says you're wanted on deck."

"Be right there, Scooter," she called and began bundling up the papers.

"I'll deal with this, my dear," Tanyth said and made little shooing motions with her fingers. "Duty calls."

Rebecca flashed a smile in thanks and disappeared through the door. Tanyth heard her footfalls pounding up the companionway and onto the deck.

She smiled and slowly gathered the bits of her life back into a neat bundle, letting her fingers trace the occasional drawing or caress a dried leaf.

At four bells she presented herself at the captain's cabin for their nightly meal.

"Come in, mum. Come in." Captain Groves answered her knock almost before she made it.

He stood when she entered. Tanyth thought he looked a bit gray in the lantern light. He waved her into a chair on his right hand. "Sit, mum. Please. I'm too tired to stand on much ceremony just now."

Jameson slipped in and latched the door behind him. "Sorry I'm late, Skipper. Evening, mum."

"Not an issue, Mr. Jameson. Come in, sit down."

Tanyth took her seat and found herself grateful for the chair. While she seldom sat on chairs, even when ashore, the shipboard habit of standing up or lying down with little in between tired her. Apparently the captain found it comforting as well. He let out a long sigh before turning to Tanyth.

"So, tell me. How'd you fare in our little blow?" Tired lines creased his face, but he managed to smile and his eyes held more life than she felt.

"I was a bit frightened for a time, Captain, but soon discovered that holdin' on for dear life takes up a great deal of attention," Tanyth said with a grin.

The two men laughed with her just as Cook knocked on the door with his cheery, "Dinner!"

"Come in, Cook! What have you for us tonight?" the captain said. "I'm hungry enough for two men, and I think they're fighting over who gets to eat first."

Cook brought in a large china tureen of soup and Scooter carried a towel-covered basket and a pile of crockery. "It's a bit of savory stew, Captain. It should warm you nicely, and Mother Fairport here helped me with the biscuits this afternoon. She'd make a fine addition to the crew, if you don't mind my sayin' so, mum."

"Thank you, Cook, but I think I might have trouble if I had to sleep in a hammock," Tanyth said.

"Oh, I don't know, mum. Hammock's not so bad once you get in. Quite comfy as a matter of fact."

Jameson eyed Scooter and said, "Getting out is sometimes an issue, I understand, mum."

Scooter colored, but Jameson smiled.

"Thank you, Cook," the captain said. "This looks—and smells—divine! Just what I needed."

"Will there be anything else, Captain?"

The captain looked around the table and said, "Is there a bit of tea?"

Cook jumped in realization. "Oh, beg pardon, Captain. I meant to have one of the lads bring it. I got so taken with Mother Fairport's biscuits, I forgot. I'll have Scooter bring that right over, sir."

The captain nodded to Scooter and Cook. "My thanks to both of you."

They scurried out and closed the door.

"You made the biscuits, mum?" Jameson had the basket and snaked out a biscuit so warm it still steamed, before handing the basket on to the captain.

"Nothing to it, really, Mr. Jameson. Been doing it off and on for a goodly spell." She accepted the basket from the captain who had found a biscuit of his own. "First time I ever made 'em at sea, but a biscuit is a biscuit."

The men laughed and the captain started ladling out the rich stew. "Cook tells me you've been rather busy in the cookhouse this trip, mum," he said, handing her a full bowl.

"It helps pass the time, and Cook is certainly agreeable company."

Jameson snorted, "Well, he's talkative enough, that's so."

"He has his quiet moments, Mr. Jameson."

"And rather a colorful vocabulary, eh, mum?" the captain asked.

"Not as bad as some drovers I've known, Captain, but he can turn a phrase until it's dizzy."

"Aye," the captain agreed, "and his listeners as well."

Scooter returned with the teapot and mugs. "Here you are, Captain. Sorry for the delay."

"Fresh tea is worth the wait, my mother used to say," the captain said with a grin. "Of course, I was mostly interested in the sandwiches that went with the tea in those days."

Scooter grinned, and even Jameson relaxed enough to smile in the captain's presence.

"Anything else, sir?" the sailor asked.

The captain looked across the table and at each of his dining companions in turn. "No, thank you, Scooter. I think we're ready to get underway here now."

"Very good, sir. Enjoy your meal." The sailor started out the door, but the captain called him before it closed.

"Oh, Scooter?"

"Yes, Captain?" He stuck his head back around the door.

"Tell Cook I said he should give you two."

Scooter's grin lit up the passageway and he nodded. "Aye, aye, Captain. Two, it is."

The captain chuckled and tucked into the spicy stew with gusto. The stew was hot from the stove and the spices that Cook used brought the heat level up so that Tanyth gasped and waved a hand.

"A bit warm, it is, mum?" the captain asked.

"A bit, Captain, but very good."

"You'll appreciate the warmth, the further we go north, I suspect."

With that warning, Tanyth tried another small bite and enjoyed it with more temperance than temperature. "Did the storm blow us off course?"

The captain shrugged. "Can't tell yet, mum. It was too rough and too cloudy to get a good reading at noon today. We'll know better tomorrow."

"The wind was from a good quarter, and the strength of it gave us quite a kick," Mr. Jameson said, "But we won't know until we can get a fix whether we were going in the right direction or not. Even a small change in course can add up to a large error at the end of a voyage."

"There's a lot of time yet, mum, and nothing out here to run into." The captain said with a cheerful grin. "With a little luck and some clear sky, we'll know soon enough."

Tanyth nodded, although she really didn't understand how they knew where they were in the middle of the ocean. The only thing to see was water, the ship, and the occasional bird.

They finished the tureen of soup, hot and spicy though it was, and the captain and Jameson both lavished praise on the biscuits. "Anytime you want to make biscuits, mum, you just tell Cook to stand back," the captain said, slathering butter on the last biscuit in the basket.

Even Jameson gave her a wink and a nod across the table.

Dinner broke up at six bells and the captain stood while Jameson escorted Tanyth back to her room.

When they got there, Tanyth placed a hand on Jameson's arm. "A moment, if you have it, Scott?"

"Yes, mum?"

"If I understand, fire's a real danger here."

"Mum, you're afloat in a craft made of wood and cloth and it's coated in tar to keep the water out. There are few things in this world more likely to go up in flame than a sailing ship, even though we're surrounded by water." He looked at her curiously. "Why? Something concerning you about fire?"

She bit her lip and gave a little shrug. "Would somebody

ship a cargo that included a lantern?"

Jameson gave his head a shake as if to rattle something loose. "A lantern, mum? Of course. People ship lanterns all the time."

"Lighted ones?"

Jameson stood very still. Tanyth could almost see the thoughts swirling in his head. "I don't even know how you'd ship a lighted lantern, mum."

"In a crate."

"It wouldn't burn, mum. The air would run out and the flame would smother if the lamp oil didn't run out first. Or the wick burn down."

"So, if there was a lighted lamp in a crate, that would be odd?"

"I'd say all but impossible, mum."

Tanyth frowned and tried to remember the dreams. It had been a few days since the last one, but the bumpy ride had her wondering what else might have jarred loose in the ship.

"What if there was holes in the crate?"

"Holes, mum? You mean like air holes?"

She nodded. "Along the bottom." She held up her fingers in a ring about the size of a gold crown. "That big."

Jameson looked at her and scrubbed the back of his neck with a hand. "Mum? You're asking some pretty hard questions and I don't like the way they're going. You know something you're not telling?"

She shrugged. "I don't know, Scott. I get these dreams sometimes. I see things in 'em."

He gave her a small nod. "Go on, mum."

"Sometimes those things are true."

Jameson blinked. "Ah, mum? That's hard to believe, you'll pardon my saying so."

She barked a bitter laugh. "Tell me about it. I'm the one's havin' these dreams and I ain't any too happy about it myself."

"All right, mum. You had a dream about a lantern in a crate?"

"Somethin' like that, yeah. A crate in the hold with something warm in it and a faint light."

"You dreamed about a crate in our hold?"

She nodded.

"And it's warm inside and has a faint light in it."

"Sounds mad, I know," she said. "Even to me."

"And it has holes in it?"

She nodded again. "At least three of 'em. Along the bottom edge."

Jameson's face took on a look of sympathy. "Mum, are you sure you didn't get tossed out of your bunk? Maybe bang your head?"

Tanyth smiled at him. "Not really, no. But I don't have any bumps or sore spots on my noggin. I didn't find any dents in the deck in here."

"But you think maybe somebody's shipped a lit lantern in a packing crate, and it's in our hold."

She shrugged. "I can't think of what else it might be. It's a faint light, and it's warmer inside the crate than out. There's a sharp smell, like lamp oil."

"You smelled lamp oil in your dream, mum?"

"Something like it."

"Anything else, mum?"

She couldn't tell if Jameson believed her or was just seeing how far she'd go with the story.

"Well, there was one more thing."

"I hesitate to ask, mum."

She smirked. "I can't say as I blame you." She paused for a moment then said, "It clicked."

"It clicked?"

"Yeah, like metal on metal. A kind of click happened kinda regular—slow. Very slow, but regular."

"I see, mum." He looked at her out of the corner of his eyes. "And when did you say you had this dream?"

"First time I saw the crate was a couple of days ago."

"And you're just bringing it up now?"

"Well, it's not the kinda thing an old lady like me can really just up and say, now is it?"

He frowned and pursed his lips in thought. "Good point, mum. It does sound a bit mad."

"I'm not mad." She must have said it with a bit more

feeling than she intended because Jameson stepped back a half step.

"I didn't say you were, mum. Just that it sounds mad."

She huffed a laugh. "You have no idea how it sounds to me."

"You have these dreams often?"

Tanyth gave a small shrug and looked the young man in the eye. "I had a few of them back at Ravenwood, but haven't had many since. Only since comin' aboard I've had two or three."

"Really, mum?" Jameson cocked his head. "They always about cargo?"

She shook her head.

"What else have you seen?"

She gave him a little smile. "You know them critters that the captain says we have none of?"

Jameson's eyes grew wide.

"Yeah. They're quite fond of the big open place below deck. One of them found an apple core down there. They like to find things to shred for their nests there, but they're careful not to come out when there's people there. Or other things that can hurt them."

Jameson stood still as an iron rod. His eyes fixed on Tanyth in something akin to horror.

She sighed. "I'm sorry, Scott. I know it sounds like I'm just bein' a foolish old woman, but I've had these kinds of dreams before. I don't understand why I'm havin' them now but—"

"No, mum. You don't understand."

She stopped and looked up at him.

"While we were loading the last of the stores aboard for Cook, we loaded a barrel of apples. He gave us all an apple for our trouble. He does that."

She nodded. "The candies. I've seen 'em."

"We all sat around the hatch coaming and ate our apples, but Ferguson dropped his. It bounced into the hold and rolled behind one of the crates."

Tanyth shrugged. "Maybe it's just a dream, but can you go look? See if there's something in the hold?"

He shook his head. "It's not that simple, mum. The hold is sealed. We'd need the captain's permission to get in there. I'd need help just to get the hatch cover off."

"And I could be mad."

"No, mum. You're not mad."

"You sound surer than I am."

He chuckled. "Maybe I do." He bit his lip in thought and gave Tanyth a glance. "Lemme see what I can do, mum. That was a good blow, maybe I can get the captain to let me check the cargo during the day tomorrow if it's calm enough."

"What if it's not calm?"

"We can't take the hatch cover off."

"Why's that?"

"Because if we take a big breaker across the bow, the water could fill up the hold and we'd go straight to the bottom."

Tanyth shuddered at the thought.

He nodded and reached over to pat her arm. "I'll think of something, mum. Don't worry."

"Thank you," she said.

"If you know any prayers, this would be the time to say 'em, mum." He knuckled his forehead and nodded once. "Good night, mum."

Tanyth crawled into her bunk and pulled the covers over her. The wheel of the year was turning toward summer, but the temperature felt colder the longer she was on the ship.

"Just bein' an old woman," she muttered and wondered if she knew a prayer for calm weather.

The temperature in the bunk seemed to shoot up and Tanyth found herself fanning the covers to release some of the heat her body generated. She sighed. "Ya had to pick now for your own private heat wave did ya?" she grumbled.

Eventually the spell passed and she wrapped the bedroll around her to capture some of the heat against the night chill.

Above her the bell rang eight times and she heard Rebecca returning from her stint on deck as she drifted off to sleep.

☽○☾

The horrible shaking and banging was over and the babies slept. She needed to find food to keep them going. She pattered out to explore. Sometimes after a shake like that, the sharp edges in the Big Place fell over and broke. Sometimes they held things for the nest, and she could find some new warm things to bring home.

Sometimes there was food. One time there was so much food that she ate until she could barely crawl back into the nest.

She pattered out of her nest and through the narrow part, up out of the hole. The male sniffed her again, but she ignored him. It wasn't her time. She watched the Big Place. It was still dark, still dim, but enough light came through the cracks for her to see. Some things were wet. A bit of water sloshed in the bottom, but she stood on top of the sharp edges and scurried along. Nothing moved. No others showed themselves.

An odor came to her, then. Food, it was, and nearby, but not in the Big Place. She followed her nose and slipped through a wet crack to the Small Place. The Small Place was more dangerous because there were others there more often. The Big Ones came there. They yelled at her and threw things and sometimes left metal with things that were good to eat but dangerous to touch.

She stayed very still. Smelling the food and sniffing for the others. There was food, but the scent was so strong she didn't smell anything else. She cast about in the dark, looking for the food. She found a round edge laying on its side. Food spilled from the top and across the ground. Big food. Enough for her and her babies for a very long time. She started nibbling at the hard, crunchy food. It tasted good and it filled her belly quickly. She ate her fill and then a little more, then crawled back through the wet crack to the Big Place.

The strange sharp edge was there. She waited and listened and heard it click. She remembered the click and scurried over to see. The holes in the bottom were there, but a little soggy now from the water that leaked in and sloshed. She stood in the damp and sniffed in the holes. The sharp smell was still there and it was still warm. The warm felt good on her face and her wet fur. She worked some more on the holes. A few more times and she'd have a hole big enough to crawl in. She'd see what made the light and what made the sharp smell. As she chewed, the thing clicked over and over.

Once she heard the ding-ding sound, but she often heard that. It didn't mean anything. She stopped anyway and looked about. Sometimes the others snuck up on her and yelled or threw things at her and she didn't like that. She didn't see anybody and went back to chewing the wood.

Eventually she had to give up. Her babies would wake and want their food. If she didn't feed them and they made too much noise, the male might eat them. She wanted to feed them.

She scurried back to the hole and found the male and one of her sisters in the hole. He wasn't sniffing her, but mounting her. It was her time. She slipped by them and down into the nest. Her full belly and her chewing made her tired. It would be good to be with her babies and sleep.

Chapter 25
The Dream Time

Tanyth awoke with the sun. The ship still rode on heavy rollers, but at least the corkscrew movement hadn't come back. Rebecca lay curled under her covers, just a bit of her brown hair showing above the blanket. Tanyth clambered out of her bunk and into her clothing, heading for the cookhouse. The sun had barely cleared the horizon and she heard four bells ring out loud and clear as she crossed the bit of open deck between the companionway and the deckhouse door.

"Well, good morning, mum," Cook greeted her with a look of surprise. "You're up and moving early enough this morning."

She hung her coat on the peg and pulled up her sleeves. "Need my tea, I think." A yawn caught her and she blinked in helpless surprise.

"Did you not sleep well, mum?" Cook asked, handing her a hot mug.

"I thought I did, but I woke up and just had to move." She shrugged and sipped, blowing a bit across the top of the mug before taking a careful taste. "Now, I'm up, I'm feelin' groggy and wonderin' what the hurry is."

"Well, you get your tea inside you, mum, and I'll just get this stove fired up. Would you like oatmeal this morning, mum?"

"Thanks, Cook. That would be grand." She sipped again. "What's on the menu for today?"

He cast a look out the cookhouse door and shrugged. "I'm planning on baking beans today. The weather should stay quiet unless that storm decides to come back and take another pass at us. I'll give 'em a nice chipped beef in gravy for lunch, I think. You feel like making biscuits again, mum?"

"Whatever you need me to do."

"Well, the lads will be looking for their breakfast soon, but the oatmeal is done. Beans don't need much work, now that they're soaked. If we give them a bit of beef for lunch, that'll make up for cold rations yesterday." He shrugged. "I can make 'em if you'd rather just lounge around today, mum. There's not much extra work to do."

She sipped her tea and thought about curling up in her bunk for the day. The idea had little appeal. "Well, let me help with breakfast at least. We'll see how my strength holds up."

"Good plan, mum. No need of overextending yourself this early in the voyage."

She laughed a bit at that. "We're not even halfway yet, are we?"

Cook shook his head with a sorrowful look. "Not unless that blow did us a real big favor, mum. We're still more than a few days out yet."

"The captain said he needs to get a fix today, assumin' the sky is clear."

Cook checked the firebox on the stove and tossed in another stick of wood for good measure. "Aye, mum. He does that every day he can. Right at noon. That's how we find our way out here. Mr. Groves usually takes a sighting along side him, just to double up and to give him practice."

"What do they take a sighting of? I didn't think there was anything to see out here."

Cook smiled over his shoulder at her. "We go out to sea to see the sea and when we see we saw the sea, we wonder what we ever saw in going out to sea."

She laughed at his bit of doggerel and waited for him to finish pouring the soaked beans into a heavy crock.

"There's lots to see out here, mum. Sun. Moon. Even stars. If you can measure good enough, and know what you're doing, you can find your way from here to there right well." He up-ended a jug of molasses over the beans and let several glugs-worth flow into the crock. "Noon sightings are for the sun. They measure it and that tells 'em what they need to know to figure out where we are."

"Sounds easy enough," Tanyth said, "but I s'pose if t'were, then young Mr. Groves wouldn't need the practice."

Cook nodded. "There's that. Wouldn't do for something to happen to the only man who knows how to navigate, now would it?"

Tanyth felt her heart beat race at that thought. "Nothin' could happen to Captain Groves, can it?"

Cook shrugged. "There's always a risk when you go to sea, mum. Sheet coulda broke and dropped a boom on him in that storm yesterday. Wave mighta caught him and carried him over." He looked pointedly at Tanyth's gray hair. "I don't need to tell you the dangers of getting on, do I?"

Tanyth thought of all the things that might go wrong and it must have shown in her face.

"Easy, mum. We've been sailing with the old man up there for years now. No reason to expect something's gonna happen to him soon."

She didn't feel much reassured.

"But we take measures to be safe even if it does, mum. Man be a fool to ignore reality." He reached into a bin under the counter and pulled up a handful of empty onion skins. "Bother," he muttered. He felt around in the bin again and then looked in several of the others.

"Problem, Cook?"

"I need to get some more onions out of the hold. Looks like some potatoes and flour, too." He looked in a cupboard and muttered a bit more.

"I thought the hold was sealed."

He nodded and looked over at her. "Main hold is, mum. How'd you know that?"

"Chattin' with Mr. Jameson last night. There was some question about how the cargo fared in the storm." She let him assume the conversation happened in the captain's cabin.

"It got a bit bumpy. That's sure," Cook said. "Ships stores aren't in the main hold, mum. That's sealed up for the voyage. We need to get to the stores underway so we've got our own hold."

"The Small Place," she muttered.

"What's that, mum?"

"Nothin', Cook. Just an odd idea." She paused before asking, "Where do you keep the stores, then?"

Cook smiled and waved her back into the corner. She stepped back and he reached down and pulled up a ring set flush in the deck. "Right here," he said with a grunt. A big square of the deck lifted up and folded back against the bulkhead. A hook and eye there latched it open. A broad-stepped ladder led down into darkness. With a grin, Cook hopped down and started rummaging around.

In a matter of a few minutes he had a sack of onions, a bag of flour, and what looked like another hundredweight of potatoes lined up on the deck beside the hatch. He reminded Tanyth of the ground squirrel that lived in Mother Alderton's back garden.

"Just need to get a tin of beef for lunch, and we'll be ready," he said and disappeared into the darkness under her feet.

"Blast it!" his voice sounded muffled and she heard him grunting and cursing.

"You all right down there, Cook?"

"Oh, aye. Just a minute."

Something thumped and then she heard three loud bangs.

"That's got it," he said and came scampering up the ladder with a big can of beef under his arm. He put the can on the work counter and reached up to release the hatch. "Watch your toes, mum."

He lowered the hatch carefully and then let it fall the last couple of inches. It landed with a heavy thump. He dusted his hands together and said, "That'll hold me for a while."

Tanyth chuckled at his performance while he poured the onions into the bin and stood the bags of flour and potatoes off to the side. He pulled a couple of the onions out and peeled and chopped them with a few economical motions, scraping the pungent onion into the pot of beans and giving the whole thing a stir.

Mr. Jameson came into the cookhouse then and looked

back and forth between Tanyth and Cook.

"Good mornin', Mr. Jameson," Tanyth said.

"Morning, mum. Morning, Cook."

"Morning, sir." Cook handed him a steaming mug.

"Well, thank you, Cook, but I came to see if everything was all right in here."

"Oh, aye, sir. Just needed to get some supplies out of stores."

Jameson sipped his tea and nodded. "I gathered that but what was all that banging?"

"Banging, sir?" Cook looked puzzled for a moment and then said, "Oh! Sorry, sir. One of the barrels of hardtack fell over and the top came off. Spilled crackers all over the hold." He held up the can of beef. "I stood the barrel back up and pounded the top back down with this. Musta made more of a racket than I thought."

Tanyth felt the blood leave her face and she was glad she was leaning against the corner of the cookhouse.

"Mum? Are you all right?" Jameson stood next to her, his concern obvious on his face.

"Yeah. I'm all right, I think." She looked from Cook to Jameson and back. "Must be hungrier than I thought."

"Oatmeal's ready, mum, if you want some," Cook offered.

"Thank you, that would prob'ly be good."

While Cook busied himself filling a bowl, Tanyth turned to Jameson. "You need to check the hold," she murmured.

He gave her a quizzical look, but Cook was already handing the full bowl to her. She took it with a smile and gave Jameson a small shake of her head.

He took the hint and didn't press the matter, turning to Cook instead. "Well, good enough then. All that banging, I didn't know but maybe Mother Fairport was beating some sense into you."

Cook grinned. "And you came to protect me, sir?"

"As if. I came to help." The men laughed, and if either one noticed that Tanyth's laughter wasn't quite jocular, neither mentioned it. With a nod to both of them, Jameson took his mug and left.

After a moment, Cook turned to Tanyth. "So, mum? Ship

secrets or would you care to fill in old Cook on what's goin' on?"

Tanyth took a deep breath and took a spoonful of the oatmeal. "You're gonna think I'm a crazy old woman, Cook."

He shrugged. "Could be worse."

"How?"

"I could think you're a crazy young woman."

She cocked her head at him. "But I'm not a young woman."

He lifted a palm up and said, "There ya go."

"How is that worse?"

"Well, mum, because then I'd be crazy, and for me, that would be much worse."

The silliness of it struck her funny and she laughed against her will.

"Come on, mum. Give. What's going on?"

She got her laughter under control. "All right, but I warned ya."

"I'm warned."

"I have dreams that I see things through the eyes of animals."

He laughed and leaned back, hands on the counter behind him. "If that's supposed to make me think you're crazy, mum? You are crazy."

"They're true."

He stopped laughing. "What do you mean, they're true?"

"What I dream? It happens."

"Like what, mum?"

"Well, lately I've been dreaming about a mother who lives down in the ship. She scampers about in the dark down below. She has four babies and is always looking for nest material and food."

"Sounds like a rat."

"Well, Mr. Jameson assures me that Captain Groves knows there are no rats on the *Zypheria's Call.*"

"Oh, yes, mum. That's true. I forgot about that." He lifted one eyebrow. "And you know this is true because...?"

"Last night, I had another dream about her. After all the banging and shaking, she went looking for food. She found a pile of food spilled out of a barrel down below."

"And then what, mum?"

"And then she ate her fill, did a little creative gnawin' on a crate in the main hold, then went back to her nest to sleep."

"That seems a long stretch from dream to true, mum."

"The food she found was a barrel of hard tack. She likes it well enough, by the bye."

Cook screwed up his face. "How can a rat know what hard tack is, mum? That's silly."

"She doesn't. She just knows it's food. But in my dream, I can see it. I know what hard tack looks like. Well, what it must look like. Can't say I've ever seen it" She put the bowl down on the counter and held up her hands. "Rectangular, about that big, and has holes in it."

"How many holes?"

Tanyth tried to picture it in her mind, but the dream was too elusive. The image of the hard tack wasn't clear enough to the rat. "I don't know. Some. Couple of rows of 'em." She shrugged. "It's dark down there."

Cook stepped back and stared at her.

"Do you believe me?"

"I don't know, mum. You have to admit it's a bit of a strange story."

She picked up her oatmeal. "You don't know the half of it," she said and took a spoonful.

"Has it happened before?"

She shrugged and then gave a little nod. "I used to see through a raven's eyes."

Cook's eyebrows shot up. "A raven?"

Tanyth nodded, chewing her oatmeal. "She liked rabbits."

"What? As pets?"

"As meals."

"She caught them?"

Tanyth shook her head. "No, dead ones. She also liked apples, frogs, and even hornets. She ate almost anything that didn't eat her first. But she liked rabbits best."

"And you saw through her eyes?"

"Yeah. It was odd at first, but flyin' was fun." Tanyth grinned at him.

"Now you're just teasing, mum."

She sighed. "No. I wish I was."

Seven bells rang and sailors started lining up outside for their breakfasts. Tanyth poured the tea and Cook doled out the oatmeal until all the sailors had bowls and mugs. Rebecca came through the line with the sailors and smiled when Cook gave her an extra helping of oatmeal.

"Mornin', mum," she said and scurried off before Tanyth could answer.

With the crew fed, they had a few minutes before they needed to start cleaning up.

Cook didn't mention their conversation the whole time, but Tanyth could see him thinking it over, occasionally shooting her odd glances as he finished putting the crock of beans together and then slid it into the oven for the long day of baking.

Tanyth finished her now-cold oatmeal and washed it down with hot tea before putting her bowl in the tray. Within a few minutes, sailors started stowing their own dirty dishes and by the time eight bells rolled around breakfast was done.

Tanyth set up her folding work surface and Cook lifted the tray of dirty dishes up for her, filled the rinse bucket with hot water from the tank, poured half of it into the tray and then placed it at her feet.

"You gonna say something?" she asked when his considering looks became unbearable.

"You're not crazy, mum."

"Why d'ya say that?"

He shrugged. "Well, granted that I've only known you a few days, mum, but you've never once struck me as a crazy, old lady. I know a few. Related to some, actually, but you're not like them, mum."

"Really?"

"Yes, mum. They're all sure they're not crazy, but then they say the craziest things like they're just normal as apple cobbler on a winter day."

"And?"

"And you say crazy things, but you know they're crazy. They make no sense. For you, they're true." He paused, looking her straight in the eyes. "And it scares ya, don't it?"

She nodded. "Yeah. I don't know what's happenin' or why. That scares the stuffin' out o' me."

He filled the tea kettle with fresh, cold water and put it on the stove to heat. He stepped back and considered Tanyth.

"So, why are you starin' at me like that?" she asked.

"I'm wondering what you're not telling me, mum."

"What I'm not tellin' you? I just told ya I dream I'm a rat."

He shrugged. "That could just be coincidence, mum. Dreams are funny things. Sometimes I dream I'm a ship sailing in the warm southern seas."

"How would I know there was a broken barrel of hard tack?"

He shrugged again. "Coincidence. There's bound to be food all around. Dreams are funny that way. They make your brain see stuff in odd ways."

"That's true enough."

"So, what else did you tell Mr. Jameson that you're not telling me, mum?"

"My lil four-footed friend thinks somethin's not right in the main hold. I want Mr. Jameson to check it out."

"What? The cargo shifted in the storm?"

She shrugged. "I'd rather not say, Cook. I feel foolish enough already. I'll feel even worse if Scott gets down there and finds nothin'."

His eyebrows shot up. "Scott, is it now? My, my."

She took a deep breath to answer but he just smiled at her.

"Finish up the dishes, mum, and then if you've still a mind to, we can make a bunch of biscuits for the lads for lunch."

"You don't think I'm crazy, then?"

He pursed his lips and shook his head. "No, mum. I don't know what you are, but you're a long way from crazy." He examined her for a long moment before asking, "How did your little friend get in to find the hardtack?"

"There's a gap between two of the planks. It's wet and a bit slimy. She slips through from the main hold that way."

His eyebrows shot up and he blinked several times in apparent astonishment. "Interesting, mum. Very interesting."

He pulled a huge cast-iron skillet down from an overhead rack in a single smooth movement. The pan was so big that Tanyth wasn't sure she could have lifted it with both hands, let alone one.

"What are you goin' to cook in that monster?"

He grinned over his shoulder and started winding the key on the tin of beef. "It takes a lot of gravy for these lads, mum. Sometimes I think a bathtub wouldn't be big enough."

The look on his face made her laugh a bit. She splashed a little more hot water into her dirty dishes and dug in with a will. "Well, you're right on one score, Cook."

"What's that, mum?"

"Dreams or not, the work still has to get done."

"Aye, mum, it surely does."

Cook set to with some onion and spices while Tanyth finished the dishes. When the last of the crockery sluiced into the rinse, Cook helped her pour the dirty water into a bucket for disposal. He stuck his head out of the deckhouse and did a double take. "Scooter? You spend way too much time lurking out there!"

He laughed at some comment that Tanyth couldn't hear. "All right, then."

Scooter slipped in past Cook, grinned at Tanyth before grabbing the bucket and disappearing again. He was back in a flash, trading the empty bucket for a sweet and scampering back on deck.

He was no sooner out of the cookhouse than the door opened and Jameson walked in with the captain right behind him. "I know, Skipper, but we've still got at least another week of bumping along. I think it would be a good idea to make sure that nothing's broken loose down there," he said.

"I'm not arguing with you, Scotty," the captain said. He turned to Cook. "A cup of tea for a pour old man, Cook? Perhaps a stale biscuit...?"

Cook laughed poured two mugs of fresh tea, handing one to each of the men. "Hold on a minute, Captain, and I'll find you a moldy crust to chew on." He pulled a biscuit out of the morning's basket and, expertly splitting it, slathered a bit of butter on each half and placed them butter side down in the heavy skillet full of onion. "Mr. Jameson? A moldy crust for you, sir?"

Jameson chuckled and shook his head. "Tea is fine for now, Cook. Thank you."

The captain turned back to Jameson. "Tell you what, we've got a waypoint coming up this morning around four bells. It should give us a bit better position on the rollers and maybe they'll even subside a bit by then."

"Thank you, Captain. Sounds like a plan."

The captain sipped his tea and nodded to Tanyth. "You keeping Cook in line, mum?"

"I'm not sure who's keeping who in line, Captain, but he finds little things for me to do that fill my empty days."

Cook grinned and handed the captain a browned biscuit. "Try that, Captain. You can just eat around any moldy bits, I think."

"Ah, thank you, Cook. I may survive after all." He turned to Jameson. "See me after we come about, Mr. Jameson."

"Aye, aye, Captain. Thank you, sir."

The captain grunted and left the deckhouse, trying to juggle his tea and catch the jam dripping off his biscuit without spilling either on his frockcoat.

Jameson gave Cook a nod and shared a look with Tanyth before taking his tea and following the captain out onto the deck.

"Well," Cook said. "I need to make some gravy and you need to make some biscuits. I think we've got about two bells before Mr. Jameson gets a chance to look in the hold and see how good your dreams are, mum."

She shivered and hoped, this time, the dreams were wrong, then she pushed up her sleeves again. Regardless of what Mr. Jameson found in the hold, the sailors would need a good lunch. While she couldn't do much about the first, the second she knew how to help with. "How much flour do you want me to use, Cook?" she asked, and got down to work.

Tanyth finished the biscuits in almost no time and soon had three full sheet pans in the oven.

"That oughta keep the lads in gravy for a while, mum." Cook looked around and shrugged. "I think that's it for this morning, mum. Thanks for doing the biscuits for me."

"You're welcome, o'course. I'm gonna go lay down and read for a bit." She snaked a mug off the shelf and poured herself some tea to take along. With a nod, she stepped out onto the deck, closing the door behind her with a snap.

After the overly-warm cookhouse, the open deck felt clean and fresh. The chill wind tried to blow the tea right out of her mug, but she found that she'd developed enough skill to walk, balance tea, and even hold her coat together with her free hand. "You might make a sailor yet," she muttered. The ship took a particularly steep wave that had Tanyth flexing her knees and trying to stay upright as the seesaw movement up and then down again jarred the ship. "If you can keep from fallin' overboard," she muttered.

A flash of white to her left caught her eye and she saw a single seabird apparently suspended alongside the ship. The bird's golden eye peered at her and she shook her head, hoping she wasn't going to start flying with gulls next.

She resumed her walk to the cabin, feeling quite proud that her path weaved only slightly back and forth with the rolling of the ship. A last stagger got her down the companionway without incident and out of the wind. She treated herself to a sip of tea. The interior of the ship always felt so quiet, even muffled, after being out on deck. She knew it wasn't true, but by comparison to the heavy winds always blowing in her ears, the relative silence struck her each time.

She found Rebecca standing beside her bunk, the surface of her blanket covered with the papers from Tanyth's bundle. Rebecca flashed her a bright smile. "G'mornin', mum. Got Cook squared away?"

Tanyth shook her head and gave a small laugh. "G'mornin', yourself. And it's gonna take more than one poor old lady to get him straightened out. How's life as a deck hand?"

Rebecca grimaced. "I think they're takin' it easy on me 'cause I'm a girl."

"Show me your hands."

Rebecca turned roughed palms up to the light. "The liniment helps some. I shudder to think of what they'd look like without it."

"No blisters?"

"No, mum."

"Well, if this is takin' it easy on ya, my dear, you prob'ly want to thank your lucky stars because much more and you'd have ground beef where your fingers should grow."

Rebecca peered at her own palms again and nodded. "Maybe it's just 'cause I'm new."

Tanyth shrugged and crossed to look over Rebecca's shoulder at the scattering of papers. "Findin' anythin' interestin'?"

"Lots. Mostly your notes about the plants and such."

"I didn't have paper to waste on the weather," Tanyth said her eyes raking back and forth across the tidy arrangements of documents.

Rebecca gave her a one armed hug. "No, mum. I s'pect you didn't. There's some odd stains on some of these."

Tanyth leaned down. "Where? Water damage?"

Rebecca shook her head and pointed. "Those there have a kind of rust on 'em. Just on the edges like."

Tanyth saw the pages in question, narrow arcs of dark eating into the margins of her notes. The date on the top page was over a decade old. Tanyth sighed. "Yeah. After that I started wrappin' them more careful."

Rebecca cocked her head and picked up one of the pages. "What is it, though, mum?"

"Blood," she said with a small shrug. "The pile was a lot shorter then, but it's blood."

"Yours?" Rebecca seemed scandalized.

Tanyth sighed again and shook her head. "No."

Rebecca started to ask another question, but the look on Tanyth's face stopped her. She put the page back on the bunk and folded her hands on the rail.

"You're keepin' them in order?" Tanyth asked after a moment.

"Yes, mum. Seemed sensible. Since you've been buildin' from the bottom of the pile—'cept for those over there that have diff'rent dates—I kept them in order as I peel them apart. These here are the newest," she pointed to the papers closest to the rail. "They get older in that direction." She waved her arm along the length of the bunk."

"That's a lot of paper to carry," Tanyth said. "I guess I never gave it much thought."

"You spent a winter with somebody named Willowton?" Rebecca said, picking a loose page off the blanket.

"Alice, yes. Alice Willowton. Not sure how many winters back now." Tanyth leaned in to look at the spidery writing on the page. "Woman was sure I'd forget how to distill oils so she wrote it all down."

Rebecca held the page up to the light and frowned at it. "Is that what this is?"

Tanyth joined her in peering at the page. "I believe so. Problem is the woman couldn't write so you could read it. Ever. But she wrote and wrote and wrote and always claimed that she could read it. Yes, look there, that word is 'heat' and I think that's 'leaves' or maybe 'loaves.'"

Rebecca cast a sidelong glance at Tanyth. "You sure this isn't a recipe for bread?"

Tanyth shrugged. "Could be, but Alice Willowton wasn't much on bread bakin'. She did like her still, though."

Rebecca caught something in Tanyth's tone and gave her a curious look.

Tanyth chuckled. "Most of the women I wintered with had something they made or grew or whatever. Just a little something to get a few coins, you know?"

Rebecca nodded.

"Mother Willowton distilled strong drink. She made the best spirits in the valley."

Rebecca laughed and held up the canvas-shrouded bundle. "And I haven't even gotten to the oldest stuff yet. You wrote more then."

"Di'n't know I was all that wordy," Tanyth said with a grin of her own.

"You didn't write anythin' last winter, mum? Nothin' about your time in Ravenwood?"

Tanyth shook her head. "Didn't learn anything new there. Nothin' to write down."

Rebecca scoffed. "Didn't think to write down about your raven dreams?"

Tanyth shot her a frown. "Not exactly learnin', is it?"

Rebecca shook her head. "No, mum, but keepin' track of all that's happening now might be useful later when you get to Mother Pinecrest's. You'll be able to tell her 'xactly when stuff happened."

Tanyth nodded and thought of the new blank book and pen in her pack. "That's not a bad idea, my dear. 'Specially now."

Rebecca cocked her head. "The momma rat, you mean?"

Tanyth gave a half shrug but didn't answer.

Above them, they heard men shouting and feet running across the decks.

"What is it, mum?" Rebecca asked, eyes wide.

"Just comin' about, I 'spect" she said. "New course again. You'll want to get your gear on. They'll be collectin' ya soon."

Rebecca shook her head in wonder. "How do you know more what the ship's doin' than I do?"

Tanyth pulled her coat off its peg and started shrugging into its heavy warmth. "I don't, my dear, but hangin' about in the cookhouse, I hear the odd bit of this 'n that."

"Lemme just bundle this back up and I'll be up in a minute. If you see Scooter or the bosun?"

"I'll tell 'em." Tanyth nodded and finished buttoning her coat. She remembered to take the mug with her at the last minute and headed up to watch the ship come about, tea in hand and feeling like a real sailor.

When she got on deck, she didn't see the men holding on to the lines and levers they needed to bring the ship about as she expected. What she saw was the full complement of sailors in the tall rigging, each one working at some activity or other that involved the sails.

The bosun saw her standing there gazing upward. "Mum, we need Becca now!" he shouted.

"She's on her way."

He waved and turned back to the crew in the rigging, bawling orders that Tanyth didn't understand but moved men from here to there. As she watched, the big canvas sails seemed to evaporate as they were gathered, reefed, and in some cases actually taken down.

Rebecca pushed up onto the deck and stepped around

Tanyth.

"The bosun's lookin' for you, my dear," Tanyth said.

"I s'pect he is, mum," she said and dashed across the deck to where the bosun stood, legs apart and gazing upwards.

He turned at her approach and clapped her on the shoulder, pointing forward and saying something in her ear that Tanyth couldn't hear above the sound of the wind buffeting past her ears.

She walked forward to the cookhouse and, in its meager protection, up-ended her mug, letting the last of the cooling tea pour into her mouth. When she brought the mug down, she saw the heavy, dark clouds working across the western sky. A flicker of lightning generated no thunder that she could hear over the roaring of the wind, but she doubted that would last very long. Even as she stood there, the mass seemed to expand, stretching gray fingers across the deep blue sky. She could make out sheets of rain hanging like some strange moss.

With an effort, she pulled her eyes away and wrenched open the door to the cookhouse and slipped inside. There she found Cook busily lashing things down. "Ah, there you are, mum. Looks like we won't be getting a peek into the hold today after all."

"Is it bad?"

Cook shrugged and didn't stop his preparations. "Bad enough, I wager." He paused to consider his handy work and then turned to the stove. He opened the firebox and stuffed two more sticks into it.

"I thought you had to secure the fire when there's stormy weather?"

He shot her a smile over his shoulder. "Aye, we do, but she's not storming yet and this hunk of iron will hold heat for hours. If I can get her hot enough before the storm hits, we'll have fresh, hot beans at midnight if we need 'em." He nodded at the trays of biscuits. "Mum? If you'd pull them off the trays and fill up them hampers?" Two covered baskets rested on the deck. "We'll be able to put some hot food in their bellies before it hits, I think."

She used a towel to hold the still hot baking sheets and dumped the biscuits unceremoniously into the baskets, throwing a bit of fresh towel in on top and slapping the lids closed. "What about the trays?"

Cook pointed to a narrow slot. "In there, turn the toggle and they'll stay in."

She found a flat bit of wood with a spike driven through the middle that allowed the wood to turn. She slipped the empty trays into the slot and turned the wood, which formed a bar across the opening. "Clever."

"Oh, we sailors are nothing if not clever, mum. Gotta keep gear from flying away, or rolling over the side, or falling on our heads every time there's a little blow. Simple is good, mum. And when you're dealing with sailors, it better be darn simple. All-Mother knows we surely are."

"Are what, Cook?"

"Simple, mum. Every blasted one of us for being out in this."

Tanyth saw his face for the first time since getting into the cookhouse. His eyes were wider than normal and his skin carried a waxy pallor.

"Anythin' else I can do, Cook?"

He looked around the galley, checking off things methodically as his gaze traversed each wall. "Well, mum, we're gonna serve up some grub here in a minute, but if you happen to know any prayers to calm the winds and flatten the seas, now would be a tip top time to say 'em."

She looked at him, but he seemed to be serious, even if a bit distracted by trying to simultaneously get a meal ready and tie down anything not in use in the galley. "First time for everythin', I suppose," she said. "Can't hurt."

She headed for the door.

"Where you goin', mum?"

"Gonna say a prayer."

He interrupted his frantic scanning and fussing to look at her, a look of surprise on his face. "A prayer, mum?"

"Yeah," she said. "You just said if I knew any prayers, now's the time to say 'em."

He barked a laugh. "And you can't say 'em in here, mum?"

She looked around the cookhouse. "Oh, prob'ly." She ducked her head to peer out of the small window at the approaching storm. "But I got a feelin' I'll need my stick for this one."

Tanyth left the cookhouse and made her way across the deck. The dark clouds grew closer by the second and the wind blew stronger than it had when she'd entered the deckhouse. Every once in a while, she felt a single drop of water blow into her face. "There'll be more where that came from, I 'spect," she muttered.

She made her way back to her compartment and staggered as the ship took a lurch just as she opened the door, nearly tumbling onto the deck with the sudden movement. Tanyth pulled her staff out from its slot beside her mattress and leaned on it for a moment, gazing out the port at the sunny sky that still showed on that side of the ship. Just the heft of it in her hand made her feel better. She took a moment to button up her heavy blue coat but left her head bare.

Staff in hand, she clambered back up on the deck and stood in the open near the center of the ship, just behind the huge main mast, and just in front of the raised bridge in the stern. It was the steadiest part of the ship and would give her the best footing. The small triangular sails at the tops of the masts had already been furled, and the three large sails that usually graced the bow of the ship had been reduced to one rather small one. The main sails were gone, wrapped and secured to the booms that held them. Above her the wind sang through the nearly naked rigging, making every line vibrate in a horrific symphony.

Out of the corner of her eyes she saw Cook come out of the deckhouse and stare at her. All around her, sailors stopped their work to gawk. She stood there, iron-shod staff grounded on the smooth, wooden deck. She glanced up to find the sun just before the advancing fingers of cloud wrapped it in a fist of angry gray. She saw Rebecca clinging to the rigging high above her. She gazed straight down at Tanyth, but instead of fear, the girl's face radiated strength and determination. Tanyth saw her set her jaw and nod once at her before she returned to her task high above the rolling deck.

"Oh, Mother, this better work," she muttered and turned

to face directly north.

The wind's passage through the rigging grew into some-thing more akin to a howl and she knew there was very little time before the storm fell over them. She took a deep breath and was just about to start when she heard the captain shout-ing behind her.

"What in the name of Farnsworth's flaming flatus are you doing out here, mum?"

She turned to see him leaning over the rail above her on the bridge. "Sayin' my prayers, why?"

"Mum, you need to get below!"

"Tell me somethin' I don't know. Gimme a minute and I'll get out of your way."

"I'm not sure you've got a minute, mum," he bellowed.

"Tell me about it," she muttered.

"What?"

She ignored him and turned to face north once more. Her feet found the place they needed and her body found the rhythm. She lifted her staff in both hands and began.

"I call on the Guardian of the North, Bones of the World, to give this ship and her crew the strength of stone to with-stand the tempest before us."

She dropped the staff to the deck with a dull thump that seemed to shake the ship and used it to pivot to her right and face the east. She raised the staff again.

"I call on the Guardian of the East, Breath of the World, to hold the winds that threaten this ship and allow us to pass through this storm in safety."

Again she dropped the staff to the deck and the dull thump felt more like a drum beat. Once more she pivoted and faced the south. As she raised the staff she saw the startled looking faces of the crew looking down at her from the raised bridge. If she hadn't been so intent, she might have laughed at their shocked expressions. Even the younger Groves staring up into the rigging looked pale under his sea-grown tan.

"I call on the Guardian of the South, Fire of the World, to grant us the gift of passion to sustain us through the storm that threatens to snuff the fires of our lives."

The staff boomed on the deck and Tanyth felt a fire growing in her middle that had nothing to do with fear. She turned again to face the west. Her staff felt heavier, or maybe she was just getting tired. She couldn't be sure.

"I call on the Guardian of the West, Blood of the World, to smooth the seas and calm the waves, to keep the force of storm from breaking this ship and dousing the lives of those aboard."

The staff boomed again and Tanyth turned, glad it was the last turn. She lifted the staff once more to the north, barely able to lift the heavy oak staff against the buffeting wind.

"May the Guardians hold the circle around this ship and all who sail her. Grant them the strength to endure, passion to live, and flexibility to survive the winds and waves and fire that drive this storm. In the name of the All-Mother, and in the name of the All-Father, I ask. So mote it be."

She brought the staff down for the last time and the sound of it crashed around her.

"Bother," she grumbled. "After all that, we get hit by lightning."

☽ ○ ☾

She gnawed on the wood some more. The hole was nearly big enough to get into, but she worried that she might not be able to get out. She could thrust her head in, but it wasn't enough for her shoulders. She needed to make the hole bigger.

The ground shook a few times and she stopped. There were no others. She heard them up above, but they didn't let the light in, so she knew she was safe. After a time, she wondered if there was still food in the Small Place or if the others had taken it away. Perhaps her sister mothers had found it and eaten it all.

She stopped chewing on the wood and cleaned her whiskers. Food would be good, she thought, and scampered toward the wet crack and had almost squeezed all the way through it when she smelled the sharp smell, the smell of danger. She froze and looked. A fat ball of food rested on the metal. The metal was danger. She knew danger and it made her angry.

She squeezed through the wet crack and walked around the food. Not touching it. Not looking at it.

She found the round edge that had spilled food. The others had come down and lifted it up, but she found spilled food in the corners and ate until her belly was full. She went back to the wet crack and walked carefully around the food. She was no longer hungry now, but the food smelled good. She squeezed through the wet crack and went back to chewing the wood.

☽○☾

Tanyth awoke to find herself wrapped snugly in her bedroll. Watery light shone through the salt-rimed glass and the ship's movement was a gentle rocking-horse motion, up and down, up and down. Rebecca stirred in the bunk across from her but seemed safe enough. She had a moment to remember the storm and wonder how she'd managed to sleep through it all before the up-and-down movement rocked her to sleep once more.

CHAPTER 26
AFTERMATH

The sound of four bells woke Tanyth again. Bright morning sun streamed in through the porthole, and her bladder told her it was time for a visit to the water closet. Rebecca stood beside the bunk, looking down on her, a gentle smile curving her lips.

"Well, there you are, mum," she said. "I was beginnin' ta wonder if you'd sleep all the way to North Haven."

Tanyth managed a weak grin. "I'm glad ta see you, too, my dear, but if I don't find the water closet, there's gonna be a problem."

Rebecca giggled and stepped back to give Tanyth room. "'Course, mum."

Tanyth untangled herself from her bedroll and clambered down off the bunk. Her knees almost gave out on her when she put her weight on them, and she leaned on Rebecca for a moment to catch her breath.

"That'll teach me to miss a meal," she said with an apologetic shrug. She wasn't sure when she was supposed to have had that meal. "It's been a long time since breakfast and here it's breakfast time again," she grumbled.

Rebecca helped her steady herself along the passageway to the water closet and back. She felt much better by the time she got back to the room. She raked her fingers through her hair to flatten it out a bit and then pulled her knit cap on over the top to hide the mess.

"What're you doin', mum?" Rebecca asked.

"Goin' to get a cuppa tea and see if Cook has a biscuit or

two for a poor old hungry woman." She grinned at Rebecca and reached for her coat.

"That's prob'ly not a good idea, mum. You're still pretty weak."

Tanyth snorted. "I'm not likely ta get much stronger without eatin' now, am I?"

Tanyth caught sight of her staff standing in the corner again where it had started the trip and she took a moment to put it back into the slot between the mattress and bunk.

She stood there frozen for several moments, hands curled around the rail, remembering the storm, remembering falling down, trying to remember how she'd gotten up off the deck. Trying out her memory to see if there were fragments that she could splice together to figure out what happened after. She couldn't find a trace and her heart banged in her chest.

"You all right, mum?" Rebecca asked, stepping up to touch her elbow.

"I'm not going mad." Her fierce whisper almost hissed in the air.

"No, mum. You're not."

She took a deep breath, then another. She willed her heart to slow.

"Tea," she muttered. "A cup of tea."

Her stomach grumbled.

"And some oatmeal maybe?"

"I'll get it for you, mum," Rebecca said, fumbling for her own outer garments.

"You'll do no such thing," Tanyth snapped.

The look of hurt in Rebecca's face captured Tanyth's attention and she took a deep breath.

"What I mean is I can take care of it myself, my dear. No need for you to bother."

Rebecca's look changed to one of soft sympathy and Tanyth wasn't sure it was an improvement.

"Of course, you can, mum." Rebecca continued putting on her wrap. "I'll just go along with you and get a cup myself."

Tanyth let out a breath she hadn't realized she was holding and nodded.

Together, they left the cabin again and made their way

across the deck to the cookhouse.

Tanyth's legs still felt a little shaky and she had to concentrate on walking across the gently rolling deck once more. She slipped through the door and found Cook staring at her, eyes all but bugging out of his skull.

She stood there for a moment, shocked by his expression before she thought to say, "Good morning, Cook. Is there tea?"

"Mum? You're up."

"Well, of course, I'm up. Where would I be?"

"In your bunk. What are you doing up?"

She blinked at him. "Well, it is morning and my bladder thought I should be. Why wouldn't I be up?"

Rebecca placed a calming hand on her shoulder. "Is there tea, Cook? Perhaps a biscuit?" she asked.

"Oh!" Cook scrambled about and grabbed a mug, sloshed tea into it and offered her the hamper of biscuits.

Tanyth had to reach well down to find a biscuit but find one she did. She propped herself in the corner and took a sip of tea and a nibble from the biscuit.

Cook offered Rebecca a heavy mug and the younger woman accepted with quiet thanks and huddled into the opposite corner.

Tanyth smiled to herself, savoring the warmth of the tea and already feeling better for having the flakey bread in her hand. She noticed Cook still staring at her.

"What?" she asked.

"Are you feeling all right, mum?"

She shrugged. "A little weak. Hungry, but it's been a long time since breakfast."

"A long time since breakfast, mum?"

"Yeah. Last thing I remember is the storm comin' and I said a little prayer and then the ship got hit by lightning. I musta slept through the storm and everything. Was anybody hurt?"

"Hurt, mum?" Cook cast a look at Rebecca who shrugged and gave a small shake of her head.

Tanyth took a deep breath and another sip of tea before she got too exasperated with him. "By the lightning? That can't be a good thing at sea."

"No, mum, we have lightning catchers on the mast heads. Sizzles a bit, but takes the lightning to water without burning up the ship and crew on the way."

"Oh, that's good." The biscuit tasted delicious and she nibbled it down.

"But we didn't take a lightning strike, mum."

She looked up at him, tearing her eyes off the biscuit, and taking a sip of the tea. "Of course, we did. I was standing right there on deck."

He shook his head. "No, mum. I was standing right there watching. You did your...I don't know what to call it..."

"Well, I call it prayer." Tanyth smiled and held out her mug for more tea.

"Your prayer, then, mum." Cook refilled her mug without stopping. "Then you smacked the deck and the whole ship shook."

"Oh, dear! I didn't hurt the deck or anything, did I? I was worried about that iron shoe. Thought it might gouge the deck."

"Mum?"

"Yes?"

"Mum, you stood there on the deck and screamed at the storm. Every time you hit the deck with your staff, the whole damn thing rang like a bell. Every time it rang louder. When you got all the way around, you smacked it one last time and then stood there with this fierce look on your face. I didn't know whether to run or hide or both."

Tanyth smiled. "That's a bit of an exaggeration, I'n't it, Cook?"

"I'm not done, yet, mum."

She blinked at his tone.

"You stood there for maybe a minute and then you just keeled over."

"Well, yeah. I remember keelin' over. I think." She blinked, trying to remember it. "I don't remember actually hitting the deck, though. I don't seem to have any bumps or extra bruises that I've found."

"Well, Mr. Groves scooped you up and took you down to

282

your cabin and tucked you in, mum." He paused. "We didn't know what else to do with ya."

"Well, sure. Silly old woman faintin' on deck just when a storm is comin'."

"Mum? That was two days ago."

She grinned at him and then at Rebecca. "Don't be ridiculous, Cook! It was just yesterday morning."

Rebecca said, "No, mum. T'was two days."

"Can't be—"

The door slammed open startling Tanyth so much she nearly spilled her tea. Mr. Jameson burst in, his eyes racing around the deckhouse. "Cook! Mother—" When he saw her standing there drinking tea, his voice cut off. "You're up, mum."

"People keep noticin' that. What's got into all of you?"

"You've been flat on your back in your bunk for two days, mum. We were getting worried."

Tanyth looked from Jameson to Rebecca to Cook and back again.

"Told ya, mum," Cook said.

"Is this a joke?" Tanyth asked. "Because if you're playin' some kinda prank, I swear I'll brain you with this biscuit." She held up the heel end of her biscuit like it was a twenty-pound hammer.

"Mum, if it's a joke, I'll get you a fresh one to use," Cook said.

"No, mum. Truth," Rebecca said. "You've been conked out in your bunk since you fell over on deck two days ago. We were all getting' rather worried that you'd hurt yourself."

Tanyth stretched her shoulders and twisted her torso a bit as an experiment, then shook her head. "I feel all right, other than a tad peckish. My knees are a little weak this morning."

"Mum, you wait right here? I need to go let the captain know you're up and about," Jameson said.

Tanyth shrugged. "All right. Sure. I wasn't plannin' on goin' anywhere."

"Thank you, mum. I'll be right back." Jameson bolted from the door and pulled it closed behind him with a slam.

Tanyth finished the scrap of biscuit and then looked to

Cook. "Is there a little oatmeal? I really am feeling hungry this morning."

"Oh, yes, mum. O' course." He spooned a healthy portion into a bowl, drizzled it with a bit of honey and handed it over. "Get on the outside of that, mum, and you can have as much as you like."

"Isn't it almost time for the lads to have their breakfast?"

He nodded. "Soon, mum, but I have a feelin' you'll be done with that before they get here."

Tanyth wolfed down the sweet, sticky oatmeal and realized that Cook had been right. In a matter of moments it was gone and she actually looked around for more.

As if reading her mind, Cook said, "There's more right here, mum."

She almost held her bowl out but the full feeling in her stomach made her think twice. "Maybe I better let this settle first."

"Might be wise, mum."

"I can't wrap my head around the idea that I slept for two days." Tanyth said.

"It's true, mum," Rebecca said.

She grimaced. "I'll take your word for it, but I never got up to use the water closet or nothing? It's a wonder I didn't wet the bed."

Cook turned to the stove, checking the oatmeal and tea. "Well, nothing in, nothing out, I guess. I was beginning to worry that there was something else wrong with you, mum, but what you did to the storm musta taken it right out of ya."

"What I did to the storm? What do you mean?" His words made Tanyth feel a bit dizzy.

Before he could answer, Mr. Jameson returned with the captain, the two of them bursting in with a rush of cool air. "See! There she is," Jameson said to the captain.

"Good morning, mum." The captain's greeting seemed a bit forced, as if she were some stranger he wasn't sure about.

"Good morning, Captain. I seem to have missed the pleasure of dinin' with you the last couple of days."

"It's quite all right, mum." The captain spared a glance for Jameson and then Cook before looking back at Tanyth.

"You were indisposed. How do you feel now?"

She shrugged. "Fine, I guess, Captain, but I'm hearing odd tales. They're a bit hard to swallow."

The captain offered a short, dry laugh. "I dare say, mum. I know the truth and I'm not sure I can fathom it myself."

The long string of seven bells rang out and the crew started lining up outside the cookhouse. The first sailor in line stuck his head in, spotted the captain, and withdrew so quickly, it struck Tanyth as comical.

"Mum? Would you come sit with me a bit in the cabin? I think we might have a bit of a chat, and the crew needs this space for breakfast."

"Well, I usually help Cook with servin', Captain."

He nodded slowly. "I know, mum, but I'm pretty sure Cook can handle this on his own."

Cook nodded furiously at the captain's glance. "Don't you worry, mum."

She shrugged. "Well, all right."

Cook held up the teapot. "Would you like a refill to take with you, mum?"

She eyed the empty oatmeal bowl, surprised that she still held it. Her tea mug was likewise empty and she couldn't remember draining it.

"Yes, Cook. Please."

She put her mug on his counter for a refill and placed the dirty bowl in the tray by the door.

"Thank you, Cook." She took up her tea and looked to the captain. "You sure you won't have some?" She held up the mug.

The captain gave a little shake of his head. "I've had my tea for now. I'll get some more in a bit. Shall we go, mum?"

He nodded to Jameson who opened the door. A crowd of curious faces peered in but pulled back as the captain strolled out. Jameson held the door for her and Tanyth followed with Rebecca by her arm. The sailors who nodded to the captain and offered him greetings as he passed became silent when she emerged from the cookhouse.

Tanyth smiled and nodded to them but couldn't help but think she'd done something wrong, the way they all just stared at her—some with bugged out eyes, others with slack jaws. One made a warding gesture with his hand, apparently thinking Tanyth wouldn't notice. Near the end of the line she found one face that offered a tentative smile.

"Good morning, mum. Beautiful day, eh?"

"Good morning, Scooter." She looked around at the clear, blue sky and the gently rolling waves. "It looks like a marvelous day indeed."

The captain waited for them at the companionway and she nodded a farewell to Scooter before joining the captain and following him down into the ship and along the passage to his cabin. He waved her into a chair and she sank into it with a sigh.

"Musta been tireder than I felt, Captain. Sittin' feels good."

The Captain took a seat and nodded Jameson into the chair across from her.

"Should I report to the bosun now, Captain?" Rebecca asked.

The captain shook his head. "He'll get by without ya for a while longer." He indicated a chair beside Tanyth and Rebecca sat.

Turning back to Tanyth, the captain said, "Well, mum, a couple days in the bunk will do that. You took no nourishment the whole time and, frankly, mum, I was getting worried."

Tanyth sipped her tea and nodded. "That's what Cook was sayin', Captain. I can't believe I slept so long or so sound." She shook her head. "Not since—" She stopped and glanced at the two men.

"Not since...?" the captain asked.

"I got hurt last winter. Cut up in a fight."

The captain shot a glance at Jameson and leaned forward, resting his elbows on the table. "You were in a fight, mum?"

Rebecca said, "Bully boys thought our village would be easy pickin's. She taught 'em different."

"But you got hurt?" the captain asked, curiosity and wonder plain on his face.

She nodded.

"Bad enough to sleep for two solid days?"

"I think it was three, but I remember wakin' up every once in a while. Fever dreams. You know how it is."

"We had to sew her up. She lost a lot of blood," Rebecca said.

The captain's eyebrows shot up and he glanced at Jameson before looking back at Tanyth. "That so?"

Tanyth gave a bit of a shrug and a nod.

"Mum, do you remember anything about...before?" the Captain asked.

"Before what? The fight in the village?"

He smiled and shook his head. "Sorry, mum. Before you fell asleep this time."

"Do I remember the storm, ya mean?"

"Yes, mum."

"Well, o'course I remember the storm. Blew up outa nowhere and stretched halfway across the sky."

"Do you remember what you did?"

She shrugged. "Why wouldn't I?"

"Humor me, mum."

"Yeah," she said, taking a moment to grab a sip of the rapidly cooling tea. "I remember what I did."

"What was that?"

"Well, I said a prayer. Asked a blessin'." She jerked one shoulder, dismissing it.

The captain flopped back in his chair like she'd hit him and glanced at Jameson who shrugged in obvious bewilderment.

"A prayer, mum? How did you happen to be on deck to begin with? In order to say the prayer, I mean."

She sipped and thought back. "Well, I thought we were getting ready to come about so I went up on deck to watch. When I saw everybody scramblin' about—and the storm—I went to see Cook. I helped him stow as much as I could and we got it all taken care of pretty fast. I asked if there was anything else I could do to help." She looked back and forth between the two men.

Each one nodded for her to go on.

"So, Cook says 'if you know any prayers to calm the wind or flatten the waves, now would be a good time to say 'em' or somethin' like that." She grinned an apology. "I don't really remember his exact words, Captain."

"That's close enough, mum. Then what?"

"Well, then I went to my cabin and got my staff and went up on deck to ask the blessin'."

"That's where I saw you, right? Just forward of the bridge?"

"Yeah. Storm was comin' fast and you can't hurry a blessin' like that, Captain. Not when you're askin' for something important."

"I see." He looked to Jameson who shook his head. "Then what, mum?"

She sipped again and squinted up her eyes to think. "I remember you yellin' at me from the bridge rail, Captain." She looked at him with an apologetic smile. "I was kinda short with ya then, wasn't I? Sorry. I was kinda busy and time was running out."

He shook his head. "Think nothing of it, mum. You did exactly right. Go on."

"So I said the prayer and asked the blessin' and then I thought the ship got hit by lightnin' cause the last boom was really loud and I passed out." She shrugged. "Cook says Mr. Groves took me below and tucked me in after that, and I've been there ever since."

"That's about right, mum," Jameson said.

The captain shot him a quelling look and he sat back in his chair.

"That's all I know, except Cook also said the ship didn't get hit by lightnin'. Even if it did, it has somethin' on the masts that catches lightnin' and feeds it to the sea or some-thin'."

The captain nodded. "Yes. Correct on both counts, mum. There are lightning catchers on the tops of the masts, and we didn't get hit in any case."

"Oh, good. I didn't dent the deck or anythin', did I, Captain? Sometimes, I get carried away. I usually do that stuff on the ground where I can't hurt anythin' and in the open so I don't hit anybody."

He shook his head. "I don't think so, mum. To be honest,

I didn't look." He turned to Jameson. "Did you, Jameson?"

"No, Captain, I didn't leave the bridge at the time and I haven't thought to look since."

The two men sat and looked at her for so long, Tanyth began to feel uncomfortable. She glanced at Rebecca and back at the captain. "Somethin' wrong, Captain?" she asked at last.

"No, mum. I'd think I might be going mad, but the crew will tell you I've been crazy for a long time." His smile belied his words.

"I know that feeling, Captain. There are days I figger I'm only addle-pated and others where I'm pretty sure that addle-pated is an understatement."

They sat quietly and Tanyth finished her tea before anybody spoke again.

"Do you have any idea what happened after you passed out, mum?" the captain asked.

"Other than what I've told ya, no, Captain. I figure it musta not been as bad as it looked since nobody's said anythin' about it."

"Give us a chance, mum. You just woke up," Jameson said with a grin.

The captain snorted a single laugh at that and nodded to Jameson. "That's about the size of it, mum."

They sat in silence for another few moments and, just as Tanyth was about to ask, the captain leaned forward in his chair again, leaning on his elbows at the edge of the table. "Mum? That storm? It never hit."

She could feel her eyebrows coming together over her nose. "But I saw it, captain. The wind was already pickin' up and I even got rained on, or the wind blew ocean on me. Somethin'. How can you say it never hit?"

"Because as soon as you keeled over there on the deck, mum, the storm just evaporated," Jameson said.

"Evaporated?" Tanyth asked, feeling a bit slow-witted. "How can a storm that size just evaporate?"

Both Jameson and the captain shrugged. "I don't know, mum," the captain said. "It was like somebody blowing on soap suds. The clouds just fell apart and blew away, taking the wind with 'em. Within half a bell, the sky was blue and clear. It's been that way ever since. Fair winds and following seas for two straight days, mum."

Tanyth looked to Jameson with a question in her eyes.

He gave his head a small shake and glanced at the captain out of the corner of his eyes.

"What?" the captain asked.

Tanyth shrugged. "That's a pretty tall tale, Captain. You think I had somethin' to do with it?"

The captain gave Jameson a hard look before turning back to Tanyth. "Well, mum, you did put on a good show."

"Well, I don't suppose you have that many little old ladies faintin' on your deck, do ya?"

The captain chuckled. "No, mum. That's true enough but I was thinking about before you keeled over. That spinning about and shaking your stick at the sky? That was impressive enough but when you hit the ship with it. That was somethin' else altogether."

"You're sure I didn't dent the deck, Captain? When I get swinging that stick around, I get carried away sometimes..."

He shook his head. "Even if you did, mum. Don't worry about it. Avoiding that storm was worth any number of dents in the decking."

They sat there staring at her again without speaking.

Tanyth shifted in her seat, growing more and more uneasy at their inspection. She turned to Rebecca who reached over to pat her forearm.

"Is there anythin' else, Captain?" Tanyth asked finally.

He took in a deep breath through is nose and blew it out the same way before answering. "I don't know, mum? Is there?"

She glanced at Jameson, but shrugged. "I don't know for sure, Captain."

"But you're worried about something, mum, and Mr. Jameson knows what it is, doesn't he."

"Captain, Mother Fairport thinks that maybe something's wrong with the cargo in the main hold," Jameson said quietly.

The captain kept watching Tanyth.

"You may remember that I asked to inspect the hold after

that last storm...?" Jameson continued.

"I remember, Mr. Jameson," the captain said without taking his eyes off Tanyth.

"I still think that's a good idea, sir."

"So do I, Mr. Jameson, but I'm curious about how this all came about. Mum?"

She gave a half shrug. "I sometimes have dreams, Captain. Sometimes they turn out to be true."

"I see," he said. "You had a dream that something's wrong in the hold of my ship?"

Rebecca said, "It's not the first time she had dreams like that, either, Captain."

"Back in the village? Where you were before?" he asked.

Tanyth sighed. "Yeah. I sometimes saw things in my dreams and usually they were real things."

"Things like what, mum?" He reached a hand across the table toward her. "I'm not meaning to pry, mum. I'm honestly curious about what's going on here and I think knowing might help me."

"The bully boys? One of them was hidin' in the woods and watchin' the village. I saw him in a dream. It was a kind of warnin', Captain."

He nodded. "What else?"

"Well, I dreamed the night they came to burn us out. We was able to stop 'em when I woke up and told everybody."

He sat back in his seat and looked over at Jameson who sat stalk-still, apparently dumbfounded by her statements.

"You didn't know this, Scotty?"

He shook his head, the movements jerky. "No, Captain. She said she had dreams but this is the first I've heard of all this."

"So what do you think is wrong in the hold, mum?"

"There's a box that don't seem right. There's a light in it. A lantern I think."

The captain glanced at Jameson who inspected his fingernails closely, but nodded.

"A lantern? In a crate? And you dreamed this, mum?"

Tanyth felt very uncomfortable with this careful scrutiny. "I don't know for sure, Captain. I can only see it from the outside. It's got some holes along the bottom and it's warm inside and there's a flickerin' light."

"Really?" his brow furrowed in thought.

"Yeah. And a sharp smell. Like metal and lamp oil."

"That's pretty specific, mum."

She shrugged. "It maybe just the rambles of a crazy, old lady, Captain."

"But you don't think so."

"No, Captain, I don't. And I'm worried that it's a warnin' that we need to take serious."

"It's easy enough to check. Would that set your mind at rest?"

"It would, Captain. I can't imagine why somebody would put a lit lantern in a box. It makes no sense to me. But that clickin' was the bothersome part, Captain."

The captain sat bolt upright. "Clicking?"

"Oh, yeah. Every so often, it clicks."

"Clicks, how?"

"Just one click like metal on metal and then a long, long pause. Then another—"

"Jameson! Get that hatch off. Now!"

Jameson all but flew out of his chair and down the passage.

"Sorry, mum. I didn't mean to interrupt you. Is there anything else you can think of? Anything at all?"

Tanyth gave a little shrug. "Nothin' about the box."

"About what, then?"

"There are rats down there."

He leaned forward and peered into her face. "Are you playing a game with me, Mother Fairport?"

The question took her off balance and she answered without thinking. "No, Captain. Not at all."

"Did you dream about the rats, too, mum?"

"Yeah. I did." She looked down at her empty mug, wishing there was something in it.

"Did you think I didn't know there are rats?" His voice carried a note of humor.

That surprised her into looking back at him. "Well, Captain, I heard that you were sure there were no rats aboard and that you weren't happy when anybody mentioned them."

He started to laugh. It began as a little giggly burble at first and then he threw back his head and guffawed.

"Captain? I don't understand. What's so funny?"

He caught his breath and pulled a huge, white handkerchief out of his pocket to wipe his streaming eyes. "It's a game I played with Benjamin when he was little. He used to sail with me when he was a boy and he'd make up these stories about how big the rats were. I'd pretend to be horrified and angry and would gnash my teeth and tear at my beard. I'd tell him there were no rats on my ship and carry on like a madman for a few minutes. It was a family thing. A joke we told each other all the time. We'd giggle about it for days afterward sometimes. Who told you about this rat mania of mine? Jameson?"

"Well, I—"

"Of course. Had to be." He took a moment to blow his nose and chuckle again. "It's fine, mum. Thank you for the laugh. I haven't laughed like that for months." He chuckled a couple more times. "Come on, Mr. Jameson should have the hatch open by now."

He stood and led the way out of the cabin. In the passageway, just before they stepped onto the deck, he turned back to her. "Mum? Don't be alarmed if I should happen to see a rat in the hold, all right?"

The request took her by surprise but nodded. "All right, Captain, but they'll hide when the light shines in."

Her comment obviously took him by surprise but he nodded in return. "Will they now? I can see why they would. Interesting, but just so you're warned, mum. Don't be alarmed?"

"Anything you say, Captain."

He grinned like a boy with a frog in his pocket and nodded his thanks. "Let's go see what we can see, shall we?"

He bounded up onto the deck and led the way forward to the main cargo hatch. Jameson and several of the crew stood around it. Tanyth saw that it wasn't one big cover as she thought, but instead consisted of broad planks across the opening with an oiled canvas cover across the top. Jameson had peeled back the cover and removed a few of the boards. They had a tongue and groove arrangement and fit tightly in the opening.

"Just pull up enough to get in there, Mr. Jameson."

"Aye, aye, Captain."

Two of the sailors pulled a couple more of the planks out and stacked them alongside the hatch. The opening was big enough that Tanyth was able to see down onto the tops of the crates and barrels stacked around down inside the ship. It wasn't as deep as she had pictured it in her mind. It looked barely tall enough to stand up in.

"Nichols, hop down there and set up the ladder," Jameson said.

"Aye, aye, sir," a heavyset sailor with muscled arms lowered himself over the coaming, hung by his hands for a moment and then let go. Tanyth heard and felt the thump of his landing. After some scraping and at least one curse, a pair of metal hooks emerged from the darkness and latched over the coaming. Nichols swarmed up the ladder and out onto the deck almost before Tanyth realized what he'd done.

Jameson started for the ladder but the captain cut him off and scampered down out of sight, disappearing into the dark almost as quickly as Nichols had emerged. Jameson went right behind him. She heard their voices speaking under the deck, but couldn't make out their words. Their voices fell silent for several long moments and just as Tanyth began to wonder if something had happened to them, she heard Jameson say, "Here!"

She heard some scrapping and bumping come from the hatch and then the captain emerged, dusting his trousers off when he regained the deck. "Nichols, Ferguson. Get a line down there and let's get our little surprise package up where we can see it. Rand, fetch a pry bar, if you please."

The ship's bell rang twice while they waited.

Then the two men pulled the crate up out of the hold and placed it on the deck. Jameson clambered right behind it.

"Step back, if you please, gentlemen," the captain said. He turned to Tanyth. "Is this the one, mum?"

She crossed to where it lay on the deck and walked around it, crouching down to look at the base. Black paint splashed the bottom third of the crate, but it looked like the right one.

Along the bottom edge, she found fresh wood showing where something had gnawed the black paint away. She nodded and looked up at the Captain. "Yeah. That's the one."

"You're sure, mum?" he said.

She nodded again. "How did you find it so fast?"

He smiled and held up one finger. After a few moments, they all heard a single, loud click.

"I took a chance that there might be only one crate that clicked," he said with a grin.

She grinned back.

"Rand?" The captain held out his hand for the pry bar and with a few deft strokes pulled the top off the crate. When he did, Tanyth heard the crunch of breaking glass and everybody froze where they stood for a long moment. Crouched near the base, she caught the tangy whiff of lamp oil and then saw a widening pool spreading out through the holes, flowing across the deck and under the captain's feet.

"Oil!" she cried and pointed.

The captain, standing with the lid half raised, looked down at his feet and froze. "Water! Douse it. Now!"

Several sailors grabbed the buckets they used for washing the deck and scooped salt water from over the side in the rapid smooth movements of long practice. In less than a minute, the deck, the crate, Tanyth, and the captain were all dripping with icy seawater.

Tanyth saw the rainbow sheen seeping away towards the scuppers in the reflected light of the morning sun.

"You think it's safe now, sir?" Jameson asked.

The captain grunted. "Don't know. Everybody stand well back, if you please. Mum? If you and your friend would get back behind the deckhouse? You've been a great help and I'd like to keep from getting you blown up."

Everybody within the sound of his voice started backpedaling as fast as they could.

"A couple of you brave lads might fill a few more buckets, just in case," the captain said with a wry grin.

They did so and stood by with them. Tanyth moved back behind the deckhouse but peeped around the corner to watch.

"Jameson, take a peep into the crate before I move this

lid any more, if you would?"

Mr. Jameson eased himself closer to the crate and peered into the dimness. "Looks like a lanyard hanging down, blowing in the breeze."

"Anything else?"

"No, Captain."

"I'm gonna move the cover. Tell me if that lanyard fetches up."

"Aye, aye, sir."

The captain rotated his upper body to open up the crate to inspection.

"Nothing yet, sir...all right, you're clear."

The captain leaned the cover against the hatch coaming and looked down into the crate. As he leaned over, it clicked again. With the lid off, the click sounded more like a clank and was loud enough to make everybody jump.

Jameson and the captain peered down into the crate and mumbled together for a few minutes. When they stood, Tanyth saw the captain's face had taken on an angry, red cast so deep it neared purple. Mr. Jameson seemed very gray, and perhaps just a little sick to his stomach.

"It's all right," the captain called. "You lot, secure the hold, if you please. We won't be putting this one back down there."

Three sailors started laying the planks back down, tapping them into place with the heels of their hands, and then stretching the oiled canvas back over the opening, lashing it down securely.

Tanyth came out from behind the deckhouse and joined the throng of sailors who clustered around the captain. "It's safe now," he said. "Thanks, again, to Mother Fairport for noticing."

He shared a pointed look with her and she nodded. "Quite welcome, Captain."

"Now, you've all got work to do, I wager. If not, I'm sure the bosun can find something...?" He didn't need to say any more as men started disappearing like soap bubbles in a high wind. The captain turned to the bosun and pointed to the crate and the mess on the deck. "Wrap that in canvas, if you please, Harcourt? Gently. Try not to bump it around too much."

The bosun nodded. "Wrapped, not bumped. Aye, aye, Cap'n."

"And then get a couple of the lads to scrub that lamp oil off the deck. No need to tempt fate, eh?"

The bosun knuckled his forehead and nodded. "Aye, aye, Cap'n. We'll take care of it."

"Mr. Jameson? Mother Fairport? Would you join me in the cabin again, please?"

They followed the captain back down the passageway and took up their regular seats at his table. Captain Groves sat back in his chair, one arm slug over the back and squinted at Tanyth. "That was good timing, mum."

"Why's that, Captain?"

"Inside that crate was a clockwork drum that slowly wound a bit of rope around and around. When the rope ran out, there was some mechanism inside that would break a jar of oil and then tilt a burning wick into it."

She glanced at Jameson who nodded in agreement.

"And why was that good timing, Captain?"

"Because the rope was almost all wound up."

"Is that why the oil spilled when you took the lid off?"

His mouth screwed into a bitter grimace. "No, that was a bit of luck there. A second lanyard was tied to the lid. Anybody prying the lid off, like I did, released the mechanism that broke the glass. The lanyard on the lid was apparently supposed to tip the lantern."

She cocked her head trying to follow what he was saying. "So, it was trapped in case somebody noticed and opened the crate?"

He nodded and rubbed a hand across his mouth. "That would have been me going up like a human torch if it had worked."

Jameson's brow crinkled in puzzlement. "I saw the lamp in there, skipper. Salt water doused it, but why didn't it tip over?"

He glanced at him before turning an amused look back to Tanyth. "It seems, Mr. Jameson, that a rat chewed through the cord."

The two men looked at Tanyth for a long, long moment before the captain asked, "Do you know who shipped that particular crate, Jameson?"

"Yes, Captain. That was the crate that Peter Robertson was so anxious that we bring aboard at the last minute."

The captain nodded. "I thought as much. It only makes sense."

Jameson asked, "Why's that, Captain?"

The captain leaned an elbow on the table and held up his fist. He raised one finger. "First, it had to have come aboard close to when we were leaving. That's not the kind of thing you can have sitting in a ship that might be tied to the pier for a week."

Jameson nodded.

The captain raised a second finger. "Second, I refused to pay the insurance premiums that the syndicate wanted. It's gone up every year, and I put my foot down. Apparently they felt it was time to make an example of me."

Jameson nodded a second time.

The captain raised a third finger. "Robertson's one of my investors. He's not been happy with that decision. He's concerned that if we lose the ship, then he'll be out a lot of money."

Jameson nodded again.

"Isn't that a reasonable fear, Captain," Tanyth asked.

He pulled his hand down and nodded. "Yes, mum, it is. But it ignores the reality that while he loses money, we lose our lives."

Jameson snorted. "And the syndicate is happy to insure a sailor's life and only charge him three times the amount he'd make in pay."

Tanyth squinted her eyes and cocked her head. "That doesn't sound like a good deal to me."

The captain barked a single laugh. "Even a landlubber can see it. They try to make out like it's a great bargain. Buy the insurance, and if you get killed at sea, then your wife and kiddies get a hundred times your pay in settlement."

Tanyth blinked at the sum. "That's a lot of money. How

often have they paid it?"

The captain shook his head. "Never as far as I know."

"But...? I don't understand."

Jameson leaned into the table. "Most sailors have their pay spent before the ship gets underway. Really, the only people who could afford the premiums are mates and captains."

"All right, so no mate or captain has ever been lost?"

The captain nodded. "Oh, aye, and some of them even had an insurance policy."

"Then, why hasn't the syndicate ever paid."

"Because the only ones who've been lost have been on ships that never came back," Jameson said.

The captain added the missing piece to the puzzle for her. "Without an officer like captain or mate to file the claim, there's nothing to pay. The wife and kiddies have no standing. If the ship doesn't come back, then the syndicate doesn't know if the corpse in question is really dead or just sailed off into the hazy distance, absconding with ship and cargo."

Jameson nodded. "So they don't need to pay."

The captain scowled and looked at Tanyth. "Some of the other captains and I have long been convinced that the syndicate was sinking ships that didn't pay the cargo premiums."

"And even some that did," Jameson added. "Nothing like a fat payout to sobbing investors to convince folks they provide a valuable service."

"But not the families?" Rebecca asked. "If the ship is lost...?"

The captain's mouth twisted into a grim parody of a smile. "Because investors don't insure the ship. They insure the cargo. If the cargo doesn't arrive, doesn't matter why. Failure to deliver is grounds for payment."

"So, some cargoes get paid for a couple of times," Jameson muttered darkly. "Send it out in an insured vessel. Ship disappears and the syndicate pays with a lot of fanfare. Meanwhile, the cargo gets off-loaded someplace quiet and the crews just evaporate into the sea fog. Voluntarily, if they know what's good for 'em."

The captain nodded, a wry smile curling his lips. "More truth than fiction in that story, too, I'm thinking." He sighed.

"I shoulda paid closer attention. I knew there was something wrong with Robertson insisting we take that crate."

"Well, we got proof now, sir. That crate is tied directly to Mr. Peter Robertson and a lot of people saw him loading it. That was a big hullabaloo in the middle of the evening, skipper. He won't find it easy to wiggle off this hook."

"I hope you're right, Jameson. That bit of clockwork and oil is pretty damning, but tying it to the syndicate could be a lot tougher."

"Well, Robertson's head on the block would probably get him to speak up right, quick, I'd wager."

The captain turned a jaundiced eye to his young subordinate.

"You don't think so, Skipper?"

He shook his head. "I think I'll have an opening on my board of investors by the time I get back, assuming I don't already."

Jameson looked startled, but Tanyth thought the captain had the right of it.

"Let me guess," she said. "Your Mr. Robertson had some financial set back that prevented him actually investin' in this voyage."

"Big loss on a corn crop last fall," the captain said. "He didn't have time to recover his fortune and the rest had to dig a little deeper to underwrite this trip."

Jameson scowled. "Does that mean they've been planning to set us up all winter?"

The captain shrugged. "Could be. Or it could be that Robertson had a handy lever for them to press on. In return for not investing in a trip he couldn't afford, and for pressuring me to buy insurance on the trip, he gets a nice little paycheck from the syndicate. When he couldn't convince me, they gave him this little present to get included on the voyage."

"You don't think he knew what was in it, Captain?" Tanyth asked.

"Oh, he probably knew, but he didn't build it. At most he had to light the wick and make sure it was on board at the last minute." The captain shook his head. "No, that's a damned clever design, right down to the artful splashes of black paint that got applied after they bored the holes. That deadman's lanyard in the top in case somebody got too nosy?" The captain shook his head. "That was just too subtle a touch for Peter Robertson. I've seen broken bottles with more subtlety than he's ever shown."

Jameson frowned. "How do you know it was painted after the holes were bored?"

"Paint on the inside of the hole. If the board had been painted before, the drill would have left nice fresh wood, like our friend the rat did with her gnawing. Somebody mighta seen that and wondered why there were air holes in a cargo crate." He sighed. "I didn't even spot the holes along the top edge until I had the cover off."

"Wait, Captain? You think there are rats on the ship?" Jameson asked, his eyes wide.

"It's a ship, isn't it? Every ship worth havin' has rats aboard. They're too smart to sail on a crappy vessel."

"All this time, and you knew?"

The captain laughed. "You'd be surprised what I know, Mr. Jameson." He winked at Mother Fairport.

The ships bell rang eight times.

"And that is lunch, I think. Mother Fairport is probably ready to pass out again from hunger, Jameson. Why don't you make sure she gets something to eat and bring me back a bowl of whatever foul concoction our poisoner has created today."

"Skipper? I thought you liked Cook's food." Jameson looked aghast.

The captain barked a laugh and clapped Jameson on the shoulder. "Sometimes you take me way too seriously, my lad."

Tanyth giggled when the captain shot her a wink while Jameson wasn't looking.

CHAPTER 27
HALFWAY DOES NOT A VOYAGE MAKE

Tanyth settled into the rhythm of the ship. She came to enjoy the regular routine. She rose with the sun and, instead of packing her gear and walking until sunset, she had a comfortable breakfast with Cook and helped him serve the crew. Sometimes she'd make biscuits and once helped with the bread.

After breakfast clean up she retired to her cabin and worked on sorting out the heavy bundle of materials that she'd collected over her many years of travel. In many ways she relived her long trek in miniature as she explored the pile, each new layer of notes and artifacts unfolding a fragile page from the book of her memory. Notes from the earliest days were the hardest to decipher. The pressure and friction of page against page had erased portions, and faded others to near illegibility. Still there was enough to amuse and entertain them for day upon day.

At midday she returned to the deckhouse to help Cook once more. Usually lunch was a hearty affair with bread and a hearty stew or fish soup. By the end of the eighth day at sea, all the food was tinned, salted, or smoked—except for those things like potatoes, carrots, and onions which held up well in storage or foods that could be created from scratch. Tanyth felt satisfied with the arrangement, having some experience with food that had gone past its prime and no desire to deal with it ever again. To make up for the lack of fresh produce, Cook made a series of fruit pasties—small crusty turnovers with a helping of cooked fruit inside. He had a barrel of apples and another of pears that he alternated with some regularity.

After lunch cleanup she returned to her compartment and the seemingly bottomless pile of notes and scribbles. Just peeling them apart could take several minutes because of their age and brittleness. More than once Tanyth found herself muttering, "Good thing I didn't wait much longer."

Rebecca smiled and offered sharp young eyes and slender fingers to aid in the process when she wasn't busy on deck or scampering about in the rigging.

In the evening, she joined the captain and one of the mates for dinner in the captain's cabin. All three men were delightful dinner companions, and Tanyth could often get them to tell stories of life at sea or along the coast. They took great pleasure in telling stories about each other and took great pains to exaggerate the stories to humorous effect. At times they'd trade off, trying to egg one into telling a more outrageous tale about the other. The two younger men took great delight in this game. Tanyth admired the way the captain managed and directed the talk, always finding a humorous note that was funny but not cruel.

As the voyage progressed, the days became chillier. Tanyth was glad for her warm trousers, heavy coat, and knit cap. The trip from companionway to deckhouse could be very raw early in the morning, although she found occasion to stroll several times around the deck for exercise when the frustration of peeling thin, delicate layers apart became overwhelming.

On the tenth night underway, Tanyth knocked on the door but failed to receive the customary "Enter!" as response. She could hear their voices as a low rumble, but couldn't make out the words through the door. After knocking again, a bit louder, she poked her head in, and found the two Groves men in heated discussion over a chart pinned down to the captain's charting table.

"Am I interruptin'?" she asked. "Cook will be here with dinner soon."

They looked up, the captain with a look of consternation on his face, the younger Groves with a look of jubilation.

"No, no, mum. Come in," the captain said. "Sorry for that. We were just discussing the navigation."

They took seats just before Cook bustled in with a pair of sailors in tow. He performed his customary delivery and, with a nod and a wink, closed the door on his way out.

"Is there somethin' wrong with the navigation?" Tanyth asked after they'd broken biscuits and addressed a bit of Cook's stew.

The younger Mr. Groves kept giving his father little looks, nudges with his eyes as if encouraging him to bring up a subject. The captain steadfastly addressed his stew with uncharacteristic single-mindedness.

Finally, with a sour look at his son, the captain tossed his spoon down. "It's our position, mum. According to the fixes we've been getting, we've been moving along quite smartly."

"Is that a problem?" Tanyth asked.

The captain shook his head, and bit his bottom lip. "The *Call* is a grand vessel, mum, but she's no sea hound. She gets us there in comfort and with a goodly-sized cargo to make getting there worthwhile." He paused to peer at her.

"But there's a problem, isn't there, Captain?" Tanyth said, more statement than question.

He gave a half shrug. "In a manner of speaking, mum."

He looked so glum, she jumped to the obvious conclusion. "Oh, no, don't tell me we've slowed down."

The captain sighed even though Tanyth thought that the younger Groves might pop a seam in his excitement. "No, mum," the captain said, "we've actually sped up."

Tanyth took a bite of her biscuit and considered the captain's expression. "You don't look pleased by this, Captain."

"Under normal circumstances, mum, I'd be delighted."

Tanyth looked across the table but young Mr. Groves wouldn't meet her eyes. "But...?" she prompted.

"But it's too much," the captain said. "According to our daily fixes, we're going almost twice as fast as we should be."

"Is that bad?"

The captain shot another sour look at his son. "Well, mum, this one thinks we've found a new current. That would explain the difference in position. We can't explain it with winds. We're not moving through the water that fast, so the water must be carrying us."

"You don't sound convinced, Captain."

He shook his head. "That's a very far-fetched explanation, mum."

"What else could it be?"

He shook his head. "All I can think of is the tables we use to translate our position from a sun sighting to an actual chart location. If the tables have some kind of consistent error, we have no way to know where we might really be."

"But, Father, what if it is a new current? We've never been in this particular part of the ocean this early in the season. It could be a winter current that hasn't subsided." His enthusiasm had him almost bouncing in his chair.

The captain shook his head. "It would be wonderful, Benjamin, of course. Even if it's only for this one trip, but if it's not, then we could be Father-knows-where."

"I'll concede the point, sir, but we'll know in a day or so whether it's real or an error."

"How's that?" Tanyth asked.

"If we're really where the fixes say we are and we keep moving at this rate, we'll spot land in another day, day and a half," Captain Groves said.

"And if not?" Rebecca asked after a short pause.

"We don't know when—or where—we'll make landfall."

"Well, it'll happen sooner or later, Father. If we keep sailing north, it's not like we can sail past the northern provinces," Mr. Groves said, his grin threatening to break free and float around the cabin.

"True enough," the captain conceded, "but I still don't like it."

"Just think of how far ahead you'll be over Malloy," Benjamin added, dunking his biscuit in the broth and nibbling the wet edges off it.

The captain shook his head. "Or not. He could be on the way back before we even get there."

"If it's a current, what's to prevent him from arriving quickly, too?" Tanyth asked.

The two Groves looked at her—the younger with a frown and the older with a thoughtful consideration.

They shared a look before Benjamin said, "It would depend on the width of the current and where they were in it. We may be in the middle, they might be on the edge. There could be a large difference in charted movement even if both ships are moving through the water at the same rate."

Captain Groves cocked his head and squinted his eyes at her. "You don't happen to know anything about this, do ya, mum?"

The question startled Tanyth. "Me, Captain? What could I have to do with it?"

He raised his eyebrows and said, "You did rather a good job on the storm. Anybody who can erase a storm could change the flow of the oceans."

"I didn't erase a storm, Captain." Tanyth felt a flutter of uneasiness in her stomach.

"Somebody did, mum," the captain said, a small smile curving his lips. "You were the only one waving around a stick."

The observation made Tanyth sit back in her seat. "I didn't mean to," she said, and realized how silly that sounded. "I mean, I s'pose I meant to, but I don't know any magic or such that could do anything like that."

"And you know how to see a firebomb in the hold?" the captain asked.

"Well, no, Captain, but that just sorta happens in my dreams." Tanyth felt flushed and flustered. She took a spoon-ful of stew to gain some time. "I didn't set out to find a bomb. It just...happened."

"So you don't get to pick what you dream about, mum?" the captain asked, genuine curiosity on his face.

She shook her head.

"Is there any kind of commonality in what you dream, mum?" Captain Groves asked.

Tanyth pondered the question for a moment. "I get two kinds of dreams that I know of, Captain. One is a kind of prophecy. I see things that happen in the future, I think. So far I've had two of those. One's come true. I'm watchin' for the second."

"And the second kind?" Benjamin asked.

"Those have been pretty specific and gen'rally have to do

with threats and warnin's."

"Do you have just regular dreams, mum? The normal ones, I mean?" Mr. Groves asked.

She shrugged. "I have my share of normal dreams, sure. The kind that make no sense if you can remember 'em at all. The special dreams. Those I remember."

With a glance at his father, Benjamin asked, "What was the last dream about?"

Without thinking about it Tanyth said, "Cook's put a trap down in the stores hold to try to catch a rat." As soon as she said it, it jarred her to her bones. "Oh, no."

"What is it, mum?" the captain asked, looking up from his stew.

"He's set a trap!" Tanyth rose from her chair. "I'll be right back."

She ran down the passageway, up onto the deck, and into the deckhouse without stopping. She found Cook cleaning up a bit, the evening meal nearly run its course.

"Mum? Are you all right? Has something happened to the captain?"

"You set a trap? Get it out of there. Now!"

He blinked in astonishment. "Trap? For what? Where?"

"By the wet crack. You set a trap. I has a bit of..." she had to close her eyes and remember it in order to figure out what he'd used for bait. "A bit of bacon?"

Cook's eyes bugged out a bit, and he said, "Oh, aye. A gob of bacon fat."

"Get it out of there now. She may step on it and die."

"She? She who, mum?"

"The rat! The one who visits your stores hold. The one that saved the ship!" she said. "You can't kill her. Not now. It wouldn't be right."

Cook held his hands out in a placating gesture. "All right, mum. All right. I'll go get it right after dinner."

"No! Now." Tanyth said. "You get it or I will!"

She started scrabbling around on the deck for the pull ring she saw him use before.

Behind her the first mate pushed into the crowded galley. "Is everything all right, mum?"

Tanyth straightened and pointed at Cook. "He's set a trap for the rat. The one that saved us. I want it removed. Now."

Mr. Groves eyed Cook with one raised brow.

"All right!" he said "All right, mum! Step back so I can get it." Cook waved her back into the corner and pulled up the ring on the deck. He latched it into place and dropped down into the darkness. After a moment, Tanyth heard him bark a laugh and he emerged with the offending trap in hand. He handed it to her. "There you go, mum, but it looks like you didn't have to worry."

She examined the trap and realized that it had been sprung and the bait gone. Some kind of gray-brown object was locked under the killing bail. She held it up and thought it should be familiar but she couldn't quite place it. She looked up at Cook with a frown as he lowered the hatch again. "What is this?"

"Why, mum, I thought you knew what hard tack looked like," he said with a grin.

She examined it again and realized it was the corner of a hard tack biscuit.

"Your lil friend must have dropped a wafer on the trap, sprung it, and then stolen the bait," Cook said, pointing at the trigger. "See? No bacon grease. It's licked clean."

Tanyth felt her heart rate returning to something like normal.

Cook handed the trap to Mr. Groves who turned it over in his hands.

"I'm sorry, mum," Cook said. He placed a hand on her shoulder and looked into her eyes, something like awe and contrition painting his face. "You really can see this in your dreams, can't you."

Tanyth nodded and felt a shiver run down her back at the thought of being in the dream when the trap struck.

Groves handed the trap back. "Thank you, Cook. Please don't do this again."

He took the trap from him. "I won't, sir." He grinned at it and shrugged. "She's too smart to fall for it now, anyway."

Tanyth chuckled and followed Mr. Groves back to the

captain's cabin.

"Are you all right, mum?" the captain asked with a glance at his son.

"Yeah, thank you, Captain. I just had to talk to Cook about a bit of bacon."

The two men shared a glance that Tanyth pretended not to notice.

$$) O ($$

Tanyth and Rebecca finished sorting through the last of her notes on the twelfth day of the voyage. The final item was a notation in Mother Dogwood's hand dated some twenty years before. After many seasons at the bottom of her pack, even being transferred from pack to pack as Tanyth wore them out over time, the folded parchment was brittle, but still legible.

"My dear Tanyth.

"Your warmth, good humor, and determination should hold you in good stead. It's a long and winding road you have before you. There is so much more to the world than I can teach you now. It falls to you to discover where your path lies and to determine whether or not you have the will to walk it.

"Most of us start out late in life and I envy you the opportunity to start walking so early. I can tell you that the path is worth walking. I suspect you will find this before you get to the end of the path and I am writing to tell you two things:

"First, I feel honored to have been the one to point you down the road.

"Second, you'll know when you reach the end of the path. Until you do, keep moving.

"May the blessing of the All-Mother guide you and the strength of the All-Father protect you on your journey.

"Blessed be. Agnes."

Tanyth read the simple note three times and then stood to look out the tiny porthole at the surging sea outside—the sparkling, blue-green ocean blurring from the moisture in her eyes.

"When did you slip this into my papers, you sly old vixen?" she murmured. In her mind she added, "And why?"

"What is it, mum?" Rebecca asked.

Tanyth handed the note to the young woman. Rebecca held it up to the light to read.

On its surface the note was little more than a message from the past, a note from a part of her life that seemed almost incomprehensibly distant. Yet, in its simplicity and in the fact that it was the last souvenir in the bundle of her life, Tanyth felt an immense weight.

"How nice," Rebecca said.

"There's a message there," she said. "If I'm only clever enough to read it."

Rebecca looked down at the brittle page once more. "A message, mum?"

Tanyth nodded.

"What kinda message?"

Tanyth leaned against her bunk, not even aware of the rocking of the ship any longer. "That's the question, isn't it, my dear?"

"What makes you say so, mum?"

Tanyth chewed her lip and held out a hand to take the paper back. "Well, Agnes Dogwood lived on the outskirts of the village. When I left my husband, I ran to her."

Rebecca's eyes never left Tanyth's face and she nodded for Tanyth to continue.

Tanyth took a deep breath and blew it out before speaking again. "I was a mess. The bruises were only part of it." In her mind, with the physical reminder of her beginning in her hand, the fall day seemed so clear. "I was scared. Scared that Roger would find me. Scared o' what people would say, me runnin' away from my husband like that. Scared o' what I was going to do next, how I'd get by in the world."

Tanyth read the letter again.

"When I showed up on her doorstep, Agnes Dogwood didn't ask any questions. Didn't even seem surprised to see me, now that I think of it."

"Was she the healer, mum?"

Tanyth nodded. "Midwife, sometimes healer. I thought

she knew everything about plants and most things about people."

"And did she?"

"Well, she knew a lot about what grew around the village, right enough, but there was a lot that I couldn't learn there. That was a hard winter, the one I spent with Agnes. I helped out by choppin' firewood, cookin' now and again. Fetched her water. Just the chores ya need to do ta keep a body and soul together through a long winter."

Rebecca nodded.

"Nobody said anything about my livin' there. None of the people from the town. Not even them that came to the house lookin' for healin'."

"Your husband never came lookin' for ya?"

Tanyth started to shake her head, but stopped—an image long forgotten, rising to her mind's eye. "He came to the door once. Mother Dogwood wouldn't let him in. Wouldn't let him talk to me." The image was of an angry-faced Roger casting invective on the white-haired old lady in the door. She just shook her head and closed the door in his face. "I don't know how, or why, but I never spoke to him again." Tanyth focused on Rebecca's smiling face. "Odd, really."

"Not so odd, mum. Not if she'd had your kinda powers."

"Oh, tut, girl. I've no kind of power."

Rebecca shook her head, giving Tanyth a sly smile. "You keep tellin' yourself that, mum. You might convince some, but you're having the Mother's own time convincin' yourself, ain't ya?"

Tanyth looked at the paper once more. "She seemed to think I was goin' on a long trip."

"And she was right, wasn't she?"

Tanyth nodded. "She started me on the road twenty-some winters ago and now I find this?"

"It was there the whole time, mum. You just never looked."

Tanyth nodded. "Guess I never thought much about stoppin' before."

"Stoppin', mum?" Surprise made Rebecca's eyes go wide.

Tanyth shrugged and looked out the porthole again. "Frank's a good man. I could do a lot worse."

Rebecca sighed. "Yes'm. He is and you could." She tugged the paper from Tanyth's unresisting fingers. "But this? This is why you need to keep goin', mum."

Tanyth looked at the girl, so young, so earnest, and laughed. "Not because I'm having dreams? Not because I see things in animals' eyes?"

Rebecca shook her head. "And not because your prayers come true, either, mum. That's all beside the point." She rattled the paper in Tanyth's face. "This woman knew somethin'. Somethin' she didn't tell you. Somethin' you need to find on your own. And I'd bet ya biscuits to bedbugs that she had that power herself."

The outburst rocked Tanyth back on her heels. "Prayers come true?"

Rebecca blinked and shook her head once. "Well, yeah. You don't remember? The storm?"

"That was just a bit of protection, nothin' to that."

Rebecca shook her head. "I was watchin', mum. You and your little prayer was somethin' to see and whatever power you got, you don't seem ta know how to control it. You don't even think you have it!" Rebecca took a deep breath and Tanyth saw her eyes filling up. "After, when Mr. Groves brought you down and tucked you in, you looked so weak, mum. So fragile. You was barely breathin'. It was like you spent your whole life out there on the deck. I was afraid, then, mum. Really afraid."

"I thought the storm was gone."

"No, mum. Afraid you were." Rebecca fumbled in her pocket for a hanky and used it to wipe her eyes and swipe her nose.

"I was what? Gone?"

Rebecca nodded.

Tanyth stared at the younger woman for a long moment. "Well, I'm not." The words sounded stilted and muffled in the small room.

Rebecca nodded again. "You coulda, though, mum." She tucked her hanky away in her pocket and looked up at Tanyth. "That's why you gotta keep goin', mum. You gotta find this Gertie Pinecrest woman. She knows. She has to know. She's the last, right?"

Tanyth gave a half shrug. "Last one I know of. She may know somebody else."

Rebecca shook her head. "No, mum. She won't. Don't you see?"

"You think that she's the end of the path that Agnes Dogwood was talkin' about?"

Rebecca gave her a look of exasperation. "Don' you, mum? Really?"

Tanyth took a deep breath and pulled her lower lip between thumb and forefinger in thought. "Well, it's easy to find reasons when you look back like that, my dear," she said after a few moments of staring out at the ocean again. "Don't mean the reasons were there to begin with. Just that they look like it in hindsight."

"But, mum, you are on this path. Things are happenin' to ya. Things that ain't exactly normal?"

Tanyth gave a small nod. "I could be goin' mad. Old people do, sometimes."

"Young people do, too, mum. Live long enough in a city like Kleesport and you'll see plenty of 'em. Point is, you're not goin' mad." Rebecca pointed at the sea outside. "You did that, mum. You stopped that storm and I'd bet you're behind this new current the captain is so concerned about."

Tanyth's face wrinkled into a grimace of denial. "That can't be. I don't know anythin' about currents and winds and all that."

Rebecca stamped her foot. "No, you don't, mum, but that don't mean you're not callin' on powers that do. Powers you got ideas about. Powers that might kill you the next time you call too much, pray too hard for stuff you don't understand." Rebecca's eyes filled again and she stopped to fumble for her handkerchief once more.

Tanyth took in a deep breath and blew it out her nose. "Well, I didn't say I wasn't gonna keep goin', did I?"

Rebecca looked up, hope in her eyes. "No, mum. You just said you was thinkin' about stoppin'."

Tanyth rubbed her own nose and gazed out at the water. "Come all this way. May as well see what ole Gertie has to say for herself," she muttered.

Rebecca surprised her by wrapping her in a warm hug.

"Now, there's 'nough o' that," Tanyth said, hugging back and then releasing the young woman. "Let's get this stuff picked up now and re-wrapped before eight bells, shall we?"

Together they carefully re-bundled the papers and notes, separating teachings and eras with bits of cloth and leather. Tanyth marveled anew as they reviewed her own words and those of her teachers. She found a wealth of pressed leaves and drawings. Each tiny sketch recalled not just the plant, but the circumstance of the drawing and the use of the material. Connections swirled in her mind as notions half-forgotten in her past suddenly linked up with ideas as fresh as Ravenwood's pine needles.

Just as they finished wrapping the bundle, the bosun rapped on their door to fetch Rebecca to duty. With a grin and a final hug, she skipped out leaving Tanyth to consider the matter while gazing out of the small round porthole at the gleaming sea beyond.

When she went to dinner with the captain and Mr. Jameson that evening, she hardly tasted the food and returned to her bunk afterward without being able to recall a word of their conversation.

"Hope you weren't rude, you old fool," she muttered as she pulled her bedroll around her against the chill and soon drifted off into sleep.

The dream seemed familiar but she couldn't place why. A tree stood in silhouette against a pale, gray sky. As the dream unfolded, the stark outline blurred and took on a pale green light. As she watched, new leaves unfolded and filled in the gaps between the branches until the whole tree stood revealed in the fullness of summer foliage, lush and green against a gray sky.

"Why is the sky gray?" she asked her dream.

The gray sky turned dark and the lush green turned charcoal against the backdrop of night.

Night seemed to last for a very long time in her dream, without even the face of the All-Father to brighten the scene.

As the night faded to rosy dawn, she remembered the

tree, knew its shape. Something was missing. Something was wrong.

She woke in the morning light streaming through the port-hole and a cheerful ding-ding from the ship's bell.

"Where's the owl?" she muttered.

"Wozzat, mum?" Rebecca's sleep muzzied voice came from across the compartment.

"Nothin', my dear. Just mumblin'."

"Mmm."

She lay there for a moment, remembering the tree from another dream. The same tree, she was certain, but that tree had been in the fall. It had bled leaves and the leaves had fallen to fertilize a new season's growth but only after lying fallow under a blanket of snow. There had been a small bird near the bole of the tree, a tiny owl. The owl had called to her from her dream. Because of that dream, she'd decided to stay in Ravenwood for the winter. There had been blood aplenty and some of it her own.

She snorted at herself. "Lazin' about tryin' to make sense o' dreams and portents," she muttered. "You used to have more sense than that, old woman."

"If you're gonna keep mumblin', mum, could you either mumble louder so's I can hear or mumble on deck so's I can't?"

Tanyth gave a small laugh. "Sorry, my dear. One minute."

With a heave, she threw herself out of the bunk and started pulling on warm clothes.

)O(

When Tanyth stepped into the deckhouse, Cook greeted her with a full mug of fresh tea and a huge grin. "Good morning, mum. Slept well, did ya?"

"Tolerable, Cook. Quite tolerable."

He beamed. "Excellent. I've decided to have an egg bake this morning, mum. It should be ready in time for break-fast, but I haven't decided what to do about lunch or dinner. Anything you'd care to suggest?"

Tanyth cocked her head to the side and gave Cook a hard stare. "You feelin' all right this mornin', Cook?"

"Never better," he said without losing the grin.

She sipped the tea and eyed him over the rim of the mug. "Well, somethin's got you giddy as a schoolgirl this morning, Cook. What is it?"

"Me, mum?" he said. "Why, I'm always the soul of cheerfulness and light in the morning."

She shook her head and chuckled. "You're usually pretty chipper, I'll grant you that, but you've got something that's tickling your whiskers this mornin'. Out with it."

"Oh, well, I heard some news this morning that perhaps has me a bit more cheerful than usual, mum."

"And that would be...?"

"Just at sunrise this morning, the mainmast lookout spotted land, mum."

"Land?" she stopped to think. "But we're not supposed to be at North Haven for another—what? Four days? Five?"

He nodded his head in a series of fast, vertical jerks so quick she feared he might dislodge his nose in the process. "If that's the right headland, mum, we'll be in port by noon tomorrow. That's a full three or four days early."

Tanyth took another sip and muttered, "Well, it wasn't an error."

"What's that, mum?"

"Oh, nothin'. The captain and Mr. Groves were chatting about some navigational thing or other. They were afraid we had some faulty charts or somethin'."

"Well, faulty or not, mum. We're almost there."

"That's wonderful news, Cook, but why are you so excited?"

"My family lives there, mum. I haven't seen 'em all winter. I 'spect me ma and me da will be glad to have me home and I can finally get a meal that I don't have to cook or clean up after!"

She laughed at his ebullience. "I'm sure they'll be glad to see you. How long will the ship stay in port?"

"Depends on the conditions, mum. Usually it doesn't take long to get the ship unloaded and then reloaded with new cargoes. Couple of days to unload. Maybe a week to load 'er up again, depending on how much is waiting to go and what it is."

"So you'll have time for a nice visit before you have to turn around again."

"Aye, mum, and when we get back to Kleesport, we'll probably all have a little extra something in profits. This first cargo of the season always pays best."

"Sounds like you've got it all planned."

"Well, no plan ever goes the way you hope, but that's not a good reason not to try to make things work out in your favor, is it, mum."

She shook her head. "No, Cook, it's not. And speakin' of workin' out in my favor, did you by any chance make me some oatmeal this mornin' or will I have to wait for the egg bake to come out of the oven."

He chuckled. "Well, mum, I know how partial you are to your oatmeal in the morning so I made you a special batch with a bit of apple and honey. You ready for it now?"

Her stomach growled loud enough for Cook to hear over the crackling of the fire in the stove and the slapping of the hull against the waves.

"I'll take that as a yes, mum."

She had plenty of time to finish before the crew showed up for their meal. The word had spread and everybody was in a cheerful mood.

As Tanyth finished the washing up, she asked, "Who'll you get to do this for you on the way back, Cook?"

He pulled a comically long face. "Unless somebody gets into trouble with the bosun, I'll be doing the washing up myself on the way back."

"Aw. I'm sorry to hear that."

Cook gave her a cheeky grin. "It's fine, mum. Having a little extra to do helps pass the time. I'm sure it won't be as entertaining has having you here to help out, but I'm used to it. Shouldn't be too bad."

When Tanyth finished, she left the deckhouse and instead of heading back to her cabin, she went forward along the rail and made her way up onto the forecastle. She pulled the knit cap from the pocket of her coat and pulled it down to protect her ears from the wind. She closed her eyes and turned her face to feel the warmth of the sun and didn't mind the icy gusts blowing in off the water and chilling her even through the sturdy wool. She looked up at the taut triangles of sail gleaming whitely against the deep azure sky and recognized another of her dreams. The feeling of the ship rising and falling and the buffeting of the wind made her feel as if she were flying. Her heart beat fast and she felt a bit dizzy. She looked to the north once more and, under a flock of puffy, white clouds, saw the smudge of land on the horizon.

A voice behind her said, "Mum? You shouldn't be on deck in this cold, mum. Mum?"

She turned to find Scooter looking concerned.

"Mum, please come down from here. At least you wore your hat. You're gonna catch your death up here, mum."

"Yes," she said, barely able to focus enough to form words. "Of course. I...I don't know what I was thinking." She took his offered hand and let him help her down to the main deck, even leaning on him all the way to the companionway.

"Are you all right, mum?" Scooter looked very concerned.

"Yes, dear boy. I think I'm fine. Just the excitement."

"All right, mum. If you say so."

"Thank you, Scooter, I can make it from here." She stepped carefully down to the companionway and looked back at him. "Sorry, I don't have any of Cook's sweets to give you."

He grinned. "'At's all right, mum. I get so many, I keep a few handy." He reached into his pocket and pulled out one of the familiar paper-wrapped sweets. "You want one, mum?"

She laughed and shook her head. "No, thank you, Scooter."

"Take care, mum," he said and closed the companionway door, cutting off the wind from outside and leaving Tanyth standing there in the dim light.

She took a deep breath and let it out slowly, trying to think, trying to make sense of the vision. She made her way into her cabin, closed the door, and crawled up into her bunk. "The last time, I almost died," she muttered. She closed her eyes against the terror.

She willed herself to take deep slow breaths and in moments she fell into sleep again.

For once she did not dream.

CHAPTER 28
LANDFALL

The town of North Haven didn't exactly fill Tanyth with enthusiasm. The slanting afternoon sun did nothing to brighten up a weather beaten collection of buildings.

"It always looks a little rough in the spring, mum." Cook stood on deck beside Tanyth as the ship picked its way into the harbor. "The weather takes a toll, but you wait. By Solstice, the winter'll be a memory. All the flowers will be blossoming. Everything will be beautiful."

The bosun yelled, "Lower tops'ls! Drop bumpers."

Tanyth looked up and had to look carefully to pick Rebecca's tanned form out of the rest of the crew swarming the rigging. The sailors furled the last of the tallest sails, leaving only one triangular sail at the bow. They'd lowered and furled the huge mainsails while still some distance from shore.

As the ship sailed neatly toward the stone pier, Tanyth saw crews putting bumpers on the side away from the pier. "Cook? Why bumpers on that side?"

He chuckled. "'Cause that's the side'll be next to the pier when we get there."

She blinked at him. "But we're almost in!"

"Looks are deceiving, mum." He jerked his chin at a sailor who stood on the bow with a heavy maul. "Nichols'll swing that hammer in a minute. Then you'll see."

Tanyth felt her brows knit as she tried to figure out what was happening.

"See where that fella's standing beside the bollard there on the dock, mum? The one wearing the green scarf?"

It took her a moment to find him about halfway down the short pier. "Yeah. What about him?"

"He'll catch the throwing line, drag in a hawser, and we'll snug into the pier right about there, if we do it right."

"There are logs in the water!"

"Camels, mum. Don't know why they call 'em camels, but that'll give us some nice wood to scrub up against instead of rock. They'll take the damage against the stone pier instead of our hull."

Tanyth heard the captain say something to Mr. Groves who shouted, "Clear away and stand-by to luff the jib."

Everybody on deck stood stock still, the last of the ship's forward motion dropping off as water resistance slowed them. Tanyth felt like the ship had all but stopped in the water but noticed that the end of the stone pier kept getting closer.

"Let go port anchor!" Mr. Groves called and the bosun repeated.

Nichols swung his mallet and Tanyth heard a horrendous splash followed by a rumble.

"Luff the jib!"

The men holding a rope at the bow let it go and the one remaining sail started flapping in the breeze even as the ship drifted toward the rocks.

"Snug it up, bosun," Captain Groves called from the bridge.

"Lash it down, my lovelies, and mind your fingers!" the bosun bawled.

Tanyth looked to Cook who pointed to the anchor line that had paid out along the water next to the ship. "Watch."

As she watched the line straightened and then grew taut. Nothing seemed to happen for several moments. Tanyth felt like the whole ship held its breath for an instant before the ship slewed about and the angle on the anchor's thick rope opened up as the momentum of the vessel brought the stern around, swinging the ship on a long, lazy arc.

"Slick as you please," Cook murmured.

Tanyth turned just in time to see the bosun throw a weighted line to the man in the green scarf. He caught it handily and, using the lighter rope, pulled a heavy mooring line over to the heavy cleat in front of him and dropped the loop deftly over the top of the heavy metal fitting.

"Spring line secured, sir!" the bosun yelled.

"Slack the chains, Mr. Montaigne!"

"Slack the chains," the bosun yelled and the ship slid backwards, using the last of its momentum and the leverage from the single line on the pier to lever in. Tanyth felt the ship bump the pier and heard a soggy squeak as the heavy rope bumpers mashed against the floating logs.

"Set the for'ard spring line. Secure fore and aft!" the bosun yelled. "Get that jib furled."

Men jumped and ropes ran everywhere. Tanyth didn't really understand it all, but the process seemed to work. In less time than she thought possible, the crew had tied the ship to the dock, pulled down all the sails, and awaited further orders.

The captain looked down from the height of the bridge and surveyed the deck and lines from his vantage. "Nicely done, Mr. Montaigne."

"Thank ya, Cap'n."

"Double up all lines, gasket sails, and retrieve the kedge, if you would, Bosun," Captain Groves called.

"Aye, aye, Cap'n."

Cook turned to Tanyth. "Welcome to North Haven."

"That's it?"

"Except for a bit of clean up and clearing away, indeed it is."

"Now what?"

He shrugged. "The captain and Mr. Jameson will talk to the harbor master and cargo lumpers. They'll figger out when we'll unload. We'll prob'ly start in the morning."

"How soon can I go ashore?"

The captain's voice came from behind her. "Soon as you like, mum, but you're welcome to stay aboard tonight."

"Thank you, Captain."

"I'll be dining ashore with my son this evening, mum, if you and Rebecca would care to join us?"

"I'd be honored, Captain."

"Excellent. We'll gather on the dock at four bells, then."
He tipped his cap and headed down the companionway into

the ship.

Tanyth stood there for a few moments. After so many days of having the deck rise and fall under her, of having to watch every step, the ship felt oddly still.

"Tea, mum?" Cook asked.

She took one last long scan of the dilapidated waterfront and the dark forest looming behind the town. A chill breeze drifted across the harbor bringing the dusky aroma of wood smoke, the tang of fish, and an unmistakable whiff of horse dung. "Love a cup," she said.

☽○☾

The bright ding of the ship's bell seemed to echo across the harbor. With the sun nearly down behind the headland, the harbor and surround was all but deserted. The sound of a concertina playing a lively jig wafted uncertainly on the light, evening breeze. Tanyth caught the redolent, green smell of pine and hemlock cutting through the smokey funk of human habitation.

"Good evening, mum. Miss Marong." Mr. Groves said, stepping onto the deck from the gangway.

"Mr. Groves," Tanyth said with a nod. "Lovely night."

"Aye, and it seems almost impossible that there's a city there tucked among the trees. Later in the season when there are half a dozen vessels in port, it'll seem a different place, but right now? I could grow to like this place."

"Half a dozen?" Rebecca took the measure of the stone pier and surrounding harbor. "Large ships like the *Call*?"

"Larger. Malloy's *Sea Rover* is half again longer and several tonnes heavier. Compared to most of the fleet, we're a jolly boat."

"Where will they put them all?" the young woman asked, eyes wide in disbelief.

He laughed. "They'll fit. Sometimes they moor side by side in the height of the season, but some in, some out, once in a while they'll lay at anchor out there and ferry crews ashore in long boats, but with that many vessels, the money flows and nobody asks questions about where to put them."

The captain opened the companionway and stepped up onto the deck. He smiled and nodded at Tanyth. "Good evening, mum. Ready for a little shore food?"

"I am, Captain, and thank you for inviting me."

He clapped his son on the shoulder in greeting. "You're more than welcome, mum. A good meal is the least we can do after all you've done for the ship."

"Indeed, mum," the younger Groves added. "We've had ladies travel with us before, but I think you may be the only one that came without a male escort. And I know you're the only one that's been on the opening voyage of the season, mum."

Captain Groves nodded. "And a good thing you were, too, mum." He kept his voice low but Tanyth heard a burr of emotion in it. "Or we'd never have arrived."

She gave a small shrug. "I had a bit of investment in the voyage, myself," she said. "Seemed the least I could do."

"And you, miss? Ready to stand on solid land again?"

Rebecca smiled and looked up at the bare spars above her head. "It's been very nice aboard, Captain." She gave a small shrug. "But yes."

Both men grinned and the captain led the way up the gangway and onto the hard surface of the pier. They started toward the town, Rebecca and the first mate leading the way.

Tanyth found herself stumbling every few steps. "What in the world," she muttered. "Is the dock shaking?"

Captain Groves offered his arm. "No, mum. It's just you're used to having the deck move under you, now. Your feet keep expecting the dock to do the same thing."

She took his arm and his steady hand kept her from making too much of a fool of herself and noticed the younger Groves provided the same service to a blushing Rebecca. To fill the quiet she asked, "Do you know who that package was addressed to?"

The captain nodded, but the younger Mr. Groves answered. "Nobody. A false name according to the harbormaster, mum. I just got back from the office." He craned his head back to speak over his shoulder. "Stevedores and cargo agents will be on the dock at eight bells in the morning, Captain."

"Thank you, Mr. Groves."

"What will you do with the..." Tanyth hesitated over saying too much where passers-by might overhear.

"The parcel in question?" Captain Groves offered.

"Yeah. The parcel in question. What will you do with it? Turn it over to the local constables?"

Mr. Groves leaned in to hear his answer, too.

"Honestly, mum? I don't know." Captain Groves screwed his mouth up and then wiped his lips with his free hand like he wanted to spit but was too polite to do it with a lady on his arm. "Constables like having things neat. We only have the box and our word where it came from."

"Why would you lie about that?"

The captain shrugged. "No reason to, but constables aren't prone to reason when they can hound you about lacking key facts in the case."

"Like what, Captain?"

"Well," he said, drawing the word out, "like who made it to begin with? That's for one thing. How did we find it, for another."

"You could just tell them you were inspecting after the squall and heard it tick," she pointed out.

"We could, but then they'd confiscate it as evidence and we'd never see it again."

"But they'd have to trace it, wouldn't they?"

The captain gave her a rather jaundiced look and asked, "Not if they work for the insurers. That would be a nice little extra bit of change if they quietly took care of any funny business here for them, don't ya think?"

Tanyth looked shocked but then realized he probably had the right of it.

"Lots of empty ocean between here and there, mum," the younger Groves added. "Plenty of room for a ship that was supposed to be lost on the way up to tragically founder on the way back."

"Aye," Captain Groves said. "About the time they get down the list of questions to 'Why aren't you dead?' That would be a stickier one to answer."

As they walked off the pier and up the main street of the town, the sound of the concertina grew louder and, with it, the sound of voices raised in celebration. Some laughed. Some sang. Some merely shouted. She couldn't understand any of them.

"That's not where we're headed, is it, Captain?" Tanyth asked.

The captain looked at her oddly for a moment before he realized where she meant. He shook his head with a laugh. "No, mum. My loud and rowdy days are long past. A quiet ale, a good slice of roast, and a few friends are more than enough for me."

Mr. Groves grinned at his father. "And besides, you know most of the crew will be up there dancing on the tables and drinking their pay away."

The captain nodded and answered with a shrug. "Tis not a pretty sight, but one they earned. It's their pay to spend and no business of mine to tell 'em how."

"And the big heads they'll earn and have to work off in the morning won't be any prettier," Mr. Groves pointed out.

"Oh, true, but the amusement value of watching them suffer will do my cold, old heart good, my boy. Be grateful you're not with 'em."

"Speaking of pay..." The first mate shot a glance over his shoulder.

"What, boy? I paid you with the rest of the crew," Captain Groves said.

"Not me, sir. Them." Mr. Groves jerked his chin at the two women, his arm still encumbered by the younger of the two.

"Oh, of course!" The captain stopped, halting the procession right in the middle of the empty street. He thrust a hand deep into his trousers, fishing around and pulling up a handful of coins. He counted out several pieces of silver in his fingers and held it out to Rebecca. "There ya go, miss. Wages earned for a job well done."

Rebecca looked confused. "But I thought I was workin' for my passage."

The younger Groves nodded. "You did, but you also earned a few silvers to help you on your way. It's customary."

"Indeed it is, girl." The captain shook his outstretched

hand. "Take it or we stand here until you do, and I'm getting hungry."

Tanyth looked at Saul Groves and saw the twinkle in his eye. "Customary? Since when?"

He grinned at her. "We'll get to you in a minute, mum. Just hold your main sheet a little longer."

Rebecca held out her hand, and the captain deposited the coins.

"Thank you, Captain," she said, with a bashful glance at the first mate.

"Very welcome, my girl, and if you ever decide to give up bein' this woman's travelin' companion, you've always a berth on the *Call*."

Rebecca seemed startled by the notion. "I didn't know women could work on vessels, Captain."

"It's not common, but it's not unheard of. You got along well with the lads and pulled your weight along with the rest of 'em. Better'n some." The old man shrugged. "Good crew's hard enough to find without getting' too finicky over the plumbin'."

Rebecca shook the coins loosely in her fist and then deposited them in her trouser pocket. "Thank you, Captain." She didn't say anything more but did spare another shy glance up to the younger Groves before reaching for his arm again.

"We're not done yet," the captain said. He counted more coins out of his hand and held his fist out to Tanyth. "You did more'n your share this trip, mum. Keepin' Cook amused is a full-time job and you did it right smartly."

Tanyth pushed the man's hand away. "No, Captain. Cook amused me on what mighta been a long and borin' trip. I couldn't."

"You will, mum, or I'll just have to hold my breath until I turn blue." He took a deep breath and puffed out his cheeks, his eyes bulging above the reddened skin.

Laughing at the staid captain behaving so childishly, Tanyth accepted the coins without looking at them. They rattled in her hand as she accepted his offered arm. They continued their stroll once more.

After a few steps, she started to deposit the coins in her

pocket. The glint of gold caught her eye. "Captain..."

"Hush, mum," he said, patting the hand he held captive under his arm.

"But this is—"

"Yes, mum." He turned to look her in the eye. "You earned much more than your passage. If you hadn't been there, and been willin' to do what you did? None of us woulda gotten to port, let alone home."

"Surely you'd have ridden out the storm," she murmured.

His lips hardened into a thin line. "I'm not talkin' about the storm, mum."

Mr. Groves looked over his shoulder, and said, "If you two don't stop mumblin' with your heads together back there, I'm gonna tell Mother on you."

They all laughed and Captain Groves led them to the front of a quiet inn a few paces off the main street. "Here we are."

He grabbed the handle and swung the door wide, ushering Rebecca, Tanyth, and his son in with a sweep of his hand.

"I always said this uniform makes me look more like a doorman than a captain, but Murial likes it."

Mr. Groves snickered at what was probably a well-worn family joke.

Tanyth just smiled and said, "Thank you, Captain," as she entered.

They stepped into the common room and surveyed the place. A large stone fireplace offered plenty of heat, and two huge wheels hung from chains from the rafters, each featuring as many as a dozen lanterns around the circumference. They bathed the room in a warm, yellow glow. Somewhere close by a joint was roasting and it filled the room with an aroma that made Tanyth's mouth water.

"Saul! Benjamin! You made it."

A pot-bellied man wearing a clean apron and homespun leggings came out from behind the bar, his arms wide. Long gray hairs scuttled about the sides of his head without offering any shade to the shining skull above.

"Perry, you old sea dog. You're still piloting the pub, I see." The captain met the man with a back-thumping embrace and then stepped back to look him up and down. "You've lost weight since the last we met, haven't you?"

A woman's voice rang out. "Don't encourage him, Saul. It just makes him more insufferable." Tanyth heard real affection in the jibe and turned to see a thin woman walk through the swinging door from the back. She carried a tray of food and smiled at Tanyth before stopping at a booth and sorting the dishes out among the denizens.

"When we saw the sails, I knew it t'was you," Perry carried on with a broad grin. "You made good time! But where are my manners? Here, sit, sit. Please. I'll find you a small somethin' to whet your whistle."

Perry ushered them to a neat, square table just off the hearth, close enough to be warmed by the fire, but not so close as to get overheated.

The thin woman came over and gave the big man a playful swat before addressing the table. "Welcome back, Saul, Benjamin." She held out her hand to Tanyth. "I'm Amanda. Perry's just the dancin' bear in this circus."

Tanyth shook the offered hand. "Tanyth. Tanyth Fairport."

Rebecca nodded in greeting. "Rebecca," she said.

Amanda squinted at the younger woman. "Just Rebecca?"

"Marong."

Amanda nodded. "You look like a Marong."

"Well, I'm the black sheep so I hope I don't act like one."

Amanda laughed at the joke that Tanyth didn't understand.

Perry returned with a large pitcher in one hand and four metal mugs in the other. He kissed the woman on the cheek on his way by. "Yes, love, but I'm your dancin' bear."

She gave him a grin and said, "For now."

Perry plunked mugs down in front of them and poured the first one full, handing it to Saul. "Try that. See if you've ever tasted finer."

Captain Groves took the mug and gave it a sniff then a swallow. He screwed up his face and repeated the process. "Ugh! What is this, dishwater?"

Perry nodded. "Right the first time, old dear."

The captain took another hefty swallow and sighed. "Someday you'll learn how to make a decent ale. Someday." He shook his head sadly.

"Well, I'll just go pour this out then..." Perry started to take the pitcher away.

"Hey!" Captain Groves said. "You might just leave that here. We'll...um...empty it for you. No need to spread the damage any farther than you already have." He glowered at the man who laughed.

"As if," he said and poured mugs for the rest. "Drink up, drink up. There's plenty more dishes need washin' so I'm unlikely to run out of dishwater to serve as ale tonight."

Benjamin lifted the mug in salute to the innkeeper and took a long swallow of his own. "Thank you, Perry. Delicious as ever."

Captain Groves slapped the table and scowled at his son. "My boy, how many times do I have to tell you."

"Sorry, Father. It just slipped out."

The general level of jocularity made Tanyth think that the odd greeting must be some part of a long-standing tradition, and Captain Groves' wink in her direction confirmed it.

She took a careful sip of her own ale and smiled. "That is delicious!" The words were out of her mouth before she could think.

"Mum, you're supposed to insult it and tell him how terrible it is. Otherwise he'll keep it all for himself!" Captain Groves explained.

"Oh! I'm sorry. I didn't know. This is my first time here."

That got a general round of laughter around the table and some from the neighboring table as well.

Amanda broke in by putting her tray against her husband's chest and pushing on it with her narrow shoulder. "Back to the bar, you. I need to feed these people. Go. Shoo." She waved the tail of her apron at him and he lumbered off, not unlike some of the bears Tanyth had seen.

"Tonight I've got a nice haunch of venison on the spit. There's some tubers and greens as well. If you'd rather something lighter, there's a nice spiced fish soup that'll warm ya up." She looked from face to face. "What'll it be?"

Captain Groves claimed her attention with "We'll have

the venison, Amanda, and are you still making those crusty loaves of sourdough?"

"I am, and I just got some out of the oven before my dancin' bear started doin' the hornpipe out here. Lemme get those for you." She turned and disappeared into the kitchen without another word.

Tanyth took another sip of the ale and felt it warm her from the inside. "Why, I believe there's a bit of bite in this beer," she commented to nobody in particular.

The captain grinned at her. "This is his ice beer. It's only available in the springtime."

"He makes beer from ice?" Rebecca asked.

"No, miss. He makes a fine ale, to be sure, but this beer he brews and then sets it out on cold nights through the winter. It's cold enough here that the water in it freezes. In the morning, he scoops the ice out and then kegs up the rest."

Benjamin said, "It's got more than a bit of a bite, mum. It'll have you singing sea chanties and dancing a jig if you're not careful."

"Trust me, mum," the captain added, "hearing me sing sea chanties and watching him dance a jig is not an experience I recommend."

"That sounds like the voice of experience, Captain."

"It is, mum. Dark and bitter experience." In spite of his lugubrious tone, the captain's eyes twinkled in the light of the fire.

Tanyth helped herself to another sip. "It is tasty."

"Oh, aye, mum. That it is," Benjamin said. "That it is."

Amanda returned with plates piled high and Perry right behind her carrying a basket of bread. With the deftness of long practice, the two delivered a feast in a matter of moments. "Enjoy, enjoy," Amanda urged and disappeared back into the kitchen while Perry circulated around the room, visiting with the diners and pouring ale from his pitcher whenever the occasion called for it.

Tanyth took in the plate full of food, the meat steaming and juicy and the ruddy tubers slathered in butter. "Mother have mercy, I'm never gonna be able to get on the outside of this."

Captain Groves dug into his meal and grinned across the table at her. "You may have to roll me back down the hill and onto the ship, but I'm going to give it my best, mum."

Mr. Groves nodded but didn't waste breath with words.

Rebecca was already carving a bit off one of the tubers with a smile of anticipation on her face.

Tanyth took the first bite of venison and found she had nothing else to say for rather a long time. When she looked up again, the two men had silly grins on their faces and nearly empty plates. Rebecca had pushed her plate back and lounged in her seat with a sleepy smile of satisfaction curving her lips. The captain used a heel from the loaf to sop up the remains of the drippings from his trencher and savored it with great gusto.

"For somebody who was not all that sure, you did very well for yourself, mum," Mr. Groves said, nodding at the plate in front of her. Only a bit of tuber remained.

"I won't need to eat for a week," Tanyth said leaning back in her chair. "But it was so good, I just couldn't stop." In truth, she felt not just full but almost uncomfortably stuffed. She took a swallow of beer to wash it all down. She was nearly mortified with the resulting belch, but the men just laughed.

"Good beer, eh, mum?" the captain asked.

She murmured an apology but nodded her agreement.

Perry appeared at her elbow and started to fill her mug again from his never empty pitcher. He went right around the table filling as he went. When he was done, he stood back and looked as pleased as if he'd eaten the dinners himself. "Now, who has room for a sweet? Eh? Amanda has a lovely squash pie she just made this afternoon."

The four of them looked at each other and uttered a collective groan.

Perry smiled and pulled up a chair, plunking himself down and placing his pitcher on the table. "All right, then," he said, and looked to Saul. "How was the trip? You made good time?"

"Just under twelve days from Kleesport," the captain said.

Perry's eyes goggled. "That's a record if I'm not mistaken."

The captain nodded. "I think so, too."

"You musta had some fair winds to make that time."

"Well, yes, and no. We ran into a bit of a blow about three days out of Kleesport. Got knocked about a bit."

"Any damage?"

"Nothing to speak of."

"Where'd you make up the time?"

"A few days later we caught a current. Not on my charts. It pushed us along right steady," the captain said. "Dead reckoning with the taffrail logs had us making goodly progress with the winds, but the shoots at noon showed we almost doubled our legs."

Perry sat back, his face slack in disbelief. "A new current?" He looked back and forth between the two Groves.

Mr. Groves shook his head. "I know. We've sailed that same course a dozen times. Never picked up anything like that."

Rebecca nudged Tanyth and gave her a knowing look but didn't say anything aloud.

The captain said, "Might be something to do with the time o' year. I don't know that I've ever been on that reach this early in the season."

"Could make getting back a bit of a bother," the younger Groves pointed out.

"Oh, aye," Perry agreed. "Don't sound like somethin' I'd like to be sailin' against."

"We'll pull off to the west'ard. See if we can dodge it on the way back," the captain said.

"So, I'm guessin' you got a jump on the rest of 'em coming out of Kleesport," Perry said with a sly smile.

"I don't think the watch flag had much more than shifted before we cast off," Mr. Groves admitted. "One bell. Two at the most."

Perry chuckled. "How far ahead of them are ya, do ya think?"

The captain shook his head. "Hard telling. Malloy and at least two other syndicate ships were waiting for wind to change. That's not saying how many were laying up without saying. Some of those ships can bend on a lot more sail than the *Call.* With the westerly winds all the way across the bight..." He shook his head again. "Hard telling."

"What if they picked up the same current?" Perry asked.

The captain grimaced. "I'm trying not to think of that."

"Well, you've got priority with the harbor master. First berth o' the season so you're sittin' in the jaybird seat on this trip."

The captain snorted. "I've learned not to count the profits until the taxman's had his due."

They all laughed at that and took another swig of ale.

Perry turned to Tanyth. "And you, mum. Sorry to be borin' ya with ole seadogs' barkin'. What brings you and your friend to our fair port?"

"We're just passin' through," she said. "Never been this far north before and hopin' to learn more about the plants and such up this way."

Perry's eyes opened wide in surprise. "You a scholar, mum? I'd never have taken you for...err...that is..."

She laughed and shook her head. "Mother, no. Just a simple herbalist. Came up to see what I can see."

"I don't know much about that stuff, mum. Other than spruce tips for bitterin' my ale, and the grains we need to make 'em, o' course."

"You know enough about apples to brew a wicked cider, don't ya?" Amanda had come up behind them and added her spice to the mix.

"Well, o' course. But that's not herbs and such, now is it?"

"Town this size must have a healer or two," Tanyth said.

"Aye," Perry said. "Three, as it happens."

"I'll pay a callin' on them tomorrow, then. If they don't know the plants and herbs themselves, they must get it from somewhere."

Perry nodded. "All three are fine gentleman. I'm sure they'll be happy to answer your questions."

"Gentlemen?" Tanyth asked.

"Oh, my, yes!" Perry exclaimed. "All from King's College, every one of 'em. Learned from the best healers in the land. Those gents got science behind 'em, mum. And they knows some stuff."

"I see."

Tanyth caught Amanda's expression and was surprised to see her weighing Tanyth with her gaze. When she turned to speak, Amanda gave the tiniest shake of her head. Tanyth held her question but made a note to speak with the woman later.

"So, how long you stayin', mum?" Perry asked. "You plannin' on going back on the *Call*?"

She shook her head. "Not sure. I gen'rally wander around a lot. A day here or there an' then move on."

"That sounds interestin', mum. How long you been doin' that?"

"Goin' on twenty-one winters."

Perry's jaw sagged and it took him a moment to recover enough to say, "Mother's mercy, mum. You musta started as a girl younger than this one." He grinned at Rebecca.

"Well, not exactly," Tanyth smiled at his compliment, "but it's been a good long time."

"Your husband must find that a mite unsettlin', don't he, mum?"

Amanda coughed loudly and so persistently that several other patrons turned to see what was the matter. She held up her hand for patience and continued to cough until whatever it was that had her released its grip.

"Well, excuse me, I don't know what came over me there." She pressed a hand to her breastbone and took a few tentative breaths. "It's passed now, I think." She turned to Tanyth. "If you need a place, mum, we have rooms up above. Two silvers a day and it includes breakfast and dinner."

"Two silvers?" Perry asked but the glare that Amanda gave him made him stop. "Oh, yes. Two silvers. Of course." He took refuge in his ale mug.

"Thank you, that would be most acceptable," Tanyth said with a nod. "I'll be staying aboard one more night, but per'aps tomorrow mornin'?"

"You just come round when you're ready, mum," Perry said. "We'll be here."

"Thank you, both," she said and shot a grateful smile to Amanda who winked.

☽○☾

In the morning, Tanyth rose in the light of dawn but missed the sun shining in the port. It took her a moment to realize that the ship now pointed south and the view out the port was of the dock and the western sky.

Rebecca groaned a bit but rolled out of her bunk readily enough and joined Tanyth at the port.

Tanyth peered out and realized that very little of the view included sky, but a rather drab looking bit of stonework crusted with small shellfish and green weed. She angled her head to look up and saw the lip of the dock well above her.

"Not much to look at, is it, mum?" Rebecca said with a snort.

"No time for sky gazin' anyway," Tanyth said. She looked around the small room that had been their home for what felt like weeks. All her goods were already tucked into the pack except the bedroll, her woolen pants, and her heavy jacket. The heavy wool trousers wouldn't fit in her pack but she rolled them up in her bedroll. As cold as people said the place was, she wasn't about to leave a pair of windproof trousers behind. The combined bundle made the bedroll a bit heavier, but wearing the heavy blue watch coat felt like second nature to her.

She hefted the pack and grimaced at the weight of it. "Gettin' soft in my old age," she muttered and then used the lip of the bunk to hold the pack steady while she slipped the straps over her shoulders. As she'd hoped, the heavy woolen coat padded her shoulders, protecting them from the straps. She had to stop and adjust the buckles to let the straps out a little to make room for the extra thickness of the jacket, but by three bells she was ready to go ashore.

Rebecca snugged the straps holding her own bedroll and hooked her pack over one shoulder, standing easily and crossing to the door. "You ready, mum?"

Tanyth nodded, took staff in hand and clapped her wide-brimmed hat on her head, before following the younger woman out of the cabin and climbing the short ladder to the deck. When she got there and saw the angle on the gangplank, she almost decided to stay aboard—at least until the tide had lifted the ship level with the dock.

"Leavin' so soon, mum?" Cook called to her from the deck-house door.

She crossed to him and surprised him with a hug. "Time for me to move on, Cook."

"I've tea here and oatmeal if you like, mum." He held the door open in invitation.

"I'll pass on the oatmeal, Cook. Dinner last night is still digestin', but I'll take a cup of tea with thanks."

Rather than trying to enter the crowded galley with their packs, the two lounged beside the door while Cook brought them steaming china mugs.

"You're not visitin' with your folks then?" she asked.

"I'll go up today, mum. I stopped by last night for a gab and an ale, but my job's here, mum."

"You don't have as much to do in port, do you?"

"More, mum. Meals aren't as big, but with the stores and supplies? Making sure we have enough flour and beans to get where we're going, mum. That takes up my time." He sipped his own tea and gave her an emphatic nod. "And how about you, mum? Now that you're here? What'll you do?"

"I still have to find my teacher. She's here somewhere. We'll find her, I'm sure, but it might take some doin'."

"Who is she, mum? Maybe I know her. I know most of the people around."

"Her name's Gertie. Gertie Pinecrest."

Cook pondered, pulling on his lower lip between thumb and forefinger. "That's a familiar name, mum, but I can't quite..."

"You know a place called Lammas Wood?"

He looked startled at the question. "Well, aye, mum. I do, but that's..." he took a deep breath and blew it out. "I don't know, mum. A couple, three, maybe four days hike out into the wild. Why?"

She gave him a small shrug. "That's where we're goin'."

"Mum? You can't." Cook's eyes practically bugged out in his alarm.

"Can't? Why not?"

"There's beasts out there, mum. Bears. Cats. Worse."

"And you know this directly?" she asked.

Cook looked into his mug and contemplated for a moment. "Well, not directly, mum. No."

She shrugged.

"But why, mum. There's nothing out there but woods and game."

"Nothing?"

He gave his own little shrug, "Well, they tell about a hermit lives out that way. I think it's just a tale they tell children to make 'em behave."

"Oh, really?"

"Yes, mum. Normal kinds of boggety-man things. 'Eat your turnips or the hermit'll get ye.' 'Mind your manners, boy, or the hermit'll teach ya some.'"

"Doesn't sound so bad."

He chuckled. "No, not from this side of twenty winters, it don't, mum. But when you're a lad of ten and your ma says, 'Do your chores, or the hermit'll come and make you chop her firewood all night and all day. You won't like that now, will ya!' Well, mum, you do it right quick."

She laughed a bit in sympathy, but filed the bit of knowledge away. They may be boogety-man stories to him, but to her they were clues to a trail. She up-ended the mug and put the empty in the tray beside the door. Rebecca followed suit.

"Thank you kindly for the tea, Cook. Fair winds and ...? What's the sayin'?"

He smiled. "Fair winds and following seas, mum."

"That's it. Fair winds and following seas, Cook." She smiled at him and took up her staff from where it rested by the door.

"We'll be in and out all summer, mum. Long as we can get in, we will—until it ices over. Maybe we'll see you again?"

She smiled and considered. "Maybe," she admitted at last. "Maybe."

They crossed the deck and Tanyth eyed the gangplank again.

"You go first, mum. I'll follow and catch ya if you slide back," Rebecca said.

Tanyth looked at the younger woman but detected no hint

of humor in the girl's face. She took a deep breath and put her feet on the treads. With the help of her staff, she managed to clamber up the steep track and stepped onto the dock without suffering the indignity of having Rebecca push her up the last few steps.

Jameson stood there at the top, facing toward the head of the pier. "Leavin' so soon, mum? G'mornin, miss."

Rebecca gave Jameson a smile and a nod. "G'mornin, Mr. Jameson."

"Seems my passage is complete, Mr. Jameson. Time to go ashore and get on with the journey."

"It's been a pleasure havin' you with us, mum, and that's the truth."

"I had fun myself," she said and realized, with a start, that she meant it. "It'd be a long way to walk, but the trip kinda blurs together now that it's over."

Jameson grinned. "Aye, mum. And when you've done the trip two dozen times, it blurs even more." He shot her a look out of the corners of his eyes. "One thing I won't forget about this trip, mum."

"What's that?" she asked. "That special little package we had?"

He shook his head. "The sight of that storm blowing away like dandelions on a summer day. That was something."

She laughed. "I wish I'd'a seen it."

"Well, it was lucky Benjamin was looking at you and not the storm, mum." He cocked his head at her. "You feelin' all right now?"

"Yeah, but I'm outa shape in carryin' my stuff about. Been too long since I took to the trails." She flexed her shoulders and grimaced.

"I don't know how you do it, mum. I don't think I could lift that pack, let alone walk with it."

"Done it a long time. Just need to get back in the habit."

"How long will you stay in North Haven, mum?"

She shook her head. "Day. Maybe two. Need to get my bearings. See what I can learn here before I move on."

"You take care, mum. Come back and see us when you're ready to go back to Kleesport."

In her heart, she wondered when that might be, but she answered, "Thank you, Mr. Jameson. Fair winds and followin' seas."

They turned toward town and passed a crowd of two dozen men following a cargo lorry with a four-horse team heading up the dock. The leadman nodded at them in greeting.

Tanyth nodded back and kept walking. At the head of the pier she stopped and looked back south one last time. The longshoremen had clustered around the ship and she saw Jameson and the lead man shaking hands. In a few days the ship would be gone, heading south across the Bight, heading home.

The thought of home struck a chord with her, sounding an emotional note she'd not felt for many winters. She thought of Frank and his steady good humor, of Ravenwood and the new inn. As much as she missed Frank's solid company, Ravenwood was not her home.

"Will you miss him, my dear?" Tanyth asked.

Rebecca glanced at her. "Miss who, mum?"

"Young Mr. Groves."

Rebecca's blush barely showed against the ruddy light of morning, but she gave Tanyth a shy smile. "Per'aps a bit," she said. "But I know where to find him again should I ever decide to set my cap."

Tanyth laughed a short laugh that ended with a sigh.

Rebecca waited silently, a small—almost sad smile—curling her lips as if she knew what was going through Tanyth's mind.

As the stevedores started lining up carts and cranes, Tanyth turned and headed up the hill towards town. "Woolgathering won't get us any closer," she muttered. "Time to get movin'."

Rebecca fell in along side her. "Mum, if you're gonna mutter?"

Tanyth shot her a sharp look.

"Do it loud enough that I can hear?" Rebecca grinned and Tanyth huffed out a short laugh.

"I'll do my best, my dear. You keep remindin' me."

"Oh, I will, mum. I will."

As they climbed up the hill toward the town, she began to think that twenty-one winters was time enough to wander. There'd always been another teacher, a new place to go. There was always somebody else to visit with, some other lore to track down. That road looked like it might have an end after all.

"You've thought that before, ya old fool," she grumbled.

She had, she knew, but things had changed. Things had been changing ever since she first dreamed through the raven's eyes and felt the lift of wind on her wings. She eyed the snowy peaks beyond the town and wondered what made a woman come out here to the north end of nowhere to live. A shiver twitched the back of her neck and she tried not to consider that notion too closely.

"Too late now," she murmured.

Mother Dogwood's words came to her mind unbidden. "Until you come to the end of the path, keep going."

"I'm goin'," she grumbled. "I'm goin'.

"This time, I'm with ya, mum," Rebecca said.

With a grin, Tanyth leaned into the shallow incline and let her feet follow her heart's path once more.

Nathan Lowell

The Golden Age of the Solar Clipper

Quarter Share

Half Share

Full Share

Double Share

Captains Share

Owners Share

South Coast

Tanyth Fairport Adventures

Ravenwood

Zypherias Call

Hermit Of Lammas Wood

Awards

2011 Parsec Award Winner for Best Speculative Fiction
(Long Form) for *Owners Share*

2010 Parsec Award Winner for Best Speculative Fiction
(Long Form) for *Captains Share*

2009 Podiobooks Founders Choice Award for Captains Share

2009 Parsec Award Finalist for Best Speculative Fiction
(Long Form) for *Double Share*

2008 Podiobooks Founders Choice Award for *Double Share*

2008 Parsec Award Finalist for Best Speculative Fiction
(Long Form) for *Full Share*

2008 Parsec Award Finalist for Best Speculative Fiction
(Long Form) for *South Coast*

Nathan Lowell

Contact

Website: nathanlowell.com
Twitter: twitter.com/nlowell
Email: nathan.lowell@gmail.com

About The Author

Nathan Lowell first entered the literary world by podcasting his novels. The Golden Age of the Solar Clipper grew from his life-long fascination with space opera and his own experiences shipboard in the United States Coast Guard. Unlike most works which focus on a larger-than-life hero, Nathan centers on the people behind the scenes—ordinary men and women trying to make a living in the depths of interstellar space. In his novels, there are no bug-eyed monsters, or galactic space battles, instead he paints a richly vivid and realistic world where the hero uses hard work and his own innate talents to improve his station and the lives of those of his community.

Dr. Nathan Lowell holds a Ph.D. in Educational Technology with specializations in Distance Education and Instructional Design. He also holds an M.A. in Educational Technology and a BS in Business Administration. He grew up on the south coast of Maine and is strongly rooted in the maritime heritage of the sea-farer. He served in the USCG from 1970 to 1975, seeing duty aboard a cutter on hurricane patrol in the North Atlantic and at a communications station in Kodiak, Alaska. He currently lives on the plains east of the Rocky Mountains with his wife and two daughters.